THE REED MONTGOMERY SERIES

BOOKS 1-3

LOGAN RYLES

Copyright © 2019 by Logan Ryles

All rights reserved.

No part of this book may be reproduced in any form or by any electronic or mechanical means, including information storage and retrieval systems, without written permission from the author, except for the use of brief quotations in a book review.

OVERWATCH, HUNT TO KILL, and TOTAL WAR are works of fiction. Names, characters, places, and incidents either are the product of the author's imagination or are used fictitiously. Any resemblance to actual persons, living or dead, events, or locales is entirely coincidental.

Print ISBN: 978-1-7323819-9-5

Library of Congress Control Number: 2019913397

Published by Ryker Morgan Publishing.

CONTENTS

Also by Logan Ryles   vii

OVERWATCH

Chapter 1	5
Chapter 2	12
Chapter 3	23
Chapter 4	30
Chapter 5	38
Chapter 6	47
Chapter 7	54
Chapter 8	61
Chapter 9	66
Chapter 10	74
Chapter 11	80
Chapter 12	86
Chapter 13	89
Chapter 14	95
Chapter 15	101
Chapter 16	106
Chapter 17	112
Chapter 18	119
Chapter 19	122
Chapter 20	127
Chapter 21	133
Chapter 22	140
Chapter 23	150
Chapter 24	156
Chapter 25	162
Chapter 26	169
Chapter 27	172
Chapter 28	174
Chapter 29	177
Chapter 30	185

Chapter 31	191
Chapter 32	194
Chapter 33	197

HUNT TO KILL

Chapter 1	211
Chapter 2	219
Chapter 3	226
Chapter 4	233
Chapter 5	238
Chapter 6	244
Chapter 7	251
Chapter 8	259
Chapter 9	267
Chapter 10	275
Chapter 11	280
Chapter 12	286
Chapter 13	291
Chapter 14	301
Chapter 15	310
Chapter 16	320
Chapter 17	325
Chapter 18	332
Chapter 19	338
Chapter 20	345
Chapter 21	349
Chapter 22	357
Chapter 23	363
Chapter 24	370
Chapter 25	379

TOTAL WAR

Chapter 1	387
Chapter 2	396
Chapter 3	402
Chapter 4	408
Chapter 5	414
Chapter 6	422

Chapter 7	430
Chapter 8	439
Chapter 9	443
Chapter 10	450
Chapter 11	456
Chapter 12	465
Chapter 13	471
Chapter 14	481
Chapter 15	486
Chapter 16	493
Chapter 17	499
Chapter 18	505
Chapter 19	510
Chapter 20	518
Chapter 21	523
Chapter 22	529
Chapter 23	535
Chapter 24	541
Chapter 25	547
Chapter 26	554
The Story Continues With...	559
Smoke and Mirrors	561
Ready for more?	567
About the Author	569
Also by Logan Ryles	571
End Page	573

ALSO BY LOGAN RYLES

The Reed Montgomery Series

Prequel: *Sandbox*, a short story (read for free at LoganRyles.com)

Book 1: *Overwatch*

Book 2: *Hunt to Kill*

Book 3: *Total War*

Book 4: *Smoke and Mirrors*

Book 5: *Survivor*

Book 6: *Death Cycle*

Book 7: *Sundown*

The Prosecution Force Series

Book 1: *Brink of War*

Book 2: *First Strike*

Book 3: *Election Day*

Book 4: *Failed State*

The Wolfgang Pierce Series

Prequel: *That Time in Appalachia* (read for free at LoganRyles.com)

Book 1: *That Time in Paris*

Book 2: *That Time in Cairo*

Book 3: *That Time in Moscow*

Book 4: *That Time in Rio*

Book 5: *That Time in Tokyo*
Book 6: *That Time in Sydney*

The Mason Sharpe Series

Book 1: *Point Blank*

OVERWATCH

REED MONTGOMERY BOOK 1

For my darling Anna

Everything I ever wrote I wrote for you.

1

Cape May
New Jersey

Jersey was cold. The first breath of impending winter blew down off the North Atlantic, whistling softly between the pilings and over the coarse sand of Cape May's south beach. Reed stood at the waterline, feeling every icy breath of wind as it whipped around the collar of his wetsuit, but he didn't shiver. He stood perfectly still, and with a pair of binoculars, he surveyed the mouth of the Delaware Bay.

Two-foot waves glimmered under the blaze of a full moon, and the water lapped against the barnacle-covered feet of pier pilings, washing back and forth across the rocky sand shore. Thirty miles to the northeast, the neon lights of Atlantic City glimmered on the horizon. In the opposite direction, the dark outline of Cape Henlopen State Park was barely visible, marked by half a dozen twinkling campfires. Red and green buoys guarded the entrance to the bay, and an occasional fish jumped into the moonlight, shining between the waves.

But it was the emptiness that hallmarked the night. The isolation. Ideal conditions for a kill.

Reed lowered the binoculars and breathed in the cold air. It stung his lungs like the prick of a million needles, but the salt breeze tasted fresh. He squinted toward the horizon, then raised the binoculars again and swept his gaze across the bay twice more. On the third pass, he paused over an irregularity in the water—a rolling wave that moved against the current, away from shore. Turning back to the left, he found the source of the disturbance—a thirty-foot yacht, running dark, without a hint of humanity on board.

He studied the boat, then crouched in the sand, depositing his binoculars into a backpack and withdrawing a small case. After snapping it open, he withdrew a Glock 26 subcompact pistol, loaded the weapon with a single magazine containing ten rounds of fragmenting hollow points, and racked the slide. Salt spray gleamed on the gun under the light of the moon. Every curve and edge of the weapon felt hard and cold, but familiar, like a favorite pair of shoes or a worn baseball cap.

With the gun tucked into the interior of his wetsuit, Reed pulled a pair of diver's goggles over his face, and the air rushed from his lungs the moment he stepped into the chilled water. One breath, then another, both slow and measured against the chills that ripped up his spine. Then he waded out until the sandy bottom slipped from under his fins. The Jersey shoreline faded behind him as he cut through the waves, drawing occasional breaths between wide breaststrokes.

Fifteen minutes of powerful kicking brought Reed four hundred yards offshore, where he stopped to tread water and reposition on the yacht. As he anticipated, it now sat at anchor outside the mouth of the bay, bobbing in the rolling waves. The boat remained dark and silent, but Reed wasn't perturbed. He floated upright in the water, treading between deep breaths as he continued to regulate his breathing. His heart thumped, but he didn't feel as cold anymore. The water trapped between the wetsuit and his skin had warmed from the vigorous exercise and now served to insulate him from the frigid water. Five minutes passed before he detected the first sign of life on board the vessel. It came in the form of a muffled shout, followed by a dull thud.

One deep breath of damp air, then Reed dove into the black water. Kicking out with both legs, he approached the boat underwater, clearing the last fifty yards in under two minutes. When he surfaced, he bobbed feet from the yacht's wide swim deck. He hoisted himself up and landed on the platform without a sound. Water drained off the wetsuit and back into the ocean as he sat, listening for any noise from inside the boat. Voices were barely audible, stifled by the thick fiberglass and teak trim of the expensive pleasure cruiser. Somewhere inside the cabin were at least two men. Both American. Both with northeastern accents.

On the platform, he twisted and then unlatched his fins, depositing them and the mask onto the swim deck. He turned and flipped over the bulkhead, his bare feet landing on the deck without a sound.

The rear of the boat consisted of a row of luxury lounge chairs followed by a narrow stairwell to the cockpit and a door to the main salon. A visual sweep of the rear of the cockpit confirmed that all occupants of the boat were inside the salon.

He unzipped his wetsuit and withdrew the Glock, subconsciously performing a press check on the chamber. The glimmer of the brass casing in the dull moonlight assured him that the weapon was hot, and he proceeded to the door of the cabin. His heart continued to thump as a rush of adrenaline charged his blood with invisible lightning. His hands didn't shake, but that was due to years of practice containing the anxiety and anticipation of an impending kill.

This is it.

The latch lifted without resistance, and the door swung inward. Lights shone from somewhere beyond the hallway. Something heavy scraped against the hardwood flooring, and the air reeked of cigarette smoke.

Stepping across the threshold, Reed raised his weapon and then rounded the corner into the lounge, where two men sat at a card table. One man was dark and slim and wore an expensive evening suit and designer eyeglasses. He sat against the far wall, leaning over the table and growling at his companion between clenched teeth.

The second man was short and broad, stuffed into a polo shirt that constricted around each layer of fat, making him look like a caterpillar fighting to break free of an undersized cocoon. He puffed on a cigarette as sweat streamed down his bold, Italian-American features.

Both men looked up when the stranger burst into the lounge. The short man with the cigarette choked and pushed himself away from the table, crashing to the floor and gurgling something unintelligible. The man in the suit glared up at the intruder with wide, panicked eyes and reached under his coat.

Reed didn't hesitate. The Glock barked twice, spitting 9mm slugs across the salon at over twelve hundred feet per second, and scarlet oozed from the folds of the man's suit. He fell limp against the wall, his hand still caught beneath the jacket, and his mouth flopped open, a trail of blood running down his chin.

The man on the floor screamed and wriggled his way backward, holding one hand out toward Reed.

"Hey! What do you want? Just chill, all right? I've got nothin' to do wid him!"

The boat swayed over another wave as Reed stepped across the salon and trained the pistol on the chubby man. Every part of Reed's body was alive with tension, now. He could feel it in his bones. In the thunder of blood rushing through his brain. In the weight of the gun clenched between his fingers.

But instead of pulling the trigger, he spoke in a calm, monotone voice.

"Where's the money?"

The chubby man frowned, swallowed, and blinked all at once.

"What? The money? Look, man. I don't know nothin' about no money! I'm just his valet, okay? I don't even know why I'm here!"

Reed squatted on the floor and leaned toward his cornered prey. He reached between the man's legs and gripped the crotch of his khakis. Without a sound, Reed tightened his hold around the wadded pants, digging his fingers into the folds of the cloth while keeping the pistol trained on the man's face.

The man's eyes grew wide, and his gut jiggled as he restrained a scream. Tears streamed down his face.

"Man, please . . . let me go!"

Reed pressed the barrel of the gun against his victim's left eye socket and laid his finger against the trigger. At the same moment, he clenched with his left hand and twisted.

"Last chance. Where's the money?"

The chubby man screamed and fell against the wall, choking on his saliva as he attempted to pull away from the gun.

"All right! All right! It's in the trunk of a taxi. New York. Medallion 7J59."

Something in his eyes—maybe it was the fear, or the shadow of truth passing through those wide windows and into his terrified soul—whatever it was, Reed believed him. He released his hold around the pants and took half a step back.

The chubby man gasped and covered his crotch with both hands, sobbing as he leaned against the mahogany paneling. "I swear, it's the truth. It's all there!"

Reed walked across the cabin to an emergency locker mounted midway up the wall. From an orange case, he withdrew a twelve-gauge flare gun and loaded a single waterproof cartridge into the chamber. He tucked the gun into his wetsuit, then zipped it back up.

"I believe you," Reed said. "It's your lucky day."

The man on the floor panted, his face still flooded with pain as he shielded his crotch.

"I swear to God, man. I wouldn't lie."

Why do the double-dipping swindlers always wait until their backs are against the wall before they tell the truth?

Reed walked to one of the salon's big bay windows, pushed it open, and sucked in a breath of fresh air. A quick visual inspection confirmed that they were still alone in the mouth of the bay, and Reed turned toward the liquor cabinet. He withdrew a pint of Kentucky bourbon, twisted the cap off, and handed it to the man on the floor.

"Drink."

"Huh?" Confusion flooded his wide eyes.

Reed pushed the pint into his hand and then raised the Glock again. "Drink," he repeated.

The man on the floor raised the bottle and took a swig of the harsh liquor. He choked and tried to lower the bourbon, but he was stopped by the pressure of the Glock jammed into his rib cage.

"Keep going. All of it."

He spluttered and gulped the alcohol in unbridled panic as more of it streamed down his chin and over his shirt. Every time he tried to lower the bottle, Reed shoved the gun deeper into his skin, twisting and biting into him through his dirty polo shirt.

At last, the bottle was empty, and it clattered to the floor amid a puddle of whiskey. The chubby man coughed and leaned back, wheezing and struggling to catch his breath as saliva dripped from his lips.

"Dammit, man. I swear I'm telling the truth."

Too little too late—like Judas apologizing to a bloody cross. Reed cocked his left fist and drove a snapping punch to the backside of the man's skull. His victim slumped over in instant unconsciousness.

Reed picked up a towel from the galley counter, wiped down the grip of the Glock, and then placed it in the hand of the man on the floor, pushing the chubby finger through the trigger guard. He stood and surveyed the scene, double-checking each step to ensure he hadn't missed something. Everything looked good, and Reed retreated to the rear deck and surveyed the horizon for any sign of other boats. As before, the bay was dark and empty.

After affixing the fins back onto his feet and pulling the mask over his face, he slipped into the cold water and kicked toward shore. When he was fifty yards away from the yacht, he drew the waterlogged flare gun from his wetsuit and aligned the sights with the main salon. He squeezed the plastic trigger. The gun popped, and the flare shot across the water, arcing perfectly through the open window and crashing into the lounge. A moment later, smoke and flames rose from the window as the flare ignited the puddle of whiskey inside.

Reed watched the scene, imagining that he could feel the heat of the fire on his icy face.

A few powerful kicks propelled his muscular frame through the water and back toward shore. He dropped the flare gun, allowing it to fade into the darkness as he closed his eyes. He pictured the flames of the yacht and imagined it sinking, slipping between the waves and carrying the bodies to the bottom of the bay and the watery grave it promised.

Twenty-nine.

2

North Georgia

The foothills and ravines rose and fell much like the waves of the night before, rising until they almost touched the morning sun, then falling again into a shadow-filled valley, carrying the road with them. Orange and brown leaves drifted down from overhanging hardwoods, bouncing across the pavement before being washed into the ditch. The last remnants of a dying summer. Everything felt crisp and clean.

The stillness of the mountain road was shattered by the roar of the black car, low-slung, with tinted windows and exhaust that shook the mountains to their roots. It blasted around a hillcrest and hurtled into a valley, every curve of the road shoving the car toward the edge, sending wide tires screaming over scarred asphalt, threatening to break free and roll into a ditch at any moment. After another bark of exhaust and a thunderous roar of the oversized engine, the car pulled out of the turn and rocketed forward again.

Reed didn't know the road. He'd never traveled that way before. Each turn was unknown, filled with hidden danger and intoxicating peril. He slammed the Camaro into fourth gear and dumped the clutch. The leather-wrapped steering wheel was damp in his hands, slipping between his fingers as he allowed the car to self-correct out of another turn. Wind ripped through the open windows, flooding the car with the mixed scents of autumn flowers and burning gasoline. It was the kind of smell dreams were made of.

Downshift back to third. Ride the brake and turn to the left. Pull out, half-throttle, just in time to break a slide and prevent the car from spinning into a ravine. The mountains clapped and shook as the exhaust backfired, a sound like a gunshot ripping through the trees. Reed sucked in a lungful of crisp air and relaxed off the throttle, allowing the car to glide to a natural halt at a stop sign. He closed his eyes and listened to the rumble of the V-8. The way the exhaust snarled, even at idle. It was like music, but better than any orchestra the world had ever heard. It was a voice that awoke the deepest parts of his soul, whispering to his heart sweeter than any lover ever could.

Freedom captured in an engine block.

Reed leaned back in the tight racing seat and slid on his sunglasses, then turned to the left and merged onto a four-lane highway. A green sign towered next to the roadway, painted with reflective letters:

ATLANTA, 127 MILES

The roar of the motor receded to a muted rumble as Reed rolled up the windows and ran one hand through his close-cropped hair. The four-lane road brought its own unique thrill: the peace of an American muscle car cruising an American highway. Another taste of freedom tainted by the irrefutable truth that it was only that—a taste.

The icy water and dancing flames of the night before receded into the back of his mind, but they would never fade away completely. They joined a slideshow of twenty-eight other bloody moments over the past three years—moments when Reed stepped into somebody's life and snuffed it out. Every night, that slideshow was the last thing he saw before drifting into oblivion. Every morning it was the first thing that flooded his mind, even before consciousness returned. He couldn't tell the difference between regret or repulsion—whether he felt guilt or simple trauma at the memories. Maybe it was all the same thing. Maybe it didn't matter. The only thing that really mattered was the other side of the list, a number that shrank each time he completed a job. A number that promised freedom when it dropped to zero.

A dull buzz rang from the console, jarring Reed from his thoughts. He hit the accept button on the dash, and the call switched to the speaker system.

"It's done," he said.

The voice that answered sounded sleepy, or maybe drunk. With Brent, there was no way to tell. It could've been both.

"Sweet, dude. I saw the news. It looks like you implemented a little arson. Good stuff."

"Did they salvage the boat?"

"Nah, man, it sank. A few locals took pictures, but there's nothing to worry about. Looks like you cleaned up real nice." The blend of spunk and dismissal in Brent's voice was the sort of casual enthusiasm only a stoned cheerleader could master. Or, in this case, a hitman's handler.

"Good. They won't find much when they raise it."

"Well, it's sitting in fifty feet of water, so it'll take time. They'll probably lift the bodies today."

"Won't be much left," Reed said. "He's got enough alcohol in his stomach to knock out a linebacker."

"Right, right. And the goods?"

"The money is in the trunk of a taxi. New York City. I emailed you the medallion number."

"You checked it out?"

"No, but it's there."

"Sure, man. Whatever you say."

Reed adjusted the phone against his ear and shifted into overdrive. The tachometer dropped, and the rumble of the motor faded into a hum. He heard Brent slurping on something. A drink, or maybe some hard candy.

"I'm ready for the next job," he said. "How soon can you line it up?"

"Um . . . dude, you haven't been paid for the last one." Brent smacked his lips. "Don't you wanna catch your breath?"

"I prefer to stay busy. What do you have?"

"I hadn't planned on booking you. I've only got one gig right now, and I didn't think you'd want it. It's a Georgia State Senator. Atlanta hit."

"That's perfect. Book me."

Brent chomped down with an explosion of wet crunching. Yes, definitely hard candy. "You sure, man? I mean, that's practically your backyard. You shouldn't shit where you eat."

"I'm not worried about it. Just book the hit and send me the file."

"Don't you wanna know what it pays?"

"Nope." Reed hit the end-call button, then dropped the shifter out of overdrive and planted his foot into the accelerator.

Atlanta: 116 miles.

"Don't twist it so hard. You'll strip it." The big greasy hand fell over Reed's, guiding him around one quarter turn of the wrench. "There. Just like that. Twist till it stops, then a quarter turn. No more."

Reed lay on the concrete and gazed up at the underside of the engine block, painted bright red with streaks of oil and grease crisscrossing it at random. His perceptions were clouded by a misted, dreamlike state, making everything he touched and each word he heard muted and distant. The big front tires hung six inches off the ground, just high enough for him to slip his little arm under. He imagined the car falling off the jack stands and jerked his arm back as a wave of thrill surged through his narrow chest.

"Hand me that socket wrench."

Reed felt the cool metal of the wrench between his greasy fingers. It was heavy and difficult to lift in the awkward position beneath the car. His hand looked tiny as he passed the wrench to the man lying beside him. Dave Montgomery took the wrench and slipped it over a sway bar link, twisted until it stopped, then gave it a quarter turn more.

"Will it be faster, Dad?" Reed asked.

Dave fiddled with the linkage, running a clean rag over the bar and toward the wheel hub.

"Speed is nothing if you can't control it, Reed. Tighter sway bars are all about control. Feeling the road when you turn. Keeping the tires planted on the pavement. You understand what I'm saying?"

Reed nodded. He watched in transfixed fascination as Dave lifted a grease gun and lubricated the joints of the front suspension. Grease dripped off the car and splattered on the garage floor.

Dave grabbed a rag and wiped up the spill.

"A good mechanic wouldn't spill grease. That means you've used too much. These tiny brass fittings here? You can tell a lot about a man by what he calls them. An ignoramus might call them a nipple. But a real motorhead knows they're called a zerk."

Reed giggled. "A zurt?"

"No, a zerk."

"That's a funny word."

Dave smiled as he picked up the grease gun again and began to crawl from beneath the car. Reed followed him, scraping his bare knees against the dirt. Dave held out his hand and helped Reed to his feet, then handed him the rag.

"Wipe off your hands. Time to give her a whirl."

The rough rag ground into his little palms as he scrubbed the grease away. Streaks of brown tarnished the red cloth, leaving his palms red. The green car with silver rally wheels sat with its front end lifted on jack stands, the hood raised to expose the big motor.

Twin white rally stripes ran over the hood and the deck of the trunk. A chrome badge, glued to the fender just behind the front wheel, read "Camaro" in graceful italics. Beyond it, just in front of the wheel, another chrome badge was accented with red trim: Z/28.

Reed touched the emblem, running his finger down the Z and beneath the numbers. His skin left a thin sheen of oil, reflecting in the dull light of the setting sun. He smiled, then looked up at his dad.

"Will we wash it today?"

Dave laughed. "Boy, you love to wash a car. No, we don't have time today, but let's turn it over and see how she sounds. Here. Hop in."

A silver key ring flashed in the air. Reed caught it with both hands, and his knees felt suddenly stiff as his fingers closed around the key. He stared down at the glistening silver, blank except for the etched Chevrolet bow tie. "Are you serious?" he mumbled.

"Of course I'm serious. Get in."

Reed didn't wait for him to change his mind. He opened the heavy door and piled onto the worn vinyl seat. It was warm from the blaze of the Alabama sun beating down through the garage door, but it felt like home. He scooted to the front of the seat and strained his left leg to reach for the clutch. His shoe slipped off the edge of the pedal, and he slid closer to the wood-lined steering wheel.

"Okay. First the clutch, all the way to the floor. Then turn it over."

The key clicked against the tumblers as Reed slipped it into the ignition. He bit his lip and pressed the clutch to the floor. It was heavy, and he had to brace himself on the edge of the seat to force the pedal against the floorboard. Then he twisted the key. The starter whined, and the car jolted as the big motor turned over. Once. Twice.

"Give it a little gas, son. Just tap the pedal."

Reed laid his right foot against the pedal and tapped the gas. The car coughed and lurched again, turning over twice more. The exhaust rumbled, and the motor roared to life, sending shockwaves ripping down the body of the car. Reed felt it in the steering wheel. He felt it in the pedals and through the seats. The Camaro shook and thundered; it was an awakened monster, alive and hungry.

"Dad! It's working. It's running!" Reed laughed and ran his hands over the steering wheel. He felt every dimple in the wood and the sharp edge of the metal spokes. He watched the tachometer dance and spike as the engine continued to cough on a bad tune. But it sounded so good. The feeling flooded his body, filling him with warmth and power.

"That's my boy!" Dave leaned through the window and grinned down at Reed. He patted him on the back, then gave his shoulder a squeeze. "You're a natural. The car trusts you. I can hear it."

Reed closed his eyes and bit his lip. His tongue poked between the gap in his teeth. The vibrations rumbled up his spine and pounded in his head. Nothing had ever felt so good.

"Can I help you?" Dave shouted over the roar of the car.

In the distance, Reed heard tires grind against concrete. Something shone across his eyes, and he snapped them open. Red and blue lights flashed in the rearview mirror, and he craned his neck to look behind him. Two black cars were stopped halfway down the long driveway, and tall men in dark suits and sunglasses piled out. They walked toward his father, and one of them flashed a gold badge. Stern wrinkles lined their jaws and foreheads, as though their faces were carved in stone.

"David Montgomery?"

"Yes . . . what can I do for you?"

"Turn around and place your hands behind your back, please."

A cold fist closed inside of Reed's stomach. The smile faded from his lips as he stared through the back glass. The men shoved his father over the rear of the Camaro and planted his face against the decklid of the trunk. His cheeks flushed red, while his eyes widened with strain. He spluttered and tried to lift his head, but the bigger man forced him down again.

"David Montgomery, you are under arrest. The charge is four

counts of securities fraud, two counts of intentional deception of a federal agent, and eight counts of money laundering. You have the right to remain silent. Anything you say...."

The voices faded into a muted blur. Reed's stomach lurched toward his throat as big tears welled, stinging and burning like fire. He jerked the door handle and sprang from the car toward the bumper. The big men hauled Dave up by the elbows and propelled him toward the sedans.

"No! Dad, no!" Reed screamed, grabbed the nearest officer by the leg, and tried to shove him away. The big man leered down at him, grabbing him by the collar and flinging him onto the concrete.

"Get out of the way, kid. We'll get to you soon enough."

They faded away toward the cars. Reed ran after them, tears still streaming down his cheeks as he pounded the pavement. But the farther he ran, the farther away they seemed, lost in the swirl of mist. Another man, tall and menacing, appeared from behind a trash can. Dressed in muted green with a giant hard-brimmed hat, he backhanded Reed across the face, hurling him to the ground.

"Where the hell do you think you're going, recruit? You better fall in before I wipe my boot across your face! You haven't got the *guts* to be a Marine!"

Reed screamed and tried to crawl away. Darkness closed around him, and metal bars sprung out of the ground, blocking his way, pressing in on every side and forcing him into a corner. Still screaming, he beat against the bars and kicked with both feet, but nobody answered. The darkness was so complete, he couldn't see his hands.

Then he heard a smooth, British voice just behind him. Reed whirled around to see a bald man with large ears, a broad, toothy smile, and deep grey eyes leaning toward him.

"Need a hand, son?" The man leaned down and offered his hand. "You're mine now."

Reed lurched out of bed, snatching a loaded SIG Sauer from the nightstand beside him and jamming it toward the leering face. He gasped for air and swung the pistol around the room, searching for a target, but none of the men were there. Not the cops, not the Marine drill sergeant, not the tall British man with big ears. They had all faded into the nightmare like every one before it.

Reed dropped the gun on the covers, pressed his face into his hands, and gasped for air again. His skin prickled, and a shiver racked his torso, chilling him under the breeze of the ceiling fan. He swung his feet out of the bed and stumbled across the loft and down the steps.

The interior of the cabin was still, and he gazed outside over the darkened forest. A night-light glowed against one wall, casting shadows across the hardwood floor. Baxter lay curled up in his favorite armchair, snoring like a dragon with sleep apnea. Drool ran out of the English bulldog's flopping lips, dripping onto the floor in a slow waterfall.

Reed stumbled to the refrigerator and retrieved a beer. He popped the cap off against the edge of the counter, and Baxter's ears pricked up. The old dog poked his head over the arm of the chair, snorting and lapping saliva off his lips, then stared at Reed with more than a hint of annoyance.

"Sorry, boy," Reed muttered. "You know how it is. Night thirst."

Baxter snorted again, then hopped down from the chair and trotted to his water bowl. He lapped up a couple swallows of water, then flopped down under the kitchen table and commenced to snoring again.

Reed watched him for a moment, smiling. Nothing kept Baxter awake. He could have slept through a tornado. The smile faded from Reed's lips as the emotional fallout of the dream sank over him. He gulped down more beer, trying to picture his father's warm smile, trying to recall the gentle laugh. As clear and strong as both had been only moments before, they now felt as old and distant as they truly were.

Almost every night for years, this same dream plagued his tired mind. At first, it was just the nightmare of his father being arrested, occasionally joined by haunted memories of the trial and conviction. After Reed joined the Marine Corps, the nightmare was expanded to include the drill sergeant—the big man with the big hat. Another shouting terror that had nothing to do with his childhood, and yet it dominated the dream as much as Dave Montgomery's violent arrest.

And then the bald man with big ears. So kind and gentle. So menacing. The kingpin killer.

Reed stumbled back up the stairs into the loft. He flipped the nightstand lamp on, then knelt beside the twin bed and reached beneath the overhanging sheets. His fingers closed around the hard edge of a box, wooden and cold, and he dragged it out then sat cross-legged on the floor. Reed took another long pull of beer, flipped the latch open, and lifted the lid.

Mementos lay inside: a few sheets of paper, five fake passports, a spare handgun, and fifty thousand dollars in cash. Reed shuffled the items aside and dug under the stack of papers. He felt the faded photograph under his fingers, recognizing it by its tattered edge, and pulled it free of the pile.

Under the soft glow of the lamp, he saw the green car sitting at the edge of a lake and shining under the sun. The chrome badges affixed to the fender glistened, half-covered by the family that sat in a neat line beside the car. A smiling Dave Montgomery on the right leaned next to his wife with one arm wrapped around her shoulders. Reed sat on his lap, barely six years old, his legs crossed much the same as they were now. The three of them radiated in that picture in a way that no amount of sunlight could fabricate. It was calm and perfect, the way they huddled together in front of that old '69 Z/28. A family together. Safe.

Reed blinked back the stinging in his eyes and shoved the photo into the pile of papers. He tipped the beer bottle up and gulped down the last few pulls of fizzy alcohol. Back in the box, he retrieved a small notebook about three inches tall with a rubber band holding it closed. He pulled the band off and flipped it open. His tight handwriting covered the first page in condensed notes.

March 17. Nova Scotia, Canada. Paul John Grier, age 37. Terminated by asphyxiation with vehicle exhaust. Body left for the police. One down, twenty-nine remaining. I feel as though I died with him.

He flipped a few more pages and then stopped at another entry, this one dated June seventh of the following year.

Marie Florence Thomas. Age 49. Panama City, Panama. Terminated by precision shot, five hundred yards. Body fell into canal. Confirmation of death obtained by secondary contractor. Twelve down, eighteen to go. This was the first woman.

Reed lifted a pencil from the box and flipped to the first blank page. He took a deep breath then scratched a new entry onto the yellow paper. His fingers trembled, and he bore down against the pencil until it bit into the paper.

October 29th. Max Chester. Middle name unknown. Delaware Bay, United States. Terminated by use of alcohol, fire, and drowning. Also had to terminate unknown man there with him. Both bodies lost to sea. Twenty-nine down, one to go. I'm almost free.

Reed stared at the note, rereading it once, then he shut the book, wrapped the rubber band back around it, and pushed the box beneath the bed. His phone dinged from the bedside, and he scooped it up. A notification lit the screen beside Brent's name. He unlocked the phone and opened the message.

Hit Confirmed. Details to follow.

3

Atlanta, Georgia

The lights of the nightclub were almost blinding. Reed sat at the bar, leaned over the counter, and stared into the muddled depths of a Jack and Coke. The ice melted slowly, and the surface of the drink pulsated with each pounding thump of the music.

Reed tipped the glass back, draining the contents, then slammed it back on the counter and nodded at the bartender.

"Make it a double."

A spunky young woman with a heavy Boston accent replaced his glass and poured three fingers from a bottle of Jack.

"Got a new Kentucky bourbon on special tonight. Wanna mix it up?"

Reed shook his head. "Last one, Jen. Gonna call it a night."

"You should stick around. We're playing live music later."

His phone vibrated in his pocket, and he pulled it out. The screen glowed, illuminating a text message from a contact labeled "O.E."

Call me.

Reed hesitated over the text, twisting the glass between his fingers and listening to the ice cubes tumble over one another. He dreaded this moment and the conversation it promised. For twenty-nine kills, his boss had maintained close tabs on Reed, checking in with him every few weeks and offering advice and training. Even knocking him over the head now and again, ensuring he was performing at the top of his game, every time. It was a strange relationship the two of them formed. Oliver Enfield was both master and friend, slaver and mentor. As the bodies piled up and Reed worked his way down the hit list, Oliver allowed him increased independence and allocated him larger paychecks.

For three years I served the U.S. Government, and I never felt as respected as I do by a total, black-hearted killer.

Reed mashed the call button and held the phone against his ear.

Oliver answered with just the hint of an English accent, abrupt but kind. "Reed. We should talk."

Reed lowered his head, covering his left ear.

"Oliver. It's not a great time. Can I call you back?"

"It's important. I want to talk to . . . about . . . kill . . ."

"I can't hear you. Oliver . . . you're breaking up."

The voice faded and crackled on the other end of the line. Reed squinted at the phone and saw one bar illuminated in the top corner of the screen. It must be the nightclub. A metal roof or something.

"Oliver, I'm gonna call you back in ten, okay? I can't hear you."

As the music stopped and the flashing lights faded, Reed drained his glass, dropped a fifty on the counter, and nodded at the bartender.

"I'll catch you later."

He pressed his way into the crowd, glancing toward the corner stage as he heard the manager rambling into the microphone.

"A sensation. A Madonna of our time. Ladies and gentlemen, please welcome the incredible Sirena Wilder!"

The manager stepped back and clapped, and the room erupted in a gentle rumble of applause. The lights focused on the stage as the manager melted into the shadows, and just as Reed started to turn back toward the door, he saw her. The club fell silent, and the girl stood in front of the mic.

Reed stopped, curiosity overcoming his better judgment. He stared over the bobbing heads as the girl picked up a guitar and settled back on a stool. She brushed long blonde bangs from her view and ran her fingers across the strings. The club was breathlessly silent as the gentle melody of the guitar rippled through the audio system. Her face shone softly in the lights, and she stared at her fingers, strumming gently and rocking back and forth on the stool.

When she smiled at the crowd, Reed's heart skipped. She had narrow, graceful features, and her high cheekbones highlighted rosy dimples. Her bright smile shone from her crystal-blue eyes, which were deep and soft, as though nothing ugly or sad had ever touched her life. She was tall and curvy, with just a hint of pudge, and she wore a spaghetti-strap top and jeans with torn-out knees. Her feet, encased in yellow converse sneakers, were tucked under the stool. Her hair fell in gentle waves over her bare shoulders, shining in the stage lights, showing just a touch of red amid the blonde.

Pressing back through the crowd, Reed sat down at the bar without taking his eyes off the stage. He rapped on the counter with his knuckles, and the bartender chuckled and slid him another whiskey.

The guitar intensified over the speakers, and the girl swayed and smiled, alight with passion and excitement. Slowly, she leaned forward and whispered into the mic.

"How we doing tonight, guys?"

The crowd cheered and clapped. Her voice was soft but clear, ringing with confidence, fun, and hint of a Southern accent. Reed swallowed his whiskey. Sirena leaned back on the stool and fingerpicked a few more chords, flooding the small room with a crescendo of melody. She grinned, then leaned forward and abruptly stopped playing. With her lips millimeters from the mic, she began to sing softly.

"He was a vagrant and I a gypsy. I lost my way when he first kissed me."

Reed sat, motionless. Her voice was unlike anything he had ever heard. It was soft, strong, and full of charm. She picked the guitar again, her voice rising with each chord change. When she hit the chorus she slapped the guitar with the palm of her hand between every strum, creating a perfect blend of rhythm and melody. She stood up from the stool and leaned toward the mic as she broke into the bridge. The crowd sang with her, swaying back and forth under the dim lights.

The song ended, and the bartender spoke over the applause. "She's from Decatur. Been playing here for a couple weeks and sings at a few bars around town. Getting kind of popular."

Reed slid his glass back down the counter for a refill, still watching the girl as she began her next song. The crowd talked amongst themselves, ordering drinks, and relaxing to the music. The girl played for another half hour, occasionally swapping the guitar for a keyboard. Her vocal talent ranged from pop to country to eighties rock-and-roll, and every song brought a new round of applause from the half-drunk audience. Still leaning against the bar at the back of the crowd, Reed joined in the show of appreciation.

When Sirena finished her final song, she waved to the audience and blew a kiss, then left through a door backstage. Reed stood and dropped another fifty on the counter. He almost started toward the stage, but the thumping club music and flashing strobe lights returned. He blinked in the blaze and shook his head.

I'm drunk. It's time to go home.

As he pushed through the crowd, he saw her again. She stood at the far end of the bar, leaning on the counter and laughing at a pair of gushing drunks. She offered them each a hug and then signed their cocktail napkins before they grinned and bumbled off. Sirena turned toward the bar, shouting something at the bartender over the blare of the music.

Reed shoved a couple drunks out of the way until he made his way to her. Sirena shuffled through her purse, peeling out a wad of one dollar bills and a handful of change. The bartender walked toward them with a cream-colored daiquiri and a fresh napkin.

Reed sat down on the stool beside her and reached into his pocket.

"May I?"

The girl squinted through the lights at his broad frame. Reed shifted on the stool, leaning down, trying to make himself look less like a killer.

She smiled. "Oh, you're sweet. But us Southern girls can buy our own drinks."

Her accent was evident now. Alabama, for sure. Or maybe Mississippi. The South never sounded so good.

Reed shook his head. "No. I insist. It was a great show."

He pulled a twenty from his wallet and passed it to the bartender. "Another, please."

Jen lifted one eyebrow. "A daiquiri?"

"Yeah . . . sure." Reed leaned on the counter and stared at Sirena as she took a deep sip of the drink then winked at him. The gesture was unexpected, and maybe it was meant to be sly, but it just looked cute.

"Where you from, cowboy?"

Reed cleared his throat. "Here and there."

"The city?"

"Sometimes. And you?"

Sirena took another long sip of the drink. "Mississippi. A little town you wouldn't have heard of."

Mississippi.

He knew it. Man, he loved Mississippi.

"Rebels fan?"

Sirena grinned. "Hell yeah! Damn right."

Reed felt the cold touch of glass in his hand and took a sip of the tangy drink. It was sweeter than he expected. "So what brings a Mississippi Rebel to the big city?"

"Fortune and fame. What else?"

She set the glass down and pulled a tube of lipstick from her purse. With practiced ease, she applied it to her lips then rubbed them together. Each motion was graceful, and confident. He liked it.

Sirena dropped the lipstick back into the purse, then laid a ten-dollar bill on the counter. "Thanks, Jen. I'll see you next week."

Reed pushed the bill back toward her. "I've got the drink. Wanna stay for another?"

Sirena laughed and winked at him. "Oh no, cowboy. I know how that game is played. This girl buys her own drinks. Thanks anyway. You're a champ." She smacked him on the arm and then stepped into the crowd.

A girl who buys her own drinks. Now that's something.

Reed stood up. "Wait. I like you."

Sirena stopped. Reed froze. What the hell did he just say? His throat was suddenly dry, and he cursed under his breath.

Idiot.

Sirena turned around, and a smirk played at the corners of her mouth. He thought she might jack slap him, but instead, she broke into a soft laugh. "Well, okay, then. Straight to the point. You ain't from around here."

His muscles relaxed, and he attempted a coy smile. "Isn't the mystery irresistible?"

She laughed again. "More desperate, I'm afraid. But there's a hint of charm . . . "

Sirena trailed off, but held his gaze. A smile played at the corner of her lips, and he wondered if she were actually intrigued.

Maybe she was as drunk as he.

"What did you have in mind?" she said at last. "I'm not going home with you. And I've had enough drinks."

Reed hesitated, his mind bogged down by indecision. He cleared his throat and motioned toward the stage. "Um . . . wanna dance?"

This time her laugh sounded genuinely amused. "This ain't that kind of club. I've got a better idea."

4

Reed followed Sirena through the tight crowd. She ducked and slipped between the sweaty bodies, occasionally pausing to return a high five or accept a drunken compliment. She moved with the grace and ease of an urban angel, her hips rocking with the beat of the music overhead. Her whole body seemed consumed by music. Even as she walked, it was still in her step. Every beat. Every riff.

The crisp air outside the club was a refreshing relief to the muggy confines of the cramped interior. Reed drew in a long breath and put his hands in his pockets. The glow of the skyline obscured most of the stars, but Sirena smiled as she stared upward.

Reed just watched her, feeling an involuntary smile tug at the corner of his mouth. She looked happy, and as soon as the thought hit him, he realized what a rare thing that actually was.

"I love the stars." Her comment seemed sudden and conclusive, as though she didn't expect or really want a response.

Reed didn't break the moment. Instead, he looked back up at the sky and suddenly wished he could extinguish the city lights. Let the heavens take over.

He'd never wished for something like that before.

Sirena started for the parking lot.

"Let's take a ride."

Reed shifted on his feet, subconsciously adjusting the SIG where it hung in a shoulder holster beneath his shirt. She beckoned him on.

"Come on, cowboy. Don't get cold feet on me now. I wanna show you something."

Reed pulled his car keys from his pocket and turned toward the Camaro, but Sirena shook her head and walked in the other direction.

"Nope. I don't get into cars with strange men. We're taking mine."

Reed followed her down the line of parked SUVs, sedans, and pickup trucks. It looked like a used car lot.

"What if I don't get into cars with strange women?" he said.

"Well, you're in luck. I'm not strange. Crazy, but not strange. Hop in."

Reed followed her around the corner of a pickup and saw a yellow Volkswagen Beetle parked on the other side. It was old. Mid-seventies, at least, with hints of rust around the wheel wells and one missing hubcap. The roof featured a rusted luggage rack, tilted awkwardly toward the driver's side. Mud clung to the tires, and the headlights were misted over with age and erosion.

"This?" Reed couldn't hide his surprise.

Sirena unlocked the door and shrugged. "You can walk."

Reed hurried to the passenger side and piled in, cramming his six-foot-four-inch frame into the confines of the vintage economy car. Sirena landed beside him with a plop and poked the keys into the ignition. She depressed the clutch and tapped the gas pedal a couple times, then twisted the key. A dull clicking sound emanated from the rear of the car.

Sirena rolled her eyes. "Hold on."

She pushed past him and dug around in the back seat. The sound of paper crumbling was followed by metal clanking on metal. Sirena emerged with a hammer and retreated to the rear of the car. She banged around under the hood, then returned to the driver's seat and tossed the hammer into the back.

"Sorry. He does that sometimes."

"He?"

"Oscar. My car. He's old and crusty. But he loves me!"

This woman is crazy.

Reed lifted his hand for the door, but he didn't really intend to open it. She twisted the key, the motor coughed, and the engine roared to life. The little car vibrated as though it were about to fly apart, but it rolled forward with surprising grace and agility.

"I'm Banks, by the way."

Reed twisted in the narrow seat and frowned. "I thought your name was Sirena Wilder."

She laughed. "That's just a stage name. You know . . . to keep the crazies away. My real name is Banks Morccelli."

Reed wanted to point out that her real name sounded a great deal more contrived than her stage name, but somehow the comment didn't seem safe or welcome. Besides, there was something charming about the unusual name. He kind of liked it.

"Chris," he said. "Chris Thomas."

"A pleasure to meet you, Chris." Banks shifted into third gear and turned the Beetle onto the highway. "I may still call you cowboy. It fits your persona better."

"My persona?"

"Yeah, you know. Leaning up on the bar with all that swagger and condescension, judging the whole universe while you sip on a Jack and Coke and hit on the bartender. Cowboy."

He shot her a sideways look, wondering if she had randomly guessed his drink of choice or had observed him consuming it. Maybe Jen mentioned it.

"I'm not judging anyone," he said. A tinge of defensiveness rang in his voice, and he winced. He should have let it go.

Banks laughed. "Relax, dude. You're too serious. Roll your window down. It's stuffy in here."

He turned the crank on the door panel and lowered the tiny

window. Banks followed suit, and the crisp fall air whistled through the little car. It felt amazing on his neck and bare forearms. Through the window, he watched the busy streets of south Atlanta pass by in a blur. Banks drove with aggression and very little grace, grinding each gear and swerving in and out of traffic. The small car would occasionally groan, and Banks would reach forward and pat the dash, poking her bottom lip out and talking to the vehicle directly.

A repressed gut instinct warned Reed that the behavior should alarm him, but he couldn't help finding it endearing. Banks seemed utterly lost in her little world—her windblown hair snapping back behind her ears as she careened around each turn. They pulled up next to a low-slung Monte Carlo at a red light, and the heavy beat of a rap track echoed across the intersection. Reed was surprised to see Banks turn toward the car and offer a "hang loose" gesture at its occupants before she broke out into an enthusiastic attempt at rapping along with the song.

It was terrible. Stifling a smile, Reed looked ahead as the Beetle groaned and bounced forward again, clearing another hill and winding into a residential section of the city.

"Where are we going?" he asked.

Banks shook her head. "Don't ask questions. Just enjoy the ride."

It was difficult to enjoy the ride when his head was continually slamming into the roof of the small car, but there was something enchanting about her careless flamboyance. He wondered how old she was. When he saw her on stage, he assumed she was in her early or mid-twenties, but now he wondered if she might still be a teenager.

Oscar bounced around another corner then slid to a stop in a small parking lot. A MARTA sign stood between the road and a set of train tracks. It read *Oakland City Station*.

Banks jerked the parking brake, then hopped out of the car. "Come on, cowboy!"

Reed pried himself out of the cabin and waited as Banks dug

through the front trunk of the car. She emerged a few seconds later with a small case on backpack straps. She slung it over her shoulder, and they jogged across the street to the station. Reed bought a MARTA card while Banks leaned against the wall, humming and gazing up at the stars.

The train arrived a few minutes later, and Banks hopped on board. Reed hurried to follow, sliding in as the doors smacked shut behind him. The computerized voice of the prerecorded MARTA announcer rang through the car.

"This train is bound for the Doraville Station."

The train started forward with a rush, and Reed started to sit, but Banks grinned and shook her head.

"No. Here, stand in the middle. Now press your feet together. All the way. Yeah, like that. Now bend with the train."

As the momentum of the car climbed, Reed struggled to keep his balance. Banks giggled and swayed with the building g-force, her sneakers remaining planted on the dirty grey floor.

"Come on, cowboy. Ride the bronco!"

Reed couldn't resist a laugh. He stumbled backward and grabbed at the overhead rail. The train stopped at the next station, and Banks urged him to try again. Once more the car launched forward, and once more Reed stood in the middle of the floor with his feet planted together. As the momentum built, he leaned back and focused on maintaining his balance. Lights flashed past the windows, and the wheels clicked on the track underneath. Reed slipped and landed in the middle of the car.

Banks laughed and leaned against the wall.

"Damn, son. You've got the balance of a rolling stone."

Reed shrugged and grinned. His face was hot, and he grabbed the overhead rail. Why did his legs feel so stiff and awkward? He watched Banks as she slouched into a seat and pulled out her phone. Stations flashed past as her fingers clicked on the screen. The light from the phone reflected in her eyes, making her whole face glow. Kicked back in the dingy mass-transit seat, she looked as content with life as anyone he'd ever met.

The announcer rang overhead. "The next station is Lindbergh Center."

Banks jumped up and shoved the phone into her pocket. The train screeched to a halt. As the door slid open, she grabbed his hand. He hesitated and looked down. Her fingers were delicate, wrapped around his, but her grip was stronger than he anticipated.

She pulled his arm, laughing again. "Come on. This is it!"

They ducked through the door and onto the platform. Reed stumbled to keep up, and she led him across the street toward a five-story parking deck. He hesitated. A distant voice in the back of his head nagged him not to wander into a dark parking garage with a stranger. What could Banks possibly want to show him? Was this a setup? Had he misread everything about the pretty blonde?

He gritted his teeth and silenced the voice. He hated feeling cynical and seeing the devil around every corner. This moment was perfect, and he wouldn't ruin that with his practiced paranoia.

Banks pulled him into the garage. "Come on. Trust me."

She slipped past the ticket booth at the entrance of the first level and walked to the elevator. Punching the top floor button, she slumped against the wall and winked at him again.

"I don't get it," Reed said with a chuckle.

"Wait for it."

The elevator stopped at the top floor, and the doors rolled open. Reed stepped out onto the broad, open-air level, and shoved his hands into his pockets. He followed Banks toward the edge of the garage, drinking in deep breaths of the cold air as he watched her hips sway with each step. Even though the only sound in the sharp night air was the squeak of the departing train, Banks still walked as though she was in the middle of a thundering concert.

"Here. Look."

Banks stopped at the waist-high wall that ran around the perimeter of the garage.

Spread out before them, the Atlanta skyline shone beneath the clear black horizon. Each building stood in independent majesty, towering over the sleepy city, glowing champions of the night. The twin peaks of 191 Peachtree Tower glowed in amber glory from the powerful beacon lights nestled at its top. A few blocks away, the cylindrical glass mass of the Westin Peachtree Plaza rose eight hundred feet above street level, glimmering in the light of the other towers as guests slept quietly within its darkened rooms.

The soft glow of the skyline calmed Reed's nerves. He rested his hands against the wall and wondered why he'd never taken time to enjoy this view before. It was both breathtaking and tranquil.

Banks grabbed his shoulder and threw her leg over the wall.

Reed reached for her hand. "Hey! What are you doing?"

"Relax, doofus." She laughed and smacked his arm. "If I were gonna jump, it wouldn't be off a parking garage."

Banks pried his hand free and slung her leg over the wall, plopping down with her feet swinging in midair over the quiet street sixty feet below. She slapped the concrete beside her.

"Have a seat, cowboy."

Reluctantly, Reed slung his legs over the wall and sat down beside her. With a grin on her face, Banks unzipped her case and pulled out a ukulele strung with four plastic strings. It was just big enough to look comical.

She nestled the little instrument over her legs and gently strummed. The melodic sound was both louder and sweeter than Reed anticipated. He folded his arms and sat quietly as she started to sing.

"City lights, city skies. The only love I know, the only place I call home. Wherever I go, these lights hold my heart. They shine in my dark. They love me so."

The world fell still around him, and he watched her. Each twist of her small hand. Her wide, beautiful smile as she sang each line. It was as though he had vanished, and she was lost. Alone in a world that only she knew.

Strumming slowly, she gazed out at the skyline and sang just loud enough to carry a tune over the ring of the instrument. She repeated the song twice, singing softer each time.

Finally, the ukulele fell silent. Banks hugged it against her body and leaned forward, still gazing at the city. For a full five minutes, she just sat, staring at the lights and the gleaming towers. Huddled beside her on the edge of the wall, Reed just watched. Her shoulders, bare under the night breeze, were covered in goosebumps, but she didn't shiver.

Who is this woman?

Between hits, Reed enjoyed the occasional one-night stand. Once upon a time, he'd even had a girlfriend. But he never recalled wanting to know somebody like he wanted to know Banks, watching her right now. A grumpy old bulldog was his family, a dirty cabin his home, and he never minded that. Life was always about the next job—the next bloody checkmark on the hit list.

Get to thirty. Don't get killed. Don't get caught. Don't think too hard about it.

They were such dry, empty ambitions. Did Banks have ambitions? Did she dream at night of being free? Of not having a gun over her head? No. She already embodied freedom, as though nothing and nobody could ever tell her she wasn't alive and as free as the wind.

Maybe that's what I see. Maybe that's what I envy.

Banks looked up at him as though she knew his thoughts, then pulled him in and kissed him on the lips, gently. Reed's heart skipped and then rushed to life. His fingers trembled as he leaned into her. Her soft lips tasted of daiquiri.

God, she can kiss.

Banks drew back and slid her hand down his arm.

"Thanks, cowboy."

Reed sat a little stunned, unsure what to say. At last he mumbled: "For what?"

She poked him in the arm. "For shutting up and enjoying the view."

5

North Georgia

The cell phone's loud buzz woke Reed, and he shoved the blankets off his legs. A hint of sunlight glowed through the east-facing window of the cabin, but the living room was still dark. Quiet. Except for Baxter's snoring, of course. The big bulldog slept on his back in front of the stone fireplace, his legs sticking straight up in the air, his tongue lolling out the side of his mouth.

Reed rubbed the sleep out of his eyes and looked down at the phone.

O.E.

He hit the answer button. "Prosecutor."

It was his preassigned code name. All of Enfield's killers had one, and Enfield picked them himself. Reed earned the title because when he first started his career as an assassin for hire, he needed more than money to kill somebody. He needed a reason. Something to "prosecute" the victim for.

Enfield probably intended the name to be derogatory, but Reed owned it. It worked for him. Except now, after all these years . . . maybe he didn't search as hard for that reason as he used to. Maybe the fact that this person, whoever they were, stood between him and his freedom was reason enough to prosecute them.

"Reed. You never called."

Oliver's voice snapped just a little, jarring Reed back to the present. The older man's tone carried a mixture of annoyance and indifference, and Reed's stomach twisted, a hot lump welling up in his throat. There was no avoiding it now. "I was occupied."

Reed stumbled to his feet and climbed down the steps, accidentally tripping over Baxter on his way to the coffee machine. The big dog snorted and rolled to his feet, bursting into a chorus of barks and charging straight for the sliding glass door. He slammed face-first into the clean glass and stepped back, snorting and swaying on his stubby legs before he fell over sideways and commenced to snoring again.

Reed decided to let Oliver initiate the inevitable. "What do you need?"

"Are you drunk?" Oliver's tone softened a little, almost as if he gave a crap.

"No. Just a little hungover. I was out relaxing last night."

"You show your face too much, kid. It's gonna bite you in the ass one of these days."

Oliver was always saying things like that. Coming from a man whom Reed had only met in person twice over the last three years, Reed wasn't too concerned with the judgment. He knew how to look after himself.

"Everybody needs a little fresh air, Oliver. You could use some yourself."

"I guess you deserved a drink. The client was very satisfied with your work up in Jersey. It should unlock quite a bit of future business for us."

Reed wasn't sure what to say to that; it was always strange discussing death in terms of sales and customers, as though Oliver were running a lemonade stand and struggling to discover the perfect balance of sweet and sour.

"Thank you." It was the only thing Reed could think to say.

"I understand you accepted a new job. The Atlanta hit."

"That's right. Just waiting on Brent to get me the file."

"Excellent. This is a big one, isn't it? Thirty?"

Here we go.

"That's right. This is thirty."

"That's great, Reed. I knew you'd do well, but I have to say you've impressed me. You're an incredible killer."

Reed leaned against the counter and picked up a bottle of whiskey. He took a long sip straight from the bottle and gazed out the front windows of the cabin. The sun rose over the Georgia pines, lighting up the surface of the forty-acre lake lying between the foothills. A glowing mist clung to the surface of the water as the sun began to burn it away.

Banks. He could still feel her kiss on his lips and smell her faint perfume. He could hear her voice and the melody of the ukulele. She left right after kissing him. She had flipped her legs back over the wall, poked him in the ribs, and winked. She'd said, "I like you, cowboy," and without a backward glance, she slung the ukulele over her shoulder and disappeared into the elevator.

Reed wanted to follow her. He wanted to chase her down, seduce her into spending the night with him. Somehow, he knew not to try.

"I think you should take a vacation."

Oliver's sudden comment jarred him out of the daydream, and Reed rubbed his eyes. "I'm glad you say that, Oliver. Actually—"

"You should check out the Caribbean. It's hot down there. Girls half-naked all the time. Get some drinks, bathe in the sun. Rent a sailboat. It's important to recharge. Keep your balance. You'll roll back in here twice the killer you left as."

This is it. I can't put it off any longer.

Reed set the bottle on the counter. "Oliver, I'm retiring. After this hit, I'm done. I fulfilled my end of the deal . . . I'm gonna walk."

The line fell silent. The hot lump returned to Reed's throat, and he shoved a cup under the spout of the coffee machine, watching while it filled. He dumped a healthy shot of whiskey into the mug, then stepped over Baxter and slid the door open.

When Oliver finally spoke, his tone was subdued and soft. He almost sounded tired. "I'm disappointed, Reed."

The wicker rocking chair next to the door had seen better days. Reed eased into it and propped his feet on the porch rail, relishing the wave of relaxation that settled over his body. The coffee was scalding hot, but it felt good on his throat. For weeks he had dreaded this conversation, but now that it had come, he just wanted to plow ahead.

"I've worked hard, Oliver. I'm very grateful for what you've done for me, but a deal is a deal. I'm holding up my end; thirty kills. Then I walk."

"You're looking at this all wrong. Your contract was never meant to be terminal. Of course, you're free after thirty, but you've got a good thing going here. Your salary doubles now, and there are opportunities for advancement. You could run this company. You're that good. Don't walk away when you're just warming up."

Just warming up. Reed tried not to internalize that statement. Tried not to overthink the fact that this man had interpreted his bloody slew of twenty-nine kills as a warm-up for a greater, more catastrophic spree.

He forced himself to sip the coffee, staring at the lake. Then he leaned forward and set the cup on the wicker table beside him. "It's not something I'm willing to discuss. You saved my life. Gave me a second chance. I'll never forget that, but I'm finished after this job. I don't want a career."

Oliver spoke in a dull monotone. "Are you sure about that, Reed?"

"Yes. Absolutely."

His boss sighed. "You're a stubborn one, I'll give you that. I'm gonna be damn sad to see you go."

A tinge of remorse loosened the knot in Reed's stomach. This was the twisted, messed up part. He couldn't make himself view

Oliver as evil. Objectively, his boss was the definition of evil. A man who made his living off the mass murder of others. A kingpin killer. And yet . . . and yet he had been there. When nobody else was. When Reed was facing death himself, alone, at the end of his rope. Oliver had been there.

"I'm very grateful for everything, Oliver. You've been good to me. It's just my time."

"If you're sure."

"I'm sure."

Oliver's voice snapped back to a confident, commanding tone. "All right, then. Let me know when you're done. I'll kick you a bonus for all the hard work."

Reed tapped the end-call button and finished the coffee. Baxter snorted from the other side of the open door, then stumbled out onto the porch for his usual scratch between the ears. He groaned and leaned against the wicker legs of the chair. Reed wondered if Oliver was anything like the old bulldog—tired, grouchy, and losing his edge.

He looked back over the lake and slumped into the chair. The faces of the twenty-nine people he had killed skipped across his memory, beginning with Paul Choc—the Latino man he killed while in prison. That kill sparked a series of events that led him here, twenty-eight kills later. That kill earned him an audience with Oliver Enfield, the kingpin assassin who offered to take Reed off death row, spring him out of prison, and give him a second chance at life. All Reed had to do was kill twenty-nine more people.

Reed closed his eyes, and for the millionth time in his life, he wondered where it all went wrong. Was it when he joined the gangs of South Los Angeles as a teenager? Was that the first misstep? Or was it when he joined the Marines and trained to become an expert killer?

No. Being a Marine pulled him out of the ugly streets of South LA.

So what, then? He rested his head in his hands, letting his mind drift back to years before—years before death row, and prison, and all the brutal realities of being a professional assassin—all the way back to that fateful night in Iraq. He still remembered the way the rifle felt in his hand. The soft kick of the weapon as each bullet left the chamber. The way the men crumbled at the end of his gun, bleeding out in the sand.

That was the moment. Iraq was when everything changed.

Reed looked up, his eyes burning in the light of the rising sun. His body ached, and his brain throbbed. Every thought, every movement was a special sort of micro-agony. And yet...

I would do it again. I would gun them down without a second thought.

Reed rubbed his eyes and set down the cup, then patted Baxter on the rib cage. "As soon as I finish in Atlanta, we're gonna hit the road. I figure we can make Kansas City in a day, and then it's all wide-open highway to California. I've got enough cash set back for us to live on for years. We'll open up that garage and tinker with cars. Maybe find you a bitch."

Baxter snorted.

"Oh, come on," Reed said. "You know what I mean. A *female dog.*"

The bulldog snorted again and waddled back into the house, leaving Reed alone on the porch. He lifted the phone back to his ear and heard it ring three times before the voicemail kicked in.

"Brent, it's Reed. Hurry up with the kill file. Thanks."

Back in the cabin, Reed retrieved the bottle of Jack and settled onto the low stool in front of his laptop on the kitchen table. With a few clicks on his keyboard, he navigated to Facebook. He never used it for personal applications, but maintained a couple fake profiles for research purposes—usually to investigate his next target.

Clicking over the search field, he typed "Banks Morchely" and hit the return key. The results were slim and mostly consisted of business pages for various community banks around the country. No personal profiles matched the beautiful blonde from the night before.

Reed took another sip of Jack and stared at the screen. He snapped his fingers and returned to the search bar. Maybe her last name was like Gucci—the *ch* sound was made with two C's.

Reed typed "Banks Morccelli" into the search field again and drummed his fingers on the table. The internet connection this far off the beaten path was shoddy at best.

A short listing of personal profiles joined the lineup of community banks. Reed scanned them, then allowed his mind to drift back through the haze of whiskey to the night before. He thought about her wide smile and bright blue eyes.

None of the pictures on his screen matched the memory.

Reed shut the laptop and stumbled to the kitchen, where he heated a skillet over the stove and opened a can of dog food. A clump of the food spilled onto the kitchen floor, and Baxter leered at it. Reed sighed and deposited the remainder of the food into the bulldog's bowl.

"Sorry, boy. Kinda hungover this morning."

After Baxter shoved his face deep into his breakfast, Reed returned to the skillet and cracked a couple eggs over the iron. As they began to bubble, he thought again about Banks's goofy, half-sly wink. Her stupid Volkswagen.

Reed reached for his phone, then stopped himself.

No. This was silly. He didn't have time for this. He had a job to do. The last job. There was no room for emotion right now.

If he hadn't been so drunk the night before, he never would have engaged with the singer, no matter how badly he wanted to. It was a pointless, reckless self-exposure. The kind of thing that got assassins killed.

Reed flipped the eggs onto a plate and dropped three strips of bacon into the pan. Baxter appeared out of nowhere, sniffing and snorting. Reed smirked at him and tossed him a piece of raw bacon. The dog slurped it down like spaghetti, then collapsed onto the kitchen rug and began to snore again.

Reed stared down at his pet.

"She would like you," he mused. He wondered what Banks

would say to the dog. Imagined how she would scratch him behind the ears and plop down on the floor beside him. Pull out the ukulele. Maybe sing a song about fat, grouchy dogs.

Reed wondered where she lived. If she had a boyfriend. If she was really from Mississippi, or if she was just passing through. Maybe she would head to Nashville or New York, keep singing, and become famous. Maybe he'd never see her again.

Reed dialed his phone, and a flat, toneless voice answered on the other end.

"Winter."

Reed didn't know if it was a man or a woman on the other end of the line. He never could tell. He didn't know Winter's ethnicity, or where Winter called home. In fact, he didn't know anything about the "analyst" who so often conducted his background checks, research projects, and scavenger hunts as he executed his diverse contracts. Winter was a ghost who knew all, yet couldn't be known. The ultimate eye in the sky. The omnipotent librarian.

If something was going down anywhere in the world, Winter knew about it. If somebody was missing or hiding, Winter could find them. If a whispered conversation took place in a bunker a mile underground, Winter could find out what was said.

Winter wasn't a person. Winter was a force of nature. Hence the name, maybe.

"I need you to pull a file for me," Reed said. "A person."

"Whose account do I charge?" Winter's voice was as toneless and neutral as ever.

"Mine. This isn't a contract. It's personal."

"Very well. What's the name?"

"Banks Morccelli. Female. American. Currently residing in Decatur, Georgia. I think."

Reed heard Winter scratching on a notepad.

"What do you want to know?" The voice sounded more than a little cryptic.

"I'm not sure. Just . . . if she's a real person. Or an alias. Whatever you can find."

"Very well. I'll be in touch."

The phone clicked. Reed chewed his bottom lip as he stared out the glass door again. The phone call made him feel like a stalker, and for all intents and purposes, maybe he was.

But it didn't matter. He had to know.

6

Brent called back fifteen minutes later to inform Reed the kill file was available on his secure email drive. The broker's typical charisma sounded muted, as though he were sick.

The email drive Reed used for work was triple-encrypted and housed on an international server. It wasn't impregnable, but isolated enough to minimize casual governmental surveillance.

He opened the file and scanned the contract. $35,000 for the successful assassination of Mitchell Holiday, without any link to the contracting party. An additional $5,000 paid as a rush fee to complete the job in the next seventy-two hours, and a $15,000 bonus for a "conspicuous prosecution of contract, rendering the target maliciously slain by intentional methods."

In layman's terms, they wanted it to be messy.

The contract was pretty standard, and the compensation was acceptable, but that last footnote, that appeal for a graphic execution, bothered Reed. It wasn't unusual to receive a special request regarding the method of death, and there was usually some form of qualifier or requirement tacked onto the contract. The last agreement requested that he mask the scene from any indicators of a professional hit, which was why he burned the boat and left the gun in his victim's hand. If any evidence remained after the boat sank, none of it would point back to a third party's involvement.

The request for a conspicuous and rushed death was both atypical and concerning, however. It indicated an emotional decision to kill made by somebody who was either rash or desperate. Rash and desperate people were dangerous. They made poor choices, defaulted on payment, and were an absolute liability if they became cornered by the police. The payment wouldn't be a problem—Brent always collected in advance. But something about the hit felt wrong. It was too . . . forced.

Reed scrolled past the outline and stopped at the target profile—Mitchell Thomas Holiday. State senator for Georgia's third district, covering the Atlantic Coast south of Savannah. He held an MBA from Vanderbilt University and owned a thriving logistics company based out of his hometown of Brunswick. Holiday was single, with no ex-wives or children. He was handsome, in his late forties, and had thick, salt-and-pepper hair, a good build, and the kind of smile that won elections—eight of them, ranging in significance from Brunswick town council, to the mayor of Brunswick, and then state senator. This was to be his last term. He had already announced his intention to retire and focus on "other pursuits," although a few pundit blogs named him as a potential candidate for governor.

Reed leaned back and rubbed his chin with one thumb as he stared at the picture.

"What did you do, Mitch? Why do they want you dead?"

Come on, Reed. Not this again. Just cap the SOB, and you're done. It doesn't matter why they want him dead.

Still, he couldn't help but feel a twinge of something in the pit of his stomach. Was it curiosity or foreboding? It was difficult to tell the difference.

The third page listed specific information about Holiday's habits and residence. Not surprisingly, Holiday owned a house in Brunswick, a vacation cabin in North Carolina, and a condominium in downtown Atlanta, which he used while the general assembly was in session. The Senate was in session for another few days, which meant Holiday should be in town.

After memorizing the downtown address, Reed shut the computer and twisted his neck until it popped. He'd take a trip downtown to do some scouting and formulate a plan.

He had seventy-two hours, one press of the trigger . . . and it would all be over.

The Camaro purred like a jungle cat as Reed directed it around the gentle curves of Highway 9 out of Dawsonville. Dawson County was beautiful in late October, with amber leaves drifting down off the foothills and blowing across the asphalt. In spite of the shedding trees, it was warm, and Reed drove with the windows down, enjoying the rumble of the motor and the touch of October on his face.

The foothills faded into city streets, and the Atlanta skyline loomed on the horizon. Small subdivisions and urban townhomes passed on either side, festooned with plastic skeletons, tree-hung ghosts, and Styrofoam tombstones. Halloween was the following day, and the city was fully engaged in the haunted trappings of the creepy holiday. Reed found the celebratory application of death and doom to be relentlessly ironic. Every year, as Halloween swept across the country, he marveled at the millions of Americans who embraced a cartoonish version of death with all the zeal and commercialization they invested into Christmas. He didn't judge them for it. How could they know how churlish the production looked through the eyes of a professional killer? Maybe he envied them and their simple joys and guarded innocence. What would it be like to laugh about fake blood on the floor and to dress up as a grim reaper? Would they laugh as much if they knew how close death might be?

He parked the car at MARTA's North Springs Station and took the train into the city, feeling a strange twinge in the pit of his stomach as he passed Lindbergh Center. It wasn't the first time he kicked himself for letting her walk away. He should have stopped her. Asked for her number. Talked her into returning home with him.

No. Something told him Banks wouldn't have fallen for that. Was she too smart, or just not interested? He couldn't be sure. And now, unless Winter could pull her out of thin air, he might never find out.

Maybe that was best. A gut instinct nagged at the edge of his consciousness, reminding him that attachment was the fast lane to getting himself killed or imprisoned. Again. How would this random infatuation serve him after his last contract? Banks couldn't come with him, and he wasn't sticking around Atlanta. There would be a girl in Idaho or Utah or wherever he finally landed; a girl who would meet the new Reed, a racing mechanic with a boring background and no greater ambitions than a house in the mountains and football on the weekends; a subdued Reed who laid his demons in a mile-deep grave before shoveling concrete over their faces.

What would it be like to have somebody?

Reed rested his head against the vibrating window of the train and pictured himself in a house by the mountains. Maybe there was a big garage with four or five cars to tinker with. Baxter was there, of course. And . . . somebody. When he pictured the house in the hills with snowcapped mountains in the backdrop, it was easy to slip Banks into the rocking chair next to his. Was that because her face was so fresh in his memory? She wasn't the first woman he'd felt sparks with. There had been one other, years before. She was a professional car thief, and they met by sheer chance in the midst of a hit. The whirlwind romance that followed over the next six weeks was overwhelming, but from the outset, Reed knew it wasn't the sort of thing forever and always was made of. Kelly was spontaneous, reckless, and exciting. But she wasn't the type of woman he could picture in the rocking chair. He couldn't imagine her scratching Baxter's ears or strumming a guitar as the sun set.

Could he picture Banks in that chair? Did it matter?

Get yourself together, Reed. This girl is stuck in your head.

Reed shook away the thoughts of Banks and departed the train at the Arts Center Station. He didn't have time for daydreams. What was that old chestnut his mother used to preach at him? Something about carts and horses—doing things in the order they should be done. First, Holiday. Finish his contract and claim his freedom, then leave Georgia behind. Build a new identity and a new life thousands of miles away. Then there would be time for all the other big gaps in his life.

He took a cab from the train station to The Foundry Park due north of town. Mitchell Holiday owned a condominium on the fourteenth floor of The Atlantic—a forty-six floor high-rise situated at 270 17th Street. Interstate 85 was less than a mile to the east, and directly across the street was a small outlet mall sandwiched between the park and the freeway. The Millennium Gate Museum stood down the street next to a small duck pond, bringing a touch of the serene to an otherwise bustling part of the city.

Reed paid the cab driver in cash and pulled a Carolina Panthers hat low over his ears before walking toward the shopping mall. He tossed occasional glances toward the high-rise, acclimating himself to the curvature of the exterior glass and the exposed framework of the post-modern building. It was beautiful, really. Exactly the kind of place a person with a healthy salary would select in North Atlanta. Not quite Buckhead, but not quite Midtown, either. A happy medium for a man who was only home a few short hours each night.

For the next hour, while settled on a metal park bench near the duck pond, Reed observed each person who passed. Locals walked dogs along the path. A crew of landscapers worked on a fall flower bed next to the museum. A mother duck and her ducklings waddled next to the waterline, quacking and butting into each other.

What do you call a mother duck? A hen? That doesn't sound right.

Reed looked up at The Atlantic. Through the glare on the tinted glass, he could just make out the silhouettes of residents bustling back and forth on the inside. Holiday's unit number indicated that it was on the fourteenth floor, but Reed didn't know which side of the building it was on. It would be a trick to figure that out without entering the building, and he wanted to avoid that if possible. There would be cameras, concierges, and old women with oversized handbags—too many people who might remember him later.

Reed dug a cigarette out of his coat pocket and chewed on the end, pondering his options. The most obvious place to isolate Holiday would be at his home. At the Capitol, there was a plethora of security personnel, cameras, metal detectors, and witnesses. Also, the Capitol was situated just south of downtown in a busy district with lots of red lights and one-way streets. It would be incredibly difficult to make a getaway without being trapped amid the traffic. Certainly, it would be conspicuous to kill Holiday on the Capitol steps, but given the right method of execution and the proper dramatic flair, any death would be conspicuous once CNN had their way with it.

The second option would be to hit Holiday someplace open and exposed between home and work. A sports bar or a train station. Someplace where the hit could be lightning quick with a clean getaway and minimal security. Such an arrangement was ideal, and it was how Reed conducted most of his hits: learn his target's patterns and habits, identify an opportunity, and then strike out of the shadows.

The problem with option two was the timing. With less than seventy-two hours to monitor Holiday's daily habits and become accustomed to the places he visited, it would be difficult—almost impossible—to identify an opportunity to make a safe and effective hit. It would require a stroke of dumb luck to hit Holiday without exposing himself. There just wasn't enough time to study the patterns.

That left option three, which was to hit Holiday at home. The high-rise offered minimal security compared to the Capitol, and Holiday's whereabouts would be easy to predict and exploit. Given only a few hours of research, Reed could locate Holiday's unit, identify an ideal method of execution, and begin planning his escape. Holiday would be home at night, providing the cover of darkness and lighter traffic for easier extraction. The cherry on top would be the horrific nature of a senator being executed in his own home. If that wasn't conspicuous, Reed didn't know what was.

Reed shuffled down the sidewalk, still glancing at the building and zeroing in on the fourteenth floor. Every unit had windows, so one side of the building had to offer an exposed view into Holiday's condo. Reed circled the building twice, examining every angle of the fourteenth floor before he realized he was making this way harder than it had to be.

He punched Holiday's address and unit number into Google on his phone and was rewarded with a Zillow listing. The condo last sold in 2016 for $428,980. The listing contained details of the unit, including square footage, a floor plan, and pictures from the inside.

One of the pictures featured the giant wall-to-wall window that framed one side of the kitchen/living room/dining room combo. Zooming in on the picturesque view allowed him to focus on the landmarks. In the distance was a flagpole featuring a small blue flag with a yellow cross. Reed studied the flag, rotated the image, then looked up and scanned the horizon. Several hundred yards away, a blue spec flew a few feet beneath a giant American flag, mounted on top of a building.

Ikea.

Reed retraced his line of sight back toward the high-rise and settled on the fourteenth floor.

"Gotcha."

7

It was a short jog to the Ikea. Reed approached the building from the north side and then turned to get a bearing on the high-rise. It stood in clear view, with no obstructing trees or buildings.

He glanced around the perimeter of the Ikea, checking for cameras, security guards, or foot traffic. The parking lot held a smattering of pickup trucks and minivans, but no police, no golf-cart security, and no rent-a-cop on a Segway.

When he made it to the rear of the building, Reed scanned the loading dock for any surveillance. The alley was quiet and littered with stray paper trash and puddles of oily runoff water. Past the loading dock, along the rear of the store, a dumpster overflowed with cardboard boxes, and directly next to it, an access ladder for the roof clung to the side of the building, its lowest rung hanging ten feet off the ground.

Reed hoisted himself onto the dumpster, and as his shoe squished against the damp edge, he slipped and then dug his fingers into the cold steel to keep from falling. He slowly rose to his feet, taking care to maintain his balance this time, and focused on the ladder.

It was mounted to the wall, four feet away, and about a foot up. After bracing himself agains the block wall of the building, he jumped, reaching out with both arms for the bottom rung. Reed missed the rung, but his hands closed around the man cage that surrounded the ladder, and he winced as the metal bit into his skin. Flakes of rust rained down over his face and into his mouth. As his legs dangled over the concrete and the full strain of his weight descended on his biceps, something in his shoulder popped. No matter how many hours he spent in the gym, he always found a way to pull a muscle and wake up sore. Reed let go with his right hand and grabbed the lowest rung of the ladder, then began to pull himself upward.

Yeah. This was gonna hurt later.

The roof was covered in pea gravel and humming air-conditioning units, and a few spots were patched with tar. At the northeast corner of the building, Reed dropped to his stomach and crawled the last twenty feet to the edge of the roof.

An eighteen-inch parapet surrounded the building, blocking his view beyond. Reed positioned himself onto his knees, then kept his head low as he approached the brink. The sun beat down on the white-painted blocks of the parapet, and Reed shielded his eyes to view the high-rise standing to the east of the duck pond.

From a small case in his cargo pants, he withdrew a digital range finder. It was black, with a magnified scope and an invisible laser which would determine the distance to any object it was pointed at, within fifteen-hundred yards or so. He held the viewfinder to his eye, feeling just a hint of adrenaline rush into his blood. This was it—the journey leading up to the press of the trigger—the suspense and cold calculation. It wasn't about the blood, and it certainly wasn't about the money. It was about pushing himself to the edge, facing death, and ushering another human toward it. It was horrific, gritty—the rawest emotional experience Reed had ever felt. He couldn't tell the difference between dread and anticipation anymore, but he didn't like the feeling. Sure, there were moments when he sat behind the rifle, stared through the scope, and felt like God himself. But that high brought a brutal hangover of darkness and despair directly behind it, reassuring him that the cost wasn't worth the power trip.

The range finder offered him a clear view of the high-rise. Reed focused the crosshairs on the fourteenth floor of the building, then depressed the trigger on the side of the scope, activating the laser. A split second later, the range was displayed in front of the crosshairs —745 yards. An easy shot.

Reed lowered the range finder and studied the high-rise. It wasn't quite square with his position. He viewed Holiday's window from a forty-degree angle, which wasn't ideal; it limited his view of the interior of the condo, and there was a chance Holiday wouldn't expose himself at all.

On the other hand, the roof of the Ikea offered unique advantages. When the coast was clear, he could enter and vacate at his convenience. There would be almost no chance of anyone else climbing to the roof after dark. Other than a handful of security cameras mounted on the light poles in the parking lot, all of which were pointed down, there was no electronic surveillance anywhere. Visually, he would be covered.

Audibly, the Ikea was also advantageous. The humming A/C units would provide moderate masking for a suppressed rifle. Contrary to what Hollywood seemed to believe, silencers didn't reduce the blast of a high-powered rifle cartridge to a puny pop. Even with a state-of-the-art suppression canister, the rifle would still make substantial noise. The A/C units, along with the vehicles in the parking lot, would help. The sound could be excused as a car backfiring or a runaway cart crashing into a minivan. An oblivious civilian wouldn't notice.

Last, there really wasn't another vantage point within range on this side of the high-rise. He could use a van or find a way to disguise his position in a park, but the odds of being caught in such an arrangement were much higher, and the field of view wouldn't be any better.

Ikea was the spot. He would set himself up a few yards behind the parapet and use a shooting mat and a bipod. A kill shot from an unseen assassin while the senator relaxed in his own home would be theatrical, and Reed would have ample time to get lost before the police arrived.

He popped his neck and returned the range finder to its case. He checked the alleyway before hurrying down the ladder and cat-dropping the final ten feet onto the pavement.

It was a Thursday, and the senator would be home sometime after dark. Reed would return to the roof with his rifle and find a place he could conceal himself on the off chance somebody joined him. The glass on the side of the high-rise was reinforced; it wouldn't stop the bullet, but it wouldn't shatter, either. With any luck, Reed would be miles away before anyone knew Holiday was dead.

Breakfast was the last meal Reed had eaten, and nausea began to set in. Packaged beef jerky and can of Coke from a gas station was a poor substitute for a meal, but it would have to suffice. Reed fumbled in his pocket for his wallet.

"That'll be five-sixty."

He nodded and checked his left pocket. Did he leave it in the car? There was spare cash in his tennis shoe, but he really didn't want to dig that out in front of the cashier.

"Think I left my wallet in the car. It'll just be a minute."

"I got you, brother," came a voice behind him.

Reed looked over his shoulder. Behind him stood a short man with a tangled beard, holding a ten-dollar bill in his right hand. He wore torn jeans and a faded Falcons hoodie that was at least a size too large.

"Excuse me?"

The man grunted and set a bottle of water and a pouch of peanuts on the counter, then handed the cashier his ten. "Semper Fi. I got this one."

Reed frowned and shook his head at the cashier, but the half-stoned teenager was already poking the bill into the cash register.

"Semper Fi?"

Reed accepted the Coke and jerky from the man, who then smiled and gestured toward Reed's right forearm, where an Eagle, Globe, and Anchor tattoo was drawn in red ink. Reed pulled the sleeve of his jacket over the tattoo and grunted.

"Let me go to my car. I'll get you your money."

The man snorted and brushed dirty hair out of his face. "Seriously, dude. I got it. Jarheads stick together."

Reed shrugged and turned toward the door. "Well, thanks. Have a good one."

As he pushed through the door back into the crisp fall air, he heard the short man shuffling behind him. "Hey, you got a smoke on you? I was gonna buy a pack, but I'm a little light on cash."

Reed sighed and dug in his pocket. He handed the man a cigarette and then started to walk away again.

"Light?"

Reed stopped half step. He crammed his hand back into his pocket, dug the lighter out, and then waited as the dirty man rolled the smoke between his fingers, dangling the tip over the golden flame.

"You look like an infantryman," the man said. "Am I right?"

"Something like that."

"I was transport. You know, the shmucks in the trucks. Two tours in Iraq. All that jazz. You?"

Reed waved his hand. "Look, man, I'm in a rush. Just keep the lighter."

The dirty man nodded. "All right. Catch you la—"

Before he could finish, a snapping sound rang out from his right leg, and he toppled forward with a grunt of pain, catching himself on the edge of a newspaper dispenser before hitting the sidewalk. Reed lunged forward and caught him by the shoulder, then helped him up. The man gritted his teeth as he leaned back against the wall.

"You okay?" Reed asked.

He grunted, then took a drag of the cigarette. "Yeah. Just my leg. It's prosthetic from the knee down. The joint keeps breaking. I'll take care of it."

Reed looked down to a dirty and worn shoe, now twisted on the end of the man's right leg, looking ready to fall apart. Through the torn canvas, Reed saw a glint of the rusting metal prosthetic, and ripped jeans exposed more of the damaged mechanical appendage.

Reed cursed under his breath. "What happened there?"

"What you think happened? IED in Baghdad."

"You didn't get disability pay?"

He snorted. "You kidding me? I was somewhere I wasn't supposed to be doing something I wasn't supposed to be doing for people who weren't supposed to be giving orders. The VA considered it 'reckless endangerment.' I get three hundred bucks a month."

It wasn't the first such story Reed had heard. Not all the refugees from the Middle East were Middle Eastern.

"Wait here." Reed hurried around the corner and ducked behind a dumpster. He pried his shoe off, lifted the insole, and withdrew five hundred-dollar bills folded neatly together in a flattened wad.

Back around the building, he handed the cash to the slouching vet.

"Here. Go find yourself a shower and some fresh clothes. And for God's sake, get a haircut. You're way out of regs, my friend."

The vet glowered at the money for a long moment, then slowly reached out his right hand. Reed accepted the firm and confident handshake, simultaneously slipping him the cash.

"Sergeant Vincent Russel," he said. "My friends just call me Vince."

"Corporal Reed Montgomery . . . Force Recon."

Vince raised an eyebrow. "Force Recon? No kidding. Reckon your retirement is a helluva lot better than mine."

"Not when you retire in handcuffs." Reed's voice was flat, emotionless.

Vince crammed the bills into his pocket. "Well, then. I guess that's two things we have in common."

"Two things?" Reed cocked his head.

Vince jutted his chin toward Reed's untucked shirt and wrinkled jacket. "Yeah. You're also out of regs."

"Regs are overrated, aren't they?" Reed smirked. "Roll easy, Sergeant."

8

North Georgia

Winter's report waited in Reed's inbox when he returned to the cabin. The single email was labeled with nothing but a capital "W" in the subject line, and in spite of his resolve to leave Banks behind, fresh anticipation and a million questions flooded his mind. Had Winter found her? Who was she? Was anything she told him true? Perhaps the most important question wasn't about Banks . . . maybe it was about himself. Why did he need to know so much? Why did he feel so obsessed over the blonde singer with the ukulele? It was petty . . . childish . . . irresistible.

The first page was blank. The next contained half a dozen color photographs, and he recognized the girl in the pictures. Blonde. Long, swept-back bangs. Bright blue eyes. That intoxicating smile. Banks stood next to an older woman in one photo, and they favored one another. Perhaps it was her mother. Another picture showed her cuddling a black cat on a couch. She smiled while the cat slept.

Reed's fingers felt numb over the mouse pad. Banks was even more beautiful than he remembered, and even more intoxicating curled up on the couch without makeup.

Reed blinked and reached for the whiskey. He took a deep swallow and scrolled to the next page. Her full name was Banks April Morccelli. Born January 14, 1994, so she was a couple years his junior and older than she looked. He was relieved that she wasn't nineteen.

Her home address was an apartment in Decatur, where she lived alone. A 1972 Super Beetle was registered in her name, with three unpaid parking tickets linked to the plate number. Her phone number and email address were both listed, but under the social media tab, Winter had typed "No accounts found."

She's a performer. Why would a performer not have social media accounts?

As he scrolled down a little farther, he learned Banks was employed at a coffee shop in Buckhead. She graduated high school from a public school in rural Mississippi and dropped out of college at Ole Miss. Her passport expired four years ago, and before Decatur, her last known residence was another apartment in Memphis, where she lived for three months.

The next page was labeled "Financials." Reed scanned the tiny notations. Banks held a checking account with a regional bank, and it was overdrawn two hundred and forty dollars. She had over four thousand dollars of unpaid medical bills in collections, her power bill was past due, and she hadn't filed taxes in two years.

Beneath the financial tab were specifics on her medical record, including two hospitalizations in the previous twelve months. Prescriptions were written for various heavy-duty antibiotics. She had Lyme disease and no medical insurance.

Winter's reconnaissance was, as always, highly detailed. Reed wasn't sure what he was looking for when he requested the file, but he wasn't expecting the graphically clear picture that was painted before him: A girl on her own, barely scraping by, and struggling with significant medical conditions. No apparent friends or family to lean on, and no career or place to call home.

He hadn't seen any of that the night before. He would have never guessed her to be broke and alone, let alone chronically sick.

She seemed so happy and colorful, as though nothing in the world could dim her glow. That made her all the more irresistible.

Walk away, Reed. Nothing in this file changes reality. This isn't the time or the woman. Walk away, now.

Reed pushed away the commanding voice in his head and unlocked his phone. It rang once before a friendly female voice answered.

"Lasquo Financial."

"The summer is hot, but at least it won't rain."

"There could be earthquakes," she answered without hesitation.

"Sure, but I have insurance."

"Thank you, sir. How may I direct your call?"

"Get me Thomas Lancaster, please."

"May I ask who's calling?"

"Reed Montgomery. Account ID 4871994."

"One moment, please."

A familiar voice with just a hint of a Cajun warble answered the line.

"Good afternoon, Reed. How are you today?"

Thomas Lancaster was the senior banker for Lasquo Financial, an independent corporation that housed a network of banking services to support the needs of the criminal underworld. The word on the street was that Lasquo was headquartered in New Orleans, but nobody actually knew for sure. Every time Reed's call was routed through their maze-like connection service, it was eventually matched with a new area code in a new city. Today it was area code 775—Reno, Nevada, which was further proof that the company was as ghostly as the people it served. While the money itself was doubtlessly stored in an assortment of Swiss, Grand Cayman, and third-world banks, Lasquo provided the daily conveniences that enabled contract criminals to exchange payments, invest in the stock market, and hide their illegal wealth. It was an orchestrated masterpiece designed to circumvent federal oversight by framing itself as a financial concierge service for elite businessmen. Reed wasn't exactly sure how it worked, and he didn't really care.

"Hello, Thomas. Another day in paradise. Could you pull my balance, please?"

"Sure. Liquid assets?"

"Just the checking is fine."

Reed heard the click of a computer keyboard.

"You have one million, two hundred twenty-two thousand, four hundred eight dollars, and forty-two cents available."

"Outstanding. I guess a payment came in?"

"Thirty-nine thousand, last night. From your last contract."

"Perfect. I'd like to make a wire, please."

"Of course. To which bank?"

"Uhm . . . it's some regional institution. Let me find it."

Reed read off the name of the bank while Thomas continued to tap on his keyboard.

"The beneficiary?"

"Banks Morccelli."

"How much would you like to send?"

"Twenty-five thousand."

"I'll have that out within the hour."

"Great. And Thomas, I'd like it to be anonymous. Is that possible?"

Thomas grunted. "Is the beneficiary not expecting the deposit?"

"No. And I don't want them to question it."

"Hmm . . . well, it's no trouble to make it untraceable. But I suspect that your average person who saw an unexpected deposit would assume it's an error and call the bank. I'll do what I can."

"That's fine. Thanks."

Reed heard the banker mumble something about wire fees, but he wasn't listening. He hung up and stared at Banks's picture. She was everything he remembered. All the grace and charm and charisma glowed just as brightly in the photo as it had under the nightclub lights. Was it wrong to pry into somebody's life? The question hit him like a bucket of ice water over his face. He'd never asked a question like that before, and why should he? Whenever he read a file like this, he was usually about to kill somebody. Digging through a sock drawer with noble intentions was virgin territory, let alone handing out money. Sure, he doled out his share of monthly guilt payments to an assortment of charities, but he never gave money to a specific person. It made him too accessible. Too vulnerable.

He thought about Vince, the homeless Marine at the gas station, and the money he gave him. This would be twice in one day that he made an erratic decision to step outside of his orchestrated comfort zone. It was dangerous, and it exposed him. It built connections he couldn't afford to have. Each relationship was a point of weakness in a carefully crafted armor of detached invincibility.

Armor that keeps me alone.

9

Atlanta, Georgia

The sky was dark and cloudless. The parking lot of the Ikea emptied slowly, and Reed waited two hundred yards away in the Camaro, watching every person who left the building. He had arrived three hours before and surveyed the parking lot, surrounding streets, and passing cars, watching every face, every police cruiser, and searching for any red flags in the quiet urban landscape.

Reed was uncomfortable with pulling off a kill so quickly. He didn't feel prepared. He didn't know the terrain and moving parts well enough. A week of surveillance would have put his mind at ease.

Chill out, Reed. It's just another job—an easy one. The last one.

Reed left the Camaro across the street from the rear of the Ikea, parked in an empty lot with no security cameras or nearby structures. He shouldered a canvas bag and walked back into the alleyway behind the store. The shadows under the moon melded with his black pullover and cargo pants, helping him to blend into the alley and fade from view.

He had learned long ago that the key to sneaking around in a public, civilian environment was not to sneak. Find out where the people are, do your best to avoid them. Act casual, and dodge any professional security or surveillance devices. The rest tended to take care of itself.

Reed stuck his arm through the bag's shoulder strap, then repeated his jump from the dumpster to catch the bottom rung of the ladder. Five seconds later, he slid over the parapet and dropped onto the gravel below. The roof was dark and still hummed with the rhythmic purring of the air conditioners. Even with the chill outside, the interior of the store would quickly become stuffy without the steady ventilation from the A/C units. Reed had counted on that.

He squatted on the roof next to the ladder and listened. The Atlanta skyline glimmered, and his stomach twisted as he remembered the last time he enjoyed that view. It was less than twenty-four hours before, but it felt like days.

Gravel crunched under his boots as he ran toward the edge of the roof. The air was thick and heavy, and his clothes clung to his body, glued by a thin layer of sweat. The moonlight that illuminated the roof outlined a handful of air conditioner units. They purred in the darkness like sleeping cats, providing just enough noise to mask the scrape of his knees against the gravel as he knelt at the edge of the roof. He set a small digital anemometer on the parapet, then drew a deep breath of damp Georgia air. It tasted like city smog.

The anemometer swiveled on its mount until it faced the wind, and the little blades whirred to the hum of the air-conditioning units. Reed crawled back to the bag. After unrolling the shooting mat across the roof, his hands moved in a practiced blur as he withdrew the rifle and locked the barrel into the receiver. He knew every part of the weapon better than he knew himself. The polymer magazine was loaded with twenty rounds of .308. The smooth, aluminum trigger guard curled around the stainless steel, three-pound competition trigger. Known as a thousand-yard rifle due to its average effective range, Reed knew the weapon was capable of slightly more. But tonight, he needed less than eight hundred.

Reed pulled the lens caps off either end of the scope and twisted the power switch. His vision blurred momentarily against the red glow of the crosshairs. He settled down behind the rifle and lifted it into his shoulder, enjoying the familiar touch of the stock against his cheek. For the first time since leaving the car, he allowed himself to relax. With his eyes closed, he focused on loosening each muscle group—his back, legs, shoulders, and stomach—drawing in deep breaths and remaining perfectly still.

Tension faded from his body with each breath, and a calm settled over his mind like a cloud passing over the sun on a hot day. This was his silent place—the moment when distractions and stressors were excommunicated from his mind, and total focus took control. It was a whole-body experience that was more than just embracing the rifle; it was the moment he became part of the weapon.

Reed laid his trigger finger against the trigger guard and gazed through the scope. The dull lights of the shopping mall illuminated his view, and he pivoted the gun to the right until the crosshairs glided across The Atlantic. The parapet blocked his view of the ground, so he counted down from the top of the building, subtracting thirty-two floors before he rested the crosshairs over the fourteen level, then twisted the zoom control to the 30x mark.

The windows of Holiday's corner unit were dark, but through the crystal-clear glass of the powerful optic, Reed could discern the outlines of furniture parked around the living room. Something gleamed beyond the living area—maybe the clock on a microwave or stove.

The fan blades of the anemometer still spun silently, and the LCD read six knots from the southwest. The breeze was barely detectable and would have little impact on a shot at 745 yards, but it was still useful information. The wind might pick up speed or change direction, and a miscalculation could easily lead his bullet off target.

Reed settled back into the stock of the rifle, pressing his cheek against the polymer and resuming his surveillance of the condo. Now there was nothing to do but wait, and hope Holiday showed up.

Hours passed, and the parking lot of the Ikea was desolate, with only a handful of cars still gathered around the front entrance. The wind picked up for a while, then died off completely, leaving the night calm, though Reed wished it would return. A steady breeze could certainly make his shot more difficult, but it provided additional masking for the blast.

Reed lay perfectly still behind the rifle, his left eye shut, and his right eye focused on the condo. Every couple of minutes, he completed a sweep of the entire building and the sidewalk around it. Residents walked their dogs. Men watched TV. Women chatted on phones. Kids played video games. A young couple made love in a shadowy bedroom. None suspected that somebody might be watching them, let alone through the scope of a high-powered rifle.

Refocused on Holiday's condo, Reed checked his watch. It was almost ten o'clock. Holiday might be out at dinner or visiting with friends. Reed wanted to catch him right as he returned home, preferably in the living room where he would be most exposed. One shot to the base of the skull. Avoid the mess of trying to tap him in the bedroom, which was less visible.

A light flashed from somewhere inside the condo, and Reed's muscles tensed. As the kitchen light flooded his optic, somebody crossed his field of view. It was a man, tall and handsome, wearing a light grey jacket and a Braves baseball cap.

Without looking away from the scope, Reed retrieved a car alarm transmitter from his bag, flipped a switch, and was answered by a barely audible beep. It was a universal device, programed to transmit a blast of constantly changing signals until one of them matched a car's emergency system.

Holiday bustled around the kitchen, smiling and talking on his cell phone. He poured himself a glass of wine and took a long sip. The crosshairs rose and fell over the senator with Reed's every gentle breath. Holiday brought his drink into the living room and flipped on the overhead light. Once Reed's eyes adjusted, he saw Holiday sitting on the couch with one leg crossed over the other, still on the phone, and taking sips of wine between animated laughs.

Reed pressed his thumb against the bolt-release button mounted on the left side of the receiver. The stainless-steel bolt slid forward over the magazine, stripping off the top round, and slamming it into the chamber. He disengaged the safety and set his left hand on the remote while holding the rifle into his shoulder with his right.

Holiday's left side was perfectly exposed to the crosshairs. Reed could make out the basic features of his face. The powerful curve of his left shoulder. The wrinkles in his jacket.

Reed lowered the crosshairs until they hovered over the base of Holiday's skull. He reached up and adjusted the windage and elevation knobs on the scope, ensuring the optic was calibrated correctly for the distance.

Holiday set down the phone and grabbed the TV remote. The room flashed as the big flat-screen came to life. Reed wrapped his hand around the grip of the rifle, rested his finger against the trigger guard, then reached down and pressed a button on the transmitter. The device beeped again, and four seconds passed. Then the parking lot below erupted with the blaring of a car horn.

Reed pressed his face against the stock of the rifle and laid his finger against the trigger. He counted silently and matched the beat of the car horn with the tempo of his mind. He would fire on the third blast.

His finger tightened around the trigger, and the crosshairs fell still over Holiday's neck as Reed drew in a half-breath and held it. His world outside the scope blurred from existence, failing to matter anymore. Only the target mattered, and the inevitable moment when that target would crash to the floor.

The horn blared. Once. Twice.

Holiday turned toward the door and smiled. Reed felt the muscles in his chest tense. Something was wrong, he could feel it in the way Holiday's shoulders rose, and his eyes flashed. Was somebody there?

The senator disappeared around the corner, back toward the front door. Every blare of the car horn matched the increasing intensity of Reed's heartbeats. He fought to restore calm to his body, removing his finger from the trigger and rolling his head back until his neck popped. As the seconds ticked by, his urge to surrender to the tension grew. Reed wanted to smash the car and silence its incessant honking.

When Holiday reappeared in the kitchen, Reed pressed his cheek against the stock and laid his finger back on the trigger. A quick twist of his arm pivoted the crosshairs from the living room back into the kitchen—back over the neck of his target. A second slipped by. He took half a breath. And then he saw her.

The breath froze in Reed's throat. He twisted the zoom to the 35x mark and stared through the glass. Her shoulder blades filled his view. Then her neck. Blonde waves fell over her shoulders, and long bangs were swept back over her ears, displaying just a shadow of rosy cheeks. Reed's hands were suddenly damp and swollen. He lifted his finger off the trigger and peeled his tongue from the roof of his mouth. His lips were dry, and his vision blurred around the woman as she turned toward him.

Banks.

The world stopped spinning, and he sat in transfixed stillness as the crosshairs hovered over her smile. She laughed and accepted a glass of wine from Holiday, and he gave her a side hug and kissed the top of her head. In the living room, they sat across from each other. Her long, elegant legs were crossed, revealing torn jeans and the white laces of her yellow sneakers.

The corners of his vision blurred. Each breath burned in his chest, burdening an already pounding heart. He pivoted the crosshairs back to Holiday, settled them over the base of his skull, and then touched the trigger.

One shot. I can't help it that she's here.

One breath. Two. He realigned with every blast of the car horn. The crosshairs twitched over his target, even though Holiday hadn't moved. Reed's breaths were shorter and more labored as he tightened his finger around the trigger . . . and then stopped. He shoved the rifle away from his shoulder and rolled onto his back, covering his face with both hands. "*Shit!*"

He lay on the roof. Whoever owned the SUV silenced the emergency alarm, and the parking lot fell quiet again. In the confused stillness that settled over him, nothing felt real. The world and every trained sense that he had honed in on this one shot only moments before were shattered. His focus, practiced calm, cold calculation—all of it was gone. All he could see was her face—the bright blue eyes, enchanting smile, the grace, and seduction of her every casual move. Each sensation tore through his mind more violently than his bullet would have ever torn through Holiday. They dominated him and reduced him to a numb and disoriented child.

Reed's hands shook as he disassembled the rifle, crammed the parts back into the bag, and jogged back to the ladder. The hangover headache from hours before returned as he dropped off the bottom rung, and every pound of his boots on the concrete echoed in his head with intensifying pain as he made his way back to the Camaro.

He dialed Brent.

"Yeah, boss?"

"Cancel the hit." Reed's voice snapped in the light breeze.

"Um, what?"

"The Holiday job. Cancel it. I'm out."

"Reed, whatever happened, just walk it off, okay? We can—"

"I said cancel it, dammit. This isn't a debate."

Brent was quiet for a moment. Reed slammed the Camaro's

door shut and fumbled in the passenger seat for a bottle of water, but there was nothing except the empty Coke can from earlier that day.

"Reed, listen to me. As your broker. You're about to make a huge mistake. This is number thirty, right? You don't wanna back out on this one. It could send a really bad message."

Reed's shoulders tensed. "How did you know about that?"

"Enfield told me. He didn't get specific, he just said you were under contract for thirty hits. Some kind of private deal between the two of you."

Reed rubbed his chin, digging his fingers into his own skin until they went numb.

"I never intended to continue past thirty. Tell them to get me another target, and I'll finish the hit list, but I won't kill Holiday."

"That's something you can tell them yourself. I'm not getting in the middle of your contract. It's nothing personal, but I won't go down with you."

Reed felt fire flood his veins. "Are you serious?"

"You might be ready to flush your career, but I'm not. These people are serious, Reed. You made a commitment. If you walk out, we can't work together anymore."

"Fine. Nice knowing you." Reed threw the phone into the passenger seat and slammed his open palm against the dash.

Why him? Why Banks? Just one shot away. Three pounds of pressure applied to a performance trigger—that was all that stood between him and the open highway.

What the hell have I done?

The Atlantic wasn't visible from where he was parked, but he could still see her face. It was forever burned into his memory. He'd never met a woman like Banks, and he didn't know why he felt this way, but there was no turning back now. Everything was on the line. He had to see her again.

10

North Georgia

Leather met leather with a wet thud. Sweat sprayed from the glove, showering the white bag in a blast of hot drops. Reed danced back on his right foot, shifting his weight over the ball of his left before lunging forward again.

Whoomp, whoomp. Each stroke jarred his shoulder. Sweat streamed into his eyes, further blurring his bloodshot vision. Another combo to the middle of the bag. Then a headlock. Two death kicks with his left shin. Another stroke on the side of the bag, just where the temple would be. Each blow fell faster than the last. The chain that suspended the bag creaked and jerked against the rafters, threatening to give way under the onslaught of enraged strokes. Reed danced back on his toes and drove a right cross, followed by a left hook, straight into the white leather. He breathed through his mouth between each blow. A hiss, and then a thud. Always in that order. So close together, the sounds melded into an indistinguishable roar, like distant thunder masked by torrential rain beating down on a metal roof.

Shhh. Whoomp. Whoomp. Two distance-testing jabs. *Shhh. Whoomp.* A blow strong enough to crush bone.

Reed stumbled back, allowing his jaw to fall slack as he gasped for air. His bare chest glimmered, and the blood pounding through his veins sent waves of dizziness through his brain, only subjected to reason by larger waves of adrenaline. Power and chaos were always at war with each other for total control of his body.

The light bulb mounted on the cabin wall shone over the back porch. As the bag continued to swing and creek, Reed collapsed against the rail. The night wasn't warm—not for an October night—but after half an hour of incessant pounding, he would have sweated in a snowstorm.

"Baxter! Beer me." Reed peeled off the gloves and tossed them onto a nearby table.

The back door hung open. Toenails clicked against hardwood, followed by the scuffling, snorting sound of the bulldog sinking his teeth into the towrope attached to the refrigerator door. Rows of brown beer bottles were conveniently stowed in the lower door pocket, right at eye-level for the grouchy pooch. A few seconds passed, then Baxter appeared on the back porch with the neck of a beer bottle clamped between his yellow teeth. He dropped it on the rough-sawn decking of the porch, then snorted and sat down.

Reed took a moment to wipe thick streams of doggy saliva off the bottle before popping off the lid against the rail.

Cold and fizzy. The light beer stung his throat and erupted like explosive sandpaper against his tongue.

Reed waved the bottle at Baxter. "That's a good beer."

The bulldog raised one eyebrow at him, then snorted again.

"No. We've been over this. No beer for you. That's animal abuse. Do I look like a criminal to you?"

Baxter closed his eyes as though the effort of staring at the quiet trees around the cabin were just too much strain. His bottom teeth jutted out between his lips, gleaming with slobber under the faint light. In spite of his disgruntled appearance, Reed knew he was content. This was Baxter's favorite time of day.

Reed finished the beer, then flung the bottle at the punching bag. It bounced off and spun into the darkness, crashing into the leaves. Waves of tension rushed through his chest, causing his muscles to tighten.

I was so close. One shot. One trigger pull. It was almost over.

Oliver would call. The kingpin killer would demand answers. There was no excuse for backing out of a hit. It simply wasn't done. Oliver's contractors *always* delivered. It was the hallmark of his company—their core belief. Whatever happens. Whatever it takes. Finish the job.

"I don't have answers," Reed spoke between dry lips. The lie tasted stale as soon as it left his tongue. Obvious and cheap. Oh, he had answers. He knew exactly why he hadn't pulled the trigger, but it wasn't an answer he could offer Oliver.

Reed could hear him now—the words snapping off his tongue like darts full of venom. *"You did what?"*

Reed stood up and placed his palms over the railing.

Does she love him? The thought snapped through his mind with all the explosive energy of an atom bomb. So clear and so obvious. *Does Banks love Holiday? Are they together? Does she smile and laugh with him the way she smiled and laughed on top of that parking garage?*

Each thought stung a little harder than the last. Reed slammed his closed fist into the railing, then drove his toe into the rough planks. Pain shot up his foot as blood dripped from a busted toenail.

What's wrong with me? Why do I care? Why didn't I just pull the damn trigger?

Once again, he saw her gliding across the kitchen, holding the wineglass between her delicate fingers. He saw the way her socks twisted when she spun over the expensive tile, and the flash in her eyes when she hugged Holiday. Was that love? Was that *love* in her eyes?

Reed shouted and drove another punch into the rail, then

glared at Baxter. The dog lifted his head and stared up at Reed with concern and uncertainty.

"Three years. Three years I've been working this job. One trigger pull away from the end, and I flip out over some damn girl? No, don't worry. I'll get it done. There's over twenty hours left. It's just the jitters . . . we've seen this before."

Reed paced the porch, running his fingers through his dripping hair. Each footfall echoed in his tired brain like the roll of a drum, regulating his breathing and helping him to focus. He couldn't return to the Ikea. There was too much risk in appearing there for a third time. He needed a new strategy—another place to strike Holiday. There was still time to formulate a secondary plan, but first, he would need to rest.

Oliver wouldn't call as long as there was still time on the kill clock. Those precious hours could be leveraged to clean this mess up, complete the job, collect the paycheck, and pack up shop—just like he planned. He'd drive far, far away from bloody Atlanta and all the bad memories it contained.

Banks's beautiful face crossed his mind and derailed his train of thought, sending it careening down a new path in the time it took him to blink. Her laugh, so bright and happy, was enough to light the darkest corner of Hell.

She feels like home.

The thought shattered the cloud of confusion around his mind as though it were made of ice. *She feels like home.* He thought again about the house at the foot of the mountains. The rocking chair on the front porch. Banks scratching Baxter behind the ears.

Home is the one thing I've never had. The only thing I want when this carnage is finally over.

Reed jerked the phone out of his pocket and dialed.

"Winter."

"Why didn't you tell me about her relationship with Holiday?" Reed shot off the question before Winter had a chance to draw a breath.

"Excuse me?"

"Senator Holiday." Reed smacked his palm against the railing. "You didn't tell me they were involved."

The line was silent. Reed didn't know if he had caught Winter off guard, or if Winter was simply giving him time to stop shouting.

"First of all"—Winter spoke in a measured monotone—"they aren't involved. He's her godfather. And second, this information was notated on page six of the report. Perhaps you didn't read the entire file."

Reed's mind spun, and he blinked through tired eyes. "Godfather? What the hell are you talking about?"

Winter paused again. Now Reed was almost sure the delay was meant to rebuke him.

"Senator Holiday was close friends with Miss Morccelli's father. They were frat brothers at Vanderbilt. The details are in the file."

Reed lowered the phone and stared into the trees, reviewing the memories one at a time. The way Holiday smiled when she entered the room, how he hugged her from the side, and kissed her on the head. His casual demeanor as he handed her the wine.

No. They weren't together, but they were clearly close—in a father-daughter way. Or, in this case, a godfather way. Holiday was a safe place for Banks—a kind, loyal friend.

And I was going to kill him.

Reed jammed the phone against his ear. "Who ordered the hit?" Once again, silence hung on the line, but this time Reed wasn't having it.

"I know you know. Who ordered the hit?"

"This is thirty, isn't it?"

The sudden question sent an icy chill down Reed's spine. He pressed the phone against his cheek and wrapped his fingers around the railing.

"*What?*"

"This is your thirtieth kill. They call it the freedom bell."

"How the hell do you know that?"

"I've contracted with Oliver Enfield's company for a long time, Reed. I've seen a lot of good contractors come . . . *and* go."

Tension shot down his arms as he dug his fingers into the wood. "What does that mean?"

Winter didn't answer. The silence was so thick, Reed felt as though Winter was sitting beside him.

"Who ordered the hit?" he shouted into the phone.

When Winter replied, the monotone was gone and replaced with a hint of menace.

"Watch your back, Reed. Freedom has a nasty bite."

The line clicked off. Reed's hands shook as he pried the phone away from his ear and stared at the blank screen. Winter had never broken character before and never expressed interest in him as a killer.

Winter had never expressed a warning.

The breach in behavior sent a sting ripping down Reed's back—an army of fire ants digging into his skin.

Who ordered the hit?

Reed snapped his fingers at Baxter and walked back into the house. Everything about this contract felt different and wrong. A voice in the back of his head whispered at him between the blasts of noise and chaos, and he couldn't discern the words, but he heard the voice, muffled and confused.

Mitchell Holiday might well deserve to die, but Reed wasn't taking the shot until he knew why. Nobody forced him into a corner, and nobody could make him take away this woman's godfather without knowing why. It was time to jerk back the curtain and find some answers.

He would start with Banks.

11

Decatur, Georgia

Glistening globes of dew still clung to each blade of browned grass, even as the sun arced toward its noon-time high, bathing Decatur in welcome warmth. The cough-rumble of the Camaro felt as blasphemous to the peace of the morning as a raunchy laugh in a graveyard, and Reed switched the car off and sat in silence as he surveyed the duplex, tired and old with peeling paint. Bits of sunbaked shingles lay in the flowerbed at random. Plastic jack-o'-lanterns guarded the entrance, their crooked smiles leering at Reed as if they knew why he had come, but they just didn't give a damn. A stray tabby cat bounced across the porch and around the house, chasing a butterfly between the bushes. But there were no people, no laughing children or bustling adults. The neighborhood, which consisted entirely of battered duplexes and brick apartment homes, was as cold and unfriendly as a warzone—decay and despair, and too little of everything.

A couple of teenagers wandered out of a side street, bouncing a basketball and talking in subdued mumbles. Reed waited for them to pass within easy earshot of the car, then he whistled. "Hey. You guys know a blonde girl who lives here?"

They stopped and stared at him as though he were an invader, armed to the teeth and ready to burn down what was left of their battered homes.

So then, Banks wasn't home. A twinge of defeat bubbled in his stomach, or was it just disappointment? Maybe he should go back to Atlanta and check the nightclub. But it didn't open until late afternoon, and anyway, if Banks left home to run errands, she would most likely do that locally. One of the numerous grocery stores or farmer's markets in the area were likely destinations for a morning shopping trip.

It was a good bet. He spotted the yellow Volkswagen fifteen minutes later, parked in front of her bank. He left the Camaro a hundred yards away in an adjoining supermarket lot and jogged toward the squat brick building. He wasn't sure what his plan was. Maybe he would pretend he was at the bank on personal business. Make it out to be a coincidence. Then ask her out to lunch and talk to her. Find out about Holiday. Figure out what the hell was going on.

His thoughts trailed off as he passed the Beetle. He stopped and stared at the rusty antique, remembering the clatter of the underpowered engine—the squeak of the suspension at every turn. The way Banks drove with reckless abandon—as though she were the only person on the road—the perpetual smile on her face, and the way the wind tossed her hair.

The front door of the bank slammed shut as a customer walked out. Reed looked back at the Beetle, then walked toward the door.

The bank was cold and sterile, and gaudy marketing covered the walls. Glass offices lined the perimeter of a crowded waiting area. A line of a dozen impatient customers stood in front of the counter, and the tellers looked distant and detached, as though they were present in body alone. It was such a stark contrast to the five-star banking experience Reed was accustomed to through

Lasquo Financial. The building was more like a title loan office than a bank.

"I don't know where it came from. It's not my money. That's the problem!"

Reed immediately recognized the thick Southern accent laden with emotion and frustration. Banks, with her back turned toward him, sat in one of the glass offices to his right. An overweight man with a thinning hairline and cheap glasses sat behind the desk, a look of exhaustion covering his chalky features.

"Ma'am, I realize you're upset. If you calm down, I'm sure we can figure this out."

"There's nothing to figure out. There's twenty-five thousand dollars in my account that doesn't belong to me. Take it out, please."

"Um, well, it's not that simple."

Banks rubbed her temples. "Why not?"

"Well, first of all, that would leave you overdrawn. You were overdrawn when the wire posted to your account."

"I'm aware of that. I'll pay you in a couple days. It's been a rough week, okay? In the meantime, take the money out of my account. You guys should be more careful where you stick money."

The banker looked ready to shoot himself. "Ma'am, I already told you. We don't 'stick money' in people's accounts. The wire was made payable directly to you, with your account number notated. We credited it to your account accordingly."

"Well, I don't want it!" Banks smacked the desk with her palm.

The banker sat forward, rubbing his eyes with a shaky right hand.

"Miss Morccelli, it's unfathomable to me that a person in your position would be so opposed—"

"My position? And just *what is* my position, exactly?" A tinge of indignation edged into her voice.

The banker backpedaled. "That's not what I meant. I'm just saying—"

"That I'm a broke-ass overdrafter? That's it. Close my account. I'm not dealing with this. I don't need anybody's help!"

Reed stood still by the door, transfixed by the scene unfolding in front of him. He wasn't sure how he expected Banks to respond when twenty-five grand appeared in her account out of nowhere. Stupidly, he assumed she would be grateful and apply the windfall toward her medical debt. He now realized how arrogant and belittling that assumption had been, but he was still taken aback by her vehement refusal to accept or even entertain a handout. It was fiercely independent. Aggressively proud.

Ridiculously attractive.

An annoyed voice grabbed his attention.

"Can I help you, sir?" A short woman wearing a crooked name badge leered at him. She looked utterly done with life.

Reed realized he was standing in the middle of the lobby with his hands in his pockets. "No. I'm good," he said as he rushed back outside.

He was a fool for assuming Banks would simply take the money. More than that, he was an asshole for tracking her down. She was independent and didn't want to be babied, which explained why she was the goddaughter of a millionaire and still drove a rattletrap of a car and was in debt up to her ears. She didn't want the help. She had it covered. More than that, she didn't have time to fix his problems. Holiday was his problem, and roping Banks into the middle of this mess wouldn't be fair to her. He would have to find the answers he needed without exposing her to whatever menace ordered the hit.

Before he could start the engine of the Camaro, his phone vibrated in his pocket. The dark screen read "UNKNOWN."

Reed hesitated, then hit the answer button and said nothing while he waited for the caller to speak first.

"You screwed up, Montgomery." The voice was computerized, like that of an automated answering machine.

"Who is this?"

"Somebody who doesn't like being let down, Reed. Somebody who feels very let down by your failure to assassinate Senator Holiday."

A rush of warmth flooded Reed's cheeks, and his heart rate accelerated. The sounds and distractions of the supermarket parking lot vanished around him.

"Look, smartass. I never fail, and I don't deal with anyone over the phone. You got a problem, call my broker."

"I'm afraid your broker is quite indisposed at the moment."

"What?"

Reed's voice was drowned out by a blood-curdling scream. Agony flooded the phone, echoing as though it came from an amphitheater. Reed jerked the phone away from his ear as he caught his breath. The screams continued, ringing as though they were voiced straight from Hell. Pleas for mercy were mixed with dull groans and shrill shrieks, all fused into one horrific chorus.

The air inside the Camaro was suddenly thick and sticky, as though Reed were breathing through a straw. He held the phone against his knee, muting the hellish voice of death. Moments felt like hours, until at last the screams faded, and the computerized tone took over.

"I sent you pictures. You have twelve hours to finish the job. Don't test me."

Reed swallowed back the dryness in his mouth and punched the steering wheel. Before he could respond, the caller hung up, leaving the screen vacant. A moment later, the first text appeared. Reed's fingers felt thick and heavy as he unlocked his phone. The ghastly image that greeted him sent waves of nausea ripping through his stomach.

Brent.

He lay on a concrete floor, tied between wooden posts, his face twisted into a death scream. Shreds of skin and flesh decorated the floor beside him, exposing an empty stomach cavity. He was disemboweled, gutted from throat to groin.

Blinding rage replaced nausea, and Reed jammed the car into

gear and dumped the clutch. The rear tires screamed against the pavement, screeching over the howl of the engine as the rear end of the vehicle swung outward. The rubber caught, and the Camaro rocketed forward out of the parking lot and back onto the highway.

Back toward Atlanta.

12

"I need you to post a hit for me," Reed shouted over the thunder of the engine. The fall breeze snapped around the mirrors and battered the headliner of the car, stinging his eyes. The wind tasted fresh and clean—a welcome relief against the smothering feeling against his chest.

Nobody answered, and Reed rolled up the windows. "Winter, did you hear me?"

A dry voice coughed, then Winter's stagnant tone flowed from the speaker.

"Who is the target?"

"Senator Mitchell Holiday."

This time the pause felt heavy, as though it were laden with unspoken thoughts and conflicting emotions. Reed didn't have time for either.

"Did you hear me? Can you do it or not?"

Another dry cough. "What's the bounty?"

"I don't care. Half a million."

Reed thought he heard the scratch of a pen on paper, but maybe it was just the squeak of whatever robotic entity Winter consisted of.

"My service fee is twenty-five hundred. I'll draft your account. Any special requests?"

"Yes. I want it posted to Section 13, dark web."

The pen tapped on the notepad. Reed could hear each slow click.

"Are you aware that Section 13 has been compromised by the FBI?"

"I am. Post it anonymously. Ignore anyone who's dumb enough to respond."

"Very well. The listing will be live in twenty minutes."

Nausea returned to the pit of Reed's stomach, boiling like a jar of sour vegetable oil. Every muscle in his body was tense. He downshifted into fourth and blew past a semi-truck. The nervousness growing in the back of his mind washed over him in waves—it was something a little worse than shock, and a little less than panic.

Brent was dead—slaughtered like a pig. It was a blatant attack on his own doorstep by a defiant challenger. Nothing like this had ever happened before. Reed wasn't particularly attached to Brent, or to anyone he worked with, but Brent was the partner he spoke to most often. He knew Brent had blond hair and loved mint ice cream and video games. The chatty broker was from Detroit and had a mother he sent checks to every month in a nursing home. She thought he worked for a military history museum in Rome. She had no idea her son was neck-deep in the mire of organized crime, and she would never know what fate befell him. He would simply vanish, gone without a trace, snuffed out like any one of Reed's victims.

The thought brought renewed rage into Reed's soul. No, he didn't care about Brent, not personally, but a line had been crossed. A line that couldn't be ignored. The contract had now spilled far, far beyond the realms of acceptable business practices, even for the criminal underworld. There was a debt to pay and a statement to make.

You don't shit on Reed Montgomery's doorstep and walk away breathing.

Reed snatched up his phone and speed-dialed the first contact, focusing on calming his nerves and backing away from a precipice of uncontrolled, rampaging madness. The answering machine picked up and greeted him with a single-word message: "Enfield." Then the beep.

"Oliver." The word snapped like a gunshot, and Reed forced himself to take another breath before continuing. "We need to talk immediately. Call me back as soon as you get this."

Reed rolled the windows down again and sucked in a lungful of air, which helped restore control over his body. He checked the clock on the dash and counted backward to the phone call with Winter.

He'd give it another hour, and then he would cancel the hit.

13

Senator Mitchell Holiday, known to his friends and foes alike as "Fighting Mitch," was feeling the wear of civil service. He sat behind the broad oak desk in his congressional office and set his reading glasses on the table. His back hurt. His neck hurt. He had a headache. And his damn knee was acting up again.

The plush leather of his office chair squeaked as Holiday leaned back. He didn't drink at the office—not anymore, anyway—but a bourbon, smooth and strong, would've really taken the edge off. He laid his hands on the arms of the chair and sat perfectly still, letting the stress and strain seep out of him.

His knee burned like fire, and he straightened his leg, attempting to relieve the strain. It was an old football injury. Holiday played for Grand Republic Preparatory School in Savannah as a running back. That was where Fighting Mitch was born. Given a chance, he always chose to run the ball straight through the defensive line instead of around. He was a sensation. Local sports commentators called him NFL talent, the pride of South Georgia. Right up to the moment the two-hundred-eighty-pound senior from Athens crashed into his shoulder and slammed him to the ground, leaving his foot caught in the soft mud. When his knee exploded, it snuffed out all ambitions of a football career in a split second.

Grand Republic was losing that night. Down twenty-one points with an Athens quarterback who had their number. But when Holiday hit the mud, vengeful fire that could've won them a Super Bowl erupted through his team. He could still hear his quarterback, Danny McKnight, shouting at the offensive line moments before the snap. He could see the explosion of glistening rainwater as shoulder pads and helmets crashed together. And then, with only seconds left on the clock, he could hear the roar of the crowd as the ball flipped between the uprights. It was the biggest upset of the season.

Holiday would never forget that night. He refused medical care until the end of the game, at which point his teammates carried him off the field on their shoulders as Danny screamed and threw his helmet into the air. Grand Republic's quarterback went on to serve in the National Guard, deployed for Desert Storm, where he was blown in half by a landmine. Holiday wasn't there, but he heard that blast in his nightmares. He imagined Danny lying in the mud, his blue eyes wide and empty, as if to say, "Where are you, Mitch? Why aren't you here to carry me off the field?"

Real life was so much colder than football. Upsets were never as simple as a field goal.

The chair groaned again as Holiday sat up. He lifted a cigarette from the desk drawer and flicked his thumb against a polished Zippo lighter. Icy waves of menthol filled his lungs, loosening his muscles and easing the tension on his strained nerves. He leaned back and dragged another cloud of smoke from the cigarette. It burned and soothed all at the same time. In the temporary relaxation of the nicotine, he could still see Danny pumping his fist in the air and grinning at the crowd. Today, in this moment, Holiday didn't feel much like Fighting Mitch anymore. He'd give anything to have Danny here, to have the whole team carry him out of the chaotic hell he called home.

Holiday walked to the window and gazed out of the Georgia

State Capitol and over the busy streets of downtown Atlanta. If he survived the remainder of the term, he would sell the logistics company. Sell the house in Brunswick, the condo here in Atlanta, and the cabin in North Carolina. Leave an inheritance for Banks and disappear out west somewhere. He'd always wanted to live out west. Holiday was a wealthy man, and for all his grandeur and resources, Georgia had chained him down his entire life. Maybe he could finally cut loose and buy a cabin someplace in the mountains of Wyoming, miles and miles from anyone and everyone. Get a dog and name him Burt, for no reason at all. Drive an old, beat-up pickup truck and hunt in the summer. Write a book in the winter. He'd always wanted to try his hand at a novel, but he just never had the time.

A trail of scarlet embers rained through the air as Holiday flicked the cigarette into a brass trash can. He rubbed his eyes with both hands, then jammed his thumb against the speaker button on his desk phone.

"Yes, sir?"

"Get me Matt Rollick."

As the smoke faded from his lungs, Holiday could already feel his chest begin to tighten again. The air in the big office was thick and hot, as though he were sitting in a sauna. He picked up a pen and clicked it. Open. Closed. Open again. Each snap of the pen was a small explosion in the still room. His fingers stuck against the cheap plastic, leaving smudges on the barrel.

"Agent Rollick." The voice, loud and jarring, crackled over the speakerphone.

Holiday switched to the receiver.

"This is Senator Holiday. I'm calling you in reference to our conversation yesterday."

After a rustle of papers from the other end of the line, Rollick's voice softened some, but he remained all-business.

"Glad to hear from you, Senator. Where do we stand regarding the FBI's offer?"

Open. Closed. The pen clicked again, and Holiday stared at the writing on its barrel. Some local pest control company. God only knew how it found its way to his desk. He ran his tongue across dry lips, then set the pen down.

"I need assurances regarding my goddaughter."

"Banks?"

"Yes. I want her left out of this. Completely. No interviews. No media. No agency attention. Nothing."

"You know I can't guarantee that, Senator."

"Then you don't have a deal. I'll burn in Hell before I watch her dragged through this mess."

"If you don't cooperate, you may very well get your wish. I can commit to distance from the agency, assuming you give us everything we need to know. I have no control over the media."

"No good, agent. I've made it clear from day one that Banks will not be involved."

"She isn't involved. I don't see the problem."

"It's her father. I want the agency's commitment that they won't turn this into a smear campaign, and that the media will be left out of it."

"I'm not in charge of media relations. I'm an investigator. My job is to investigate. If you're not willing to cooperate, you may be facing media attention of your own. Your hands aren't clean, Senator. Don't forget that."

"Are you threatening me?"

"I'm reminding you of the cards you've been dealt. This could be your last chance to step out of this alive. When this investigation sees the light of day, I won't be able to protect you if you're not on my side. Do you understand what I'm saying, Senator?"

The room was suddenly calm as if the world were holding its breath. Holiday sucked in the thick and stale air and tapped his finger against the desktop. His mind raced, but really, there wasn't much to decide.

"Banks is given protective custody. Complete isolation from the media. And Frank is a hero. Do you hear me? No smearing. The man died a hero."

Rollick sighed. "I'm not going to make promises I can't keep. You either trust me or you don't. There are no guarantees."

"Then there's no deal. Good luck unraveling this cluster on your own."

Holiday slammed the headset back onto the hook and clenched his fist. Exhaustion overwhelmed his mind. It was the sort of total, crushing fatigue that no amount of rest or nicotine could relieve. It was death itself knocking at his doorstep.

He sat in perfect stillness for what must have been half an hour. Rollick would call back. The investigator couldn't drop a witness this crucial. He would make some calls and find a way to meet Holiday's demands. And then he would call back.

Holiday suddenly wondered if God was listening. He hadn't prayed in twenty years. Not since his high school sweetheart and the love of his life, Mary Truant Anderson, wasted away on an Atlanta hospital bed, eaten alive by what should have been a curable cancer. None of the medications had any effect, and none of the treatments slowed it down. It devoured her body in a matter of weeks, draining her away to a mere shadow of her old self before the life breath finally left her lungs.

It was as though God himself had sucked the life out of her and struck her down right in the prime of life, for no reason or purpose. She was a beautiful soul. A loving, kind-hearted angel. Somebody who truly didn't deserve to die.

If God wouldn't listen to prayers for somebody as beautiful as Mary, there was no way he would hear prayers for somebody as battered and war-torn as Mitchell Holiday. There was blood on these hands.

The intercom buzzed, jarring Holiday back to the present.

"Senator, there's men here from the FBI. They want . . . Wait! You can't go in there!"

The door slammed back on its hinges, crashing into the mahogany wall with a thunderclap. Holiday jumped up and shoved the chair in front of him, his fight-or-flight instincts kicking in with a wave of panic. Four men wearing black suits and stern glares barged through the door. The lead guy flashed a gold badge and stomped right up to the desk.

"Agent Wes Harper, FBI. You need to come with us, Senator."

Holiday clutched the back of his chair, and his knuckles turned white. He took a slow breath and forced himself to assume the diplomatic confidence that won his elections. Calm. Southern. Just a little indignant. "Agent, you can't just bust in here. I've already told Agent Rollick I'm not going anywhere until my demands are met. That's the final word on this matter."

Harper's brow wrinkled. The hand holding the badge fell to his side, and he turned to one of his colleagues, who only shrugged.

Holiday swallowed, feeling his stomach twist into a knot. The moments ticked by in slow motion.

Harper turned back. He shoved the badge into his pocket and stepped to the side, motioning to the door. "I have no idea what you're talking about, Senator, but you need to come with us. There's been a credible threat to your life. You are now under the protective custody of the FBI."

14

North Georgia

The fall wind blowing off the mountains brought a bite with it when Reed stepped out of the Camaro. Leaves rattled across the gravel driveway and tumbled over one another, and the chill penetrated his jacket, sending a slight shiver down his back. He shoved his hands deeper into his pockets and kicked at the steps of the porch, knocking dirt off his shoes. Baxter lay just inside the door, snoring like a troll with a lake of drool gathering around his snout. Reed knelt beside him and scratched behind his floppy ears. Baxter's snores became more regular, and his body fell limp under the gentle stroking.

There was something singularly peaceful about a sleeping dog. Reed often found himself envying the simple life of his pet, and he couldn't help but smile as he thought how far the fat pooch had come from the mangy stray that showed up on his doorstep two years before. That dog had been only days from death, and more than a little gun shy of humanity. But as the weeks passed, a strange connection developed between them. Maybe they were both beat-up and scarred and scared of the world. Maybe they both needed a friend who didn't ask too many questions.

The gas stove hissed and clicked as Reed flipped it on then set a skillet over the flame. He dropped a thick ribeye into the pan and was rewarded by the sizzle of red meat frying on hot iron. The little cabin was flooded with the greasy aroma of quality beef, followed by the sound of Baxter rolling to his feet and wobbling into the kitchen.

"Nice nap?" Reed flipped the steak and sprinkled seasoning from an unmarked bottle over the browned side. Baxter snorted and sat down beside him, panting and staring at the pan.

"There's been a problem," Reed muttered. "Somebody took a dump on our front porch. Gonna have to do something about it."

Grease sizzled and spat from the pan. Reed flipped the steak onto a plate and then dumped a can of green beans into a saucepan before setting it on the stove. Soon the water began to bubble and steam as the beans danced beneath the rolling surface.

"The thing is . . . there's this girl. I met her the other night, and I was gonna tell you about her. I don't know, man. She's something else."

Reed opened a can of dog food and kicked Baxter's bowl out from under the cabinet before dumping the slop into it. Baxter snorted and looked at the steak.

"You ever met a girl—or dog—who just made the world go 'round? You know. Maybe a French bulldog. I could see you with a Frenchie."

Water bubbled over the edge of the pan. Reed lifted it off the stove and dumped the water into the sink before emptying the beans onto the plate. An icy cold German lager from the fridge completed the menu. Reed sat at the table and wiped the grease off a fork and knife from his dinner the night before. The first bite of steak tasted perfect. Tender and red, with just a trace of blood oozing from the center.

"I don't know, man. Right now, there are more pressing issues.

Somebody took out Brent, and I'm not sure what to do about it. What would you do?"

Baxter sat beside the table with his head tilted to one side, and his lower teeth jutting out over his lip. Drool dripped down the side of his face. Reed cut a piece of ribeye from the edge of the steak and dropped it over his nose. Baxter wolfed it down in one swallow and returned to his previous pose.

Reed took a bite of green beans and waved his fork at the dog. "This is my steak. You want steak, you get a job. I've had about enough of your freeloading. You don't even sweep the damn porch."

The old bulldog woofed spit over Reed's leg then wandered back into the kitchen and contented himself with slurping up the bowl of dog food. Reed pulled the phone out of his pocket. He tried calling Oliver, and once more was sent to voicemail. It was unlike his boss to not answer, and even more out of character for him to not call back.

Oliver remained highly connected to his organization. Even though his contractors operated with a certain level of anonymity, Oliver kept close tabs on their activities and needs. His unexpected distance was disconcerting.

The last bite of steak, washed down with a swallow of beer, made a perfect finale to a delicious meal. Reed set the plate on the floor for Baxter to lick clean, then relocated to his desk and powered on the laptop. He needed to learn everything he could about Mitchell Holiday. Usually, he would short-circuit the research project and assign the job to Winter, but Reed was starting to feel unsure about the ghost, who typically made it a practice to remain detached and neutral in all business dealings. Winter's cryptic warning from the night before left Reed feeling more than a little uneasy.

Google would have to take Winter's place for now. A quick search produced a handful of old blogs, social media posts, and even pictures of Holiday in grade school. An article from a Savannah newspaper detailed Holiday's tragic football injury and how it derailed multiple collegiate scholarships. A few sources mentioned legislative actions and business dealings, but nothing was very helpful. By all accounts, Holiday was a traditional, low-level politician, hallmarked by occasional controversy and a handful of red-letter moments. Nothing special. Certainly nothing worth killing a man over.

Whatever Holiday had stumbled into, it wasn't a public matter, and that wasn't surprising. Reed's contracts usually involved underhanded deals gone bad.

By now, the FBI would have red-flagged the hit listing on the dark web and placed Holiday under protective custody, probably in one of the Capitol Police buildings downtown. Reed appreciated the breathing room that provided him, but he knew it wouldn't last. Whoever killed Brent had already demonstrated vicious intolerance for being defied, and placing Holiday under the nose of the FBI was far from checkmate.

"They'll come after me next," he said aloud. "A dominance kill. Probably back off on Holiday for a bit. Wait for things to cool down."

And then I'm going to burn their party down. His thought wasn't an emotional decision—just an inevitable one. When this was done—when the smoke settled and he checked off the thirtieth kill and disappeared forever—he couldn't leave any loose ends behind.

The last drops of beer tasted warm and bitter. Reed tossed the bottle into the trash, stood up, popped his neck, and started toward the bathroom.

The phone rang.

Reed pried it out of his pocket, feeling his stomach tighten. Only one word illuminated the screen: "UNKNOWN."

He hit the green button, and didn't wait for the computerized voice to speak first.

"All right, jerk-off. Now he's under protective custody. Your turn to listen."

The speaker echoed with a hissing sound—slow breaths from a dry throat. To Reed's surprise, the voice wasn't computerized. The tone was calm and icy cold. A hint of a South American accent dampened each word. Venezuelan, maybe. Or Colombian.

"You're clever, aren't you?"

A cold sweat ran down Reed's neck. He leaned over the table and dug his fingernails into the wood. "Who the hell is this?"

"You can call me Salvador. I'm the man who resents being toyed with. You're toying with me, Reed."

The derision in the voice was as thick and heavy as the tone was sharp.

Reed balled his fingers into a fist and slammed them into the table.

"You think I'm toying with you? Well, let me clue you in on our next playdate. I'm going to rip your face off, one bloody strip at a time. By the time I'm finished, you—"

A shriek broke the silence. "Stop! Back off!"

Reed's palms went cold. He knew that voice. How could he ever forget it?

Banks.

"Do I have your attention, Reed?" The speaker was still calm, but Reed could hear the impatience in his tone.

"What are you doing?" Reed hissed.

"I think you know. I have Miss Morccelli. You know Miss Morccelli, don't you? Two nights ago, you sat on the edge of the parking garage at Lindbergh Station while she played the ukulele. It was a beautiful song. I still have a copy of the recording if you're interested."

Bile welled up in Reed's throat, tasting both acidic and bitter at the same time. It was all he could do not to scream. He felt his windpipe closing, and he focused all of his energy on controlling his response.

"What do you want?"

"The same thing I've always wanted. I want you to kill Mitchell Holiday. It's going to be a lot harder now, thanks to your little stunt with the dark web. But that's your problem. You'll find him on the fourth floor of an FBI field office at the corner of 5th and Washington. It's an unmarked support office. Blow up the whole building if you want. Just get it done. You have until sundown. Every fifteen minutes after dark, I'm going to cut off one of Banks's fingers. If she runs out of fingers, I'm going to begin filleting her from the neck down. That sounds deadly, but it's not. It could take hours for her to bleed out, and I won't be in a hurry. Do you understand me, Reed?"

The cabin fell silent, and a chill filled Reed's soul. He closed his eyes and focused on each breath, each muscle movement. The dark clouds in his head began to dissipate, and his fighting instincts and the cold calculation of a natural killer took over.

"I need assurances that she won't be harmed before sundown."

"You have them. But this is your last chance. Finish the job."

15

Light flooded the basement and dust hung in the air as Reed pounded down the stairs and walked straight to the gun safe. His hands were damp and numb as he spun the dial three times to clear it, then entered the combination and twisted the bolt handle. Fire and a blinding rush of something between rage and hatred flooded his veins. He reached into the safe and pulled out a KRISS Vector submachine gun chambered in .45 ACP.

One thing rang perfectly clear through his muddled mind: He could not think about Banks. It was all he could do to push the sound of her agonized screams out of his mind and focus on the task at hand, but he knew if he didn't try, the rage would overwhelm him.

Rage puts you in the fast lane to dying hard. Oliver said it a thousand times.

Reed set the gun on the table. With only four hours until sunset, there was no time to strategize or create a subtle plan of attack. He had only one option—kick down the door, clear the room, and find Mitch Holiday. The senator was his best bet of finding Banks.

Reed peeled off his sweat-drenched jeans before retrieving a pair of cargo pants pre-strung with a heavy leather belt. A black T-shirt, black boots, and a set of body armor plates completed his outfit, masking his frame into the classic picture of an American killer. He checked the straps of the body armor and cinched them down further until it hurt to breathe. His chest was already tight, and his mind numb. Every action was practiced and mechanical. There was no time to think.

Reed returned to the safe and selected a drop leg holster. He strapped it to his right thigh before sliding a loaded and chambered Glock 31 pistol inside. Another belt holding two full pistol mags, a Ka-Bar knife, and a flashlight went over his gun belt. Next came the chest rig, loaded with six submachine gun magazines, each filled with lead-nose cartridges. Above the magazines, Reed clipped three flashbangs and a smoke grenade to the chest rig.

A sudden rush of blood fell from Reed's head, leaving a wave of dizziness behind it. He grabbed a shelf to steady himself, and for a moment focused on catching his breath.

They took her. And it's my fault.

Reed shook his head, forcing the thoughts out of his mind.

Go in cold, come out cold. Emotion is for suicidal assassins.

The heft of the KRISS Vector felt good under his calloused hands. Reed ran up the stairs and walked past a sleeping Baxter as he approached the front door.

"Don't wait up."

The roar of passing cars echoed through a supermarket parking lot three miles north of town, situated right next to the highway. Reed parked at the edge of the lot and carried his gear toward a silver SUV a few yards away. The Camaro was too impractical for the mission at hand, and he didn't want to risk having the plates photographed. The Toyota that sat by itself next to a shopping cart corral sported political stickers and the words "wash me" written in greasy finger smears over the back glass. It was a few years old, with a peeling clear coat and a cracked front bumper.

Reed set the bags down beside the SUV and dug into the pocket of his cargo pants. He produced a folding slim-jim and slid it between the glass and the water seal of the driver's window. A few minutes of careful manipulation with the tool were rewarded by the click of the lock. Reed opened the door and tossed his gun inside, then piled into the driver seat. The SUV was cluttered with fast-food wrappers, empty soda cans, and sales brochures for some real estate company. The stale stench of week-old French fries and sour cheese hung in the air like the ghost of drive-thru past, making him cough and wrinkle his nose. Reed tried to ignore the smell and dug beneath the steering column. He flipped a knife out of his pocket and worked for a couple more minutes before the starter clicked, and the engine whined to life.

As Reed put the car into drive, the congealed remains of some food byproduct stuck to his hands. He wiped his palms against his pants and piloted out of the lot and back onto the highway. Cars flashed past as he accelerated into the fast lane and drove toward the east side of Atlanta. Orange lights blanketed the city as the sun began its westward journey toward the ends of the earth. The knots in his stomach tightened, and he rolled the windows down.

Banks was alone. Afraid. Hurting. They had tortured her. He saw those big blue eyes again—so wide and deep—and he imagined them full of fear. Was it worse to know she was in pain, or worse to know he couldn't do anything to stop it?

In cold. Out cold. Clear your head, Reed.

He took the exit onto I-285 and pressed the accelerator deeper into the floor. The Toyota had half a tank of gas. He would get to the field office, take a few minutes to survey the situation, and then pull the trigger. There weren't a lot of options. He needed Holiday alive—at least for now. Unless and until the status quo changed, Reed wanted the senator as insurance, and possibly as a source of intel.

Why is Holiday still with the FBI? Why didn't they turn him over to Capitol Police?

The FBI building on the corner of Washington and 5th wasn't the bureau's primary facility for the city. Their official field office sat on Flowers Street, with a big lobby and an army of agents. He figured this building must be an off-grid secondary location used for more subtle operations. Did that mean the FBI knew why Holiday was wanted dead? Did Holiday have connections in the bureau?

No possible answer was a good one.

Anger and frustration boiled in Reed's veins as he approached the field office. He was cornered and forced into a hand of cards he didn't want to play. From the moment he accepted this damnable hit, everything had spun out of control. He was a puppet on a string, being jerked around and dragged toward an inevitable demise.

It would end today. He would recover Holiday, then retreat to a safe house. Sit down with the senator. Get to the bottom of this entire mess. Then negotiate for Banks's safe release. There would be time for vengeance later.

Reed parked the SUV in an alleyway between a gas station and a shopping strip, one block from the field office. After he cut the engine off, he sat in silence and surveyed his limited view of the street at the end of the alley. He couldn't see the field office. He hoped they couldn't see him.

What are you going to do, Reed? Storm the building, snatch him up, and haul ass? That's a horrible plan. You'll be gunned down.

Oliver's commanding voice echoed in the back of his mind, a lesson the hardened killer had pounded into Reed's skull from day one: *Always be ready to walk away.*

The steering wheel was rock-hard under his grip, and his knuckles were white. He let go and rubbed his numb fingers. Oliver was right—the only course of action that ended in his favor was to walk away, torch the cabin, cash out some savings. Steal a car and go to ground—Mexico, maybe—and fade off the map. Vanish like the ghost he was.

He gritted his teeth. Why couldn't he walk away? He wasn't a hero, and he wasn't interested in becoming one. He made his living by pulling triggers and snapping necks. He never asked why, and he never harbored regrets. A man in his shoes didn't need honor, and he sure as hell didn't need a conscience. All he wanted was to be finished. To wash his hands and disappear forever.

Reed reached for the ignition wires. Their bare copper tips gleamed in the sunlight, promising freedom and security—everything he treasured and clung to.

Then he heard it faintly in the back of his mind, like the muted melody of an orchestra playing on the other side of a brick wall. It was the soft strumming of her ukulele. The enchanting murmur of her sweet voice, just above a whisper, singing to the Atlanta skyline. In an instant, every desperate, prehistoric impulse ignited within his body. The memory of her intoxicating smile. The touch of her lips on his.

The way she felt like home.

Reed slung the gun's harness over his neck and slammed the door shut, then reached into his cargo pocket and jerked out a three-hole ski mask. He pulled it over his head and checked his wristwatch. Two hours until sunset.

16

Glass shattered under Reed's boot as he kicked the door open and raised the gun. The receptionist didn't scream. She stood, stepped back, and reached for her handgun. Reed pulled the trigger twice. The bark of the submachine gun was deafening, and the bullets slammed into the wall just inches from the woman's ear. She blinked and stumbled, fumbling with the retention strap on her holster. Reed raced across the lobby and grabbed her by the back of the head, slamming her face into the desk before she could draw her weapon. She collapsed to the floor as blood streamed from her forehead.

An alarm blared, ringing through the building like the bugles of Hell. Reed's heart thumped, and each breath was strained beneath the constricting body armor. He knelt and snatched the keycard from the hip of the unconscious agent, then held the gun into his shoulder and orbited the corner toward the hallway. Steel doors guarded the entrance to the elevators and the stairwell. Both were controlled with keycard access.

Reed slid the card at the stairwell and waited for the green light to shine, then jerked the door open and thundered up the stairs. With each footfall, fresh adrenaline surged into his system.

Thoughts of Banks and the ukulele on top of the parking garage faded from his mind and were replaced by the overwhelming urge to conquer. Combat was what he knew best. It didn't matter if he was kicking down wooden doors in Iraq or glass office doors in Georgia; the explosive thrill of fear and anticipation felt the same. It was a high like nothing a narcotic could deliver.

Overhead, agents shouted, and the continuous honk of the alarm filled the stairwell. He took the steps two at a time, making it to the landing of the second floor just as the door burst open and a sandy-haired man wearing a suit and wielding a pistol appeared. The agent wrapped his finger around the trigger and squeezed. Reed slid to his knees, raised the KRISS, and fired twice. The bullets smacked home, directly into the agent's exposed chest. He was knocked off his feet and catapulted out the door. The pistol clattered to the floor, and Reed jumped back to his feet, breaking into a run up the next flight of stairs. More agents confronted him halfway to the next landing, both screaming for him to stop.

They opened fire, and one bullet smacked Reed in the middle of the chest, slamming into the body armor at over a thousand feet per second. The next slug grazed his right arm, shredding the thin shirt and drawing blood. Pain erupted from his torso in torrential waves, ripping through his body and almost knocking him off his feet. Reed grunted through gritted teeth, then lunged forward and grabbed the first agent by the forearm. He ducked low and jerked backward. The agent lost his balance and tumbled over Reed's back before crashing down the stairwell.

Reed stumbled backward and dropped the gun. It dangled from the sling as he delivered a lightning punch to the second man's exposed rib cage. The agent collapsed forward, screaming in pain. He fired again as he fell, but the round flew wide and struck the concrete wall in a shower of white powder.

Everything descended into a blur of blood and pain and adrenaline. Reed followed the punch with a palm strike to the agent's ear, driving his head into the block wall, and bone met concrete with a sickening crack. The agent's eyes rolled back, and he slumped to the floor.

Next level. Cover your ass.

Reed jerked his weapon free of the fallen agent's sport jacket and raised it to eye level as he ran around the next landing. His arm throbbed, and blood dripped from his elbow. Each inhale was agony from the massive bruising inflicted by the chest-armor strike. He wouldn't die, but it would hurt like hell for a few days. He felt the smooth contour of the trigger under his finger, and the fear faded from his mind—a receding tide, leaving nothing but blinding determination behind it.

A large number four was painted on the wall in gleaming white stencil. Sirens and shouts echoed from the other side of the door as Reed fired three rounds into the lock. It blew to pieces in a shower of sparks and shrapnel, and he kicked it open.

The noise on the other side of the door was much louder. Red lights flashed overhead, and complete chaos ruled the room around him. Reed raised the rifle and flipped the selector switch to full auto before unleashing a string of rounds over the tops of a dozen cubicles. Somebody screamed over the familiar popping of a 9mm handgun. Bullets skipped against the wall nearby, and Reed slid to his knees and redirected his line of fire at a short female agent who stood ten yards away between the cubicles. Reed trained the gun on her chest and squeezed the trigger, delivering a 255-grain, lead-nose bullet into the center mass of her Kevlar body armor. She crumpled like a rag doll.

The air hung thick with gun smoke. Blood puddled on the floor around Reed as he opened fire on the walls and the ceiling, shattering lights and alarm sirens. Sparks and drywall debris rained down on the office in a cloud of white before the gun's bolt locked back on empty. Reed pulled himself to his feet and dropped the mag. He slammed a new one in place, smacked his palm against the bolt release, and raised the gun again.

Chaos ruled. Through the smoke and dust, the distinguishable features of the room were seen only through the flashes of handgun fire. The stock of Reed's weapon ground against his cheek as more agents appeared around the corner, fifteen yards away. Both went down before they could even raise their Glocks. The hellish roar of the submachine gun filled the office space and rattled the windows as brass showered down over the bloody carpet. Reed broke into a run between the offices, leaping across the fallen agents and turning toward the next hallway. A heavy steel door bolted closed with no window or latch blocked the way. Reed dropped the KRISS, allowing it to swing on its harness. Digging into his right cargo pocket, he retrieved a small wad of C-4 and slapped it onto the wall beside the door. He pressed a detonator into the sticky white explosive, flipped the switch, and dove for the floor on the other side of a cubical.

The C-4 discharged with a floor-shaking blast, and an avalanche of concrete, drywall, and rebar cascaded over the carpet around him. Reed felt something slam into his leg, and at first thought it was a piece of debris. Then he heard another gunshot. He groaned and rolled over. Blood coated his leg and mired the carpet, causing him to slip as he struggled to get to his feet. His vision blurred, and the room around him swayed and danced as though an earthquake had erupted under the building. His hands shook, and he spat dirt and saliva onto the carpet.

Reed fought to raise the rifle, but the sling was tangled around his arm and hung on the gun belt. He could see the shooter now, standing next to the elevator and firing from the cover of an upturned desk. Muzzle flash lit up the smoke-filled room in little orange bursts as bullets smacked the wall around him. Reed clawed the Glock out of his drop holster and raised it, firing five times. The fast-shooting .357 caliber slugs sent splinters of fake wood flying as the agent dove for better cover.

The room was dark now and clouded with dust. Reed coughed and holstered the handgun, jerking the KRISS back to his shoulder before turning toward the hole left by the blast of the explosives. It was about two feet across, torn through the block as though a giant had put his fist through the wall. Lights flashed on the other side. Agents shouted, and footsteps pounded the carpeted floor.

Stepping up beside the hole, Reed winced at the pain in his leg. It throbbed and burned. His fingers trembled with the mad rush of adrenaline and the unbridled desire to survive as he jerked a flashbang from his chest rig, pulled the pin with his teeth, and flung it through the hole.

The grenade detonated with an earthshaking blast only a moment later. Reed didn't wait. He held the KRISS close to his chest and dove through the hole.

On the other side of the wall, a large and linear room with stark-white walls and a series of reinforced glass partitions greeted him. The floor was covered in concrete and dirt, and a small table lay on its side. People shouted from somewhere on the other side of the room. The air smelled dirty and burnt, as though he were breathing in ashes. His lungs were clogged with the filth.

Reed rolled into a crouching position and raised the gun. He fired into the glass panels separating him from the far side of the building. They shattered, leaving the wire reinforcements floating in midair behind them. Glass rained down, and people continued to shout. Gunshots rang out from the far end of the building, and this time they weren't the rapid pops of a handgun. This gunfire was both faster and louder. It was from an assault rifle.

More glass shattered, and pieces of foam exploded from the cubical partitions under the raking fire of the rifle. Reed pulled another flashbang from his chest and flung it as far toward the other end of the building as possible. Before it detonated, he followed it up with the smoke grenade.

The room reverberated with the blast of the first grenade, followed by the slow hiss of the second. The fire alarm overhead began to scream, the sprinkler system kicked in, and cool water showered down. Reed jumped to his feet and ran toward the end of the hallway, where he held the rifle up to his cheek. Agents coughed, and somebody shouted for backup. Reed slid around the corner of one of the glass partitions and saw a tall man leaning over, coughing onto the floor with an assault rifle held loosely in his arms.

Before he could lift the weapon, Reed twisted the butt of the submachine gun in an elegant arc and slammed it into the agent's face. The man went down like a house of cards, crumpling to the floor without a sound.

More gunfire rang through the room. Reed returned fire, though he couldn't see what he was aiming at through the dense smoke. Somebody shouted, and he heard the familiar thud of his bullets striking body armor.

A body hit the floor. Bullets whistled past his ear.

This is going sideways, fast. I've got to move.

The roar of a shotgun shook the walls of the narrow room. Two rounds of the heavy buckshot struck Reed in the stomach of his body armor panel. He choked and stumbled as bile and chunks of steak spewed from his mouth. He squeezed the trigger of the KRISS, the gun jerked, and then the bolt locked back on empty. Extreme pain cascaded through his body, but Reed repeated his reloading routine. Saliva dripped from his lips, and his knees wobbled under him as he staggered forward again.

The smoke began to clear, and Reed saw two men huddled behind a copy machine. A third man lay against the wall in the corner, clutching his chest. A woman was crumpled on the floor next to another reinforced door. This time, though, the door wasn't locked. It hung open a couple of inches, and through the gap, Reed saw the frightened eyes and washed-out face of Mitchell Holiday.

17

Holiday sat in a folding chair with his hands cuffed to the tabletop and his face spotlighted beneath the LED lights. In a millisecond, Reed noted every detail of the predicament, and his stomach fluttered.

Why is Holiday handcuffed?

Gunshots popped from the crowd of disoriented agents. Reed rolled behind a desk and jerked his last flashbang from his chest rig. He hurled it over the desk and covered his head. The room shook, and glass showered the dirty carpet. Reed jumped up, raised the KRISS, and placed a string of shots just over the heads of the stumbling FBI agents. They ducked and screamed, raising their hands over their heads as the guns began to drop.

Reed rushed the disoriented agents and slammed the butt of his gun into the stomach of the nearest one, causing her to double over. He followed the blow with a palm strike to her exposed head, and she collapsed to the floor just as a bullet slammed into his backplate. As if he were hit with a sledgehammer, waves of agony ripped through his torso. He twisted to the left just in time to miss the next bullet.

The shooter stood ten feet away, firing from between the

cubical walls. Reed jerked the Glock from his thigh and shot twice. The agent crumpled to the floor with blood spraying from his right arm, and the final agents clawed their way out of the room, coughing and falling over each other.

I've got to extract. Now.

Reed turned toward the metal door and kicked it open.

Holiday stood up, jerking at the cuffs. He stumbled over his own feet and shouted, "Don't shoot!"

Reed jerked the submachine gun back to his shoulder and fired twice. The chain linking the handcuffs shattered, and Holiday collapsed against the wall with a panicked shout.

The folds of the senator's collar were soaked with sweat, and Reed dug his fingers into Holiday's neck, hoisting him to his feet before jamming the muzzle of the gun into his ribs. "Do exactly as I say. Don't scream."

The look in his wild eyes told Reed he wouldn't resist. This man was beyond terrified and on the verge of a total psychotic breakdown. Reed shoved him toward the nearest window and looked out over the senator's shoulder. Fifteen feet below them, just across a five-foot alley, was the flat-topped roof of a two-story shopping strip. A ladder hung off the far side of the building, leading down to where Reed parked the SUV.

Boots thundered up the stairwell behind them. Men shouted, and more sirens blared.

I'm so sick of sirens.

Turning back to the window, he fired three rounds into the thick glass and was gratified to see it shatter. A few swift kicks removed the remaining shards, leaving a wide hole into the open air outside.

"Hold your arms to your chest," Reed snapped. "Run and jump."

Holiday shook his head. "No way!"

Reed pulled the trigger of the gun twice, and the laminate flooring erupted in a haze of dust next to Holiday's feet. The senator jumped and held up his hands again.

"Jump. Now!" Reed shouted.

Holiday hesitated, then glanced toward the stairwell and back at Reed holding the gun.

The senator flung himself through the window, and Reed watched him hurtling through the air like a lame duck, arms and legs flailing before he crashed onto the pea gravel of the flat roof. There was a snapping sound on impact, and Holiday screamed and grabbed at his knee.

A flashbang detonated from the other side of the door. Reed's ears rang, and his head was light, as though it were filled with helium. He blinked back the mist of confusion, then launched himself through the window. Clear air and bright sunlight flashed past him as he fell forward, preparing himself for a parachute landing as the roof of the shopping center rocketed toward him. Gravel and dirt crunched under his shoulder, and he rolled once before hauling himself to his feet, just yards from Holiday. His head still swam, and every step was uncertain, as though he were walking on a cloud.

Blood coated the gravel under Reed's boots as he stepped over Holiday and grabbed him by the collar again. "Get up! Move!"

Holiday's eyes were clamped shut, as though he had decided the world couldn't hurt him if he couldn't see it. He cried out in pain at the pressure on his neck but limped to his feet.

Reed shoved him toward the ladder, continuing to shout and prod him with the submachine gun. "Move, Senator!"

Holiday went down the rusty ladder first, fumbling with shaky hands and groaning with each step on his right knee. Reed followed just above him, keeping the gun pointed at his head. The ladder stopped ten feet above the sidewalk, and Reed pressed his boot into Holiday's shoulder, forcing him to drop. Even Reed winced when Holiday landed on both feet and screamed in agony.

His knee must be shattered.

Torrents of pain ran through Reed's body as he fell to the street.

"Let's go!" He hoisted Holiday into a semi-standing position and dragged him around the corner of the shopping mall to the SUV.

Holiday's shoes scraped on the ground, and the blood drained from his face, leaving him ashen white and barely conscious.

Reed jerked the rear door of the Toyota open and hoisted Holiday into the back. He crashed into the cargo space with a pained groan, and Reed shoved Holiday's legs in, then lifted the butt of the gun.

"I'm sorry, Senator."

Another flash of fear crossed across Holiday's face, but he didn't have time to shield himself. The butt of the gun smacked him in the base of the skull, and he fell limp in the cargo space. Reed slammed the door shut and then ran to the driver's seat. His fingers trembled as he fought with the ignition wires. Fire alarms still rang from the building and were now joined by the whine of a fire truck siren. The SUV sputtered to life, and Reed planted his foot into the accelerator. In the rearview mirror, the FBI field office was shrouded by smoke. The slow whoop of a police siren joined the fire truck. Or was it several sirens? They were closing in on his position like hounds racing after a rabbit.

For all of that, no black SUVs swerved to follow him. No helicopters buzzed down on him like vultures, ready to gun him down in a shower of lead. The street ahead lay empty, providing a clear avenue of escape.

Reed winced as a stabbing pain shot through his rib cage. His lips were dry, and he dug a half-empty bottle of water from the door pocket of the SUV and guzzled it down. The fresh taste washed away the dust and bile, dampening his dry throat and promising new life for his battered body.

Blood loss. Bruised ribs, or maybe broken ones. At least one definite bullet strike in his lower leg. Plenty of strained muscles. All things considered, Reed felt lucky. The element of surprise mixed with overwhelming violence and three flashbangs made for a winning cocktail.

He pulled the ski mask off his head and sucked in the fresh air. The SUV didn't smell half bad after the warzone behind him. He turned onto I-85, and the warmth of the sun blazed down on the back of his neck. It was strangely relaxing, in spite of the reminder that darkness was barely ninety minutes away. With a little more luck, it would be time enough.

The buildings around him gradually gave way to rising hills and trees as he passed through Buckhead and turned toward Doraville. Ten minutes later, the green signs on the side of the highway advertised exits for Duluth and Lawrenceville. Reed took the ramp onto Georgia State Highway 316 and continued east. Occasional cars passed him, piloted by tired men in business suits and stressed soccer moms with frazzled hair. Nobody gave a second glance to the stolen Toyota or the killer who sat behind the wheel. As the cityscape gave way to horse fields and peach orchards, the BMWs were replaced by pickup trucks and large SUVs, but the faces remained the same: detached and uninterested.

After another half hour, he turned onto a dirt road and drove a couple more miles. Pine trees and dense, dying undergrowth clogged the fields on either side of him, encroaching on the orange roadbed like the claws of nature, ready to swallow it whole. An armadillo scampered across the road, its tail dragging in the dust and sending orange clouds rising in the face of the Toyota. Birds flitted between the trees, singing songs of impending winter and nesting down for the night. The isolation was perfect, and it brought calm back to Reed's strained mind. He relaxed in his seat and loosened the body armor, which allowed him to take his first real breath in hours. It hurt like hell, but the oxygen brought welcome relief to his frayed nerves.

I'm not dead, neither is Banks, and neither is Holiday. I'm regaining control.

Reed turned the SUV off the road and onto a narrow trail, barely marked by shallow ruts. Branches scraped against the side of the SUV as he lurched over potholes and fallen tree limbs. Around a bend, a locked cattle gate blocked the way.

Reed got out of the Toyota and pulled a key from his pocket. The rusty lock binding the gate to a half-rotten fence post squeaked and stuck, but Reed jerked it open and shoved the gate out of the way. Back in the SUV, he wound his way another half mile into the trees.

The single-wide trailer sat by itself in a clearing barely large enough to hold it. There was no driveway or parking space, no mailbox or front lawn. Faded yellow sheet metal clung to the sides of the trailer, showing traces of rust amid the dents and scratches. Pine needles and small limbs were piled high on the flat roof, and what was left of a narrow front porch leaned to one side, with a chunk of the rail missing. The battered home looked tired and broken as if nobody had laughed or shared a beer with a friend in this place for a long, long time.

Reed got out of the SUV and looked up. The sun descended into the western sky, sending stunning rays of gold, orange, and red streaming through the trees like a continuous burst of fireworks. He opened the rear hatch and pulled Holiday out. The senator was still unconscious, with saliva draining out of his mouth. Reed checked his pulse, then slung the inert lawmaker over his shoulder and dragged him up the front steps and onto the rickety porch. The damp smell of rotting wood and musty insulation filled his nostrils, and he coughed as he shoved another key into the deadbolt. It twisted with a dry squeak, then the door swung open, revealing a pitch-black living room on the other side. Reed drew the flashlight from his belt and flipped it on, then dragged Holiday inside.

The trailer belonged to Oliver's company; one of a network of safe houses and hideouts littered across the country. Both the trailer and the half-acre it sat on were registered in the name of a Georgia LLC, which was owned by a Kansas LLC, which was owned fifty-fifty by two Montana LLCs, and so on—a typical procedure for company property. Reed had never used it before, but he always kept it in the back of his mind in case there came a time when he needed to lay low close to Atlanta.

A time such as this.

The floor shuddered and creaked as though it might collapse as Reed dropped Holiday onto the torn linoleum. He walked into the kitchen and shuffled through the drawers, dumping plastic forks and rat poop onto the counter, until he found a wooden spoon. He drew the Ka-Bar from his belt and whittled the end of the spoon's handle into a sharp point, about the same diameter as a .30 caliber bullet. Then he returned to the living room and knelt beside Holiday.

Empty darkness filled the senator's eyes. He lay on the floor with his arm twisted under him, his jaw slack. Reed drew a small bottle of ether from his pocket and held it under Holiday's nose, waiting for his breaths to become more consistent. When he was confident the senator was well and truly incapacitated, he stretched the front of Holiday's dress shirt and lifted the sharpened spoon. Two swift stabs to the chest left twin holes just above Holiday's heart, about half an inch deep and three inches apart. Blood pooled out of the holes, soaking the shirt and draining onto the floor.

Reed stood and tossed the spoon into the corner, then drew his phone from his pocket and held the flashlight over the body. The LED glow shone on Holiday's face, washing his skin in a chalky pallor. Reed snapped a few pictures from different angles then reviewed each one. The effect was perfect. Holiday lay on the floor with two bullet-sized wounds streaming blood over his chest.

A thick wad of stuffing from the broken armchair in the corner subdued the bleeding. Reed bound it in place with strips from Holiday's undershirt and propped his body against the wall so the blood would run downward and away from the wounds. Then he selected the unknown number from his recent-callers list and sent a string of photographs followed by one message.

IT'S DONE.

18

Outside of Atlanta, Georgia

The last rays of sunlight faded through the pines. Reed stood amid the trees and lit a cigarette, enjoying the tangy flood of nicotine as it washed through his lungs, bringing fresh waves of relief along with it. The throbbing ache in his body subsided a little, and he exhaled through his nose. So many times, he swore off cigarettes. So many times, he enjoyed a "last smoke ever." The habit started in Iraq, where booze was restricted and tobacco was cheap. That first smoke became a pack a day in less than a month. Careful restraint reduced the addiction to a pack per week, but he couldn't fully surrender the comfort of the smoldering drug. Not yet.

Not until I'm home.

Careful inspection of his body confirmed that he wasn't seriously injured. His chest and back were bruised, and his ears rang. The bullet strike on his leg was a graze, and quick attention with the first aid kit in his cargo pants pocket stopped the bleeding. For now, that would have to suffice.

His cell phone buzzed. UNKNOWN lit up the screen. Reed took

another slow pull of smoke, then hit the green button. "It's done. Where's Banks?"

Salvador spoke calmly, disguising a hint of venom beneath his words.

"Impressive work, Montgomery. I'll be honest. I wasn't sure you could pull it off. He certainly looks dead . . ."

Salvador let his voice trail off, leaving the sentence hanging. The suspicion was evident in his tone.

"He's dead. And you will be too if you don't hold up your end. Where's Banks?"

"Hmm . . ."

Reed's heart pounded, and he slammed his clenched fist against the nearest pine tree, but he didn't speak. This was a battle of nerves, and he wouldn't be the one to break.

"In your original contract, you may recall we had a stipulation for the manner of death."

Reed searched his memory, trying to remember the details of that first contract.

"You wanted him dead within seventy-two hours. And he is."

"Right. But we also specified that the death had to be *conspicuous*."

"I just knocked down a freaking FBI stronghold, you cheap shit. How much more conspicuous can you get?"

"Granted. But we're going to need more. Where's the body now?"

"Someplace the FBI isn't."

"I figured as much. We're going to need more concrete assurances of his death. Along with a more public . . . spectacle. Are you following me, Reed?"

"No. I'm not. And I'm done playing games. He's dead. I'm coming for Banks. Where is she?"

Salvador sighed. "Reed . . . you challenge my patience. Hit her."

Reed heard an abrasive popping sound . . . an unearthly scream . . . a muffled crashing . . . another scream.

"Stop." Reed didn't shout. Blood thundered in his ears, and his throat was dry, but he forced himself to focus. There was no card for him to play. He could bluster and threaten all he wanted, but at the end of the day they both knew he was helpless.

The screaming faded, and Salvador returned. "As I was saying. We want a spectacle. I'm feeling generous. It's just now five o'clock, and I'll give you until ten."

"What do you want?"

"I want you to tie a rope around Holiday's ankles and hang his body off the west side of the 191 Peachtree building."

Ice-cold dread washed through Reed's body, landing in his stomach and triggering a wave of nausea. "*What?*"

"You heard me, Reed. I want you to present his body in front of CNN headquarters."

"That building is secured access. I can't get inside. I'll display the body in Centennial Park. Or on the Capitol steps."

"No. I want it done at 191 Peachtree. And I want it on an upper floor. Shall we say the forty-fifth floor? That seems reasonable."

Reed slammed his closed fist into the hood of the SUV, clenching his jaw to avoid screaming. The frustration and tension in his body overwhelmed him. It rushed through his blood and clouded his mind in a wave of total rage.

"I can't get inside. It can't be done."

Another laugh. It was a dry, humorless sound.

"Reed, you just knocked down an FBI stronghold. An office building should be a walk in the park. You have five hours. Oh, and Reed?"

"What?" Reed spat the word.

"Make it bloody."

19

Special Agent Matthew Rollick sat in his windowless cubical and watched his computer screen in silence as the soundless security camera played footage in black-and-white with poor resolution. Parts of it were obscured by smoke, and some of the camera angles prevented him from viewing the face of the man in the ski mask. He wondered if that was intentional. Did the masked attacker purposefully dodge the cameras, or was it just his own crappy luck?

Rollick clicked the ballpoint pen in his hand and replayed the tape. His T-shirt clung to his skin, and he flipped the desk fan to a higher speed. It didn't help much. The AC unit was out again.

First, he viewed the receptionist. As the glass door of the field office swung open, she had stepped back, assumed a fighting stance, and reached for her gun. There were two flashes from the muzzle of the submachine gun in the attacker's hands, and she went down. Then the stairwell. The cameras provided a limited view of the gunfight between the first and fourth floors. More gunshots. Three agents down.

And then—in what couldn't be described as anything less than a massacre—the entire fourth floor was overtaken and subdued by the one man and his gun.

Rollick punched the blinking call-waiting button on his desk phone. The name flashing on the screen read "Fleet, L."

"Okay. I watched it," Rollick said.

"What do you think?" Agent Lucas Fleet's voice carried an oppressive Boston accent, mixed with the rasp of too many cigarettes.

Rollick leaned back in his chair and hooked his forearm behind his head. "I think, whoever he is, he eats his green vegetables."

"No kidding."

"How many causalities?"

Lucas grunted. "That's the crazy part. None."

"Say what?"

"None. I mean, we've got some pretty banged-up agents. Lots of broken ribs, shattered eardrums, etcetera. A couple gunshot wounds in the shoulders and arms, but no fatalities."

"I don't understand. He shot at least four agents, center mass."

"Yep. But the only bullets that struck a vital area were all stopped by body armor. They shattered some bones and left some bruises, but they didn't penetrate. We're still running tests, but initial impressions are that they were lead-nose bullets."

Rollick scratched his jaw. "That's a miracle."

"Maybe. Or maybe not."

"Come again?"

"Every round was placed squarely in the center of the vests, right where the Kevlar would absorb the bulk of the shock. It's unlikely that any .45-caliber cartridge would penetrate body armor, but it's almost certain that a lead-nose bullet wouldn't. If I'm going to war, and I'm trained well enough to take out a dozen FBI agents, I'm not loading my gun with lead-nose bullets."

"Unless you didn't actually want to kill anyone." Rollick finished the thought.

"Exactly."

"You did say there were some gunshot wounds."

"Yep. A few. All flesh wounds, nothing fatal."

Rollick unwrapped a peppermint candy and popped it between his lips. "What's your theory?"

"I don't have one. That's why I called you. You've been working this Holiday case for three months. I hoped you might have some ideas."

Rollick placed his right hand behind his head and twisted his neck until it popped, providing moderate relief for his sore muscles. His head hurt. He knew there were dark circles under his eyes, and he wasn't really sure what day it was. Friday, maybe? He couldn't remember his last shower, either, but none of this was unusual. He had indeed worked the Holiday case for three months, and holy mackerel, what a nightmare. Endless dead ends, missing emails, corrupted surveillance footage, silent witnesses, and vanishing suspects. It was the most frustrating, exhausting case he had ever worked. Holiday had been a top witness—and possible suspect—for the previous ten weeks, but he was impossibly hard to crack. Rollick's fifteen years as an investigator taught him the unique stench of fear. Holiday was drenched with it.

"I don't know, Lucas. I talked to Holiday for about half an hour before your boys picked him up. He was agitated, but that's typical with him. He's got this goddaughter that he's really close to. Frank Morccelli's girl. He wanted all these guarantees of her isolation from the case and the media. Of course, I couldn't promise that, so he hung up. An hour later, I got word that you had him under protective custody for the death threat."

"Hit order," Lucas corrected him. "And yeah, I'm sorry I didn't advise you beforehand. There wasn't much time. He was a bit contentious, also. We had to restrain him in the safe room."

"It's fine. I can assume that whoever is on the other side of this mess got word Holiday was about to squeal, and they wanted him buried. That would make the fifth witness to vanish or bite the dirt right before they talked."

"You think our gunman is employed by your suspects?"

"I don't have any suspects. Just a series of crimes that feel linked to me, and a gut feeling that there's a bigger picture behind it all. Holiday claims he has insider knowledge about a massive conspiracy, and he also claims to have damning proof. But he won't share it until I meet his demands. This incident adds fuel to the fire, but even so, I'm not sure this gunman works for whoever Holiday wants to rat on."

"Why's that?" Rollick could hear Lucas grinding his thumb against a cigarette lighter.

Geez, the man never quit.

"Because he didn't kill him," Rollick said. "If they wanted him eliminated, it would've been easy to do. I mean, our security obviously isn't an issue. So why kidnap him?"

Lucas breathed out, and Rollick imagined he could smell the sordid odor of cigarette smoke. Seconds turned into minutes, punctuated by occasional puffs from Lucas. He must've been rewatching the security footage for the umpteenth time.

"Maybe they wanted to talk to Holiday first. Make sure he hadn't leaked anything."

"That's possible, but most of my witnesses have a habit of simply winding up dead. Still, he's a state senator. Maybe they're being more surgical this time."

Lucas was quiet a moment longer, and Rollick heard the clicking of a computer mouse.

"What strikes you about him?" Lucas said. "The gunman."

The security footage played on loop now, starting with the carnage in the lobby and moving to the stairwell. Rollick studied the attacker's moves—the way he managed his weapons, his stance, dress, and tactics. They weren't the stuff of an action movie, but they were brutally effective.

"Military," he said.

"Yep. And look at his stance. Adjusted Weaver-style, maintaining his hold on the grip of the gun when he changes mags, leaning low against the walls . . ."

"He's one of ours," Rollick finished.

"Looks that way. Not your average GI, though."

"So, we have another rogue spec ops commando on our hands."

Lucas grunted. "Yep. Okay, Roll. I'll keep you posted if we make any progress. Get some shut-eye. You sound like death."

The line went dead, and Rollick leaned back and rubbed his eyes. Coming from Lucas, the prognosis was as good as a terminal illness.

20

Darkness blanketed the forest, saturating the clearing and leaving Reed alone in the cold. The air was thin but smelled heavily of pine needles. As the last of the sun vanished over the horizon, the tension in his chest increased, and cold sweats ran down his back. The Kevlar suffocated him, and he jerked it off and hurled it to the ground with a scream.

"*Dammit!*" Reed drove his fist into the hood of the SUV again, leaving a large dent. He gasped for air and leaned over the Toyota, resting his forehead against the cool metal. A light breeze whispered through the forest, and it felt good to breathe it in.

Banks was alone. A captive of the freak from South America. A madman with an obsessive desire to destroy her godfather. *Why?* The thought wouldn't leave his mind. Why the *hell* did they want him so publicly executed? Of all the twisted, depraved crap they could come up with—hanging his body off the side of a skyscraper? It was beyond bizarre and worse than twisted. It was sickening.

Pine needles and dry sticks crunched under his feet as Reed straightened. He paced in front of the trailer as his eyes adjusted to the darkness. His mind raced as he considered his options—not that he had many. He couldn't kill Holiday, of course. And he couldn't throw him off the 191 building.

Again, the keystone of the problem was the request itself—their obsession with a conspicuous death didn't add up. Holiday's violent kidnapping and disappearance were conspicuous enough—maybe the most conspicuous thing Reed had ever done. By sunrise, every news outlet in the country would carry the story. The nation would dissolve into a state of shock as pundits and talk show hosts fanned the flames of public uncertainty into a roaring blaze of fear. The president would make a thoughts-and-prayers speech, then call the director of the FBI and demand immediate answers.

So why inflame things any further? Amplifying the horror of the murder now only stacked the deck against these people in every possible way. A gruesome and public display of the body would all but ensure that the killer was run down and . . .

Reed stopped pacing, and a tingling sensation rippled up his arms. There it was. It was so painfully obvious. They *wanted* the killer to be caught. And that killer was him. The whole thing was an elaborate setup. Salvador wanted him to be apprehended at the FBI building. He probably laid a trap at the Ikea, also. When Reed evaded capture both times, they had no choice but to up the ante once more. Naming the place and time of Holiday's post-mortem display was a perfect way to ensure success. Reed would be cornered on the 45th floor of a secured-access building with no route of escape. One call to the Atlanta PD, and the music would stop. Reed would be caught in the act, as guilty as sin.

Like cops closing in on an escaped prisoner, the darkness enveloped his mind, making him feel suddenly smothered. Reed fell to the ground and slumped against a tree, burying his face in his hands. Images of Banks's bright smile flooded his mind, pushing past his most desperate attempts to block them out. He imagined the face of her captor, his teeth narrowing into fangs as he pressed a knife into her stomach. Her smile turned to screams as she fought, begged, screamed.

Reed was cornered, and it was his own fault. Every step over the last twenty-four hours had led him deeper into the muck. It was a trap from the start, and his moronic refusal to look after his own interests had ensured that he fell head over heels into the pit.

He jumped to his feet and turned back to the trailer, flipping the flashlight on. The dark living room still smelled musty and stale, with a hint of blood in the air. Reed shuffled through the kitchen drawers again until he located a bottle of water and half a roll of duct tape. Both were old and dirty, but serviceable.

Strips of tape secured Holiday's hands to his thighs, and a third locked his ankles together. Reed slipped the ski mask back on, then opened the water bottle and dumped it over his prisoner's face while smacking him on the cheeks. The senator coughed and blinked bloodshot eyes full of fear when he recognized the black ski mask, and he mumbled a panicked plea before recoiling from the water. Reed shoved the bottle into Holiday's mouth.

"Drink," he snapped.

Holiday didn't object. He gulped the water, spluttering as it streamed down his chin. Reed let him consume all but the last swallow, then finished the rest himself.

"Where am I?"

It was a predictable question.

"West Virginia," Reed said without hesitation. He needed Holiday to talk, and he guessed the senator would respond best to open dialogue.

"Why?"

Reed squatted in front of him. The senator still appeared confused, as though he wasn't aware that he had been kidnapped. But the rasping breaths and rigid posture betrayed his terror.

"I brought you here. Now you're going to answer some questions. Do you understand?"

Holiday grunted. His eyes began to clear, but he still wouldn't meet Reed's gaze.

"A hit was placed on your life," Reed said. "Do you understand what that means?"

Something flashed across Holiday's face. Uncertainty? A distant connection, perhaps? He glared at Reed.

"Who are you?"

"I'm the man hired to kill you."

Holiday leaned back and tried to jerk his hands free. It was a futile effort, and Reed pinned him against the wall with one hand.

"Why do they want you dead, Senator?"

Holiday shook his head. "I don't know. You don't want to do this!"

"You're right. I don't. So, answer my question. Who wants you dead?"

Holiday looked away and coughed over the floor. "Look, this isn't worth it. Just walk away while you can."

"Walk away from what?"

"I'm not saying a damn thi—"

Reed cocked his right arm and dealt Holiday a quick punch to the jaw. The cracking sound of bone on bone popped through the small room. Holiday's head smacked into the fake wood paneling of the walls, and blood streamed from his lip as he cried out in pain.

"Don't test me, Senator. Who ordered the hit?"

Holiday spat again, spraying blood and saliva over the dingy linoleum. "How would I know? You think I have any idea how deep this goes?"

"How deep *what* goes?"

Tears mixed with blood as they dripped off Holiday's chin and splashed on his pants. He shook his head again, looked up, and started to answer, but his eyebrows furrowed, and the sobbing faded. He stared at Reed as though he were seeing him for the first time.

"Did you kill Frank?"

The question took Reed off guard. "Who?"

"You son of a bitch. You killed him, didn't you?"

Holiday spat blood in Reed's face. He began to kick out with both legs, thrashing around on the floor of the trailer. His bound feet struck Reed in the knee, and Reed stumbled back with a grunt of pain. The next kick landed in Reed's lower back, sending waves of pain ripping up his spine. Reed threw himself on top of Holiday and sent another powerful punch into the senator's throat. Holiday choked and coughed up blood, gasping for breath. Reed hit him again in the face, leaving a swollen red welt on his right cheekbone.

"Who are they? Who wants you dead?" Reed shouted.

It was pointless. Holiday slumped forward, his face as white as a corpse. Reed grabbed his wrist and felt a pulse, but the senator was out cold.

Perfect.

Reed let him fall to the floor with a meaty thud, then stood up and jerked the ski mask off. He paced the dingy carpet, his heart thumping. He pulled his phone out and redialed Oliver. This time it went directly to voicemail.

There was no hiding from the truth he'd suspected all day. This whole miserable mess was an elaborate puppet show designed to end the moment Reed pressed the trigger outside of Holiday's condo. Whoever ordered this hit—whoever was behind the fear in Holiday's eyes—that person wanted Reed to take the fall for it. They wanted a clean, clear-cut killing. An execution.

Reed leaned against the counter and tried to control his breathing, forcing himself to take slower, calmer breaths. His heart rate slowed, and his mind began to clear. It wasn't all at once, but the thoughts that screamed inside his head became more orderly. More discernible.

I'm alone. Mitchell Holiday is a dead man walking. After him, they'll kill Banks. Then they'll do their best to kill me. The only way out is to run. Cut bait. Leave Holiday and Banks to their fate and get the hell out of Dodge.

The fire in his blood burned through every part of his body. A numbness overcame his urge to flee, followed by a flicker of hatred. The visceral reaction grew into an inferno of outrage—a blinding desire to destroy. He heard her laugh, and he felt a warm rush at the sound of her beautiful voice. It was a feeling he'd long forgotten in the cold, dark world he lived in. It was a feeling he didn't know existed anymore—a beauty he wasn't sure was real. But he felt it, standing there on the top of that parking garage staring out at the city. It *was* real.

He wasn't walking away from this. He wasn't walking away from anything. He'd burn the whole damn city down if that's what it took. He would kick down every door until he ratted Salvador out of his hole and tore out his throat. He was going to find Banks.

Reed set Holiday in the armchair and stretched a strip of duct tape over his mouth. He locked the trailer and started toward the SUV.

There would be no going back. No chance to disengage from the carnage he was about to unleash. Now that Salvador dragged Banks into this mess, war was the only option.

21

North Georgia

The cabin was a shadow in the darkness. Reed parked the stolen SUV in the driveway, then pounded up the steps and shoved the door open. Baxter snored on the rug in the living room. He jumped to his feet when Reed burst in, and erupted in angry barks, running to the window and snarling at whatever invisible threat had awakened the monster inside his human friend.

Reed jerked the drawers of his desk open and dumped a pile of books and papers on the kitchen table. He pulled a map of Atlanta from the stack and unfolded it, tracing his finger through the streets of downtown until he stopped at the intersection of Andrew Young International Blvd and Peachtree Street. He stared at the block, his mind racing like a freight train careening off its tracks.

191 Peachtree. Right in the heart of the city.

His heart thumped, and he reached for the bottle of Jack sitting on the desk. After a deep swig, he looked back at the map.

There has to be a way to draw them out. Find a way to corner them.

If he attempted to breach the fifty-story skyscraper at that intersection, he would be in handcuffs with his face in the concrete as soon as he exposed the body. Maybe Salvador even had a few Atlanta cops on the payroll. Perhaps they were standing by, even now, waiting to catch a killer attempting to hang a body off the side of an Atlanta landmark.

Reed checked his watch. Six fifteen. This wouldn't be his first operation executed under the torment of a ticking clock, but this one felt different. The strain on his nerves wore at the corners of his focus, infringing on his ability to think outside the box.

They need a spectacle. They need me cornered. So, I have to corner them.

Reed ran a hand through his hair.

What if I do it? What if I hang Holiday off the tower? If he were unconscious, maybe...

No, that was moronic. Salvador wanted Reed caught, and executing the ridiculous assignment as instructed wouldn't result in Banks's release. They would kill her. The only way for this to end would be for Reed to turn the ambush into a counter-ambush somehow. Find a way to catch the tiger by the tail and run him back to his cave.

Reed took another sip of whiskey. What if he traced the call and found out where it was made? No, anybody smart enough to block the caller ID would be smart enough to avoid being traced. He had to lure the tiger out. Catch him in the open.

That's it. It's so simple.

He didn't have to lure the tiger out. The tiger would already be out, on the prowl, waiting and watching to make sure Reed was caught. Reed had evaded capture twice, and Salvador couldn't afford to fail again. He would have men planted downtown—not in the tower, but close by within easy viewing distance.

I'll draw them out. If they think I'm escaping, they'll have no choice but to expose themselves. I'll need to see them before they see me. Someplace close. Someplace tall.

Back to the map. The surrounding blocks were marked with tiny icons, indicating the towers that built the Atlanta skyline. He traced the streets around 191 Peachtree, moving out in every direction. Then his finger stopped at the intersection of Peachtree and Luckie Street.

Perfect.

The pine planks of the cabin floor creaked under his boots as he ran through the kitchen and into the pantry, back through the fake wall, and down the narrow steps into the basement. The single lightbulb still glowed overhead, illuminating the dust that hung in the air. He snatched an empty backpack off the wall and began sweeping gear off the shelves and into the bag. A chest harness with a rappel slide, five hundred feet of static climbing rope, a case holding four encrypted radio headsets, a lock pick kit, a bottle of water, and three magazines loaded with twenty rounds each of .308.

The last item of his gear lay in a case on the table: the sniper rifle. It was heavy under his tired and battered grip, but the weight comforted him. It was his weapon of choice—a precise instrument of judgment.

After closing the entrance to the basement, Reed whistled for Baxter. The bulldog bounded off the couch and trotted into the kitchen. His little eyes blazed with curiosity, and maybe just a hint of fighting fury, almost as if the dog were saying, *Come on, we can take 'em!*

Drool dripped from Baxter's bottom lip, and he cocked his head in confusion. Reed knelt beside him and scratched behind his ears, then rubbed him between his shoulder blades, right where he liked it. Baxter groaned and dropped his butt on the floor.

"Yeah. Guess you know it's going down. In case I don't come back . . . Well, you go get that Frenchie, friend."

Reed patted him on the head, then walked out the front door. The last thing he needed was a little ground support, and he had a pretty good idea of where to find it.

Reed loaded the gear into the SUV and drove back into the city. It took him over an hour to fight his way through traffic and back to where he left the Camaro. After parking the SUV, he retrieved a roll of hundred-dollar bills from the Camaro's glove box and laid them in the seat of the Toyota before pressing a sticky note on top of the money. He retrieved a pen from the console and scrawled a brief note on the yellow paper.

Sorry for everything.

The adrenaline from the maddened afternoon began to wear off, and the extreme pain from his injuries started to rip into his body again. His stomach and chest ached like hell from the bullet strikes on his body armor, and each breath sent a streaking pain shooting down his right side—probably from bruised ribs. The pain would be a lot worse in the morning, and his whole body would be stiff, assuming he lived that long.

Reed shifted into gear and roared back onto the freeway. The Camaro shook, and the exhaust growled like all the demons of Hell reciting a war chant. He loved that sound. It helped him focus on something other than the pain in his body and the strain on his mind. He loved that car.

I hope it's in one piece when this is over.

The familiar hallmarks of Buckhead faded into those of Midtown. Reed exited the freeway and turned the car past the Ikea and toward an older part of town. As he passed a gas station, he stepped on the brake and lowered the windows, surveying the streets and small parks. It took him ten minutes to find a homeless man lying on a park bench; a worn blanket was stretched over his thin body. Reed stopped the Camaro at the edge of the park and climbed out, then pulled the Panthers jacket over his shoulder holster and jogged to the bench.

"Excuse me."

The man sat up and waved a dirty fist at Reed. "Leave me alone! Can't a man sleep in a free country?"

Reed held up one hand. "Chill. I'm just looking for Vince. Do you know him?"

With narrowed eyes, the man tilted his head to one side. "Who's asking?"

Reed drew a couple twenties from his pocket and held them out. "Here. Take this. Where is he?"

The homeless man curled his lip. "You think I'd rat on a brother for forty bucks? Go to hell!"

He stood up and shuffled toward the park.

Reed cursed and started to follow, but a crackling voice rang out from behind him.

"Well, well. If it ain't mister big shot, harassing an honest American down on his luck. You're way out of regs, Marine!"

A short, stocky man with his arms crossed stood twenty feet back. He wore a tattered Falcons hoodie, but his hair was neatly cut, and his face cleanly shaved. He didn't look older than thirty-five, but he had dark eyes and a brutal scar that ran down his left cheek.

Reed took a cautious step forward. "Vince? That you?"

The stocky Marine laughed. "You said to get a haircut."

Reed sighed in relief. "I've been looking for you, Sergeant."

"Well, you found me. What do you want?" Vince was abrupt, but there was no aggression in his voice. Reed offered his hand, but Vince kept his arms crossed.

Reed cleared his throat. "I'll get straight to the point. I'm mixed up in some shit. It's not legal. Somebody I care about is in trouble, and I need your help."

Vince continued to stare, his face blank and emotionless. Reed saw the spiderweb of scars tracing his neck and scalp. A burn mark twisted the flesh beneath his right ear, and discoloration marred his shaved cheeks.

Leftovers from the IED?

Vince grunted. "Who's asking?"

"A fellow Marine," Reed said.

The answer seemed to satisfy Vince. He unfolded his arms and shoved his hands into the pockets of the jacket. "What do you need?"

"I need a diversion. If you have some friends, I could use their help, also. I'll make it worth your while."

Vince let out a low whistle, and Reed looked up to see a small group of men, all dressed in shabby, torn clothes, materialize out of the darkness around him. Their faces were cold and hard, one man was missing an arm, and another wore an eyepatch. They were all filthy, but they all sported impeccable haircuts.

Vince waved his arm as though he were presenting Olympic medalists. "Meet the rifle squad, Jarhead. Somebody need their ass kicked?"

Reed indulged a small smile. "I'll take care of the ass-kicking. I just need help with the smoke and mirrors. I have to warn you; somebody could spend the night downtown for this."

A ripple of condescending laughter passed through the small crowd.

"You mean a warm bed and a hot meal?" somebody said.

"Fair enough. I'm just saying, the police are certain to turn up."

Another ripple of laughter. Reed deemed it to be a good sign and jerked his head toward Vince. The sergeant stepped a few feet away from his men, and Reed lowered his voice.

"I have to make sure you understand. There could be use of deadly force."

Vince motioned to the men, now standing in a circle, their hands in their pockets while they talked quietly. "You see that kid over there?"

A scrawny young man with a neck tattoo stood beneath a tree, huddled over in a threadbare sweatshirt. He laughed at a joke, but the mirth didn't make it to his empty eyes.

"That's Private Becker. He's from Milwaukee. Served in Iraq and got shook up pretty bad. Has all kinds of mental crap going on."

Vince reached into his pocket and drew out a cigarette. He lit it with a brand-new Zippo lighter and took a long pull. After blowing smoke through his nose, he continued.

"Two nights ago, this gangbanger from across town jumped Becker. Tried to take his blanket. Cracked a rib."

Vince met Reed's gaze and spoke without a hint of hesitation. "We crushed his skull and slung his body in a dumpster."

The sergeant's battle-weary face gleamed in the soft glow of the streetlamps. Reed wasn't sure what he expected when he first met Vince, but this wasn't it. This was cold. Brutal.

Vince took another long pull of the cigarette, then sighed. "America has left us with nothing except each other, Corporal. But what we have, we look after. So cut the crap and tell me what you need."

Reed dug the car keys out of his pocket. "Well, Sergeant. Can you drive a stick?"

22

Atlanta, Georgia

As Atlanta's business district closed shop and commuted home, the nightlife of the old city began to stir. The highways, loaded to capacity with overnight shipping traffic, wound their way through Atlanta like giant snakes, one red and one white. Lights flashed from nightclubs. The spire of the Bank of America Plaza and the crowns adorning the top of 191 Peachtree glowed with amber fire, lighting up the night sky with a blazing reminder that the Empire City of the South was as vibrant and alive as ever.

It was the *alive* part that bothered Reed the most. There would never be an ideal time to execute a plan this bold in the heart of downtown. But at nine p.m., with cops patrolling the downtown streets, couples walking hand-in-hand between ice cream shops, and city buses rolling in and out of their downtown garages, the deck felt stacked against him. Reed's only advantage was the shield of nightfall, but even the darkness was beaten into submission by the blazing streetlamps and flashing headlights.

Reed stood at the edge of the park, huddled close to the shadows, as he stared up at the impending mass of 191 Peachtree, rising from the concrete jungle five hundred yards away. The granite-faced tower stood 771 feet tall, dominating the skyline with imperial majesty. The crowns sitting on top of the building looked like haunting beacons against the grey sky, shining in golden light from the powerful lamps housed within. Everything about the structure boasted power and stability.

Empire.

Reed ducked his head and adjusted the backpack on his shoulder. He still wore the Carolina Panthers jacket and carried a duffle bag in his left hand. It was less conspicuous than the rifle case, but it accomplished the same task. The familiar rush of adrenaline flooded his system as he stepped across Centennial Olympic Park Drive and started down Luckie Street. It was a feeling he'd felt twenty-nine times before, but this time it was different. It wasn't just the weight of impending death tugging at the edge of his focus; the stakes were bigger this time—as was the stage.

A bicycle cop whirred down the sidewalk, and Reed nodded a brief greeting before hurrying past. Dark solar panels adorned the block to his left, lined in ghostly rows under the dark sky. One block farther on, the Holiday Inn Express rose from the sidewalk, its windows gleaming with yellow light as cars passed quietly in front of it along Cone Street. A homeless man stood on the corner, his gaunt cheeks caving in under sharp cheekbones. Reed handed him a ten-dollar bill before he could ask, then he accelerated his pace.

Two more blocks passed under Reed's combat boots before he stopped at the corner of Forsyth and Luckie Streets and tilted his head back.

The Equitable Building dominated the block with 453 feet of tower. Everything about it was dark. Ebony sheathing framed heavily tinted windows. Black doors guarded the main entrance like gates to Hell. Only the tall letters, glowing in soft white light and gracing the top of the tower, broke the pattern: EQUITABLE.

The building looked like the corporate headquarters of a billionaire mob boss—strong, silent, and brooding.

Reed shifted the backpack on his shoulder.

This is it. You can't lose this time.

The thin wire headset was flimsy over Reed's ear, and he twisted the mic close to his mouth, breathing into it until the radio activated. "Vince, you with me?"

"Who's Vince? This is Falcon One, your driver."

"Right. Of course. And my tower team?"

"Call them Falcon Two. Falcon Three has the van. What about you?"

"Prosecutor," Reed said. "My call sign is Prosecutor."

"Roger that, Prosecutor. We're standing by."

The earpiece clicked as Reed muted it. He hurried around the corner and onto the tower's service alley. Shadows danced under the streetlamps as a decorative tree swayed in the night breeze. Machinery hummed from the loading dock, and a black cat scampered across the alley. But there were no people. No security. Reed moved deeper into the shadows and climbed onto the loading dock. His torso erupted in waves of pain as he pulled himself back to his feet. The injuries burned beneath his skin, sending bursts of agony into his skull. The dock wavered under his feet, and Reed leaned against the wall to steady himself. He'd suffered bruises and broken ribs before. There was little to do besides suck it up and press on.

Even though the breeze dropped into the low fifties, Reed was clammy with perspiration as he approached the service door and tried the latch. It was locked, and a cheap, plastic card key reader with a single flashing light was mounted next to the door. Reed flipped his pocket knife out and began to pry the cover off.

"So, Prosecutor." Vince's voice crackled over the headset. "What happened in Iraq?"

Reed paused over the card reader. "Iraq?"

"You said you left the Marines in handcuffs. Sounds like a hell of a story."

Reed hesitated. "Your point?"

"We've got time to kill. What happened?"

The plastic cover snapped off, exposing a small circuit board and several multi-colored wires. Reed stuck his flashlight between his teeth, and with the tip of his knife, he began removing the tiny silver screws that held the circuit board in place.

Reed spoke around the flashlight. "Let's just say . . . the right thing and the legal thing aren't always the same thing."

Vince grunted. "So, you did the right thing, and you went to prison for it."

"Yeah." Reed's focus blurred for a moment. He paused over the card reader as momentary flashes of that dark night in Baghdad reentered his mind. They were as fresh as the moment they transpired. The gunshots. The bodies on the ground. The resulting whirlwind of a court-martial, a prison sentence, the hopelessness of death row.

And then, Oliver. Reed's one chance at freedom.

"Thirty kills in exchange for your freedom."

"Wanna tell me what went down?" Vince asked, jarring Reed out of his thoughts.

Reed blinked his way back into focus and cleared his throat. "Not really."

Vince grunted again. "I get it. Backstory then. Where you from?"

"You first."

"Montana! Big Sky Country. A ranch with a few thousand head of cattle. Grew up wrangling beef and raising hell."

Reed's thoughts cleared as the circuit board fell off, further exposing the wires. Reed slipped the blade under an orange wire and pressed his thumb over the rubber jacketing, applying just enough pressure to expose the copper wire beneath. Two more precise twists of the knife revealed the yellow and black wires. He severed the red wire next and pressed the other three together across their sides. The light flashed green, and the latch clicked.

"You eat a lot of steak in Montana?" Reed said.

"Best damn steak you ever stuck a fork in. I'm a ribeye man myself, but I don't mind a filet now and again."

Reed opened the door and hurried inside, holding the light at shoulder level. A hallway opened up in front of him. It was dark, with thick wooden doors lining either side. Storage closets, maybe. The floor was slick with wax, and his rubber boots squeaked with each footstep.

"Amen to that. Slap it on a plate with a baked potato and salad. Beer or sweet iced tea."

"Iced tea?" Vince laughed. "That's a Southern tradition. You from 'round here?"

Two turns in the hallway brought Reed to an intersection with elevators and a service door. The elevators were locked by card key, as was the stairwell. He could breach them again, but unlike the dock door, these access points probably recorded entry, and there would be surveillance inside the elevators and stairwells. Reed approached the service door instead.

"I went to high school in LA, but before that, we lived in Birmingham. My dad was from a little town called Sylacauga. I wouldn't say I'm Southern."

"You said *was*. Did your old man pass?"

Reed paused at the service door, his hand hanging over the handle. For a moment, he didn't answer, then he reached into his cargo pocket and pulled out a lock pick.

"Something like that. My mom moved us to California. But you know ... sweet tea follows you."

Vince grunted again. Maybe he knew when to stop pressing. The lock pick slipped into the keyhole, and Reed manipulated the tiny tool with practiced ease. His ribs throbbed with each slow breath, and sweat dripped off his nose and onto his boot. One twist, then a flick of his wrist, and the lock clicked.

"You got a lady, Falcon?" Reed asked.

"You take me for a motard, Prosecutor? I got a whole busload of ladies!"

A flood of musty air rushed from the service room as Reed stepped in. A quick scan with the flashlight revealed a large storage area with mop buckets, tool boxes, and cardboard boxes littering the floor. On the far end of the room a small door about three feet square was framed in the middle of the wall, with a row of buttons lining the wall beside it.

"No, I'm talking about *the* lady. You know. The face you saw when that IED went off."

Vince sighed. It was a quiet sound. Softer than his usual rumbling growl. "Danielle Taylor . . . the most gorgeous woman in Montana."

The twin doors of the service elevator squeaked and groaned. Reed smacked the button to the top floor, then tossed the duffle bag inside the car before bending over and cramming himself in alongside it. A shiver of misery ripped through his body with the motion. It was all he could do not to scream. Each shallow breath further inflamed his swollen and torn muscles. Every tiny movement was a bolt of lightning flashing through his torso, ripping and burning as it went.

"Brunette?" Reed hissed the word through gritted teeth. The elevator groaned then started upward with a screech of metal on metal.

"She was. Chemo took that. But damn, son, it couldn't take her smile. That's the smile I saw when the IED went off."

Somewhere far overhead, the whine of the winch echoed down the elevator shaft. The cramped interior of the car smelled of oil and cleaning supplies, but the metal was refreshingly cool against his skin. *There's always a silver lining.*

"Did she make it?"

"Oh yes." Vince's words were still soft. "For three years. Breast. Lung. Spine. It finally went to her brain. That's what took her. But she gave it a hell of a fight. Not many a jarhead could've held on like my Danielle."

The radio fell silent, and Reed felt the stillness between them hanging over the invisible distance. It was the kind of stillness that falls between two old men sitting over a beer, too rich to be broken.

"You should be proud, Falcon."

"Damn right, Prosecutor. Heaven is proud to have her."

The elevator screeched to a halt. Numbness overwhelmed the sharper edges of the pain now, providing welcome relief but reducing his ability to make precise motor movements. He would need that precision before this night was over. The green LED letters of his watch read 9:39. Only twenty-one minutes until the deadline. His heart thumped, and he adjusted the pistol on his belt, then he pried the doors open. A cool breeze washed over his face as he piled out of the elevator, dragging the bag behind him. Hard concrete, mixed with the grimy crunch of loose dirt, clicked against his combat boots. Reed flipped the flashlight on and scanned the space around him, taking a moment to catch his breath.

The floor was mostly open, with half-built partitions rising at odd intervals between wooden columns. Cans of paint were stacked next to the wall, and piles of rolled carpet lay in what looked like a future hallway. Bare wires hung from the skeleton of a suspended ceiling. The breeze blew in from somewhere overhead, and the air was fresh—cleaner than the gasoline smell of the city streets far below.

"What about you, Prosecutor? Whose face will you see right before this shit plan of yours explodes?"

Reed slipped between the piles of construction materials, testing the floor with his toes before placing his weight on it. A few yards ahead, the primary elevator shaft shot upward through the floor and disappeared into the ceiling. Unfinished drywall clung to the side of the shaft with gaping cracks and water damage decorating the bland white. A single door stood in the backside of the shaft. It was metal and painted brown, with clean white letters stenciled over the middle of it.

ROOF ACCESS.

"I'm alone," Reed said. "It's just me."

"Aw, come on, Prosecutor. There must have been somebody."

Reed hesitated, then sighed. "There was, once. It didn't last long."

"A fellow Marine?"

Reed chuckled. "A car thief. Her name was Kelly."

"Ah. So, this would have been after your little visit to the lockup."

"Yeah, bad company, and all that. Like I said, it didn't last."

Reed stepped up to the door and reached into his pocket for the lockpick.

"What about the other girl?" Vince asked.

"What girl?"

A short, condescending laugh filled the mic. "The girl we're pulling this moronic scheme for. The one you're obsessing over right now."

Reed hid a smirk as he pressed the lockpick into the keyhole and began to manipulate the tool. "I don't know what you're talking about, Falcon."

"Don't bullshit me, kid. There's only one kind of thing that motivates a man to act the fool. It's love. Love of country, love of money, love of something. The only thing I see you loving is another human."

Reed stared at the door, manipulating the lockpick without looking at it. Seconds passed, then he sighed.

"All right. You got me."

"Brunette?" Vince asked.

"Blonde."

"Girlfriend?"

"No. More like . . . somebody I let down. Somebody I should have protected."

"Hmm . . ." Vince's thought trailed off.

Reed guessed that the sergeant wanted to ask more but now wasn't the time or place.

The lock clicked. Reed pulled the door open and hauled himself up the stairs on the other side. Twelve steps, then he reached another metal door. This one was locked from the inside, and a quick flip of his thumb defeated the bolt. As the hinges squeaked, a blast of wind tore through the small gap, flooding his lungs with life. Another fifteen steps lay on the other side of the door, and then the rooftop. Reed sucked in a long pull of fresh air as he pressed through the doorway and stepped onto the tower's roof.

Atlanta lay at his feet, stretching out for miles on every side. As far as he could see, the lights of every suburb, shopping mall, and streetlamp glowed in the darkness as a star-filled cityscape of towers and hotels, office suites and bus stations. The wind carried the distant bustle of six million residents, their barking dogs, and honking cars. A child laughed from somewhere far away, and a door slammed. Reed imagined he could hear music—maybe the thump of a disco. He could hear the hum of a city bus. A city alive with passion and secrets.

And there, towering in the middle of it all, as a proud monument of Southern tradition, was the 191 Peachtree building. Only a few hundred yards away, its flame-finished granite face gleamed in the light of the other skyscrapers. The shadow of each passing cloud flitted across the tinted windows, gracing the majestic structure with a light show of mottled yellow streetlight and white moonlight.

Reed thought it was nothing short of magnificent.

His head swam, and his legs were wobbly as he approached the edge. If you wanted to make a statement the world would never forget, dropping a body off the side of 191 Peachtree was a good place to start.

He stopped, taking a moment to clear his mind before looking down, 453 feet below him, to the cold outline of Forsyth Street. The pavement wavered, making him feel suddenly dizzy. He stepped away from the edge and closed his eyes, releasing the tension in his muscles and calming his pulse.

Dammit. Why couldn't this have been a ground job?

Reed could take the darkness, the blood, the murky water and suffocating heat. Snakes, spiders, and snapping dogs didn't even bother him, but heights . . . heights he could do without.

The duffle bag thudded against the concrete rooftop. Reed pried out the rifle, snapped it together, and then flipped the lens caps off the scope and locked the bipod into place. His hands trembled with anticipation as he settled down behind the weapon and lifted the butt to his shoulder. It felt good to rest his cheek against the stock, and the cool touch of polymer against his skin was more familiar and comforting than a soft pillow. He felt powerful and in control again.

"Prosecutor to all channels, I have obtained overwatch. Operation is a go."

Vince's voice sounded strong and commanding. "Very good. Falcon Two, this is Falcon One. Confirm, operation is a go. You may breach the granite dildo."

Reed blinked. "Granite dildo? That's what we're calling it?"

A crackling laugh rippled over the headset. "Welcome back to the Corps, Prosecutor!"

23

The wind bit straight through his Panthers jacket, and Reed avoided looking at the clouds, which would only reinforce the illusion that he was about to crash to the street below in a gruesome puddle of blood and gore. Instead, he focused on his position, nestling himself five feet from the edge of the roof. He lay on his stomach with his legs splayed behind him for extra stability. The cold concrete pressed into his rib cage, sending new waves of pain shooting down his spine. Normally, he would have packed a pad of some kind for overwatch duty, but there hadn't been room for it.

Reed flipped the scope's illumination feature on, then swept the red crosshairs across rooftops until they came to rest on the west face of 191 Peachtree.

Drawing in a long breath, he focused on relaxing each muscle group. First his toes, then the soles of his feet. He breathed through his mouth, relishing the relief of each muscle as it loosened. It brought moderate relaxation to his aching body, promising the possibility that he might not die from busted ribs after all. Each breath became deeper and slower than the last, and his heart rate slowed along with them. His entire body rested in a state of calm. Not comfort, by any stretch. But control.

"Falcon Two, this is Prosecutor. Sitrep, over."

"'Sup, Prosecutor." The man on the other end of the radio didn't suppress his heavy Arkansas accent. Vince introduced him as "Snort," a former assistant squad leader during the Vietnam war. Snort was now pushing seventy, but he moved like a man twenty years younger.

"We have gained entry and are preparing to stroke this shaft."

Reed blinked. "Come again?"

Vince laughed, breaking onto the radio without offering a call sign. "They're gonna ride the elevator."

The radio fell silent, and Reed nestled his cheek against the stock again. He looked down at his watch. The green numerals glowed at 9:52. He wanted to urge Snort to hurry the hell up, but he didn't want to deal with the storm of innuendos that would unleash.

Seconds ticked by. Reed swung the crosshairs down the building and toward the east, surveying the streets. A motorcycle passed by on Ellis Street, and a couple of cars cruised in front of 191's primary entrance on Peachtree Street. The rest of the avenues were quiet. A final stillness was closing over the city, bringing with it a welcome release of tension over Reed's nerves.

I know you're out there. I know you're watching. I'm gonna run your rat ass to ground.

"This is Falcon Two. We have reached the forty-fifth floor. All silent so far. Setting up now."

Reed continued his surveillance of the streets around the tower. He paused over every rooftop, every window, and every parking garage—any place that provided the slightest vantage point over the west face of the tower. He saw no one. No dark cars, no men with binoculars, and no snipers hiding in the shadows.

One more pass, and then Reed swung the optic back to the tower and ran the crosshairs down the building. He paused at the entrance. A black Chevy Impala pulled up to the front door of the office building, while across the street, two patrol cars sat at the intersection of Ellis and Peachtree.

"This is Prosecutor. I have three police vehicles in position at the main entrance . . . possibly a fourth bearing southbound on Andrew Young. Yes, he's pulling over. It's a cop. Black Chevrolet Tahoe."

"Roger that, Prosecutor." Snort spoke into the mic as though he were talking through a mouthful of pudding. "We are T minus ninety seconds."

Reed twisted his hand around the familiar grip of the rifle. The rubberized texture rubbed against his palm, loosening his muscles and reminding him of each time he pressed that trigger—the way the weapon lurched into his shoulder, and the puff of red that flashed across his scope before the crosshairs jumped upward. Sitting a thousand yards away and executing judgment on the guilty was the closest feeling to total power.

"Hey, Falcon One," he whispered.

"Yeah, Corporal?"

"That fake leg of yours can still pump a clutch, right?"

Vince snorted. "There's no end to the things this Marine can pump."

"Ooorah!" Falcon Two shouted.

Reed rolled his eyes. "All right. Just making sure. Because if you scratch my car, I'll take it out of your battered jarhead ass."

"I'd welcome you to try, Corporal."

The crosshairs settled over the forty-fifth floor as Reed relaxed his shoulder. The familiar buzz of his cell phone erupted in his pocket, and he pried it out to see the screen illuminated with the all-too-familiar caller ID.

UNKNOWN.

One tap on the green button, and Reed held it to his ear, but he didn't say anything.

"Reed . . . it's three minutes 'til ten. I hope you're not about to disappoint me again."

Reed gasped for air as though he had just climbed a few hundred stairs.

"Listen . . . I'm almost done. Just a couple more minutes."

Salvador grunted. "Ten o'clock, Reed, or Miss Morccelli will be picking her ukulele with three fingers."

The phone clicked off. Reed shoved it back into his pocket and growled into the mic. "Falcon Two, let's go already."

"Just a few more seconds . . . wiring the explosives now. This is some good junk, Prosecutor. You must have the hookup."

Reed didn't respond. He closed his left eye and focused on the forty-fifth floor. Behind one of the windows, he saw a shadow moving in the darkness. It was graceful and silent. Snort's men may have lost their homes, but they clearly hadn't lost their training.

"All right, Prosecutor. Falcon Two is ready to rock."

"Falcon One?" Reed said.

"Falcon One is in position and ready to roll, Prosecutor."

Reed settled his cheek into the rifle and took one more measured breath. The night fell still and silent, and all noises and distractions were blocked from his mind in this final moment before the storm.

"Falcon Two, execute."

A half second passed, then a loud bang ripped through the quiet night. The window exploded beyond the crosshairs, raining down in deadly shards over the street hundreds of feet below. A body wrapped in dark clothes shot out of the window and fell through empty space, its feet tied by a rope that disappeared back inside the tower. The body soared out from the building with its arms dangling before the cord became taut, and the corpse fell back and slammed against the tower. Crimson blood gushed from the torso, streaming down the building as the arms hung limp next to the glass.

Reed maximized the zoom on the rifle, focusing on the dangling body. He started at the feet, then worked his way down. The legs were covered in dark jeans. The body was wrapped in a dirty denim jacket, now saturated in crimson. Fake blood from the busted reservoir inside the chest streamed over its face. The face was white, distorted by a crushed jaw.

It was a damn-convincing Halloween prop.

Blue lights flashed from the street below. The patrol cars parked on Ellis shot forward, rocketing to the front entrance. Officers piled out of the Impala and Tahoe, while spotlights from all four vehicles blazed over the gaping hole. Reed indulged in a brief smile, enjoying the moment of truth. *It's good to be right.*

"This is Prosecutor. I have four vehicles bearing down on the main entrance. Ten officers closing on your position. Move it, guys."

"Roger that, Prosecutor. We are pulling out."

Reed grinned.

He centered the crosshairs over the main entrance, and they hovered there as cops stormed the door. Dressed in black and clutching assault weapons and tactical shotguns, they were much more heavily armed than your average patrolman. Much too prepared to call it a coincidence.

"Prosecutor, this is Falcon One. I am ready on your mark."

"Wait a moment, Falcon One . . ." Reed looked down at his watch and waited as the seconds ticked by. Ten seconds. Thirty seconds. One minute. He focused on each flash of the digital watch, matching the tempo of time with every pound of his heart, and waiting until the moment felt right.

The tower was bathed in spotlights. Another patrol car screeched over the pavement from the northeast, a bullhorn squealed, and then a voice barked orders at the tower from somewhere amongst the vehicles. Noise and chaos reigned.

It was time.

"All right, Falcon One. Execute."

A split second passed. Reed swung the crosshairs away from the tower toward the east, and the scope settled over the parking lot that sat between Ellis Street and the Georgia-Pacific Tower. Lights flashed out of the darkness, and an unearthly howl filled his ears. It was the sound of 505 American horses roaring to life.

The Camaro rolled out of the parking lot, then took a gentle turn onto Peachtree Street. Reed imagined he could feel the rumble of the pavement under the uncorked exhaust, shooting up his legs and forcing his body into the rhythm of the engine. He could almost taste the oily flavor of exhaust on the air and feel the familiar leather knob of the shifter under his palm.

The beast slipped down the street at a calm twenty miles per hour, its windows black and its lights dark. Reed traced its path with the scope, zooming out so he could keep the surrounding blocks in view. He bit his lip, held his breath, and then swept the surrounding streets again.

His gaze caught on a glint of steel. He flipped the rifle's safety off and hissed into the mic. "Falcon One, this is Prosecutor. Haul ass."

24

Thunder ripped between the buildings and pounded off the sides of the skyscrapers as the front end of the Camaro lifted off the ground, and the back tires spun against the pavement. A familiar thrill flooded Reed's brain as the car took off, rocketing down Peachtree Street toward Plaza Park. Two more engines, higher-pitched, with shrieking blasts of exhaust, screamed to life fifty yards behind the Camaro. Reed traced Peachtree Street with the crosshairs, back toward the tower, and back toward the police. This was it.

Two suited figures, bent low over Japanese sports bikes, flashed out of a darkened street. They shot through the crowd of cops without so much as a pause, then raced after the Camaro. The air was alive with the roar of the American V-8 and the hellish scream of the bikes.

Reed swung the rifle to the right, following the bikes as they turned into a curve where Peachtree passed the Georgia-Pacific Tower. The motorcycles vanished out of sight behind the silhouette of the Residence Inn, and Reed jumped to his feet and sprinted to the far side of the Equitable Building. He slid back into a prone position behind the rifle, a couple of feet from the southern corner of the tower. Barely a second passed before the Camaro's taillights flashed across Decatur Street, crossing through the scope in a millisecond, and then they were gone again.

"Falcon One, this is Prosecutor. Take a left on Wall Street, then another left onto Peachtree Center Avenue."

"Roger that, Prosecutor."

Reed retraced the Camaro's trail until the crosshairs settled over the sports bikes. The two lean figures bent over the handlebars with the practiced grace of true athletes. He could take them out—a clean shot to the back of each helmet and lay them down in the middle of Peachtree Street, but that wouldn't bring him any closer to Banks.

Vince spun the Camaro around the corner onto Wall Street, then disappeared behind a row of buildings. The bikes followed a hundred yards behind, with no hint of suspicion or hesitation marking their turns. The men in hot pursuit of the Camaro were truly convinced that Reed Montgomery sat behind the wheel and was putting pedal to the metal to make his escape.

The intersection of Wall Street and Peachtree Center loomed ahead of the Camaro. A hundred yards. Then fifty. The car jolted and almost slid into the sidewalk as Vince negotiated a turn. Reed held his breath, then saw the back tires bite concrete and break the slide at the last moment.

"Falcon Three," Reed whispered. "You ready?"

"I'm all yours, Prosecutor."

Reed laid his finger on the trigger. The first bike flashed into view, crossing the intersection of Peachtree Center and Gilmer Street, right in front of Hurt Park. Reed drew half a breath, the crosshairs froze, and he pressed the trigger.

The front tire of the lead motorcycle exploded. Reed pivoted the crosshairs to the right and pressed the trigger again. The rear tire of the second bike burst. Both bikes slid out of control, slinging their riders into the empty street as the powerful motorcycles spun across the pavement.

Another press of the trigger and a bullet struck home in the left thigh of the first rider. A fourth crack of the rifle blew the second rider's ankle apart, and he convulsed in pain. Both men clawed at their helmets, writhing on the asphalt as blood sprayed from their legs.

"Falcon Three, execute!"

A white utility van roared out of the darkness of Hurt Park, driving against the one-way arrows painted on Gilmer Street. It slid to a stop beside the two fallen men. Reed watched through the scope as a tall man wearing a ski mask jumped out. He stuck a Taser into the rib cage of each man, then dragged their unconscious bodies into the rear of the vehicle. The doors slammed shut, and the van rocketed out of the intersection.

"Prosecutor, this is Falcon Three. Be advised, I have the, um . . . people you wanted."

"Roger that. On my way to the rendezvous. Prosecutor out."

Reed jumped to his feet and ripped the headset off. He ran back to his bags, shoved the radio inside his backpack, and then jerked out the thick bundle of rope. Sparks flashed between the synthetic cord and his damp hands. He ran to the west face of the tower, where a bank of air-conditioning units sat in a six-foot recess on the roof. Reed hurried down the access ladder, then ran to the backside of the humming AC units. His fingers worked in a blur of sweat and rope—a quick flip, and a jerk of both arms to secure the knot. His head pounded again, but the pain was a distant memory overshadowed by the gravity of what came next.

Back on the roof, he flung the rope over the edge and watched it unravel four hundred feet down the side of the tower until it hit the ground. He didn't have time to think about the swimmy feeling in his stomach or the wobble in his knees; everything just blurred together in a series of practiced motions—one foot through the harness, then the next foot. The cinch strap clicked against the buckle as he tightened the harness around his waist, then he slung the backpack over his shoulders, followed by the rifle on the nylon sling. Both were heavy against his back, dragging on his shoulders and making each breath feel short and shallow. Or was that the height?

Reed set the duffle bag beneath the rope, right on the edge of the rooftop. It provided moderate protection against the sharp edge of the concrete—hardly a professional solution, but hopefully it would suffice. The rope felt heavy as he locked it into his harness, checking each connection and buckle one more time.

Surges of adrenaline drowned out the feeling of absolute terror as he approached the brink of the building. His stomach convulsed, and he fought the overwhelming urge to vomit. Some biological fire alarm wired in his brain erupted in a screaming chorus of warnings. *Get back. Don't do it. Danger! Danger!*

First one foot on the edge, and then the other. Reed's knuckles turned white as he closed his eyes, clutched the rope, and forced himself to lean forward until it became taut. In the distance, he heard police sirens, the blare of the bullhorn, a honking fire truck, boots clapping against the pavement to the pulse of his heart so loud and insistent, he thought it might explode. Bile bubbled up in his throat, but he didn't vomit. He didn't jerk back from the edge.

The white EQUITABLE lights gleamed a couple feet beneath his toes. His hands shook, and he took a long breath between his teeth. It whistled like the blast of the wind in his ears. His knees were locked, and he felt frozen in time, like the moment before the trigger clicked and the rifle cracked.

Go.

The rope slipped through the harness as Reed fell forward. His body rocked over the side of the building until he hung ninety degrees out, suspended by the rope, then continued to plunge. One foot in front of the other, he was a superhero, defiant of gravity or geometry. The rope dangled beneath him, and his heart thundered as his boots pounded down the face of the tower. With each strike of rubber on glass, unshakeable resolve overwhelmed his fear. It was anger now—the kind of anger he felt when he dominated his fears and realized how weak they truly were. He stretched out his legs and leaped forward, allowing fresh yards of rope to hiss through the harness at an ever-increasing speed. He was barely in control, only one false step away from sudden death.

His boots slipped on the slick glass, and Reed tightened his hand on the brake, feeling his shoulders sling forward and his heels fly back. Bile and spit sprayed from his lips as he kicked out at the windows beneath his feet. His toe caught the underside of a windowsill just in time to keep him from plummeting toward the ground in a total free fall. He regained his footing then pushed downward again, rocketing toward the street in a series of hopping leaps. Reed gasped for air, realizing he had been holding his breath since he left the rooftop. Windows and floors flashed past like a blurry slideshow.

The halfway point vanished beneath his feet, and he relaxed his hand on the brake, allowing the rope to slide more quickly through the harness. The brake was hot from the friction, but he didn't let go. He pushed out from the building and released tension, plummeting down another forty feet before his boots struck the glass again.

Almost as quickly as it began, it was over. The rope ran short, and Reed free-fell the final twelve feet onto the hard sidewalk below. His knees absorbed most of the shock, and he stumbled forward, feeling dizzy and disoriented. The cool night air helped to clear his head as he stumbled away with the rifle bouncing on his shoulders. He tipped his head back to survey the tower, and euphoria overwhelmed his better judgment as he screamed and pumped his fist. "Hell yeah!"

Reed ran up Forsyth Street, pounding the sidewalk in long, smooth strides. He didn't even notice the heavy rifle bouncing on his back or the harness still strapped around his waist. He was consumed by full operator mode and could run through a brick wall if he had to.

Almost there. Just a few more blocks.

Sirens blared from somewhere behind him. The police force would be in a state of total chaos by now. Especially the clean cops, who were unaware of the botched setup that was falling apart and taking their city down with it. Reed hated it when clean cops got mixed up in the dealings of the dirty ones. He could only hope the smoke cleared without any casualties.

Two more blocks passed under his pounding feet. Centennial Olympic Park loomed ahead, and just before it on his right, a small parking lot stretched out between the office buildings. Reed rushed between parked cars, then spotted the utility van parked in the back corner. Its lights were off, but he could tell by the small cloud of vapor building behind the rear tires that the engine was running.

A few quick strides and Reed stopped next to the driver's door. His legs and chest burned from the exertion.

The door opened, and one of Vince's displaced Marines stepped out. Ellis, a former fuel-truck driver and two-tour veteran, wore a broad smile as though he'd just won a wrestling match.

"They're all yours, Prosecutor. I've got them subdued, but they'll come around soon enough."

Reed offered his hand, his chest still heaving. "Thank you. I owe you guys . . . big time."

Ellis shrugged. "Don't worry about it. We don't have a lot to lose. It felt good to have some excitement for a change."

"It still means a lot. Next Monday afternoon, you'll find a man sitting on the park bench where I found Vince tonight. He'll leave a suitcase and walk away. Split it up with the guys."

Reed handed him a black card with a ten-digit number printed on one side in silver ink. The rest of the card was blank.

"This is me. I'm one call away."

Ellis offered a casual salute. "Good luck, Prosecutor. Give 'em hell."

As the battered Marine disappeared around the corner, Reed shoved his gear into the van and then piled in after it. Hell was a good word for what lay ahead.

25

Atlanta, Georgia

The van coughed and lurched forward. Reed looked over his shoulder to see the motorcycle riders laid out in the rear, unconscious amid shelves of electrical wire and fallen hand tools. The van belonged to a local electrical contractor, and Reed stole it from their service lot an hour before breaching the Equitable building. Vince would leave the Camaro at a pre-arranged drop point, but for now, the van would be less conspicuous.

Once again, the phone buzzed in Reed's pocket, but this time he didn't bother to check the caller ID.

"What's up, creep?"

Salvador's smooth voice was taut with anger. "Reed, you just made a very costly mistake."

"Help me out here, Sal. Was it a mistake to kick your goons in the nuts, or to evade your underhanded attempt to frame me? It's difficult to keep up with your games."

Short, hissing breaths blasted through the speaker. "All right. If that's how you want it, cut off her hand!"

"You're not good at blackmail, are you?"

The line fell silent. Salvador's tense breathing paused.

"Take notes, Sal. The first rule of blackmail: Never threaten a person you can't control."

"You think I'm scared of you, Montgomery?" Salvador's voice snapped like a bullwhip.

"Apparently not. But you're about to be."

"Listen, you shit. I'm about to filet this girl like—"

Reed hung up and tossed the phone into the passenger's seat. It buzzed again, but Reed ignored it. He turned off the highway and drove through the quiet streets of a neighborhood, taking increasingly more isolated streets until he found a long, desolate road leading out toward a garbage dump. Dust fogged the air around him as he bounced over potholes and swerved around deep ruts, driving another three miles before stopping in front of the dump's main entrance. A single streetlight buzzed over the gate, washing the chain link fence in a pool of orange warmth. The motor died, and the empty space around the landfill became still. Reed surveyed his surroundings for any sign of electronic surveillance, but he saw none. This far from the city, isolation ruled.

Dried mud crunched under his feet next to the van, and the air was thick with the smog of rotting garbage and pervasive diesel fumes. The motorcyclists groaned in agony as Reed jerked them through the back door and allowed them to collapse onto the ground. A few layers of duct tape bound their hands and sealed their wounds, moderating the flow of blood. Pale faces flooded with fear were framed by small features and blonde hair. European, clearly, and probably from east of Germany. One of the old Com-Bloc nations, maybe. Desperate men so long lost in the mire of the criminal underworld that they wouldn't be recognized by their own mothers. Reed knew the type.

Quick jabs to the gunshot wounds with the toe of his boot brought both men back to full consciousness. Groans turned to screams, and they began to kick. Reed dealt each a swift blow to the jaw, slamming their heads back against the rear of the van, then he squatted in front of them and drew the Glock.

"I haven't got a lot of time. Who do you work for, and where is Banks Morccelli?"

"To hell with you, man."

The accent was exactly as Reed suspected—thick, Eastern European, laden with heavy L's and rolled R's.

Reed laid the muzzle of the pistol against the man's left kneecap and pressed the trigger. Blood exploded from the leather pants, and the man screamed and jerked away, slamming his head into the back of the van. A waterfall of agony streamed from his eyes, drawing wavering lines through the dirt on his cheeks.

"I think I have your attention." Reed's tone remained level and focused. "Whoever talks first gets to live. Who do you work for?"

The men glared at him in defiant silence, and the one on the left groaned and shook in pain, but still didn't speak.

"Damn you people. You're only hurting yourself." Reed holstered the pistol and walked around to the side of the van. He dug through the pile of tools until he located a pair of electrician's cable-cutters—thick, heavy-duty pliers with rusted handles. He returned to the rear of the van and placed the righthand man's index finger between the cutting jaws of the pliers.

"What the—"

The landfill echoed with agonized screams as Reed clamped down on the pliers. Bone was no match for his grip.

"Who do you work for?"

His victim shook like a tree in a hurricane, then beat his head against the back of the van, leaving smears of blood on the dusty white paint. Reed cocked back his fist and dealt him a swift blow to the jaw with the pliers. Bone cracked. Reed struck again, and the man on the left cursed in protest. Reed switched fire and beat him over the face, collapsing his nose.

"Do you know what they call me?" Reed asked. "They call me The Prosecutor. Because when I've got a job, I prosecute the hell out of it until I get the results I want. You two dirtbags made a huge mistake getting in my way."

Reed wiped his forehead. His stomach was ready to bust each

time he looked down at his bloody handiwork, but the resolve in his mind was as inflexible as iron.

"One of you has a chance to walk away. Who do you work for?"

The men sat trembling, blood puddling on the ground around them. Reed waited. Sometimes the fear itself was more powerful than waves of pain.

The man on the right spoke first. "I do not know name. He—"

"Shut up!" His partner sank his teeth into the man's shoulder.

Reed snatched the pistol from his belt and fired twice. Blood sprayed across the rear door of the van. The body toppled to the ground.

"Continue." Reed's voice was dull and emotionless.

"I do not know him! We get contract, just like you. He tell us police will arrest you. We stop you if you try to escape. This is all, I swear!"

Reed holstered the gun and squatted in front of him, toying with the pliers.

"How were you paid?"

"Cash. American dollars."

"Who paid you?"

"Nobody. We get job through Swiss broker. They call him Cedric. We were told to pick up the cash in locker at train station. This was all!"

"You're lying." Reed lifted the pliers.

"No! Okay. Okay. We work for him before. The man in Georgia. I do not know his name."

"Salvador? Is he called Salvador?"

"Salvador? No. He is English."

"English?" Reed cocked his head. "You mean he's white?"

"I don't know!" He looked away and slammed his head into the van again.

Reed grabbed him by the collar and jerked him forward, forcing him to meet his gaze.

"What did you do?"

Breath whistled between his bloody teeth. His eyes reminded

Reed of the way pupils looked after being dilated at the optometrist —wide, vacant, and unnatural.

"There was girl. I do not know who. He wanted her taken."

"Describe her."

Again, he tried to look away, but Reed dropped the pliers and sent his fist crashing directly below his victim's left eye. Knuckles met flesh with all the vengeance and power of the practiced blows back at the cabin. Once, then twice, then came the third stroke, driving the man's head into the rear of the van.

Reed leaned closer and screamed into this ear. "What did she look like?"

The man sobbed. "Blonde. Pretty. Young twenties."

"Where did you take her?"

"Train! Train place. I do not know name! No trains come. Only empty."

Reed shook him by the collar then raised his fist again. "Abandoned? It's abandoned?"

"Yes! Is abandoned."

"In the city?"

"Yes . . . yes. In the city."

Reed knew the location. It was the last place anyone would look —empty and isolated, with plenty of places to hide a kidnapped woman. He tossed the pliers into his left hand and drew the pistol.

The prisoner stared down the muzzle.

"No! You said if I talk, I live!"

Reed's eyes stung, and he swallowed hard. "I did, and you would have. But you touched Banks. I'm sorry."

The pistol cracked, and the man fell to the ground. Reed's arms trembled, his vision fogged, and the world tipped under his feet as he stepped away from the bodies and leaned against the van. Nausea and vertigo overwhelmed him, washing down his body like a tidal wave of illness. Vomit hurtled through his throat and splashed over his boots.

God, forgive me.

The bodies crumpled over each other in the back of the van.

Reed tossed the pliers inside, then shut the door and kicked dirt over the pools of blood under his feet. He drove back to the four-lane highway and turned east. The pavement drummed under the cheap tires, and occasional cars flashed past in the oncoming lanes. Reed's head spun, but he forced back the feelings of confused remorse. There was no time to feel sorry for the guilty.

He pulled the van into a dark, abandoned shopping mall southeast of town. Broken and abandoned shopping carts sat at random throughout the lot, while paper bags and bits of trash skipped over the pavement. Reed parked behind the main building and grabbed his gear. After digging through one of the dead man's pockets, he located a cell phone. It was locked but still allowed him to dial 911.

"What's your emergency?"

The sleeve of his jacket tasted bitter as he pressed it against his lips and spoke in a dull monotone. "You'll find Senator Holiday in a trailer off of Grimley Road. Bring medical."

Reed hung up before the operator could respond, and he threw the cell into the back of the van. He drew the Glock and bent over under the rear bumper. One shot to the bottom of the plastic gas tank resulted in a stream of fuel gushing over the pavement. The gasoline gurgled and splashed over the asphalt and tires, and filled the air with the thick aroma of petrol. He stepped back a few feet, holstered the gun, and lit a cigarette. His fingers trembled as he lifted it to his lips, but the nicotine brought relief to his strained nerves. His joints loosened, and he relished the fog that consumed his brain—not really a distraction, and barely a shield. It was a filter that blocked out the worst of the last hour, clearing his thoughts of the screams and carnage.

What have I become?

Reed flipped the smoke beneath the van. The gas exploded into a red-hot ball of fire, lifting the rear tires an inch off the ground before consuming the vehicle in flames. They were hot on his face, singeing his skin like a summer sun. Reed turned away.

The Camaro sat in the shadows, melting into the darkness like a ghost. He opened the trunk and deposited the rifle and gear, then slid into the driver's seat. Pain ripped through his legs and torso, reminding him that his adrenaline high was receding. There was nothing he could do about that. There would be time for painkillers and whiskey later.

Reed slammed the car into gear and took the on-ramp onto I-24 East. He planted his foot into the accelerator and listened to the roar of the wind and motor meld together in a bellow of hellish defiance that matched the rage building in the back of his mind.

It was time to finish this.

26

The miles passed under the belly of the Camaro in a dark blur. Reed circumvented the heart of the city, knowing it would still be hot with police activity. There was almost certainly an APB on the Camaro, which left him only a few hours before the investigative net of the Atlanta PD tightened too much for him to enter the city at all. By sunrise, both the car and its driver would need to be far away.

After taking the bypass around the southern side of the city, Reed turned north along State Highway 23 through Thomasville. His heart rate quickened as he closed in on East Atlanta. A lot of railroads cut between the streets and houses, and there were plenty of rail yards, also. Several of those were abandoned, the skeletons of an industrial age now passed. But when the tortured goon mentioned an empty rail yard where Salvador held Banks, only one place came to mind.

Pratt-Pullman Yard.

The streets around the Camaro grew darker and more desolate. Old houses with faded and peeling paint lined the sidewalks, many of them abandoned with shattered windows and boarded-up doors. Giant oak trees leaned over the streets with wiry branches hovering over rotting rooftops. Many of these trees remembered the Civil War; they were the survivors of the flames that consumed Atlanta, and they felt unwelcoming to Reed's violent intrusion, as though this place had seen enough of conflict and only wanted to sleep.

Reed stopped the car where he could see the rusty rooftops of the train yard a few hundred yards ahead. Just beyond it, MARTA's Blue Line ripped through the neighborhood and toward the east, lit by soft streetlights and red track lamps. Everything was unmoving and reserved, as though the trees and the darkness housed a terrible secret. There was an unnatural calm that promised awful things to anyone who broke it. Could that secret be Banks?

The body armor was heavy and restrictive as Reed pulled it on. He didn't tighten the straps as much this time, but he tucked an extra magazine into the elastic straps of the chest plate. The KRISS Vector, fully loaded, hung from a single-point sling around his neck. Half-dry blood stuck to his hands and forearms, and it was splattered over his pants and covered his shoes.

Reed slammed the trunk closed and stepped around to the side door of the Camaro. For the first time since hanging up on the unknown caller three hours before, he looked down at his phone. There were four missed calls, all from the same number. Reed hit redial.

The voice that answered was the furthest thing from the calm and controlled speaker of the last twenty-four hours. Salvador was consumed by anger, and his South American snarl muddled the clarity of his words, converting them into a stream of verbal vomit.

"It's too late, Montgomery. We've killed her!"

Reed forced himself to remain calm. "If that were true, you wouldn't have answered."

A crashing sound erupted from over the phone. "I'm going to rip her limb from limb!"

"Shut up." Reed's patience snapped like a strained rubber band. "I'm giving you one chance to walk away. Leave Banks, and get out while you're still alive."

"I'm not scared of you, Reed! You want her? Come get her!"

Reed hung up and pulled the charging handle of the submachine gun. The heavy bolt cycled back and rammed a fresh round into the chamber. His body was tense and charged, his mind sharpened, and he focused on the metal building rising over the shingle roofs three hundred yards away. The battered tin was painted with graffiti and full of holes, and the moonlight illuminated Pratt-Pullman as though it were a stage. Reed thought about the way Banks laughed and the overwhelming obsession he felt the second her lips touched his. The sound of her fingers strumming the ukulele, looking out over Atlanta. A city she loved. A place she called home.

Reed broke into a run toward the train yard.

27

Banks couldn't see. Her head was numb, and her eyes stung like they were filled with pepper juice. She knew there was some type of sedative in her veins, and it caused her mind to work in slow motion, as though each thought was its own private marathon. She blinked and tried to focus on tangible concepts, things she could work with, information that was relevant.

Her hands were tied behind her back and around the chair. She could work with that. What kind of bonds were they? Hard and narrow. Cable ties, maybe? Her feet were also bound, locked to the chair's legs with more cables. A dirty cloth that tasted like gasoline filled her mouth.

Her heart pounded like a war drum. Even through the drugs, the fear was palpable, building into a driving force that urged her to embrace the panic and descend into mental anarchy. She tried to identify her last clear memory, but everything was fuzzy. Was she in the Beetle or just near it? No, she wasn't in it. She was walking toward it. In a parking lot? Yes, it was a parking lot. There was a shopping bag in her hand. New socks and a bag of potato chips. That detail rang ironically clear in her crowded mind.

She remembered a split second of fear before the world erupted into chaos. There were men . . . two of them. Maybe more. They jumped from the side of a van and ran toward her. She fumbled with her purse, reaching for the Smith & Wesson 637 buried inside, and she struggled with the holster. The hammer spur caught on the inside of the bag, and panic overwhelmed her mind.

And then there was blackness. Had they hit her? Her head didn't hurt, but her neck throbbed.

Banks sank her teeth into the towel and pulled at the bonds. Nothing loosened. She tried to scream past the wadded cloth in her mouth, but the muted moan sounded more like a grunt than a cry for help.

Light flooded her face, and she blinked and tried to focus through her blurred vision and numb mind. She could see a door on the far side of the room, and two men stepped in. They moved in a blur of black clothes and stomping boots, lifted the chair off the floor, and carried her across the room.

A third man, short with dark skin, appeared and snapped angry commands at the others. "Hurry! Put her on the train. If you don't hear from me in ten minutes, go through with it."

Banks kicked against the chair, and a gloved fist slammed into her cheekbone. She tried to scream, but everything hurt. Panic surged through her mind, but this time it was accompanied by rage.

Another fist to her temple and she choked and slumped forward. The world spun.

28

Reed held the submachine gun to his chest and leaned low as he ran northward along Rogers Street. Everything was deathly silent. He checked the rifle for the third time as Toomer Elementary School loomed to his right. The school was dark and the parking lot empty. On the far side of the schoolyard a row of trees blocked the south edge of Pullman Yard. Reed jogged across the lot and slipped into the trees, and his boots fell in soft thumps on the leaf-covered ground.

He ducked under a limb and paused at the edge of the tree line. The bulk of Pratt-Pullman stood directly ahead in a cluster of large warehouse buildings. The space between consisted of a mostly empty field with a few abandoned structures and shallow ditches. To his right, the trees became thicker and looped their way along the east side of the field and toward the warehouses. The foliage was dense and tangled, ensuring a difficult and time-consuming approach. The alternative, however, would be to make a direct dash across an exposed three-hundred-yard stretch.

He opted for the trees and turned right, working his way through the brush for fifty yards before turning north and moving along the east edge of the field. The forest floor was littered with dry sticks and shallow holes, making it difficult to walk without sounding like an army of squirrels bouncing through the leaves. Reed bent under the low-hanging limbs and held the gun just under his line of sight, his finger extended over the trigger guard. Each breath was shallow. Every movement charged with nervous excitement.

As he approached the warehouses, the trees began to thin, and standing just twenty yards from the tree line was the first of the metal structures. They consisted of four narrow buildings, with sloping tin roofs, built directly next to each other. The walls were rusted and full of wide holes, exposing nothing but darkness on the other side. Reed slipped up next to the first structure and swept the muzzle of the rifle over the landscape around it. There were no signs of life. Moonlight played hide-and-seek with the shadows as the trees swayed in the wind. In the distance, an owl hooted, and some kind of nocturnal rodent bounced through the leaves. Reed's arm trembled with tension.

Thirty yards across a small field littered with trailer parts and manufacturing paraphernalia stood the train yard's primary structure. Over a hundred yards long, it dominated the field in rusty red —a relic of another era. The eastern end of the building was buried in the trees, with foliage and kudzu vines growing over the side and onto the roof, threatening to consume the building back into the belly of nature. The southern wall faced Reed with a series of twelve garage-style doors. Half of them hung open, gaping like the hungry mouths of a sleeping beast. Windows ran along the sloping rooftop, and most of them were busted out, leaving shards of dirty glass glistening in the moonlight. Graffiti covered every exposed inch of the building, blasted in gaudy shades of spray paint over the metal and brick. Nothing about the shadowy structure was hospitable. Reed realized there would be no chance of breaching it without exposing himself. Once inside, it would be dark. The floor could be concrete, strewn with machinery and sections of railroad iron. Worse still, the floor might be constructed of rotting wood ready to give way under the slightest provocation. He understood why Salvador chose this spot. It wasn't isolated or hidden or even defensible, but it was utterly impossible to approach without complete exposure.

Reed disengaged the safety and laid his finger over the trigger. He cast a wary look around the open field, checking for any new signs of surveillance or defense. Then he launched himself out of the trees and toward the building.

29

Three strides into the field and one leap over a ditch. That was as far as Reed made it before the first gunshots shattered the stillness. They were small-caliber, fully automatic, and blazing from one of the windows near the roofline. The ground exploded around his feet, sending rocks blasting into the air as though a land mine had detonated. Reed ducked and dashed to the left, and the gunfire continued, spraying the field with a deluge of lead.

It must be some kind of com-block submachine gun, inaccurate beyond fifty or sixty yards, clapping and thundering like some kind of deranged DJ hooked on a bass loop. Reed raised the KRISS and flipped the thumb switch to fully automatic, then pressed the trigger. The gun rattled like a firecracker, dumping twenty-five rounds of .45 ACP slugs into the building at random. The gunshots from the warehouse ceased, and Reed accelerated toward the building. He dropped the empty magazine and slammed a new one into the mag well, then smacked the bolt release with the heel of his left hand. Every sound rang in his head, pounding and echoing as though individually amplified. Reed skidded to a halt next to one of the gaping garage doors, pulled the gun into his shoulder, and ducked through the door. The inside of the warehouse stretched out before him, lit by the moon shining through the holes in the roof. As soon as his foot crossed the threshold, the gunfire resumed. He pivoted toward the sound and raised the KRISS. Muzzle flash blazed from a catwalk a few dozen yards away, suspended high above the concrete floor. Reed aligned the red dot over the spot and pressed the trigger twice. Something blunt struck his left calf, tearing through his pants like a red-hot spike. Reed grunted and fell sideways to the floor, still firing at the catwalk. The warehouse thundered with the sound of gunfire, reverberating off the tin walls. Somebody screamed, and a body hit the floor with a meaty crash. More gunfire erupted from the far end of the warehouse, ripping through the open space toward Reed.

He rolled to the left and forced himself to his feet. Sticky hot blood streamed down his left leg and over his boot as he pivoted toward the gunfire and pressed the trigger. Before he could fire again, something struck his right shoulder, and he collapsed to the ground. A tall man wielding a nightstick loomed over his head, and Reed rolled to his right just in time to dodge a sweeping blow from the baton. A boot landed on his knee and pressed down with over two hundred pounds of force. Reed jerked his leg free, then jammed his left boot into his attacker's shin. The submachine gun lay tangled in the sling under his arm. Reed grabbed the Glock instead and fired twice at the man's face. The attacker clattered to the ground. Reed fought his way to his feet, and the world turned as though he were on a carnival ride and being slung in and out while being forced to listen to a drumbeat of hell the whole time.

He holstered the Glock and lifted the submachine gun. A quick sweep of the warehouse revealed two bodies lying on the ground thirty yards away. One of them writhed in pain, clutching his stomach as blood puddled around him. The other lay still.

Reed conducted two more sweeps of the building, ensuring that no blind spots might hide additional assailants, then broke into a run toward the wounded man on the floor. The gunman blurred out of focus, fading in and out of a red mist. Reed kicked him in the ribs.

"Where is she?" he screamed.

The gunman's eyes narrowed. Reed shoved his heel into the bullet wound, pressing until the building echoed with screams of agony.

Reed jammed the muzzle of the gun into the man's right eye socket and screamed again.

"*Where is she?*"

"Do it."

A calm voice with a thick, South American accent rang out from behind him. Reed spun on his heel and raised the submachine gun. The man standing twenty yards away was framed by the shadows. He was barely five feet tall, dressed in a heavy overcoat and fedora, with his hands jammed into his pockets.

Reed laid his finger over the trigger. "Game's up, Sal. Where is she?"

Salvador's laugh rumbled and then thundered from his throat. It was a full, gleeful sound of triumph. The blaze in his eyes intensified, as though he didn't control his own reactions—as though he were the slave of an invisible drug.

"Put down the gun, Reed. This is checkmate."

A crimson flash caught Reed's eye, and he looked down, relaxing his trigger finger as he did. The red dot that hovered over his chest twitched back and forth, forming X patterns over his heart. Reed traced the laser sight up and onto the roof of the building where an unseen shooter lay in overwatch—his sights fixed on Reed.

"You could have made it simple, Reed," Salvador said. "But honestly, we thought you'd respond this way. It's why we had a backup plan."

Reed lowered the gun and ran his tongue over dry and cracked lips. The unbendable iron in his mind returned, bringing control back to his anger.

"Whoever you are, you're in way over your head," Reed snapped. "When you screw with me, you screw with my company. It's not a game you can win."

"*Your* company?" Salvador tilted his head. "Don't you mean Oliver's company?"

A knife of uncertainty sliced through his chest. Then he heard a familiar footfall clicking on the concrete. The moonlight cut through the roof overhead, illuminating the new figure emerging from the shadows. He was tall, slender, and balding, with a thin grey beard.

The gun trembled in Reed's damp fingers as his heart thundered.

"*Oliver?*"

Oliver Enfield shoved his hands into his pockets and stepped beside Salvador. His battered old face was set in hard lines, and his brow furrowed into a stony frown—every inch of him looked the part of a disgusted killer.

"I gave you a chance, Reed." Oliver's voice rumbled like distant thunder. "This wasn't my first choice. I would have given you the world, and all you wanted was to walk."

The shock gave way to untethered rage, and Reed remembered the words of the bloodied biker at the landfill—how he had called his employer "English." He didn't mean white. He meant British. He meant Oliver Enfield.

"Thirty kills," Reed screamed. "That was the deal. Then I'm free!"

"That's right, Reed. Free to continue working for my company as long as you draw breath."

"So, it's all a racket." Reed spat the words as though they were venom. It was all he could do not to sling himself forward and tear Oliver's throat out, even as the red dot continued to dance over his chest.

"No, Reed. It's a company. A company you work for until you die. And you had that chance. You could have climbed as high as you wanted. Maybe one day, you would have taken my place. *The Prosecutor,* my brightest, most ruthless killer. But instead, you threw that back in my face. You ungrateful, whiny child!"

"You kidnapped Banks. You killed Brent. You set me up from day one!"

"No." Oliver shook his head. "The Holiday hit was a legitimate job, a contract made for the legitimate people that Mr. Salvador works for. You were the one who ruined a good thing. Do you think I could just let you walk away? Kill thirty people and then just leave with all you know and all you've seen? Of course not. So, Mr. Salvador and I decided to kill two birds with one stone: Senator Holiday . . . and you."

Reed snorted. "Don't kid yourself, Oliver. After your man guns me down, your whole world is going to cave in. Didn't you think I'd hedge my bets? I've dirt on you, stored away someplace where the FBI will find it. Enough to send you straight to death row for Holiday's death."

It was a bluff, all of it. Reed was a killer, not a chess master. He never thought to question Oliver, and now he was going to die for it.

Oliver stood in silence, his hands still jammed into his pockets. The groans of the wounded man had faded, and even the wind outside the warehouse died down. Oliver stepped forward, his expensive leather shoes tapping the concrete with grace and precision. He stopped in front of Reed, faced him eye to eye, then calmly put one hand on his shoulder and smiled.

"You're the perfect killer, Reed. Cold. Brutal. Nothing to lose. You've only got one problem: You can't appreciate the shades of grey—the cunning of an old man. Holiday isn't dead—I know that. But I'm not going to kill you. I could have done that from day one, but then I'd have to explain to the whole company that I'm not a ruthless backstabber. How can I expect to maintain the trust and effort of my contractors if I gun down their colleagues? It's not good for morale. So no, I've got other plans for you. I'm going to let *you* clean this up."

Oliver squeezed his shoulder and stared at Reed, cold and emotionless. The smile faded, leaving nothing but the ashen glare of a relentless monster. Oliver slapped him on the shoulder, jammed his hands back into his pockets, then turned and jerked his head at Salvador as he walked toward the door.

"Enjoy prison, Reed. You might recall that I have a lot of influence when it comes to incarceration. Correctional facilities are funny places full of all kinds of people waiting to throttle a man in his sleep." Oliver laughed. "None of my other contractors could blame me for that, could they?"

Police sirens rang in the distance, blending with the thunder of a chopper from someplace overhead. The Atlanta PD was closing in on the train yard like a pack of bloodhounds eager to sink their teeth into the red-handed killer standing inside. Reed remained silent as Oliver stopped at the door and then twisted his neck. It popped like a gunshot.

Reed spoke calmly, with no hint of malice. "I'll take you down with me." It was a promise.

Oliver glanced back at Reed. His smile was wide this time, exposing a row of perfect teeth. "Wanna bet?"

A truck roared to life outside, and the gunman in the shadows lifted his rifle and vanished behind Oliver and Salvador through the doorway. The police sirens screamed from somewhere in the east, bearing down on the warehouse. Tires spun, and rocks clanged against the building as Reed ran to the door, raising his gun and searching for a target. But the truck had already disappeared around the corner; its fading taillights passed out of view and into a hidden path between the trees.

Reed coughed on the dust and started to run, but then he heard the screech of metal on metal, the whistle of air snapping around each car, and the clack of wheels rattling on a train track. By themselves the sounds heralded nothing more than the routine passing of the nearby MARTA train, but then he heard the scream—ripping and unearthly.

He knew that voice; he would've recognized it anywhere.

Reed bolted toward the far end of the warehouse, slid through a gap in the tin, and ran. Forty yards away, he saw it: MARTA's Blue Line train rocketing out of Edgewood Station toward Indian Creek.

The lights on the train flashed, and passengers locked inside the row of cars pounded against the windows and clawed at the sliding doors. The train hadn't stopped at Edgewood. It barreled down the track at full speed, sparks flying from the wheels. The windshield of the driver's booth was shattered, with blood sprayed against the glass, and there, handcuffed to the doorframe, was Banks.

Reed's heart slammed into his throat, and in the split second it took to recognize Banks, it all made sense. *Checkmate*—Oliver's final ploy to frame Reed and send him back to prison, there to be executed at the hands of an endless network of criminal butchers. It was the ultimate maneuver. Even if Reed ran for the hills, everything would be hung on him now. Oliver would feed the FBI and the media whatever they needed to pin the carnage on Reed and run him to ground, with no risk of anything undermining the stability of the company.

Reed could drag it out, of course. He could hide and manipulate, and raise hell for Oliver. Do everything he could to burn the world down. That was why they handcuffed Banks to the front of the train—so Reed never had the option to run.

The roar of the train pounded in his head, and every other noise and stimulant faded away as he ran toward the track, watching Banks flash past. Her blonde hair was torn by the wind, and her screams were drowned out by the train.

Reed slid to a stop at the chainlink fence that barred his path to the rail line, watching as the last car flashed past. He knew the train wouldn't stop. All MARTA cars were fitted with automatic braking systems to prevent derailing in an emergency, but Oliver would have disabled them. Nothing would keep the train from hurtling the last seven miles to the track terminus, there to explode in a wreckage of twisted metal and shattered bodies.

He dashed back toward the warehouse, tripping over a piece of railroad track along the way. His right leg ignited in pain, and thick blood oozed over his cargo pants. There were three dead men inside the warehouse, and not all of them could have arrived in Oliver's truck. There must've been another vehicle.

Think.

Reed charged through the rail yard, searching behind stacks of machinery and rotting railroad timbers. Entire portions of the yard were consumed by vines and undergrowth, slowly dying as winter approached. Dry dirt crumbling under his boots filled the air around him with a red cloud. Reed clawed the flashlight from his belt and clicked it on. He saw footprints, ruts, shallow ditches, and then the tracks. They crisscrossed the thin dirt, then disappeared into one of the sheds. A red taillight glimmered through the holes in the tin, reflecting against the powerful LED.

He dashed back into the big warehouse, slid to his knees next to the fallen gunman, and ripped through his pockets. There was a watch, a knife, and a wad of dirty cash. And then he found the keys.

Reed's left leg was numb as he pulled himself back to his feet and ran. The earth rang with dull thuds as his boots struck the packed dust. He couldn't hear the train anymore, and police sirens screamed down Rogers Street only a hundred yards away.

Reed slung his leg over the big Japanese sports bike, jammed the key into the ignition, clamped his hand down on the clutch, and kicked the starter. The engine roared to life with a devilish scream. The rear tire spun on dry concrete, and Reed flashed out of the shed as police cars skidded into the empty lot between the buildings. Floodlights blinded him, and somebody screamed for him to stop. A pistol popped, followed by rifle shots. Reed gunned the engine, and the front tire lifted off the ground. He clung to the bike as the KRISS bounced on his back, riding on the ends of the sling.

He skidded around the corner of the building and shot onto Rogers Street. The bike shook as he slammed it into second gear and swerved around a black SUV loaded with SWAT responders. Everybody shouted at him to stop, and a bullhorn blared. The road opened in front of the bike, and houses flashed past, followed by Toomer Elementary. He leaned into a sharp left turn onto Hosea L Williams Drive and twisted the grip to max throttle.

30

Reed gunned the bike past ninety miles an hour as he rocketed through subdivisions and small shopping strips. MARTA's Blue Line led through the East Lake Station before diving beneath Decatur. On the far side of the city, Avondale was the first place the train resurfaced and traveled above ground. Reed remembered a low bridge that crossed over the tracks just past the station. If he could get to that bridge before the train, he might have a chance of stopping it.

He hit the brakes and planted his boot on the ground, sliding into a left turn before he downshifted and hit the throttle again. As the motor whined and the bike surged northward onto Howard Street, time stood still.

The trees and the houses under the night sky faded around him, and he could feel the hot California breeze on his face. He heard the thunder of his old 1992 Suzuki, smelled the salt wind blowing off the Pacific coast, and felt the surge of panicked adrenaline as a squad car closed in on his tail. He remembered the rush of blind recklessness as he gunned the big bike and pulled away from the cop. The world and all of its problems were no longer concerns. The only thing that mattered was clearing the next block, sliding through the next traffic light, and vanishing back into the sweet freedom of south Los Angeles.

Reed refocused on the dark street and hooked a right onto College Avenue North East. There were no traffic lights and no stop signs. The avenue opened up as far as he could see, disappearing into the darkness toward Decatur. Reed shifted up and wound the engine out. As the RPM meter rose, the speedometer passed one hundred miles an hour. The neighborhood faded into the dark corners of his vision, and the street became a grey tunnel leading forward between the trees. Lights flashed over either shoulder as Decatur rocketed into view, and the speedometer hit one-forty as the RPM meter hovered close to redline. Reed leaned forward and pressed his body into the bike. The wind blasted his face, almost blinding him as the bike bounced over the slight imperfections in the road.

East Lake Station passed on his left, and there was no sign of the train. He pressed the throttle harder, but the big Japanese engine was pushed to its max. The train tracks on his left vanished into the ground as MARTA's Blue Line dove under the city toward Decatur Station. There was a chance that MARTA headquarters had been able to apply the brakes remotely. Even now, the train might be screeching to a stop deep beneath the pavement, but Reed couldn't take that chance. College Avenue stretched out perfectly straight in front of him for miles. The train would make seventy miles an hour under full speed, and the bike was locked at a hard one-forty.

Maybe enough.

Seconds passed. Avondale Station was five hundred yards ahead, and just to his left, the Blue Line rose out of the tunnel and back to ground level. Reed's heart skipped a beat as he saw the train flash out of the darkness, still flying eastward at full speed. He caught sight of Banks clinging to the front of the train, her hair whipping as the car careened forward. Her left foot had been knocked off the front bumper, and she clung to the front door handle as one leg dangled inches above the tracks.

Reed looked forward just in time to swerve and miss an oncoming truck, then he leaned to the right and applied the brake as he rounded a gentle curve on College Avenue. Avondale Station flashed past on his left, and he could hear the clacking roar of the train just over his left shoulder, a hundred yards behind him. A large four-way intersection lay directly ahead, connecting College Avenue with Sam's Crossing. The bridge that spanned the Blue Line waited there.

Reed released pressure on the throttle and leaned to the left, then slammed on the brake. The bike shuddered and slid, and he struggled to keep it upright as the g-force almost slung him off the seat. The intersection flashed around him, and he turned the bike left on Sam's Crossing and clamped down on the brake again. The motorcycle slid onto the bridge, and he saw Avondale Station beneath him, a hundred yards west. The headlights of the train flashed into view, coming out of the station and rocketing toward the bridge.

The bike screeched to a halt and slammed down on its side. Reed screamed in pain and fought to free his leg from underneath the piping-hot engine block. He heard the train crashing along the track as it passed beneath the bridge. He jerked his leg free, tearing fabric and flesh against the side of the bike, and leaving the air reeking with burning rubber and singed cloth.

Reed jumped to his feet and limped to the edge of the bridge. He didn't have time to think. The last car passed under the bridge, and Reed grabbed the guard rail and flipped his legs over. The open air whistled past his ears as he free-fell ten feet. His boots slammed into the metal roof of the last car, his legs slipped from under him, and he landed on his side, sliding backward over the slick sheet metal toward the rear of the car. Reed shouted and grabbed at the ridges in the metal, clawing for anything to hold onto.

His fingers caught on a ridge in the roof, slowing him down just enough to keep him from flying off the side. The wind roared in his ears as the car rose and fell beneath him, clacking against the metal rails. His legs spun off the roof, hanging in midair before slamming down against the side of the car. Reed clawed his way forward, and a fingernail split. With a Herculean effort, he slung his left leg up and over, and pulled himself back onto the roof. He lay five feet from the tail of the train, and began to claw his way toward the rear emergency door.

Reed twisted and grabbed the rear rim of the roof, then pulled himself toward it. The train rattled over a joint in the track, and he looked forward just in time to plant his face against the metal. A bridge flashed overhead, inches above his shoulder blades. He looked up again toward the front of the train and felt the cold claw of fear sink into his heart. Another tunnel was rapidly approaching, and he could already tell there wasn't enough clearance for a man to lie on top of the car.

Reed grabbed the top rim of the train and slung his legs over the edge, free-falling toward the track. His knees slammed into the rear of the car as his full weight descended on his fingers, and he kicked out with his feet, fighting for any hint of a purchase. The rifle sling caught on the top of the emergency doorframe, tying him to the rear of the train and tightening around his neck, choking him as the train rocketed into the tunnel. He jerked at the sling, but it wouldn't tear free. Reaching down, he grabbed the butt of the rifle and pressed the quick-release. The sling snapped free and slid around his neck just as his boots caught the edge of what must have been the rear bumper. The rifle dangled against the side of the train, then the sling slipped free of the doorframe and the gun disappeared into the darkness.

Reed gasped for air and let go of the roof with his right hand. He grabbed the exterior handle of the emergency door and jerked it up. The door opened, and he shoved his right foot into the gap before sliding to the right, allowing the door to swing open. He let go of the roof and slung himself inside the train. The door slammed shut behind him, and for a moment, everything was shockingly still.

His head spun as he looked up to see terrified commuters standing at the front of the car, staring back at him with wild eyes.

Reed clawed his way to his feet and stumbled forward, shouting over the clacking rattle of the train.

"Get to the back! Hold on to something. Help the others!"

No one responded. Reed raised his voice and pointed to the rear of the car. "Stand in the back! We're going to crash! Grab the rails!"

He shoved past the remaining commuters and to the front of the car. The tunnel disappeared around him as he jerked open the emergency door at the front of the car and stepped out onto the coupling between the cars. As he burst through the next door, he was already shouting.

"Go to the rear car! We're going to crash! Hold on to something!"

The commuters screamed and fought their way past him.

Reed pushed ahead and ran through the next two cars, shouting at the passengers and waving toward the rear of the train.

"Move now! Get to the back!"

The passengers moved with increasing urgency, pushing past him and fighting through to the back of the train. A baby screamed. A woman cried. Somebody shouted a blatant refusal to step out between the cars.

Reed ignored them all and burst into the last car. Lights flashed outside the windows—they were passing through Kensington Station. As the lights of the city glowed in ambers and reds, gleaming in muddled blurs through the windows, the prerecorded voice of the announcer kicked in overhead.

"The next station is Indian Creek Station. This is the end of the line."

Reed grabbed the handle into the driver's pod. It was locked. He drew the Glock from his belt and fired four rounds into the handle. Screams burst from the crowd behind him, and he kicked the door, breaking the latch, and then jerked it open.

Blood covered the floor. The driver lay stretched out in front of him with two bullet holes in her chest. Reed lunged over her, and then he saw Banks standing to his left, outside of the dirty windshield, with her face pressed against the glass. Her hands were bound by cuffs to the security latch at the top of the door.

Reed shoved past the driver's seat and pulled the first red lever he saw. Something snapped, and the train lurched and slowed a little, but it didn't stop. He jerked the lever again. This time it was limp, flopping in its channel like a broken arm.

One mile ahead, under a highway overpass and just beyond the offloading deck of the Indian Creek Station, red lights lit up the outline of the metal train stop.

The end of the line.

31

Reed fired twice into the window to the left of the door, then sent his fist crashing through the glass. Wind whistled through the interior of the car, carrying Banks's scream with it.

He pushed his arm through the hole and grabbed her by the arm.

"Banks! Come toward me!"

The wind tore the long blonde hair out of her face, and she looked up at him. "Chris?"

"Come toward me!" He pulled on her arm, but she shook her head.

"I can't move! I'll fall!"

"I'm going to cut the handcuff. I want you to move to your right so I can open the door!"

She shook her head again. "No, I can't—"

Reed didn't wait for her to finish. He jammed the pistol through the hole with his left arm and pointed it toward the chain of the handcuff. He fired once. The chain burst and Banks started to fall backward, but Reed grabbed her by the arm and pulled her toward the left of the train.

"Hold on!"

She wrapped her hands around the rubber of the window frame. Shards of glass still stuck from the edges, and she cried out in pain as they sliced into her hand, but she didn't let go.

Reed jammed the Glock into the holster and shoved the handle on the emergency door. It popped, but the door was pinned closed by the force of oncoming wind. He pushed it forward, forcing it open far enough for him to slip through. He fought for purchase on the front of the car until his boot found the same narrow lip that he had used on the other end of the train.

Banks screamed over the roar of the wind. "Let me in!"

Reed shook his head.

"We're about to crash! We've got to jump!"

"Are you insane?"

Reed looked over his shoulder. Indian Creek Station was a hundred yards away, and less than four hundred yards farther, the train stop loomed up out of the dirt.

He didn't have time to argue. He wrapped his powerful right arm around Banks's torso and pulled her into him, twisting her around until they faced each other. He inched his way along the front of the car, clinging to the broken window frame with his left hand.

"Grab my chest rig and hold on!"

Her eyes were wild with panic, but she grabbed the chest plate, planting her face against the rough fabric. The train station flashed past them on the right, and nothing but a wide-open ditch and trees stood to the left of the tracks. Reed let go of the window frame, wrapped both arms around Banks, and then launched himself away from the car.

As the train rocketed past, they flew through the air, spinning over the ditch. He clung to Banks like she was the only person left on Earth, holding her close with his arms wrapped around her back. An unearthly slamming and screeching sound exploded behind them, and then they landed.

Reed hit the dirt first, then tumbled over Banks as they crashed through the leaves and low underbrush. Dirt filled his mouth, and he lost his grip on her as his legs flew over his head and he continued rolling. His hips collided with the base of a tree, bringing his rampage through the undergrowth to a sudden stop.

The sky spun overhead. He twisted his neck and saw the train lying in a pile of mangled cars. All but the last two had flown off the rails and rolled into the ditch. The passengers were piled in the last car, and nobody moved.

Reed tried to roll to his knees, but the pain was too much. He could barely see, and his mouth filled with blood. Banks lay face up on the ground, still and silent, blood streaming from her temple.

"No . . ." Reed hissed. He rolled onto his stomach and crawled toward her. Every part of him burned with pain, but he put his palm against her throat and felt for a pulse. Nothing.

He clawed the phone out of his pocket and fumbled to unlock it before pressing the first contact.

A female voice answered almost immediately. "Where are you?"

"Indian Creek . . . Station. MARTA."

"Don't move. I'm coming."

Reed collapsed.

32

He heard the rustling of sheets first, then the faint sensation of something prodding his feet. His eyelids felt like they were weighted down by a ton of bricks.

Reed tried to open his mouth, but his tongue was dry. He coughed, then he felt a tube prodding between his lips. Cold water flowed over his tongue, wetting his throat, and he gulped it down. The stream continued for a few seconds longer before it was removed.

A grey ceiling filled his vision overhead, and he heard the faint whir of a fan, but he couldn't see it through his blurry vision.

"Can you hear me?" It was the familiar voice again.

"Kelly. I can hear you."

"Excellent. Take your time."

Reed couldn't remember anything. "Where was I?"

A soft laugh. "The usual. Lying in the middle of a cloud of dust and chaos."

That sounded right. His mind was fuzzy, but details began to return. "Banks."

He twisted his head and saw a short, brunette woman in her late twenties sitting on a stool next to him, her arms crossed as she stared back. Wavy hair was pushed behind her ears, and her brown eyes flashed.

"You mean the blonde girl?"

"Yes."

Kelly grunted. "She's alive. They had her in ICU at Grady, but I think they moved her to a regular room today."

Reed let out a sigh and slumped against the pillow. "Thanks, Kelly."

She snorted. "That's it? You don't want to know your situation?"

He attempted a shrug, but the movement sent searing pain across his chest. "I assume I'm alive."

"Yeah, you're alive. You don't deserve to be, but there's nothing new in all that. You've got fractured ribs, a seriously sprained ankle, a deep bullet graze on your left leg, severe lacerations over your back, a definite concussion—"

"How long?"

Kelly raised an eyebrow. "Until you and I can take a tumble between the sheets or until you can get back to blowing people away?"

Reed forced a smirk. "Is there a difference?"

Kelly stood up, retrieving a purse and shoveling personal effects into it. "You can go home tomorrow. I'll have you loaded up with some heavy-duty pills. You're beat up pretty hard, but nothing life-threatening. I stitched up your leg and put a brace on your ankle. Ideally, you should stay off your feet for a few days. But of course, you're not going to listen to me."

Reed tried to smile. "You're the best, Kel."

Kelly lingered next to the bed, the keys dangling from her fingers. She stared at him a long time, then slowly shook her head. "Dammit, Reed. This is the last time. I'm not patching you up anymore. I'm engaged now. I'm gonna settle down. Have a family. I can't have you barging into my life every two months needing illegal medical care."

Reed closed his eyes and nodded. "Don't worry. I won't call you again. I'll set you up with a sweet engagement present."

She smacked him with the keys, and when he opened his eyes, he saw that hers were rimmed with red. She leaned down and gave him a hug, then kissed him on the cheek.

"I would have married you if you weren't such a walking disaster."

She walked toward the door, her tennis shoes squeaking on the linoleum. The keys rattled against the lock, then she turned back.

"Let her go, Reed. Whoever she is. I saw the look in your eyes when you said her name. Take it from me . . . you break hearts a lot better than you break necks."

Reed stared at Kelly. Her deep brown eyes were sad and quiet, but there was peace in them. Kindness. It was a peace he hadn't seen there in a long time, as though her warning came from a place of quiet confidence, not bluster.

He closed his eyes and leaned back into the pillow. The door shut, and Kelly was gone. As silence filled the room, Reed tried not to think about her. He tried to push out the memories of the blonde girl with the ukulele—the smile on her face, her beautiful voice. The way her eyes flashed in the city lights.

But as his mind drifted into oblivion, those eyes were the last thing he saw.

33

Atlanta, Georgia

Grady Memorial Hospital sat in the heart of the city. It rose above the tangle of concrete structures and streets, towering in all of its old glory as one of Atlanta's keystone hospitals. Reed stood outside the main entrance and tilted his head back, staring up at the tall building. His neck hurt. Actually, his whole body ached, but Kelly's drugs were working all the magic he could hope for. They numbed enough of the pain so he could walk, and the rest would fade in time.

Reed looked toward the northeast. He couldn't see the west faces of 191 Peachtree or the Equitable Building, but he knew they were both laced with crime scene tape. The blown-out window on the forty-fifth floor of the 191 building was patched with thick plastic, pending a full replacement. The bleeding mannequin was gone, as were the ropes from the Equitable Building. The news stories Reed read earlier that morning postulated on every possible explanation for the bizarre events just days before, including drugged-up vagabonds, terrorists, and even a satirical article blaming it all on Batman.

The explanations for the derailed train were much more sinister, which was to be expected, considering the dead driver and all the mortified civilians on board. Several of the passengers sustained broken arms and concussions, but nobody died. Reed was thankful for that.

The investigations into the events around the towers and the train would turn against him. Cameras inside the trains would have captured his face. They wouldn't know who he was, and part of Oliver's detailed recruitment program involved washing Reed's fingerprints from national databases, so when the police found the abandoned submachine gun in the tunnel, they wouldn't be able to trace it back to him. But it was only a matter of time. Oliver would feed them what they needed to know, step back, and let the law do his dirty work for him.

Reed knew he should've been gone already. Everything about his training and the voice of survival in the back of his head commanded him to go. Even now, at the front entrance to Grady, Reed almost turned away. By midnight, he could be in another country. Within twenty-four hours, another continent. Far, far away from the claws of the FBI.

But he had to see her again. One last time.

He adjusted the shoulder holster under a new Panthers jacket, pulled the ball cap low over his ears, then stepped through the sliding glass doors. The busy main floor of the hospital hummed around him, and he pulled the jacket closer around his torso as he walked to the elevator. With the heel of his hand, he pressed the button to select the fifth floor, and then pulled a stick of gum from his pocket and jammed it between his teeth. The elevator rose slowly, and Reed chewed and tapped his foot with methodical nervousness, feeling suddenly closed in.

The doors opened, and he shuffled towards the nurses' station, waiting for them to acknowledge him.

"Can I help you?"

Reed glanced around the hospital hallways. The squeak of a

wheelchair passed behind him. Computers beeped. A keyboard clicked.

"Sir?"

Reed clamped down on the gum, then without a word, shifted on his feet back toward the elevator.

"Chris?" The excited voice rang from behind, and Reed stopped. He almost walked forward again. Almost hit the elevator button.

But instead he turned, and there she was. Banks stood across the room wearing a loose T-shirt. Her left arm was held in a sling, both hands were bandaged, and on the outside of her sweatpants, she wore a brace around one knee. Her hair fell down behind her ears, and she wasn't wearing makeup.

The breath caught in his throat as he stared at her. Every noise he had obsessed over only moments before faded, carrying the stress and paranoia about being captured with them. She had never been more beautiful.

Banks broke into a big grin and limped toward him. Without hesitation, she wrapped him in a one-arm hug, pulling him closer toward her. "Chris! I couldn't find you."

Reed shifted, keeping his hands in his pockets. He could smell her hair and wanted so badly to sweep her off her feet. He could imagine her cheek pressed against his shoulder, her body cradled in his arms. His own person who cared for him and wanted him as much as he cared for and wanted her.

A home.

But Reed didn't move. He remained stiff and awkward. Unsure.

Banks smiled. "I'm glad you're okay."

For a moment, he couldn't do anything but stare, but he swallowed the gum and coughed. "I was, uh... at another hospital."

"Are you okay?" The concern in her voice was so sincere and innocent. She *did* care about him.

"Yeah, I'm great. Just a few bruises."

Banks reached up and touched his cheek, stroking it with the tips of her fingers, then she stood on her toes and kissed him softly. Sweetly.

Lost in the kiss, the world around him no longer mattered, and everything faded into perfect bliss.

Banks leaned back. "Thank you."

Those simple words knocked the wind right out of him. He wondered how the hell this girl could be so calm. She was strapped to the front of the train and sent hurtling toward her death before jumping from the moving car and rolling into battered unconsciousness. She was kidnapped, probably harassed, and mentally tormented. She almost certainly thought she would die.

Thank you?

Reed didn't know what to say. The knot in his stomach was like molten iron.

"Who are you, Chris? Why were you there?"

This was the question he dreaded. The one that kept him away from the hospital all morning, and probably should have kept him away altogether.

"I was at the station," he lied. "I saw the train pass. I just . . . did what I could."

The words stung him, and he wondered if she saw through the paper-thin sham.

Instead of pressing for specifics, Banks tilted her head toward the hallway.

"Come on. There's somebody I want you to meet."

Reed hesitated, but she grabbed his hand. They walked down the hall until she stopped at a closed door. Blocking the way was a Georgia State Police officer, glaring at him and cradling an AR-15 in his arms. Reed thought he was about to get frisked, so he tucked his left arm closer to his shoulder holster and started to turn back.

Banks pulled him forward. "It's fine, officer. He's with me."

The officer grunted and stepped to the side. Banks opened the door, and Reed ducked his head, slipping into the room. Another officer sat in the corner with a pistol strapped to his hip and a rifle leaning against the chair next to him. A tall woman dressed in a dark business suit stood next to the bed. She held a tablet and was busy tapping on the screen.

Lying in bed, bandaged up with tubes and wires strapped to his arm, was Senator Mitchell Holiday.

Reed relaxed his shoulders and allowed Banks to lead him toward the bed. The senator broke into a big smile when he saw Banks. She smiled back, and Reed forced himself to further relax his defensive stance.

"Uncle Mitch, I want you to meet someone." She turned toward Reed, and the smile she offered him was as warm and soft as the Caribbean sun. "This is Chris. He's the one who saved me."

Holiday's face was tired and sported a couple dark bruises. Reed knew where those bruises came from, and he also knew why the senator's chest was bandaged. He stared directly at Holiday and waited, bracing himself to run.

Holiday's face broke into a wide smile, and he offered his hand.

"Chris. Such a pleasure. I can't thank you enough for what you did. You're a hero, son."

Reed took Holiday's hand and offered a small smile. "It's an honor, Senator. I'm glad you're okay. I understand you've been through quite an ordeal."

Holiday laughed. "You could say that. Mostly I'm just dehydrated. Hence all this crap stuck in my arm. But nobody wants to talk about that. Tell me about yourself. My goddaughter thinks you hung the moon."

Reed hesitated, but Banks grabbed his hand and led him to the single empty chair. She perched herself on the left arm, and Reed reluctantly sat down beside her.

"What do you do, son? You military? You've got the bearing."

Reed tried to smile. Holiday talked like a politician. "No, sir. I'm . . . a venture capitalist."

Holiday raised one eyebrow. "Really?"

Reed decided to run with the lie. "Yes. I work with small firms. Mostly out west. Invest and promote growth. It's all pretty boring."

Holiday tilted his head and squinted. "Have we met before? Something about you is familiar."

Reed forced a laugh and leaned back in the chair. "I get that a lot. A familiar face, I guess."

Holiday nodded slowly, then smiled again. "Well, I'm so drugged up, who knows? I'm a bit of a businessman myself, though. I'd love to hear more about your work. We should have lunch sometime."

Reed glanced at Banks sitting beside him. Her cheeks glowed, and her shoulders were relaxed into a casual slump. She looked happy, and he marveled at that. How could anyone experience the total terror she had been through and walk away so bright and alive? Maybe they gave her a sedative.

"Banks tells me you met at a bar," Holiday continued. "Hell of a second date."

Reed shifted on the chair and looked up at Banks. He wanted to scoop her up and kiss her, take her by the hand, and run like hell. Make her his. Love her and protect her and spend the rest of his life making her happy. They could escape this place and all the menacing dangers it held. Run so far into the sunset that nobody, not even his darkest enemies, could find them. Forget the west. They could leave the country, move to Asia or Africa, and build a simple home where he could be with her every day. Hold her and protect her and spend every morning staring into those eyes.

The daydream built in momentum, consuming him until his heart thumped. He stared at her so long, picturing every detail of her gorgeous face, that Banks tilted her head and squinted, dampening the innocence in her eyes.

In that moment, the daydream shattered. It fell around him like a glass statue exploding into a million pieces. Kelly's warning echoed in his mind, and he knew it then as clearly as he had ever known anything: he was a killer. This woman was an angel. As desperately as Reed longed for a home—a peaceful place to call his own—and as much as Banks felt like home, it wasn't fair. She was innocent and beautiful, a priceless artifact from an untarnished world, so far removed from his own that he didn't even speak the same language. His life was one of deceit and shadows and bloodshed—a violent, unpredictable, hostile world with deathtraps and menace at every corner. A harsh, cold place that was no habitat for love, and no home for happiness. He might escape that life, eventually, but he could never escape the reality of what it had done to him or who he had become.

That was a reality that this goddess from another life could never, ever be touched by. She deserved more.

Reed looked away.

"Actually, Senator, I have to be going. I've got some business in Europe. I just wanted to stop by and check on Banks."

Holiday frowned, and Reed wasn't sure if the senator was angry or just confused. Either way, he offered his hand again, and Reed stood up and shook it. Banks got up, and the soul-crushed look on her face was more than he could bear. He nodded at her and then pulled the hat down over his ears and walked toward the door. The guard let him out, and Reed accelerated toward the elevator.

He heard the door shut behind him, and another set of footsteps rang in the hallway.

"Wait!"

Reed stopped and felt the burn of tears sting his eyes. Everything in his body begged him to stop and turn around. To scoop her up. To hold her close and never, ever let go. He wanted that more than he wanted his next breath. He turned around, and she stared at him with red-rimmed eyes.

"That's it?" she mumbled. "You're just . . . leaving?"

The molten feeling in his stomach felt like a hurricane, but the feeling still wasn't strong enough to wash away the inescapable truth. He couldn't be hers, and she could never be his. He was at war now. A war that would be long and brutal and would get people hurt. Banks couldn't be one of those people. She had already suffered too much at the hands of Reed's dark underworld.

"Take care of yourself, Banks. You're an amazing woman."

Without another word, he turned and pushed through the doorway to the stairwell, leaving Banks standing in the hallway. The steps clicked under his feet, matching the tempo of his pounding heart.

As he shoved his way through the crowded waiting room and back onto the sidewalk, the cold breeze stung his face and chilled his cheeks. He looked up at the sky and felt the warmth of the sun on his face, remembering the touch of her lips on his and her amazing eyes shining with so much life and passion.

Nothing had ever felt so much like home.

Reed shoved his hands into his pockets, and without looking back, turned away from the city and walked to the terminal. The white MARTA bus was just pulling up as he arrived. Reed paid the fare and took a seat in the back, where he settled in and jammed his hands into his pockets.

He took one final glance at the hospital as the bus turned northeast and drove out of the city. He imagined Banks standing in a window, staring down at him, and waving goodbye. And he realized, just then, that he was leaving a part of him behind that he didn't know existed. All his life the world had taken things from him—his parents, his integrity, his freedom, his identity. He didn't think he had anything left to lose, and yet, in this moment, he realized just how much anyone could lose. The home that he longed for wasn't a building or an address on a quiet street. It was so much simpler than that—so much more internal.

He just wanted to belong.

Reed closed his eyes. He took a deep breath, and when he opened his eyes again, he forced out the memories, the hopes, the daydreams, and clenched his fingers around the arms of his chair.

He may not have a home, but that didn't mean he didn't have a place to go. Reed had a promise to fulfill—a promise to complete thirty kills. With twenty-nine down, Reed knew exactly who his next target would be.

He pictured the face and imagined the crosshairs settling over the base of the neck behind the balding head. He imagined the touch of steel beneath his trigger finger and the snap of the gunshot.

Twenty-nine kills. Oliver would be thirty.

HUNT TO KILL

REED MONTGOMERY BOOK 2

For 2LT I.R.K., Alabama Army National Guard.

My original fan.

1

November 24, 2014
United States Military Court
Washington, DC

"Reed Montgomery, on the charge of conduct unbecoming a United States Marine, you have been found *guilty*. On the charge of five counts of first-degree murder, you have been found *guilty*. You are hereby stripped of your rank and dishonorably discharged from the United States Armed Forces."

The judge paused over the conviction papers, his weary shoulders dropping a little but his tone remaining resolute.

"The murder of Private Jeanie O'Conner was a deplorable act. But I nevertheless find your deliberate execution of five US citizens to be a crime of the worst character, and I am unconvinced of any remorse on your part. I am therefore compelled to sentence you to death. Sergeant, take the guilty into custody!"

The gavel rang like a gunshot. The sharp *shrick* of the corporal patches being torn from Reed's sleeves filled his ears, screaming over the pounding of blood. Cold cuffs closed around his wrists, and the tall military policeman wearing sergeant's patches grabbed him by the arm and shoved him toward the door. Boots clicked on the tile, and the air was thick and hot, like the oppressive nights of Baghdad.

Private Rufus "Turk" Turkman, Reed's long-time brother-in-arms, stood next to the door. Reed met his gaze and mouthed a single word: "Goodbye."

"Next!" The stocky sergeant behind the desk bellowed at the line of white-clad prisoners without looking up. His face was pale and blotchy, betraying a life spent sitting behind that desk, away from the sun, and barking at convicts.

Reed shuffled forward, twisting his wrists against the tight cuffs. His footfalls rang against the blank block walls, leaving dark black scuffs on the dirty concrete. In the corner, a desk heater's electric coils glowed red in a futile attempt to provide warmth to the uninsulated space.

"Name," the sergeant demanded.

"Montgomery. Reed."

A pen scratched on yellow paper. The metal table squeaked under the pressure, and Reed swallowed back the knots in his stomach. He twisted his wrists again and tried to keep from shivering.

God, it's cold. The whole place can't be this cold.

"All right." The sergeant spoke without looking up. "Listen carefully, and don't speak until I'm finished. You are a prisoner of the United States Armed Forces. While renovations are completed at Fort Leavenworth, you will be housed at this facility. As such, you are our guest and will behave accordingly at all times. Is that clear?"

"Yes."

"Excellent. This institution is the property and function of the state of Colorado, and you can expect it to be operated according to our laws. Colorado does not automatically isolate death row inmates such as yourself. You will be confined in gen pop with other max security prisoners. This housing arrangement is a *privilege*, and can and will be revoked at any time should you become insubordinate. Do you understand?"

"I do."

"Good. You will abide by all daily functions, including lights out, waking hours, housekeeping duties, and any commands given to you by correctional officers. Any insurrection, insubordination, contraband, violence, or disruptive behavior will be swiftly and severely punished. Is that clear?"

"Yes."

The sergeant laid down the pen, and for the first time, he faced Reed. "You carry a death sentence. Men such as yourself often find themselves feeling desperate. Listen to me carefully when I tell you we do not tolerate desperate behavior. No matter who you are or where you came from, I promise you, you *do not* want to test us. This isn't a white-collar resort with a chain-link fence. We have the power to make your life absolute hell. Do you understand me?"

The heater hummed in the corner, providing the only variance to the silence. Those wide, bloodshot eyes didn't blink, and neither did Reed's. Seconds dripped by as though they were falling from a slow-leaking faucet.

"So, you're one of those." The sergeant nodded and tapped his pen against the table. "We'll see how long that lasts. Officer Yates! Show the convict to his cell."

An iron grip latched around Reed's arm, and he was propelled out of the room through a back door and into a long hallway. The CO's boots clicked amid the shuffle of the ankle chains, and with each step, Reed's chest constricted a little tighter. Dim lights shone down over him, barely illuminating the black dirt packed into the floor's cracks or the scratches in the paint along the walls. Dingy yellow ceiling panels hung overhead, completing the mood of the most utilitarian, unwelcoming place Reed could imagine.

"Move it, con." The correctional officer snapped and pushed harder. The chains caught on his ankles, and Reed stumbled around the corner. Two more halls, one flight of steps, and then a tall metal door with no window. Voices and footsteps rang out on the other side, pounding through a cavernous room beyond. Reed tripped over the threshold and fell to his knees, crashing against concrete. White pants flashing back and forth across the floor filled his vision.

A hundred yards ahead of him, standing in neat two-story rows, were dozens of small cells. Steel bars with open sliding doors guarded them, and a hundred white-clothed convicts wandered around the floor. Fluorescent light glowed from someplace far above, joined by a single bar-covered window at the top of the wall. The floor was as hard as the block hallways behind him, and there was no other way out. No doors. No color. No warmth. Only cold, brutal containment.

The CO grabbed him by the arm and hauled him to his feet. His fingers dug into Reed's arm, sending waves of pain shooting up to his shoulder. He fought to find his footing as he was shoved forward.

"Welcome to Rock Hollow Penitentiary, Number 4371."

"What's your name?"

Reed sat on the edge of the bed, his feet resting on the cell's chilled floor. He rubbed his bare wrists, massaging the bruises left by the cuffs. The thin white coverall suit he wore was incapable of blocking the bite of impending winter. Nothing could stop that scourge.

"Hey. You deaf?"

Reed looked up. A tall, skinny man with a shiny bald head and no hair on his pale face stood in the doorway to the cell, one hand resting on the wall, the other jammed in his pocket. His eyes were grey and hollow, like twin black holes frozen over.

"I'm Reed." The words left his lips as a dry monotone. He swallowed and tried to clear his throat.

The tall man nodded, still expressionless. "Is that right? Well, what the hell are you doing on my bed, Reed?"

Reed placed his hands on the thin blanket stretched over the cheap mattress. The stiff plastic sheathing crackled under his touch. He stood up and stepped away, offering a small shrug. "I'll take the top."

Reed placed his palms on the top bunk, preparing to lift himself onto the mattress, when cold fingers wrapped around his wrist, tightening into his skin.

The tall man leaned in close, his breath, reeking of garlic and cheap food, misting just inches from Reed's face. "That's my bed, too."

The comment felt distantly preposterous to Reed, as though he should laugh. But through the fog of disorientation, he couldn't make sense of it. He tilted his head and stepped back, gesturing toward the small cell. "Where the hell do I sleep?"

The man laughed, then jerked a thumb toward the stainless steel toilet mounted against the wall. "Sitting up. Like the bitch you are."

Reed stared at the toilet. The comments didn't register. Was this a joke? Was this man insane?

"Hey! What'd I tell you about coming in here? Get your skinny ass back into the hall!"

A snapping, high-pitched voice filled the cell, coming from behind the tall man. Reed started and stepped back as a short guy with dark hair barreled through the door. He wore the same white coveralls, but they fell low around his ankles and almost covered his hands. He couldn't have been more than five and a half feet tall, but his shoulders bulged, and even through the loose outfit, Reed could see the power of his muscled core.

The short man grabbed the tall one by the back of his coveralls and shoved him toward the door with another curse. "Go back to your hole, creep! I catch you slinking around here again, and you'll catch a shiv in the ribs. You hear me?"

The tall man cast one more sinister look toward Reed, then

vanished down the hallway. The sound of barking voices from the crowd of convicts drowned out his footfalls. Reed leaned against the wall, feeling all the more disoriented.

The short man ran his fingers through dark curls, still glowering at the door. Then he shot a semi-interested glance at Reed. "You must be the fresh meat. Welcome to the pen." He extended his fist, then waited for Reed to bump it. His knuckles were hard with thick callouses built over them. He nodded at Reed once, then turned toward the bed and began to stretch the wrinkles out of the blanket. "I'm Stiller. You can call me *Still* if you want. I'm your celly. You want top or bottom?"

Reed placed his hand on the rail of the top bunk and ran his finger against the smooth surface. Flecks of ancient lead paint and grime rained onto the floor, and the stench of unwashed bodies and years of sweat filled his nostrils. The edge of the rail dug into his finger, and he dropped his hand back to his side.

I've slept on concrete that was more welcoming.

Stiller waited, then chuckled. "The fresh meat daze! Still can't believe it's real, huh? Well, take it from me, homie. It's real. Sooner you own it, the better your life will be. You take the bottom bunk. I won't sleep well with a dude your size hanging over me."

Stiller kicked off his shoes before hoisting himself onto the upper bunk. "You got a name or what?"

"Reed. Reed Montgomery."

"A pleasure, Reed. What'd you do?"

Reed folded his arms and leaned against the wall. The concrete bit into his shoulder blades, but he didn't move. He clenched his fists into his armpits and closed his eyes.

Stiller laughed again. "So, you're one of those. Whatever makes you feel better. Myself, I got busted dealing dope. I got a dime, still eight to go."

Reed pushed his hands into his pockets, searching for warmth to thaw his numb fingers.

"At least tell me how long you're in for," Stiller said.

Reed hesitated, then slumped over. It didn't really matter, he guessed. "Until they finish renovations at Leavenworth. I'll be there until . . . it's over."

Stiller frowned, tilting his head, and then an apparent realization dawned on him. He sighed. "Damn sorry to hear that, Reed. May you find favor with the appeals gods."

Reed shrugged and looked out into the hallway. "Who was he? The tall guy."

Stiller grunted. "They call him *Milk*. No idea what his real name is. Even the COs call him that."

"Is he dangerous?"

Stiller chuckled again. The sound was strangely comforting.

"Dude, you need to understand something. *Everyone* in here is dangerous. Milk isn't particularly burly, but he's shady and ruthless, and he's got a lot of friends. A lot of bitches, too—people who fear him and run his errands. My guess is, he was here to test the waters with you."

Reed stared into the hallway, rubbing his fingers together inside the pockets. They were still numb, but a hint of warmth built between the folds of the fabric.

"Did he try to push you around? Demean you?" Stiller said. Reed grunted, and Stiller leaned back into the pillow. "Yep. He's testing you. Better deal with it, Reed. It's not something you wanna leave hanging."

Reed kicked off his shoes and sat on the edge of the bed, looking at the blank, merciless floor between his feet. "I'm not here to fight. I just wanna—"

"Do your time and be left alone." Stiller finished the sentence with another snort. He rolled over on the bunk, and then his head appeared upside down next to Reed's. He had a handsome face with two days' worth of scruff on his cheeks. "Let me give you some advice, Reed. Best case scenario, you get off death row and spend the rest of your life inside a cell. Worst case scenario, you work through the appeals courts for the next ten years, and they still kill you. Either way, you're gonna be in prison for a hot minute. It's up to you how hot that minute is." Stiller slid off the bunk and shoved his feet back into the shoes, then shuffled through the open door.

Metal and shoes rattled outside the cell, and the grey walls around Reed blurred out of focus. Everything closed around him, drawing in toward his skull. Reed staggered to the sink and splashed water on his face, gasping for air as he clutched the edges of the basin. His reflection in the dirty mirror showed the white pallor of his cheeks and the panic in his eyes.

I can't stay here.

2

Rock Hollow Penitentiary

"Lights! Lights!"

The sharp *pop, pop* of the industrial switches preceded a flood of light blazing into the cell. Reed blinked and groaned, pulling the blanket over his face.

Stiller crashed to the floor beside him, then smacked him on the arm. "Get up, Reed. It's not an option."

More clanging resounded outside, this time on the second level, and growing closer. Reed pushed his feet out of bed and dropped to the floor. The shoes were tight around his toes, and a new shiver ripped through his body as he shuffled toward the locked door.

Two grey-clad correctional officers stomped in front of his cell, and a metal flashlight clicked against the bars before blasting his face with light. The beam swept over both bunks before the guards disappeared toward the next cell.

"They'll open the doors and order us out. Fall in behind me. Keep your hands out of your pockets, and walk with the others. Don't talk to the guards."

Reed reluctantly pulled his hands from his pockets and shifted on the hard floor.

What time is it? How long did I sleep?

There was no time in this place. No concept of day or night. It could've been three in the afternoon for all he knew.

"Open full block!" The command snapped from the end of the hallway, and the electric controls of the doors squeaked and groaned. Each steel door slid open.

"All convicts, *fall in*!" The voice boomed over the speakers, buried out of sight in the ceiling high above. Stiller stepped out of the cell and turned left. Reed followed him and stood behind, looking down the long line of white-clad prisoners. Nobody spoke. All eyes were directed at the line of COs standing on the ground level, brooding and swinging nightsticks on the ends of leather lanyards.

"*Move out!*"

Jumpsuit legs swished against one another, releasing body odor down the hallway as the column of convicts migrated toward the door. The lights flickered, and sweat filled Reed's palms as he clenched them against his sides.

Someone shoved him in the lower back, and Reed looked over his shoulder.

A tall, cross-eyed man gave him a crooked grin. One eye stared at Reed while the other twitched at random. "Fresh meat," he hissed.

Reed shot him an icy glare and faced forward again. Doors and hallways flashed past—one flight of stairs, then two metal gates that opened into a wide courtyard outside. Block walls topped with razor wire surrounded them, canopied by a black sky without a hint of sun. White spotlights drove the shadows into the far corners of the yard.

"Line up on the grid," Stiller whispered.

Reed followed him down the sidewalk and stopped on a wide white line. The other prisoners followed suit, forming into eight neat rows of twenty men standing shoulder to shoulder. The air was bitter cold, biting straight through the thin coveralls and into Reed's bones, making every joint feel stiff and brittle.

"*Count off!*" the lead CO shouted from the end of the first line.

His cohorts walked between the lines of prisoners, tapping each one on the arm as they counted. Reed stiffened as a nightstick smacked against his elbow, and the CO passed without making eye contact.

The private from the end of the line called back to the sergeant at the front of the courtyard. "All prisoners present and accounted for, sir!"

"You may begin the drill, Officer."

Reed's stomach fluttered, and he looked at Stiller. "Drill?"

Stiller squeezed his eyes shut. "Contraband. They found contraband. This is what happens."

"All right, you cons. On the ground!"

The men around him fell on their stomachs. Reed followed, placing his hands beneath his chest as the private began to count off. One, two. Each pushup burned, sending prickling heat shooting down the backs of his arms. Within minutes, a pool of sweat built on the concrete under his nose. Stiller pumped up and down beside him without a sound, his face down, vision fixed on the pavement.

Reed gritted his teeth and continued as the CO at the end of the line shouted the count. They passed the thirty mark and kept going. The ache building in his back ran toward his tailbone, but Reed's hardened muscles tightened and delivered.

"On your feet! *Move it!*"

All one hundred sixty men scrambled up, and a clapping resounded from the nearest CO.

He jerked his arm toward the nearest block wall. "*Laps!* Let's go!"

The crowd of sweaty men piled in along the walls and began to circle the courtyard, running as the CO continued to shout commands and urge them onward. Reed had run many times in his life. It was his favorite exercise during boot camp—simple, rhythmic, and predictable—but this was totally different. Men slammed into his back and shoved him sideways, making it almost impossible to maintain his pace. The crush of bodies around him was like a swarm of fish, all piled on top of each other and desperately trying to escape the wide, open mouth of a killer whale.

"*Faster! Let's go!*"

Reed gasped for breath and pushed back the mental revulsion to the burn in his legs. The world spun around him, still covered by a black sky. One lap followed another, broken into segments of a hundred yards by fifty yards. Some of the men flagged and stumbled, but were driven on by shouting COs.

"Halt!"

The long column fell over each other as they collapsed against the fences and the ground. Reed held his stomach and gasped. A tinge of orange slowly brightened the sky over the mountains.

"Fall in! Showers!"

The column of prisoners slipped through the gates and back into the hallways, working their way up two flights of steps. The prison was alive now with blazing lights and the clamor of guards and workers. As they passed one of the dining rooms, the sour stench of stale grease took away any appetite Reed might have had. Everything was old, dingy, and utilitarian. No hint of beauty or life touched this place. It was like a graveyard for the living.

One more hallway opened into a wide room with tile floors and rows of showerheads on the walls. There were no partitions, and a draft blew in from someplace overhead.

"Strip! Let's go!"

The prisoners shucked their sweat-soaked coveralls and dumped them into a line of laundry carts. As Reed peeled off the sticky garment, he searched for Stiller, but his undersized cellmate had already disappeared somewhere in the line of naked bodies that formed between the carts and the showerheads. Reed stepped back to the end of the line and held his hands loosely at his sides, flexing his toes over the cold tiles.

Where the hell am I?

He joined the Marines to get out. Get out of Southern California, out of the gangs, out of his mother's boyfriend's stinking apartment. To be free. Be on his own. How had that vanished so quickly?

Nothing was what he expected. Not that he gave a lot of thought to what prison would be like. He assumed it would entail long periods of downtime, sitting in a cell by himself, staring at a wall. Forced PT, mass showers, and screaming COs hadn't entered into that equation.

He thought back over the past year, back before the courtrooms, the trial, and the handcuffs. Back to Iraq. Back to the sand and the heat and the bullets. And O'Conner. He saw her lying dead in the dirt with a bloodied face and the haunted, empty eyes of a woman who hours before had held enough spirit to tame a dragon. Now gone. Crushed like a roach against hardwood.

The hard edge of a nightstick smacked Reed on the arm, and a CO glowered at him. "Move it, con! Let's go!"

Reed hurried to close the gap between himself and the end of the line. As the room began to empty, a shower became available. The water that streamed over his back was lukewarm at best, but still eased the tension in his taut muscles. Flakes of greasy soap broke off the bar as Reed rubbed it against his armpits. He tried not to think about how many dozens of smelly bodies had collided with that bar since it assumed residency at the top of a mildew-encrusted ledge next to the showerhead. Somehow, soap still felt more sanitary than water alone, no matter how greasy. He spat a stream of over-chlorinated water against the wall and replaced the soap on the ledge.

I'd do it again.

The thought rang as clearly in his head as it had the past July, right before he chambered a round into his rifle and aligned the scope with the base of Commander Gould's neck. He pulled that trigger because he had no choice. Something snapped inside of him when he first saw Private O'Conner's brutalized corpse. From that moment, everything that happened was automated.

Inevitable.

And now this.

"Well, well... Looks like it's just you and me again, bitch."

Reed blinked away the soap and water. The voice was familiar, smooth, and venomous.

Milk stood five feet away, his wet hair dripping over a naked, bony frame. One hand draped over his exposed crotch, slowly rubbing back and forth, while his eyes blazed at Reed over a twisted smile. "You *are* a bitch, aren't you? You look like a bitch. A lot like the bitch I took back in Nebraska. Oh, but she wasn't as smart as you. She screamed bloody murder like she wasn't even enjoying it. You're smarter, aren't you? You know what's good for you."

Reed cast a quick glance around the shower room. The COs were gone, as were the remainder of the prisoners—all except two tall, beefy men with thick arms that swung next to bulging guts as they closed in a few steps behind Milk. Reed recognized one of the goons by his cross-eyed glare, one eye fixed on his prey while the other roamed the room at random. Their bare feet smacked against the tile as water droplets cascaded over still-dirty hair.

Milk took a step forward, running a skinny tongue over his lips. "All right, then. Make it quick and strong if you know what's good for you." He took another step and touched Reed's arm.

Reed slid to the right before grabbing Milk by the throat and placing his other hand against the base of the man's skull. A lightning twist of his torso propelled Milk's face directly into the wall. Flesh met tile with a crack, and blood exploded over Reed's hands. He stepped back and grabbed Milk by the shoulder, then swept his left foot across the floor and into Milk's shins at the same moment he pushed down on the shoulder. The creep crashed to the floor with a scream.

Before Reed could turn, Milk's goons were on top of him, throwing him into the wall a millisecond before one of their meaty fists slammed home into his gut. He clutched his stomach as another fist caught him in the chin, followed by a knee to the groin.

An eruption of pain flooded through him, weakening all other sensations as Reed flailed out with both arms. Another blow to his stomach and his vision began to tunnel. Thick fingers closed around his throat, choking out the air and forcing his head into the tile.

"Night-night, bitch," the voice rumbled, half-chuckle, half-snarl.

No. Not this way.

Reed launched his fist forward in one more blind attempt to dislodge the grip on his throat, and he felt the satisfying crack of a nose collapsing beneath his knuckles. The fingers fell off his throat, and he gasped for air. Then a fist flashed into Reed's view just as it tore through the air and crashed into his head.

3

Lights from overhead burned through Reed's eyelids. His clouded eyes felt both crusty and moist, blurring out the big, blotchy face that leaned over his. A medical mask was stretched over the nose, just below dark eyes. Reed tried twisting to get a better view, but his body was restrained by some thick strap circumventing his stomach. The familiar bite of handcuffs on either wrist secured his arms to the table.

The distinct sting of a needle pierced his face once, then twice. With each push of the needle, fingers twitched against his skin, stitching one thread after another into his cheek. The pain restored his memory, and he saw Milk's sneering face leaning over him again. The anger returned, along with maddening frustration.

"Is he conscious?"

The man in the mask grunted, and a new face appeared beside his. It was the desk sergeant who checked Reed into the prison on his first day.

"I knew you'd be trouble, Montgomery." There was no hint of sympathy in the cold voice.

Reed grunted and tried to twist again, then remembered the restraints. "They jumped me."

"Is that right? By the look of it, you were happy to join in on the fun."

There was nothing Reed could say. The sergeant would either believe him or he wouldn't. Either way, not much was likely to change.

The sergeant barked at the medical officer. "What's his prognosis?"

The man in the mask grunted again, then snipped the end of the thread with a pair of scissors. "Cuts and bruises. He'll be fine."

"Very good." The sergeant snapped his fingers. "Officer!"

The door opened, and another CO stepped in.

"Take 4371 to isolation. Book him for three weeks. Minimum rations."

The private slid the handcuffs and belt off of Reed. As he stood, head spinning, the private closed his hard fingers around his arm.

"Learn your lesson, Montgomery." The sergeant's voice was unsympathetic. "There's no forgiveness here."

The CO shoved him forward through the door and into a hall.

Another oversized pair of white coveralls swished against his legs with each step, but his feet were bare. Bruises and aching joints fogged his mind, making each step agony. His head ached harder than ever, and his tongue stuck to the roof of a dry mouth.

Light flooded his eyes as the private pushed him out into another courtyard. This one was much larger than the first, with grass and park benches. Small crowds of convicts stood around the perimeter, talking or milling about. Sneers and smirks, mixed with a handful of blank stares, met Reed's gaze. The CO pushed him along the sidewalk, down the fence line, and toward the isolation ward. As Reed stumbled on he noticed a scrawny man bent over a park bench with his back turned. Two other men stood nearby with their arms folded across their chests. Reed squinted against the bright sunlight, watching as Milk turned toward him, his face wrapped in a thick bandage.

Reed jerked free of the guard and made a dash toward the table before the nightstick descended over the back of his head. A light crack, just sharp enough to send disorientation and nausea washing through his body.

He shoved the guard back and stumbled toward Milk, wrapping his fingers into a tight fist. "I'll rip your throat out!"

Another blow from the nightstick crashed into his arm. Fingers dug into the collar of his jumpsuit, pulling him off balance as more COs rushed in to subdue him.

Reed kicked out with both feet, swinging his elbow backward until it connected with somebody's chin. "Let me at him! He started it, dammit!"

"Shut up, con!"

Two more COs piled on top of him, and Reed jerked free of the first, launching himself out of the pile and back onto his feet. Milk stood ten feet away, his eyes alight with devilish glee as he twisted his head backward and stuck his tongue out as though he were strangling at the end of a noose.

The guards grabbed Reed, overpowering him and dragging him backward. He gave up the fight, but found Milk's eyes one last time and mouthed a warning: *"I'm coming for you."*

"Don't do it, Reed. Whatever happened. Whatever you know. You can't come back from this."

Grey mist swarmed and danced around Turk's face. His words were distant, as though they were coming from the other side of a cavern—echoing, but familiar. Reed touched Turk's shoulder and imagined the rough, dirty texture of the military jacket, but it felt thin and wispy, as though Turk were a ghost. But it wasn't a ghost. He knew this marine. Turk was his best friend and the last surviving member of his fire team back in Iraq. His right-hand man.

"Neither can she." Reed's own words echoed through the mist and darkness, and his body felt detached from his voice.

The words tasted bitter. God, why are they so bitter? They flew from his mouth like venom. Reed shoved past Turk as fireworks burst, lighting up his path as he weaved between the barracks. Dry sand crunched beneath his feet. The rifle was heavy, but with each stride, fresh confidence—and fresh anger—flooded his body.

Where am I? Why is it all so familiar? And so distant?

Men in black with beer bottles and cigarettes were gathered around a table—smoking, drinking, laughing. One of them leaned over the table, pumping his hips into its edge, dramatizing the motion while the others laughed. These weren't marines. No, they were contractors. Mercenaries.

"Give it to her! Smack that bitch!" The shout was slurred, laden with alcohol.

Five of them. Reed squinted into the scope of the rifle, aligning the crosshairs with the base of the first man's neck.

Commander Gould. The prick.

That first gunshot shattered their laughter but was lost amongst the blast of Independence Day fireworks overhead. Gould went down, blood gushing from his stomach over the Iraqi dust. Reed stepped ahead and fired again. There were shouts, and then a handgun popped. Something ripped into his shoulder.

The thunk of the bolt locking back over an empty magazine resonated through Reed's arm. Through the blur of rage and adrenaline, he saw four bodies lying in the swirling mist with gaping mouths and pale cheeks. The fifth man lay on his side with blood gushing from his hip as he clawed at the sand, pulling himself away from the corpses of his comrades.

Reed knew his face—a strong brow line, low cheekbones, a bold chin. Even in the darkness that hung around him, he recognized Commander Gould's defiant glare.

The shriek of metal against metal rang through the stillness as Reed's knife cleared its sheath. Someplace on the other side of the fog, men shouted. There were gunshots, too—short and popping, the familiar voice of a handgun. A bullet hissed past Reed's ear as he stepped over the last body and placed his muddy boot against Gould's shoulder, pinning him into the dirt.

"Remember me, Gould?"

The commander's face twisted into a smile, then his features morphed *as his teeth became fangs and his hair horns. It was no longer the face of a civilian contractor. It was the face of a demon, snarling back at him in blatant defiance.*

Reed plunged the knife into the demon's throat. The gunshots roared behind him now, and bullets tore through his back, blasting holes in his chest that gleamed like stars as he jerked the knife free and plunged it home again. The blood that gushed free of the demon's throat wasn't red—it was inky black. Thick and hot.

Reed sat up with a scream. Cold sweat ran down his face as he fumbled through the darkness. The tiny isolation cell was complete and consuming. He grabbed to his right and felt the block wall. As his feet hit the floor, he focused on the opposing wall, only four feet separated from its twin.

He dug his fingers into the mattress, holding on as he imagined the walls closing in around him.

No. I can't do it. I can't do it.

Reed stood up and slung himself against the steel door, driving his fist into it. The tiny cell rang with the clatter, and he screamed for the guard. No lights flooded on, and no boots rang against the hallways. Only silence answered his desperate outburst.

The mattress squeaked as he collapsed back against it, and at once, the visions returned. Blood. Carnage. Bodies everywhere. Eyes open or closed, he could still see their faces—the haunted stares of the slain. He didn't feel regret, and no hint of remorse haunted his soul, but he felt the burning desire to destroy the last remaining traces of the ghosts from Iraq.

Reed clamped his eyes shut in an attempt to extinguish the flames dancing behind his eyelids. But even here, in the darkness and silence, there was no peace—only anger and the crushing reality that his life was a joke. Maybe it always had been. His earliest memories weren't like this. They were happy. His father was a free man and a successful finance professional. His mother was a local environmental activist, and she was sober, still something of a basket case on her worst days, but nothing like the slobbering, skanky drunk she became after her husband was hauled off to federal prison for money laundering.

Reed tried to calm his nerves by remembering those days when his family was a family. They lived in Mountain Brook, Alabama, an upscale suburb of Birmingham. Tabitha Montgomery used to make Toaster Strudels in the morning before Reed got on the bus, and ham and potatoes on Sundays for lunch. She always fussed about feeding him sugar first thing in the morning, but Dave Montgomery came to his son's rescue. Dave was like that. Fun and happy. He told cheesy jokes and was friends with all the neighbors—the kind of guy you might ask to borrow a hand tool from and wind up sitting on the back patio sipping beer and swapping war stories with. Everybody loved him.

Maybe that was why she left, Reed thought. Maybe that was why, after her husband's conviction and sentencing, Tabitha couldn't stay in her beloved hometown anymore. Too many people knew her, knew Dave, and knew little Reed. There were too many patronizing stares at the grocery store, too many whispering gossips at the local Baptist church. It was a level of shame and displacement she couldn't handle, so she did the next logical thing: pack up her son and what was left of her belongings after the federal confiscations, and move as far away as she could.

Reed opened his eyes and stared at the dark ceiling. He imagined his mother's face: the bags under her bloodshot eyes, another glass of vodka held between thin, greasy fingers. Los Angeles hadn't been kind to her, just like it hadn't been kind to him. At eighteen, Reed was only weeks away from being accepted into a south LA gang when the Marine recruiter confronted him outside a restaurant.

The sergeant wore green camouflage and a glare that could melt stone, but when he looked at Reed, he smiled. "You're about to screw up your whole life, kid. What a shame. A guy like you could make a hell of a Marine. Guess the apple doesn't fall far from the tree, huh?"

Reed rubbed his finger against the steel rail of his bunk and closed his eyes again. He never asked the recruiter how he knew about his father. He never asked him what the pay was or what career opportunities he would have in the Corps. He didn't even ask where they would send him. He just walked after him, caught the recruiter by the sleeve, and said, "You're wrong. Where do I sign?"

The edge of the bedrail sliced into Reed's thumb, and he snatched his hand back. The tiny cell closed in on him again, and he sucked in a humid breath.

All that sacrifice. All that war. And they threw me in here without a second thought.

He pressed his thumb against the dirty sheets until the bleeding subsided. He couldn't see Tabitha's face anymore. He couldn't hear the Marine recruiter challenging him with that gruff, disgusted voice. All he could hear was a single thought, pounding through his skull as loud and insistent as a war chant.

I have to get out of here.

4

The dining hall clattered as plastic plates were set onto steel dining tables. Reed rubbed his wrists.

The CO standing at his side raised an eyebrow then jerked his head toward the mess line twenty feet away. "Get to it, 4371. No talking."

Reed stepped into the back of the line and waited his turn to fill his plate. The dining hall rang with the clinking of utensils and the murmur of voices. COs stood in the corners, their narrow eyes surveying the crowd of convicts. A few of the prisoners looked at Reed with detached curiosity, but nobody spoke to him.

A cafeteria worker slopped runny mashed potatoes piled high next to dry ham and a wilting salad onto Reed's plate. He remembered eating with Turk in Baghdad at the military mess halls. That food was a feast compared to the stale slop on his plate now.

He took a seat at a table near the back of the room and ate quietly, searching the room for any sign of Milk or his comrades. A few faces were familiar, and the others were men with big shoulders and stern glares, tattoos adorning their skin, exposed by rolled-up sleeves. Nobody smiled. Nobody laughed.

Ignoring the slimy texture of the salad and dressing, Reed shoveled more food into his mouth. At least he could see what he was eating. That was an improvement over the lightless dungeon of solitary confinement.

The door at the far end of the room opened, and a CO stepped out first, followed by a small crowd of prisoners. Reed immediately spotted Milk standing at the back, a surly smirk playing at the corners of his mouth. When he saw Reed, his smile widened and his eyes flashed as before, but he turned away and shuffled toward the meal line. Reed watched him over the top rim of his water cup, taking slow sips and muting out the chaos around him. Only the pale man in coveralls mattered.

"He's not worth it. Trust me."

Reed recoiled, clenching his fist and raising it to defend himself. A short white man in a prison jumpsuit stood behind him, his stubby arms jammed into his pockets. He squinted at Reed, and without breaking eye contact, tilted his head toward a nearby CO.

Reed traced his gaze to the correctional officer, then lowered his fist.

The short man shuffled forward and sat down on the bench across from him, his hands still in his pockets. "You're quite the fighter, in spite of your total lack of discretion. That's why you're here, isn't it?"

"Who the hell are you?" Reed spat the words, surprised by his own aggression.

"I don't know, 4371. *Who are you?*"

Reed scoffed and stuck his fork into the last clump of cold potatoes. "Get lost."

Silence hung between them for a moment, but the little man didn't move.

When Reed looked up again, the narrow black eyes were still locked on him, and his fork rang against the plate. "I said, beat it!"

The short man withdrew his hands from his pockets and placed them on the table. One finger was missing from his right hand, and his other fingers were short and stumpy like the rest of his body.

"Think very carefully about what you're about to do," he said. "I know you can kill him. *You* know you can kill him. He probably knows it, too. But you'll be caught. And when you are, there'll be zero chance of your death penalty being lifted."

Reed's fork hung in midair, a piece of leathery ham stuck to the end. "How do you know about that?"

"I know a lot of things, Reed. A lot of things you'd like to know."

Once more, Reed let the silence hang in the air between them as he waited for the man to either blink or look away. He did neither.

"All right," Reed said. "I'll bite. What do you know?"

The little man drummed his fingers on the table, then smiled. "I know how to get you out of here."

Reed snorted. "Let me guess. Through the door?"

"It's not a joke, Reed. I know how to get you out."

This time the silence was palpable, like the emptiness of a tomb. Reed stopped chewing, once more trying to force the man to blink, but he wouldn't. His gaze was as unbroken and relentless as the block walls that encased them.

"Who are you?" Reed demanded.

"Call me Gould."

Reed slammed the fork against the plate, wiped his mouth on his sleeve, then clenched his fist over the tabletop. "Okay. So you know all about me. What do you want?"

"I want you to do what you do best. I want you to kill somebody. Somebody in this prison. Except this time, I want you to get away with it."

"And why the hell would I do that?"

"Because after you do, you'll walk out a free man. No death penalty. No FBI hounds on your heels. No criminal record to hide from. A fresh start."

"You know something, *Gould*? When something sounds too good to be true, it is."

"I thought you might say that. And maybe you're right. So go ahead and finish your ham. Go on and kill Milk. Rot in prison for another ten years before they shoot you up with a load of potassium chloride. Won't be my loss."

"Military death penalties are automatically appealed," Reed said. "They're appealing mine right now. The sentence could be lifted. Why would I throw that away and trust you?"

He shrugged. "You were ready to throw it away to kill an underweight pervert. But fine. If that's how you feel, appeal your sentence. Take life in prison instead. You're not yet thirty, the next fifty years should glide right by."

A knot twisted deep inside Reed's stomach, and he rubbed his thumb against the tabletop. His breath was short and shallow, like he was inhaling and exhaling through a straw. "All right, fine. Explain yourself."

"There's nothing to explain. I work for a powerful man who has the resources to restore your freedom. Somebody in this prison doesn't deserve to be alive, and that's a problem for my employer. You fix his problem, and he'll fix yours."

"So, you want me to murder somebody in cold blood?"

"No. I want you to execute justice. Just like you did in Baghdad. Just like you were about to do with Milk. I want you to be the hand of long-overdue karma."

Reed dropped the fork and wiped his mouth on a greasy section of paper towel. He folded the napkin and laid it on the table, smoothing it against the stainless steel as he noticed its flower pattern contrasting sharply with the scratches in the metal. He studied the faded blues and yellows as prisoners around the mess hall began to shuffle into line. COs barked commands. The racket felt unimportant, as though it were happening on the other side of the world.

Reed whispered between his teeth, "Who do you want me to kill?"

A smile spread across the man's thin lips. "Now that's a good question. But you need to sleep on it, Reed. When I know you're fully committed . . . then we'll talk."

He stood and shuffled off, leaving Reed sitting alone. A CO grabbed Reed by the arm, dragging him to his feet and shoving him toward the line of men. Still, the noise was distant. Irrelevant. One thought rang through Reed's tired mind: *I can be free.*

5

Rock Hollow Penitentiary

Weeks dragged by in a muddled blur. Each day was the same: Up before sunrise to march out to the yard and stand in line while the COs counted them off. If there had been any infractions from any prisoner the day before, they would be forced to exercise. Sometimes they would be left to stand for an hour, huddled in the cold while the COs did whatever it was COs spent their long days doing. Then they would be shoved into the showers.

Midday was consumed with prison housekeeping duties, while the afternoon was contained within the confines of the cell block, and nighttime hours were restricted to individual cells. Usually, the guards would let them out for an hour or so in the yard right after lunch, but sometimes an entire day would slip by without leaving the prison block.

The short man had vanished like a ghost. Reed spent days searching for him amid the crowd of prisoners and uniformed guards, but he was gone as quickly and suddenly as he appeared. Stiller had never seen him before and gave Reed a twisted frown when he asked. None of the other prisoners would talk to Reed. They avoided him like the plague, knotting around Milk in the yard and giving Reed long, foreboding glares.

"They're plotting," Stiller warned. "Probably because of the shower fight. Milk was banged up pretty good. He can't lose rep over you."

The wind that howled over the high block walls brought spits of snow with it. Reed leaned against the chain-link fence and folded his arms, watching the goons across the yard. Milk sat in the midst of them, his eyes flashing death at Reed. Without a word, the pale prisoner lifted a long index finger and ran it slowly across his throat.

"Bastard," Reed whispered.

"You need allies, man," Stiller said. "The COs won't do anything until there's a fight. By then, it could be too late."

Reed stared Milk down as he adjusted his feet against the hard-packed dirt of the yard. Neither man blinked.

Stiller sighed and leaned against the fence, facing through the chain link to the next prison yard. "What's your deal, Reed? You're dark, man. Like there's a hurricane just beating you to pieces from the inside."

Reed spat into the dirt without taking his eyes off of Milk. "This is prison, Stiller. It's a pretty dark place."

"Right. But it's like . . . you're not accepting it. You're *here*, man. You're in prison. Own it. Stop making it so hard on yourself."

"I'm not staying."

Stiller shot him a sideways look. "Say what?"

Reed folded his arms. "One way or another, I'm not wasting away behind these walls."

"Dude." Stiller lifted his eyes heavenward as if he were employing supernatural assistance. "*This* is what I'm talking about. You're in denial or something. I'm not judging, but it's not real, man. This prison *is*. Do you understand me? You're in prison."

Reed watched Milk saunter across the yard, pretending to ignore the ex-Marine that was glaring daggers at him.

"Just tell me why. Explain why you're the exception."

Reed wrapped his fingers around the chain link and spoke through gritted teeth. "Because I did the right thing. The men I killed were murderers, thieves, and rapists, and that's why they died. I went to Iraq to prosecute justice, and the government didn't bat an eye at the body count until Americans started falling. And you know what? To hell with them. But I'm going to keep fighting this thing until I get out."

Stiller stared at him through tired, exhausted eyes, and shook his head. "You're not a prosecutor, Reed. Let alone a judge and jury."

"You're right. I'm not. Not like the people who put me here. I'm the kind of prosecutor nobody wants to admit that everyone needs."

Silence hung between them, their eyes still locked. With every passing moment, that silence felt heavier.

"Number 4371! Fall out!"

The voice boomed from across the yard, breaking the tension between them. Stiller shot Reed another exhausted look then shuffled off toward the fence line, leaving Reed to march across the yard toward the CO.

"Come on, con. Your attorney's here."

The CO led Reed down a hallway, through the cellblock, and into a small and windowless room on the third level. A table sat in the middle, with metal chairs on either side while a flickering yellow light buzzed from overhead, washing the room in an uneven glow.

"Sit. He'll be here shortly."

The guard snapped handcuffs around Reed's wrists, then left him alone. A chill washed through him. The bite of winter cut straight through the block walls, coating the prison in frosty discomfort. Reed could only imagine what his cell would feel like in the summer months.

The door groaned on its hinges, and a tall man in a crisp brown uniform shirt stepped in. A Marine Corps judge advocate—

similar to a lawyer—here to represent Reed during the appeals process. He wore round glasses and the kind of detached, disinterested expression of a man who was already done with his day. The judge advocate set his briefcase on the table, then sat down without a word. He opened the case and shuffled through a stack of papers, spending a full five minutes scanning the file before he looked up.

My God. He hasn't even reviewed my case yet.

"You're Reed Montgomery?"

Reed nodded once, interlacing his fingers and laying his hands on the table.

The attorney returned to the papers and proceeded to read again, then folded and shoved them back into the briefcase. "I'm Lieutenant Graves, your appeals council."

"What happened to Lieutenant O'Hara?"

"She was reassigned. I'll be representing you for now."

"*For now?*"

Graves pushed the glasses up his nose. "The appeals process will be lengthy. It's possible I may be reassigned as well. Don't worry. We'll find somebody to replace me."

Reed sat back in the chair. "Okay. So what happens next?"

"Right. Well, first we'll file a motion of appeals on your sentence, then—"

"Wait. *File* a motion? You mean the motion hasn't been filed yet?"

Graves tilted his head, staring at the wall as though he'd just been asked to solve a trigonometry problem. Then he dug through the case again, shuffling through the papers. Half of them spilled onto the floor, and he didn't bother to pick them up.

"Um, no. I don't think so."

"You don't *think* so? Lieutenant, this is my life you're playing with."

The lieutenant's blue eyes flashed, blazing into a sudden glare. "You'd do well not to use that tone with me, Reed. I'm the only friend you've got. It's a lengthy process, okay? If we do well, we should have you in court within eighteen to twenty-four months, then we—"

"*Two years?* Are you kidding me?"

Once more, the perplexed frown washed over Graves's serious features. "I'm not kidding. It's not a joke."

Reed lowered his face into his hands and rubbed his thumbs into his temples. Another headache, an all-too-familiar plague, settled into the base of his skull.

"Don't worry, Reed." Graves scooped the pages off the floor and began to cram them back into the briefcase. "I'll file that appeal right away. We'll get this thing moving again. One of the Supreme Court judges is getting old. With luck, by the time we make it that far, we'll have an anti-capital punishment justice on the Court. That could be a game changer."

Reed clenched his fingers around the edge of the table. "Wait. You're already planning a Supreme Court appeal?"

Graves snapped the case shut and smiled a tight, awkward smile. "Well, Reed. The reality is the judges between here and the Supreme Court aren't very lenient. We'll do what we can, of course, but we have to be realistic. I'll see in you in a few weeks, okay?"

Graves shuffled to the door and let himself out.

Reed's heart hammered in his chest, and the room shrank around him, becoming at once stuffier than it was moments before. The flickering yellow light went out, and he laid his head on folded arms.

They've abandoned me. It's already over.

The floor felt unstable beneath his feet, as though the entire prison were swaying beneath him.

The door opened again. Reed waited for the hand of the CO to close around his shoulder, to pull him up and away from the table and back to the narrow cell he now called home. Back under the watchful eyes of Milk and his minions. At this rate, Reed would never make it to the appeals court. Milk's henchmen would mob him long before.

"Isn't he a gem?"

Reed sat up with a jolt at the familiar soft voice. The short man with nine fingers stood on the other side of the table. This time he wasn't wearing the white coveralls of a prisoner, but a brown pinstripe suit and a beige tie, complete with a pocket square poking out of the breast pocket. His close-cropped hair was gelled and combed to one side, glistening over his bright eyes.

"You!" Reed snapped. "Who the hell are you?"

The man slid into the opposite chair as Reed looked out for the guard, but the door was closed, and the room quiet.

"I'm here to discuss my proposal."

"You're not a prisoner," Reed said.

"No, I'm not. Do you want to be?"

Reed heard his own breath hissing between his lips. Each inhale tasted dry, and each exhale sour. The blood pumping through his neck surged toward his brain, clarifying the moment and driving back the confusion and questions. It didn't matter who this man was. It didn't matter what he wanted. The answer to his simple question was just as simple.

"No," Reed said. "I don't want to be a prisoner."

"What *do* you want to be, Reed?"

Reed ran his tongue over dry lips then clenched his fists. "The hand of overdue karma."

The man's smile kindled a fire of dark flames in his eyes. "Now, that's something I can help with."

6

"You have twenty-four hours. His name is Paul Choc."

From outside his cell on the second-floor landing, Reed surveyed the block. Small knots of prisoners stood scattered around the first and second floors, talking in low whispers and swapping various paraphernalia: candy, magazines, stamps.

The guards at the main entrance paced a short path back and forth in front of the door, tapping their nightsticks against their thighs while surveying the prisoners the way a man might survey week-old leftovers in the fridge. Every few minutes, one of them would yell, correcting some minor infraction. Other than the murmur of voices and occasional shouts, the block was relatively quiet—a welcome break in a busy afternoon.

Twenty-four hours. I've already blown three.

Back in his cell, Reed held his hand under the sink faucet, cupping a swallow of water in his worn palms. It tasted crisp and bitter, laden with chlorine and God knew what else.

"Stiller... You know a guy named Choc?"

His cellmate sat on the bunk, legs crossed under him as he flipped through an outdated magazine and shook his head without looking up.

Reed waited for a moment, then slouched against the wall, forcing himself to appear casual. "Paul Choc. I think he's housed here. Was a buddy of mine."

Stiller grunted, then flipped the magazine around. "Dude, check out the jugs on this one."

The magazine was dirty and worn with smudged fingerprints on every page.

Reed lifted an eyebrow. "Still . . . that's a cooking magazine."

Stiller laughed. "Right? Who knew cooks could be this hot."

Reed wiped his mouth with the back of his hand and cleared his throat. "So about my friend. I'd like to find him."

"I don't know a Choc. But most guys here have nicknames. What's he look like?"

I asked the same thing.

"He has a tattoo on his left forearm. An eagle with burning wings."

The magazine crackled as Stiller twisted the dry pages into a tight roll and shoved it under his shirt, scratching his back with short strokes of his muscled arms. "Blazer. I've seen him."

Reed's heart rate quickened, and he tried to remain calm, still leaning against the wall. "Where?"

Stiller cocked his head and ran his index finger under his lip, picking at a chunk of food stuck in his back teeth. "Hmm . . . I don't know, man. It's been a while. Think maybe he got out. Or maybe they moved him to another block."

"Did he have any friends? Anyone he talked to?"

"Friends . . . hmm. I mean, I guess he hung out with the other chicos. But again, it's been a while."

"Chicos?"

"Yeah, man. The Latinos."

"Choc is Latino?"

Shit. Why did I say that?

Stiller shot him a confused frown. "I thought this guy was your friend."

Reed attempted a casual shrug. "I mean, yeah, I guess I just don't think about that kind of thing."

Stiller's frown intensified. "You good, man? This isn't about yesterday, is it? You know, I've been thinking about what you said, and—"

Reed waved his hand dismissively. "Don't worry about it, Still. I don't want to talk about it."

He stepped back out of the cell and scanned the crowd of inmates. Most were white or black. Milk and his crew slouched in one corner, talking in low voices while staring at each other through half-closed eyes—doped up on something, it seemed. Another pass of the packed cellblock, and Reed settled on the small group of prisoners sitting on the floor in one corner, playing cards with a worn-out deck. These men were slightly shorter than the rest, with olive skin and thick, dark hair.

Gotcha.

Stiller lay still on his bunk, his chest rising and falling in a smooth rhythm, and Reed slipped up beside him, running his hand along the side of the bunk and feeling between the bed frame and the mattress. Two more passes and he felt the soft edge of something that wasn't cloth or metal. Watching Stiller for any sign of a disturbance in his breathing, Reed gently lifted the mattress and pulled at the edge of the object. A moment later, he produced a small envelope from beneath the sheet, and a quick survey of its contents produced two dozen stamps, a five-dollar bill, and a couple baseball cards. Reed dumped everything into his pocket, then returned the envelope.

The Latinos looked up as Reed approached, surveying him through narrow, suspicious eyes. Trying to remain relaxed and slumping his shoulders, Reed walked slowly toward their small crowd. There were six guys, all fit and trim, with a definite aura of confidence about them. Even the smallest sat with a straight back and a bold, unwelcoming glare.

"You guys got room for one more?"

The dealer leaned against the wall, his knees propped up at

chest level as he shuffled the cards. His brown fingers moved like lightning, cutting the deck twice before shuffling again. "Move along, man. We don't want nothing to do with your drama."

Pretending to be surprised, Reed frowned and looked behind him as if he were trailing some invisible baggage. He tilted his head back and nodded. "Oh, you mean that shit in the shower bay. Yeah, that wasn't my choice, man. You know how it is. . . . Gotta stick up for yourself."

"Yeah, well, stick up for yourself someplace else. Table's full."

Reed dug the stamps out of his pocket, then tapped the roll against his leg, rubbing his thumb over the glossy surface of the American flag. "You sure?"

The small crowd exchanged glances, then one of them grunted, "Let him play, Rigo."

The dealer motioned to the floor. "Ante is five flags. You won't last long."

Reed dumped five stamps onto the floor and accepted a hand of cards. They played without a sound, shuffling bets back and forth as the dealer flipped cards onto the bare floor. Reed's first hand was a bust, and he dumped more stamps onto the ground as new cards circulated the group.

"I'm Reed," he said.

Rigo snorted. "Nobody cares, man."

A round of betting passed through the circle. Two cards landed face-up. A couple players folded, and Reed dropped the five-dollar bill in the circle, resulting in raised eyebrows from the other players. The dealer flipped another two cards, and Reed dropped his to the floor. Low curses punctuated snorts of disgust as Reed shoveled the pot into his lap and sorted through the assortment of stamps, coins, and cigarettes.

"I'm looking for a friend of mine. Short dude, eagle tattoo. Goes by Blazer."

The circle fell deathly silent. Reed resisted the urge to look up as he finished sorting the loot, then dumped five fresh stamps into the middle of the floor.

Rigo began to hand out cards, slower this time, while staring at Reed. "This ain't the lost-and-found, man. If you're looking for a friend, you can look elsewhere."

More cards hit the floor. Reed tossed fresh collateral into the pile, barely looking at his cards as he bet. The first flop passed, then the second. Once again, Reed scooped the pile into his lap. Fresh curses and glares rippled through the group, and one man tossed his cards onto the floor before shuffling off.

"I think you know him." Reed pushed a cigarette into his mouth and chewed the filter, rolling the smoke between his teeth.

"Is that right?"

"Yep. And I think you know where he is. So, what's the big secret?"

Another round of sharp, suspicious glares circulated.

The dealer shoved the cards into a tight stack and leaned forward. "Who the hell are you, man?"

Without looking up, Reed continued chewing on the smoke while sorting through his pile of winnings. "I'm just a guy who'd rather serve his time with a friend around. Don't see what the big issue is."

Rigo leaned back. "Blazer is nobody's friend. If you knew him, you know that."

Reed shrugged and checked his cards. His hand was weaker this time, which was good; a third straight win wouldn't earn him any charity from his fellow players. "Of course not. But I still know him. He stay in this block?"

The final flop hit the floor, and the man to Reed's right scooped up the pile of winnings. A black snake tattoo rippled along his neck as he began sorting the captured loot between his knees.

"If he did, he wouldn't put up with your white ass sitting here." Snake spoke through dry lips, dropping stamps into the pot before accepting new cards from the dealer.

"So, nothing's changed?" Reed forced a laugh, trying to make it sound both strained and nervous.

I can work this angle.

Rigo tilted his head, and a slow smile spread across his tight lips. "Oh, I see. You scared, aren't you? You're making sure he's not around."

Reed shrugged. "It wouldn't break my heart if he were in another cellblock."

An alarm rang out, blasting through the block like the screech of a tornado siren. Wood clanked on metal as guards slammed their nightsticks into the bars of the lower cells.

"All right, you cons. Let's go! Back into the cells!"

Rigo scooped up the cards with a practiced flip of his fingers, shoving them back into a stack. Reed dumped his winnings into his pockets, lingering at the edge of the circle.

The playing cards clicked and hissed under Rigo's practiced fingers, and he stared across the room at the guards. "Did I see a baseball card in that pile?"

Reed flipped out the card and passed it to him. It disappeared amid the playing cards, then into the pocket of Rigo's dirty coveralls.

"All right, man. You can sleep easy tonight. Blazer is housed in E Block. They moved him over there after a fight with some of the guys here."

Reed grunted and extended his hand. "Thanks."

Rigo glared down at the extended hand, then spat on the floor next to Reed's feet. "Get back to your cell, man. And don't come down here no more. We don't want any of your white-ass drama."

Without another word, Rigo disappeared into his cell. A hard nightstick rapped against Reed's shoulder, and one of the guards snapped from behind.

"Move it, 4371. Lights out in ten!"

Reed stomped back up the steps, casting a quick look back as he went. At the end of the cellblock, beneath the roofline high above, a narrow window provided light and a limited view of the yard outside. Just past the main rec field, a tall fence topped with razor wire separated the yard from the one next to it. Across that small field, nestled next to another fence, was an identical block building, topped with an A-frame roof. It was dark and brooding, with a short row of bold letters painted on the exterior wall: CELLBLOCK E.

As he settled into his bed, Reed allowed himself to embrace a moment of confidence. This could be his chance—a one in a million shot at freedom. The government would give him life behind bars, at best. He remembered the short man in the pinstripe suit—his suave appearance and quiet confidence.

"Don't question yourself, Reed. Paul Choc deserves to die. You have the opportunity to execute justice for his victims, and we have the power to reward you for it."

Reed closed his eyes and relaxed. He was going to do it. He was going to prosecute the man they called Blazer.

7

"You seen my stamps, man?"

Reed lay on the bottom bunk. The underside of Stiller's mattress was brown, stained, and sagged in the middle. The thin outlines of support wires that crossed on the other side of the fabric were barely strong enough to keep the abused mattress from collapsing onto the bottom bunk.

"Something dropped off your bed last night. I don't know what it was."

Stiller hopped down from his bunk and poked his head under Reed's. A moment later he reappeared with a small pile of stamps and folded bills clamped between his fingers. Reed had already removed the cigarettes but couldn't do anything about the missing cash or baseball card.

Stiller counted the collection twice, scratched behind one ear, then shrugged and replaced it beneath his pillow.

Redirecting his attention to the bottom of the mattress, Reed studied the crisscross lines of wires. He chewed his bottom lip, twisting his fingers beneath his head.

Ten hours. I have less than ten hours.

"Hey, Still. Do the guys from E Block ever come over here?"

Stiller was busy shoving his inflated treasure back into the envelope. "I dunno, man. E Block is for the troublemakers. Surprised they haven't sent you over there."

I could stir up more trouble and make them send me over there. But I don't have time for a visit to solitary in between.

Reed pulled one of the smokes from his pocket and stuck it between his lips, biting into the paper and sucking the flavor of the nicotine out of the dry tobacco.

"Their yard is next to ours," Reed said. "Nothing but a chain-link fence separating us. You have to see them during rec sometimes."

Stiller shook his head. "I told you, man. They're troublemakers. Guards never let them out at the same time as us."

Reed suppressed a curse and closed his eyes. *There has to be a way.*

"Do they ever transfer guys over to E Block? I mean, temporarily?"

Stiller flopped back onto his bunk and unrolled the same cooking magazine, starting at page one. "Dude, I don't know. Why do you care so much about E Block? Trust me, you don't wanna be over there."

Reed sank his teeth deeper into the cigarette, cutting through the paper and exposing the tobacco. The sting of the drug seeped onto his tongue, and he imagined the vapor filling his lungs, flooding his body, and bringing welcome relief. What he wouldn't have given for a lighter. Of course, no lighters were allowed—no fire of any kind—making the cigarettes an odd and pointless commodity in the strange and volatile marketplace of prison trade.

Just a little flame. Just enough to light up an ember and generate a good cloud of smoke.

Reed's eyes snapped open. He stood up and flipped the cigarette into the toilet, then walked to the closed cell door, peering out and up toward the ceiling. He could see the air vents lined up high above, pouring warm air into the dank prison block. Far below, on the first floor, nestled in the corner next to the main gate, another grill was bolted to the blocks. But this one wasn't a vent; it was an air return where all the smelly, used air was sucked out and filtered through the climate control unit before being pumped back into each cellblock.

Reed wrapped his fingers around the bars, his eyes fixed on the air return. For the first time since being shoved off the prison bus, the tension faded from his stomach, and his muscles relaxed.

Perfect.

Darkness descended over the prison, broken only by the systematic rhythm of boots as the guards conducted their circuits. Reed lay awake on the bottom bunk, listening to Stiller snore. As the minutes drained into hours, the snores became deeper and more relaxed, blending with the creak of the wind against the metal roof far above.

Every twenty minutes, a CO passed the entrance to their cell, casting a lazy glance over the occupants before moving on. Reed lay perfectly still, counting each second in his mind and matching the beat of the boots with the tick of a nonexistent clock. The method wasn't perfect, and neither were the circuits. Sometimes the CO would pass five minutes early, and sometimes ten minutes late. Sometimes his boots rang sharp and clear against the floor, and sometimes he slipped up in front of the cell with a lazy creep that was all but silent.

Reed didn't think the tactical advantages of this irregular method were intentional. More than likely, the CO was simply tired and bored and conducting his job at random to keep himself awake. Either way, it made Reed's task that much harder.

Slipping his fingers under the thin sheets, Reed felt along the edge of his cheap commercial mattress. It was made entirely of foam, but not the fancy kind. More like the kind you find in the seat of a tractor: thick, yellow, and spongy, encased in a thick waterproof sleeve that looked like the tarpaulins FEMA spreads over busted roofs after a hurricane. Along the bottom edge of the mattress, a seam ran in the tarp, manufactured of rough stitches and plastic rolled on top of itself in a thick strip. As Reed ran his hand along the seam, he twisted the plastic beneath his fingers, gratified to find it stiff and inflexible—a little too inflexible for plastic alone.

The swish of pant legs echoed down the balcony. Reed froze and closed his eyes, waiting for the guard to pass. He counted to a hundred just to be certain, then rolled sideways and leaned over the side of the bed. The plastic tasted like sweat, grime, and pure body odor between his teeth. He bit down on the seam, grinding it in his mouth with increasing pressure and pulling on the plastic with both hands. His stomach convulsed, and he wanted to vomit, but he kept chewing—another bite, and then a twist. The plastic tore and slid back, exposing a thin wire core as thick as a coat hanger, but more flexible.

Reed spat plastic and saliva and twisted his fingers around the wire. It was perfect—malleable but strong—and made out of cheap steel. He slipped his fingers into the hole of the plastic and tore it back, exposing a wide section of dirty yellow foam and several inches of the wire. Careful pressure with his fingers caused the wire to bend around the bed frame. Reed rolled the wire and bent it in the opposite direction, back and forth, until it finally snapped under the heat and friction. He tore the seam another few feet down the length of the mattress, masking the ripping of the plastic with Stiller's violent snores, then repeated the process of bending the wire until he broke off a three-foot section. It was flimsy in his hands, but the weight and strength were sufficient. He coiled the wire around his fingers, being careful not to bend it too harshly, then slipped it into his pocket.

The foam felt as dirty as it looked, sticking to his fingers as he pulled it apart. Little chunks broke free of the mattress and filled his hands, leaving smudges of grease and grime on his palms. Reed pressed handfuls of the petroleum product into his jumpsuit, packing it in around his waist. It was hot and sticky next to his body and filled his nostrils with the stench of more body odor. He wrinkled his nose and zipped the coveralls shut, then rested his head against the pillow.

A full six hours remained between him and the morning wakeup call, and eight hours left until the deadline.

It has to be enough.

The cell door shrieked back on its hinges, grinding under the whine of the electric motor. Reed's eyes snapped open, and he propped himself up on his elbows. The lights that snapped on blazed without the familiar scream of COs shouting, *"Lights! Lights!"*

Something was wrong.

The footsteps that filled the air like the rumble of a freight train were much louder than usual. Dozens of metallic shrieks ripped through the silence as more cell doors were electrically opened, followed by the squeal of the intercom from the ceiling high above.

"All prisoners, fall out! Assemble on ground level! Fall out!"

Reed peered out over the railing to the lower level, where no less than forty COs gathered around the bottom units and shoved prisoners out of their beds and onto the floor. Another twenty guards were pounding their way directly toward him.

"What's this?" Reed shouted.

Stiller stumbled out of bed, yawning. "Shakedown, dude. They do it once or twice a month. Checking for contraband."

Shakedown. Shit.

"All prisoners! *Fall out!*"

Stiller hit the floor. "Let's go, man. Get to the ground floor."

The mattress was barely covered by the blanket, leaving the hole where Reed had dug the foam and wire out partially exposed and easy to find.

"Dude, let's go! You don't want to be here when they are."

Reed stumbled out onto the balcony, his legs feeling suddenly wobbly. He joined the long line of sleepy prisoners, listening to the guards shouting and turning the cells upside down. As he stepped off the stairs and onto the main floor, Milk caught him by the arm. "I'm coming for you, bitch."

Reed jerked away and pressed into the crowd of prisoners gathering around the far end of the cellblock. Most looked half-awake, only half wore shoes, and the fat ones had their coveralls tied around their waists, exposing broad and sweaty chests.

"Let's go, cons! Against the wall!"

Reed forced his way to the back of the crowd, feeling his shoulders rammed against the blocks as the entire population of the cellblock pushed him backward. He inched his way sideways along the wall, feeling with his right hand until his fingers closed around a hard metal edge—the frame of the air return.

The leg of his coveralls clung to the surface of the vent as the heating unit sucked sordid air back into the conduits. Like the rest of the prison, the surface of the grate was grimy to the touch, but there was a full one-inch gap between the slats. Reed pushed himself downward, kneeling against the wall before he dug inside his coveralls. The noise inside the cellblock became deafening—a combination of shouting guards and grumbling prisoners. The suffocating smell of body odor was overwhelming at this height, but nobody noticed him. Nobody looked down as Reed shoved wads of mattress foam between the slats and into the mouth of the air return.

Where are the Latinos? I need the Latinos.

He pressed the last wad of foam through the grill and stood up again. Nobody had noticed, but when he looked down at the grill, the pile of foam was clearly visible. Smaller chunks of the mattress had already disappeared inside the conduit, sucked away by the pressure of the returning air, but a sizable mound remained behind, lying just on the other side of the slats.

Reed grabbed the nearest prisoner by the sleeve and gave it a soft jerk. "Hey, where are the Latinos?"

The big man glared at him, then jerked the sleeve free and stumbled off. Fighting his way through the packed crowd, Reed shoved elbows and thick arms aside as he searched for the shorter crowd of men from the day before. The shout of guards and grumble of the prisoners grew louder in his ears, pounding in a constant chorus. Each breath of the filthy prison clogged his lungs.

Reed saw the ringleader first: short with curly black hair and wiry brown arms—the stuff of south LA—every bit the hardened gangster. He pushed through two more half-naked convicts and tugged on Rigo's sleeve. "Amigo."

The short man spun on him. "Who you calling *amigo*, gringo?"

Reed brushed the bluster aside and leaned down to make himself heard over the ruckus. "I need your lighter. You can have everything from yesterday. Everything I won."

Rigo wrapped his fingers into fists and took a step back. "I don't know what you're talking about, white boy, but you better clear out of here before I put a hurt on your ass."

Reed gritted his teeth. "Look, *dude*. Nobody carries that many smokes without a flame. I know you've got one, and I know you've got it on you. You wouldn't leave it in your cell during a shakedown."

Rigo shook his head. "Move along, man. If you know what's good for you—"

"*Number 4371!*" The voice boomed out from the second floor, cascading over the crowd with all the terror of a direct thunderclap. Reed's mouth went dry. A guard stood outside his cell, bellowing into a bullhorn. The man's face blazed red, and he searched the crowd below him.

"Number 4371! *Fall out!*"

"Oh no, white boy." Rigo's lips twisted into a smirk. "Looks like you got busted."

Panicked adrenaline surged through Reed's body. He whirled back around and grabbed Rigo by the neck, pulling him in close before driving his fist full force into the Latino's jaw. Bone met bone with a sharp crack, and blood sprayed across Reed's white jumpsuit. Somebody shouted, and chaos erupted.

Reed grabbed the collar of Rigo's jumpsuit and ripped it open, pulling it down over his shoulder before running his hand down Rigo's back and feeling between his butt cheeks. His fingers closed around the hard edge of the lighter. Though barely conscious, Rigo spluttered and tried to fight. Reed swept his feet out from under him, then turned and launched himself back into the crowd. The COs shouted. The bullhorn blared. Every noise bounced and echoed off the bare walls as though the entire prison were caught in a giant blender, and Reed was slipping toward the blades.

He slid to his knees at the grate, ground his finger against the wheel of the Zippo lighter, and waited for the flame to dance. The metal fins of the air grate sliced into his skin, drawing blood as he pressed the lighter through the vent and onto the pile of greasy petroleum foam.

Bright light and heat washed over Reed's face, singeing his eyebrows and sending him stumbling backward. He fought to regain his balance, but his right foot slipped, and he crashed onto his tailbone as fresh clouds of smoke billowed into the air return.

"Number 4371! Show us your hands!"

8

The snarling, acne-covered guard closed his hand around Reed's arm, but Reed pulled himself free, launching himself back into the crowd and hiding amid the packed prisoners as the COs closed in on all sides. The bullhorn barked, and fresh guards burst into the cellblock. Reed ducked and tried to push himself farther into the crowd, but the attempt was futile; there was no more room to move.

Reed tipped his head back, gazing at the ceiling where rows of AC vents lined the exposed ductwork. A trace of smoke escaped the suck of the air return, wafting toward the ceiling. A moment later, the shrieking ring of the fire alarm overtook the blare of the bullhorn. Red lights flashed from the ceiling, and panic overwhelmed the entire prison.

"Fall into line. *Fall in, convicts!*"

Reed pressed himself behind a short man with one ear, ducking low to avoid detection. The COs crowded around the prisoners, shoving them toward the hallway that led into the yard and pushing them along with snapping shouts and the crack of nightsticks against concrete.

"Evacuate Block D! All convicts, move into the yard!"

The commands were barely audible over the scream of the alarm. Ducking and stumbling through the door and into the yard, Reed shielded himself against the mass of swinging body parts around him. The yard was still clothed in the inky black of the early morning hours. Even the spotlights of the towers were directed elsewhere, back onto the roof of Block D as the guards searched for the source of the smoke.

Reed turned away from the crowd and walked toward the fence near E Block's yard. He waited, drumming his knuckles against his thigh as he stared at the sister block standing tall and dark under the black sky. The moments that ticked by felt like hours. He placed his hand against the chain-link and dug his toes into the mud. The air smelled crisp and clean, but there was still the undertone of dirty bodies from the cage designed to house them all until the end of time.

Red lights flashed from the upper windows of the cellblock, and another fire alarm shrieked, this one ringing from inside E Block's walls. An unknown thrill, a rush he had never felt before, washed through his veins. It wasn't excitement or even nervousness; it was vindication—the sort of self-justice you feel when against all odds, you got something right.

Prisoners poured out of E Block. They stumbled into one another, groggy and confused, leaning forward and rubbing their eyes as a smaller group of COs evacuated them. They dispersed into the yard, looking for places to sit while they awaited their return to bed. Reed scanned each face in the crowd, searching for any sign of a Latino, checking every arm for the eagle tattoo. Because of the white jumpsuits, most arms were obscured from view, and those that were exposed were too wreathed in shadow to be discernible.

Then he saw him: short with bulging muscles and a bald head, his sleeves torn off, revealing thick arms covered in tattoos. On the left one, just beneath his elbow, was the feathery face of a screaming bald eagle wreathed in fire.

Reed reached into his pocket and closed his fingers around the wire, lifting it out and unwinding it, leaving the strand hanging at his left side in a gently curved strip. "Blazer!"

The muscular Latino looked up immediately, squinting through the yard lights, and took a half step forward.

Reed called again. "Blazer, don't you remember me?"

Another few yards closed. His face was scarred, betraying the hardened features of a longtime resident of the prison. He stopped five feet from the fence and glowered at Reed. "Who the hell are you, man?"

Reed forced a laugh. "Dude, it's me. Travis. From back home?"

Blazer took another step toward the fence.

The gaps in the chain-link were just large enough for Reed to slip his wrist through, and he held out his hand, fingers open, waiting to shake. "Blazer. . . . Don't break my heart, man. I don't have friends around here."

The Latino squinted and leaned forward another two inches. It was two inches close enough.

Reed shot his arm through the barrier and dug his fingers into the collar of Blazer's jumpsuit, then pulled him in until his head crashed against the chain-link fence. With a flip of his left wrist, Reed ran the wire through the fence and around Blazer's neck, catching the tail end with his right hand and pulling it back through the chain-link. Blazer twisted and shouted as he tried to break free. He twisted on his feet, turning until he faced away from Reed.

It was a fatal mistake.

With the wire closed around his throat, Reed pulled back and jerked right in one powerful motion. The wire sliced right through the skin and cut through Blazer's windpipe, sending a spray of blood over the loose gravel as Reed finished the stroke and released the wire. Blazer collapsed to the ground, and Reed stumbled backward. His hands were sticky, now coated with a thin layer of blood. Blazer choked and thrashed, his hands flying to his throat as his panicked eyes stared at the sky. Several of the other E Block inmates shouted and rushed toward him, but the damage was already done.

Blazer choked out in just over a minute, his dead eyes still staring heavenward.

What the hell have I done?

For the first time, Reed thought of cameras. Guards posted on surveillance. Other prisoners. Who might have seen him? He fell to his knees and began to grind dirt against his palms, rubbing away the gunky crimson of death. He was only vaguely aware of other prisoners shouting and running away from the prison block. Every noise and sensation was dampened, muted by the reality sinking into his bones.

I just killed a man.

"Well, what do we have here? A little bitch, all by himself."

Reed scrambled to his feet and whirled around. Two big men stood behind Milk, only ten yards away. Rigo appeared out of the crowd to join them, his lips lifted into a deadly snarl.

Mud crumbled beneath his bare feet as Reed stumbled back, kicking out and swinging with his left hand. He missed, and Rigo darted in, sending a swift kick to his stomach. The world spun, and Reed lashed out, connecting with somebody's face before a sharp object sliced into his arm, followed by another blow to his wounded stomach. The leering sneer of the cross-eyed Hulk appeared in the corner of his eye just before a massive, meaty fist came crashing down, straight into the base of Reed's skull.

The greasy smell of the room reminded Reed of hydraulic fluid or engine oil. It was distinct. Heavy. It didn't smell like the prison. His arms, neck, and most of all, his skull hurt as he fought for consciousness. Agony washed over him, the claws of a dragon digging into his flesh and ripping the muscles straight off the bone.

"Give him another."

Like the bite of an insect, something stung his arm and

burrowed into his skin. Warmth flooded his blood, and his mind began to clear. He could see a dim light in the otherwise dark room with metal walls and that thick, greasy smell. He sat in a chair, unrestrained at a metal table. Two men bustled around behind him, and two more sat on the far side of the table. He recognized the man on the left immediately. It was the short, stocky man from the prison. The one who vanished then reappeared in the brown pinstripe suit. He didn't know the second man, tall and lean, with a carefully trimmed beard and not a hair on his scalp. His green eyes flashed, and the stub of a cigar glowed between his fingers.

I didn't smell the cigar.

It was such an odd thought, such a pointless thing to notice, especially since he smelled it now—thick and sweet.

"Welcome to the land of the living, Number 4371."

Sarcasm tainted the familiar voice of the man on the left. Out of his pinstripe suit, he now wore a tight black T-shirt and silver chain necklace with a dangling golden crucifix.

Reed raised his fingers to his face, rubbing his tired eyes. "Where am I?"

"Right where I promised you'd be. You're on the outside, Reed. You're free."

The fight outside the prison. The staged fire. The feeling of the wire slicing through skin as it tore into Blazer's throat. A sick feeling settled into his stomach as every detailed memory flooded back into the forefront of his mind.

"You're wondering how you did it."

For the first time, the man on the right spoke. His English had just a hint of refined London drawl. He looked to be in his late fifties, Reed thought, with a mostly white beard and some wrinkles, but his eyes were still strong. Still potent.

"That's always the question," the man continued. "*How did I do it? How did I kill a man in cold blood?*"

Everything felt as though it were happening in slow motion, just quick enough for Reed to make sense of one action as it related to another.

"I'll tell you how you did it, Reed. You did it because it's who you are. You're a born killer. A natural wielder of justice. That's how you killed those contractors in Iraq, isn't it? Because they deserved to die. And that's how you'll kill your next dozen targets, too."

The words rang clearer now, and the mental fog began to fade. "Who the hell are you?"

"My name is Oliver Enfield. I operate an independent contracting agency. We supply professional killers for hire."

The words were so frank, so direct that Reed knew he should've felt surprised, but he didn't. The only thing he felt was confusion. "You got me out of prison?"

"I did."

"That's not possible."

"It is, and it happened. It's all a matter of influence. Something you'll come to find I have a great deal of."

"They're coming for me. Whoever you are, they're coming for you, too."

Oliver laughed. It was a deep, confident sound. Not at all uncomfortable, either. It was more like the warm chuckle your grandfather makes when you tell a cheesy joke.

"Reed, when I say it's all a matter of influence, what I mean is, *everything* is a matter of influence. Nobody is coming for you. In fact, as of this moment, nobody knows you exist. Your record is gone. The court-martial files. The prison manifest. Even your fingerprints. Like I said, I am a man of tremendous influence."

The words made sense, but they didn't quite compute. The claims were either too radical or too absurd to feel true.

"What do you want?" It was the only question Reed could think of.

Oliver took a puff on the cigar, then faced Reed dead in the eye. In an instant, all the warmth and gentleness faded from his features, replaced by cold calculation.

"I want you to do what you do best. I want you to kill. And you're going to do it for me."

The room was suddenly quiet. The man in the black T-shirt

interlaced his fingers and leaned forward, staring at Reed without blinking. The goons in the background stood out of sight, also silent.

"I already did that," Reed said. "Choc is dead. I cut his throat."

"Yes. A very inventive method, I will say. We'll have to work on your subtlety—because you don't have any. But in the meantime, suffice it to say that I'm impressed."

"Okay. Good. So you let me go now like you promised. He's dead. You got me out of prison. We're done."

Oliver puffed on the cigar again. "No, Reed. We're not done. One life gets you out of prison. Thirty more *keep* you out of prison. I'm not looking for a one-time hit inside a pen full of the world's most violent killers. I could have done that myself for free. I'm looking for a lethal weapon to join my growing enterprise. Somebody ruthless. Somebody like you."

Reed clenched his hands over the table. "I'm not killing thirty people for you. He said I kill and I walk. *That was the deal!*"

Oliver exchanged glances with his companion, then ground the cigar against the tabletop. "If that's how you feel, I can have you back in prison before nightfall. They'll put you straight into solitary while they prepare a trial for the murder of Paul Choc. They don't know you did it, but I'll make sure they learn. Or maybe I won't. Maybe you won't have to worry about death row. I own half that prison. By the end of the week, you could be in a white body bag lying in the morgue."

There was no deceit in Oliver's stone-cold eyes. No bluster. This man was absolutely serious. He would kill Reed in a heartbeat, and without a second thought.

Oliver tapped his finger on the table and narrowed his eyes at Reed. "They tell me you have a word for what you did in Iraq. They say you called yourself a *prosecutor*."

Reed didn't answer. He returned the stare with as much confidence and bluster as he could muster.

"I like that word," Oliver said. "I like the spirit behind it. The idea that you can pursue justice independently of a corrupt judicial system. That's pretty much what my company does all year long." He leaned forward. "Come with me, Reed. I'll make you the scourge of a world that is long overdue the sword of justice. I'll make you rich. I'll make you terrible. I'll make you more deadly than the strongest spec ops soldier on the planet. I'll give you a home and a purpose and something to call your own. I'll make you more than free. I'll make you God. I'll make you the Prosecutor."

Reed sucked in a long breath through his nose, and the muscles in his back began to loosen. A calm swallowed his soul like the eye of a hurricane passing over a storm-battered city. It wasn't peace. It didn't feel like security. It just felt like a momentary reprieve from the blast of the storm—an opportunity to find shelter.

"Thirty kills?" he asked.

Oliver's mouth twisted into a glistening smile. "Thirty kills."

9

Three years later
43 Miles Northeast of Atlanta

Orange flames licked up the side of the cabin, racing along the darkened stains of gasoline that saturated the timbers. Sparks and pine splinters fell from the walls, raining down on the wet earth beneath. The rain that fell through the trees in a gentle shower wouldn't stop the blaze, but there was no danger of the fire being blown into the surrounding trees. Within minutes, the roof began to creak, then it collapsed into the living room amid a rush of sparks.

Baxter whimpered. His bottom teeth jutted out, and his head tilted to one side as he watched the flames. Reed patted him behind his ears, feeling the greasy hair matted between the rolls of fat that hung to the bulldog's neck.

"I know, boy," Reed whispered. "We knew it could end this way."

The dog snorted and pawed the ground, then stood up. Without a backward glance, he walked down the hill toward the pickup truck parked at the end of the driveway. Staring into the flames a moment longer, Reed watched his longtime home disintegrate. Not for the first time, his aching mind wandered back to Banks—the stunning blonde he met at a nightclub only hours before all hell broke loose and his world feel apart. He saw her eyes, her smile, the way her whole body glowed when she sang. He imagined her lips on his and remembered the way they tasted. How she felt. The way she made him feel.

He closed his eyes. Ignored the cold wind on his back conflicting with the warmth of the fire on his face. It took every ounce of willpower and determination to walk away from Banks. To leave her out of this hellish war he had fallen into. He opened his eyes and clenched his jaw. The aching in his heart to find her again, to be with her, couldn't wash away the burning reality of who he was and what he had to do. No matter how desperately he longed to hold her again, just for a moment, there was a deeper, more burning desire in his soul—a desire for vengeance.

Without another glance, Reed shouldered the backpack and started after the dog. Each step brought new resolve to his mind. New anger. For three years, he believed a lie. Believed that after thirty brutal kills, he would be a free man with nothing but a wide-open road in front of him. That was the snake oil that Oliver Enfield sold him when he shook Reed's hand and designated him *Codename Prosecutor*. Reed wanted to believe it was for real—a genuine opportunity for belonging, for something bigger than himself. But at the end of the day, that too had faded into a lie as quickly as the cabin turned to ash behind him.

Three weeks had passed since the train wreck in east Atlanta when Reed first learned that his mentor and employer had sold him out to an unknown enemy. Reed spent those weeks bouncing from one grimy hotel to another, laying low and giving his injuries as much time as possible to heal. Then he returned to his cabin to scrub the place, removing anything and everything that could be traced back to him. He packed the bulk of his gear into the trunk of the Camaro, then stashed the car in a storage shed. He paid in cash and gave the clerk a fake name and South

Carolina driver's license. Nothing could be traced back to him. The FBI would search for the black Camaro last seen at the site of the Peachtree Tower. Of course, Reed removed the license plate before that operation, but the car was still too conspicuous for him to risk. The black pickup truck from the rental car company would be easier to hide in and easier to ditch if things went sideways.

And things were almost certainly about to go sideways.

He opened the door of the pickup and Baxter jumped in, landing in the passenger seat and settling down for the ride. Reed tossed the backpack in the rear seat on top of the rifle case. The pack contained his standard rush kit, loaded with everything he needed to vanish. Fake IDs, straps of cash in three different currencies, survival gear, spare burner cell phones, and enough ammunition to lay down a battalion of Marines. Or maybe a kingpin killer and his army of goons.

Gravel crunched under the tires of the truck as it bounced down the unpaved road back toward town. It took almost twenty minutes to reach the blacktop again, and Reed turned southwest toward Canton. The sun crested through the treetops, blazing through the thinning clouds and into the pickup, covering his bruised skin with welcome warmth. As the mile markers ticked by, more cars joined him on the ever-widening highway. The daily grind of metropolitan Atlanta was underway, bringing fresh bustle and noise to drown out the chaos of days before.

Baxter rested his head on his paws and stared into space. A trail of drool drained from his bottom lip and onto the seat, but he didn't snore like he usually did while relaxing. His whole body was still and quiet.

Large brick houses lined the streets of a neighborhood, complete with postage-stamp lawns, brown privacy fences, and identical Bradford pear trees. All the driveways were pressure-washed white, and the few cars that sat outside the garages were all new and clean, white and black, mostly SUVs and sport sedans with the occasional Japanese minivan mixed in. It was a quiet

Caucasian neighborhood, still asleep prior to the impending rush of weekday life.

The truck squeaked to a stop in front of a home at the end of a cul-de-sac. The flowerbeds in front of the brick were packed with bright fall colors, and the lawn was clean and raked. A black sedan sat in the driveway with a blue bumper sticker plastered just beneath the left taillight: My Cat Should Be President.

Reed switched the truck off and admired the car and the house and the perfectly clean yard. It looked peaceful. Maybe not happy. Definitely not exciting. But certainly peaceful. The kind of peace that a quiet, simple, boring life promises.

He checked the gun under his unzipped jacket, then walked across the lawn and up the spotless sidewalk to the front door. The neighborhood was quiet and calm, making his knuckles sound like gunshots as they collided with the door. He shoved his hands into his pockets and waited, drawing a deep breath of the fall that was much colder than a typical November morning in North Georgia.

Moments ticked by until he heard the soft patter of footsteps and then the thump of a forehead resting against the door. The peephole darkened. The chain rattled in its slot, then the bolt snapped back. The door glided open on silent, greased hinges.

Kelly wore hospital scrubs and tennis shoes, both a minty green, and her thin brown hair was swept back behind her ears. She stared into Reed's eyes with silent, reserved calmness, then sighed and stepped back. "Come in."

A tasteful assortment of accents and framed pictures hung on the walls of the home. Dim light shone from the living room, glinting off the dark-brown tile. He didn't see a cat, but a bowl labeled "kitty dinner" sat on the floor next to a water dish. Coming from someplace upstairs, Reed heard the sound of water splashing in a shower and the muted tone of a man singing. He pulled the coat a little tighter over the gun and followed Kelly down the hall and into the kitchen. With each step, uncertainty overwhelmed his confidence. He'd never been there before, and he hadn't seen Kelly since she patched him up after the train wreck. Before that, it had been almost twelve months. But the way she walked—the look in those dark eyes—it still made his head go light. He remembered when that feeling was the only thing that got him out of bed in the morning, but now it ignited only guilt.

Kelly led him into the kitchen, and without a word, she filled a coffee cup from the pot and passed it to him. Reed sipped it in silence while she propped her elbows on the counter and calmly watched him.

"Seems like you're back on your feet, in spite of my directions."

Reed shrugged. The hot coffee warmed his chilled fingers.

"Leg healing up okay?"

"Yep." Through the back window, he saw a flowerbed and a swing set, new and still glistening with bright paint that the first summer would burn into dullness. One child's swing with tiny straps hung from the bar. It was yellow.

Reed turned back to Kelly and raised both eyebrows. She nodded once but didn't say anything.

"Congratulations. I'm happy for you." He wasn't sure if he meant those words or not. They were just what he needed to say. The best way to stay numb was to suppress his feelings.

"I asked you not to come around anymore, Reed. I was very clear about that." An edge crept into Kelly's tone.

"I know. It's not about the medical. I—"

A skinny man with blonde hair stepped off the staircase and into the hallway. Water dripped from his hair, and there was a towel wrapped around his waist. Steam still rose from his flushed skin, and a big smile hung on his lips. "Kelly, I was thinking—" His smile faded when he saw Reed, but there was no defensiveness in his posture—just surprise.

"John, this is Reed." Kelly poured another cup of coffee, and John stepped forward and took the coffee before extending his hand toward Reed. The grip was firm and confident, but not all that strong.

Reed shook once, then released.

"Reed is my realtor. He sold me the house." Kelly stared into her cup.

"Oh, cool." The smile returned, and John took a deep sip of the coffee. "Sorry to come down dressed like this, man. Didn't know we had company."

Reed forced a tight smile. "It's early. My intrusion."

John shifted on his feet, then flashed another nervous smile. "Well, I better get dressed. Good meeting you, Reed." He disappeared back up the steps, coffee in hand.

Reed turned back to Kelly and raised one eyebrow. She flicked her hand at him and turned away, wiping down the counter with a dry cloth.

"He seems nice," Reed said. He hoped the insincerity in his voice wasn't as obvious as John's awkwardness.

"He is."

"Is he ... umm ... ?"

Kelly rolled her eyes. "A Christian?"

"Well, yeah. I guess."

"Yes. I met him at church."

"I'm happy for you."

Kelly flung the cloth into the sink and shot him a glare. "You don't have to lie, Reed. I know what you think. He's not like you. He's not big and blunt and brutal. Not everyone has to be."

The room fell silent with that awkward, tense mood like an invisible fog.

Kelly leaned against the counter and wiped hair from her face. "I'm sorry."

Reed rubbed his finger over the mosaic pattern of the mug, tracing each spiral and shard of colored glass. "I never hated you for what you believe. I just don't feel the same."

"I know." She stared at the floor, and once again, the silence felt thick.

Reed imagined he could feel each second slipping by, punctuated by a heart rate that shouldn't be so pronounced. He looked into the backyard again and studied the swing. Bright yellow.

Gender-neutral. The kind of thing only an overzealous future parent would buy before they even knew the sex of their child. That was Kelly, always jumping ahead.

"Why are you here, Reed?"

The sudden question jarred Reed out of his muse. He dumped the coffee into the sink and leaned on the counter. "I need you to keep Baxter for a couple days. He's in the truck." He shoved his hands back into his pockets and rested against the kitchen island.

"I told you I was done. I'm not getting mixed up in your chaos anymore. I'm an honest woman now."

"You were always an honest woman, Kelly. That's what made you such a shitty thief."

She rolled her eyes. "I wasn't half bad in my better days."

"Does John know about your better days?"

She looked away. "What do you think?"

"I doubt he'll ever ask. Doesn't impress me as an inquisitive person."

"What about when I tell him my realtor's dog is staying the week?"

Reed grinned. "Hey, you set yourself up for that one."

Kelly's dark eyes were rimmed with red.

Reed stepped across the room and placed one hand on her arm, squeezing softly. "This is the last time. I swear to you. There's something I have to clean up, but when I'm finished, I'll come back for Baxter and then I'll be gone. You'll never see or hear from me again."

A single tear spilled out of her eye. She looked away, glaring at the back patio through the sliding glass door. "You think that's what I want?"

"I think it's what you need."

Reed brushed the fallen bangs out of her eyes, then leaned down and kissed the top of her head. He gave her arm another squeeze and then walked toward the door. "Three days, Kel. Maybe four."

"I charge for pet sitting!"

Reed paused and shot her a wink and a grin. "Maybe I'll pay off the house."

As the door closed behind him, Reed faced north toward the mountains. The breeze that stung his cheeks unleashed fresh resolve in his veins. He pushed back the thoughts of Kelly and her quiet life, and he remembered Atlanta—the wrecked train, the bloody bodies, and the ultimate backstabbing. He was only one kill away from a quiet life like this—one of retirement and solitude—or at least he thought he was. But that had all been a farce. Oliver's promise of thirty kills in exchange for his freedom was a lie from the start, and it was a lie Reed would never swallow. He worked as a professional killer under the condition that he killed people who deserved to be killed. It was a cheap, clichéd excuse for his bloody profession, but it was how he justified the relentless slaughter.

Oliver made a terrible miscalculation when he turned on Reed, failing to realize that a man they called *Prosecutor*—a man who made his living gunning down injustice—should be the last man he tried to backstab.

I'm coming for you, Oliver.

10

Western North Carolina

"... It's twenty-eight degrees here in beautiful Cherokee County and not showing any signs of warming up. This is truly radical weather for late November. We've got a cold front sweeping down from the Midwest, with temperatures expected to fall into the single digits overnight. You're gonna want to get home early tonight and make sure you bundle up. It's gonna be a cold one. From channel—"

Reed cut the radio off and settled back into the cloth seat of the pickup. The heater hummed on low, pumping hot air over the windshield to keep it from fogging. Even though the cab of the truck was warm, Reed could feel the chill from the other side of the glass. It hung in the trees as a semi-frozen mist, frosting over the tips of the limbs and collecting on the grass. Chunks of ice cascaded down the gurgling brooks that crisscrossed beneath the county road, and what leaves remained in the trees were stiff with the sub-freezing temperatures. The brunt of impending winter was hitting North Carolina early, and even the animals had taken shelter. The mountains felt still and silent, almost as though a brooding force lay in the shadows between the trees, waiting and watching, haunting every passerby who defied the claws of the cold.

The two-lane mountain road wound back on itself, weaving its way farther into the mountains. Every ten or fifteen minutes, another vehicle passed him, slipping by on the narrow space between the yellow lines and a hundred-yard cliff, dropping down into the depths of an empty ravine.

Reed left the town of Murphy over an hour before, skirting Hiwassee Lake before working his way through the back roads and into the wilderness. Oliver's cabin headquarters lay deep in the heart of the North Carolina Appalachians, far off the beaten path, where no hunter or hiker would ever stumble across it. Reed discovered the location by accident while reviewing kill contracts almost two years before. It was a secret, and at the time, he didn't mention it to Oliver to avoid his employer's possible wrath. Now the secret carried an entirely new value. With any luck, Oliver would be holed up in his safe house, half-drunk and sitting by the fire when Reed closed in. It was equally possible that Oliver was on the other side of the world, negotiating contracts with Indonesian warlords, but Reed was willing to take the chance that his former employer wouldn't leave the States until the Prosecutor had been put to bed. They had to know he was coming.

Reed turned off the blacktop and onto a back road. Using the GPS, he rechecked his position relative to the cabin: six miles out, separated by two ravines and one river. The river would be the greatest challenge. There was a bridge, sure, but it was an obvious point of weakness for Oliver's defenses. At two miles from the cabin, it was almost certain that the old killer had some surveillance at the bridge.

Reed would have to figure something else out when the time came. He would leave the pickup in the woods, three miles out, wait for the cover of darkness, then approach the cabin from the west. Oliver might not be alone and could have dogs or tripwires crisscrossing between the trees around the cabin. It would be a painfully slow process to make his approach, and Reed was ready to take his time.

The digital thermometer on the dash read twenty-two degrees when Reed cut off the truck fifty yards from the road, buried in the trees. He settled into the seat and waited while the heat slowly vacated the cabin, replaced by an icy temperature that seeped straight through his thick black jacket and into his bones. He rested his head back against the headrest, crossing his arms, and embraced the discomfort. It burned, then it ached. Soon his mind would numb it out, just like it had a thousand times before, and then he'd be ready to conquer the wilderness and beat it into submission.

"*You are God. Everything is subject to your will. The day you stop believing that is the day you die.*"

Oliver's admonition rang in Reed's mind—a distant echo of three years before during his intense training. Fresh out of prison, with nothing to lose and everything to win, Reed followed Oliver into these very mountains. It was winter, snow lay on the ground, and for a Marine fresh out of Iraq, this new ice demon was an unprecedented threat. Here in these mountains, miles away from civilization, Oliver and his goons took Reed to the edge of death, forcing him through a four-month pressure-cooker course designed to remove the humanity from his soul and make him the ultimate killer.

"*I'm going to destroy you. And if by some miracle you prove to be indestructible, I'm going to hire you.*"

Reed guessed that the challenge was meant to be horrific, but it wasn't. He'd already been on death row, so the thought of losing his life here in this frozen wilderness was less than terrifying. It was more annoying than anything because when he accepted Oliver's thirty-kill deal, he was under the impression that he *was* hired. The sudden change of events in North Carolina felt like backtracking, but these mountains hadn't killed him then, and they wouldn't kill him now.

The sun slowly faded over the western horizon, vanishing amid the trees and leaving the forest in a ghostly glow of moonlight and shadow. Reed would have preferred perfect darkness, pierced by the illumination of his night vision goggles, but there was no time to waste defying the clear sky and full moon. He would have to make do with the shadows.

Reed's wristwatch read nine thirty before he slipped out of the truck, shutting the door softly behind him. The ground was frozen, and brittle mud crunched with each footfall. Thin fog drifted down from the tree limbs, further distorting the darkness and making every shadow morph under the shine of the moon. In the distance, an owl hooted. Amid the leaves to the north, a chipmunk scampered through the forest. Or maybe it was a squirrel. The cold that cut through his jacket no longer bothered him; it felt natural to feel this numb, even with the added discomfort of a glacial breeze drifting out of the west.

I dominate this. This cold is mine.

Reed opened the back door of the truck and dug through the bags. His handgun was already strapped beneath the jacket, accompanied by two spare magazines and a Ka-Bar knife. He withdrew his custom-built AR-10 sniper rifle, chambered in .308. It was the same weapon he had wielded from the top of the Equitable Building in Atlanta a few days before. He slipped a twenty-round magazine into the receiver, then dumped two more magazines into the oversized pockets of his jacket. Last, he pulled an oversized backpack on a metal frame from the back seat and secured it to his shoulders. A black baseball cap pulled low over his ears completed his ensemble. There was too much moonlight for his nightvision goggles to be truly effective, and they would respond poorly to muzzle flash. He'd rather just let his eyes adjust and trust his instincts.

Reed looked up at the night sky, searching amid the glistening pinholes until he located the North Star, then he shouldered the rifle and stepped into the trees. The owl began to hoot again, and another nocturnal mammal bounded through the leaves. The terrain, littered with rocks and fallen logs, rose and fell beneath him. His body began to warm as he fought his way up the mountainside, hiking toward the ridgeline. The strain and pressure felt good.

"Fight through. Kill or die. Dominate or be a slave. There is no middle ground, Reed."

The top of the ridge burst into view as the trees parted, and Reed knelt behind a boulder, lifting a pair of binoculars to his eyes. The forest that clung to the next ridge was thick, allowing for very little view of what could be hiding amongst it. The cabin sat on the end of the ridge, right at the top of a fifty-yard cliff, while the river cut through the valley in between. It would be impossible to slip down to the water, find a way across, then scale his way to the cabin without being detected. Certainly, there was a method to Oliver's design.

Reed lowered the binoculars and bit his lip. He could position himself on the top of the next ridge and establish a decent overwatch over the cabin, but at seven hundred yards in the dark with all the trees, it was doubtful he would obtain a clear shot. If he approached the cabin from the south along the long and winding driveway that ran along the ridgetop, he would be discovered before he was within half a mile of the mountaintop hideout.

There was really only one option. He would have to run Oliver out of his hole, and there was no subtle way to do it. It was time to launch the fireworks.

11

The top of the next ridge was covered in a dense thicket of evergreens and scrub brush, providing ideal cover as Reed slipped up to the edge and returned the binoculars to his eyes. Two hundred yards below, down a steep hillside covered in rocks and brush, the river wound its way through the ravine. It was about twenty yards wide and surged through the valley floor in a black tide speckled with ice. The far wall of the ravine shot upward in a slope so steep it was almost a cliff. At the top, nestled on the very end of the ridge right before another drop-off, Reed focused the binoculars on the cabin. It sat under the shade of towering pines, built low to the ground out of thick spruce logs. An awning hung off the back, sheltering a green pickup truck and a large stack of firewood. Smoke rose from the chimney, barely visible against the black sky as it drifted into oblivion.

Reed lowered the binoculars and tapped his index finger against them. He'd never seen the cabin before, but he knew the pickup. There were no bumper stickers, scratches, dents, or identifying marks of any kind. It was just a plain Chevy, but he would've recognized it at five hundred yards anywhere in the world. The vehicle was wider than a regular Chevy of that year and sat one inch closer to the ground. That was because of the thick bulletproof plates built into the body beneath the paneling—the daily driver of a kingpin killer.

The cold faded out of Reed's mind as he unslung the backpack and dug into it. He retrieved his Bushnell rangefinder, clicked it on, set the crosshairs over the cabin, and hit the trigger. Oliver's front door sat 367 yards away, at a comparable elevation to Reed's current position. The next item from the backpack was long and dark, consisting of three metal tubes held together by bungee cords. Reed unstrapped them and clicked each one together, then unfolded a metal bipod and locked the tube into it. The weapon was an M224 60mm mortar, and he was well acquainted with its capabilities. Back in Iraq, he'd spent many long hours using identical mortars to shell ISIL entrenchments, and more than a few times, he'd been forced to take cover himself as captured M224s were redirected back at the Marines.

The mortar was heavy, and the metal felt so cold to the touch it almost burned. His fingers stuck to the controls as he adjusted the bipod, squinting through the iron sights as he aimed the weapon toward the cabin. His breath came in short bursts, and his heart rate accelerated with that familiar rush of excitement. Anticipation.

Reed never remembered regretting a kill. From the moment he pressed the trigger on that first contractor in Iraq, to the execution of Oliver's East European thugs at the garbage dump outside of Atlanta. To him, it was all the same. These men deserved to die, for one reason or another, and he was here to prosecute that justice. But tonight, sitting behind the mortar, staring at Oliver's cabin, things felt different. The excitement was a little stronger than the usual rush of anticipation and nervousness. Reed felt eager. Hungry. This was more than an execution—this was a statement. Oliver had broken his own rules, and Reed was going to prosecute him for it.

He checked the elevation of the bipod once more, then reached into the backpack again, more gingerly this time. In the bottom of the pack, carefully wrapped in thick foam padding, were three

60mm mortars. Two were marked with red paint, and the third in a bright green. All three were smooth and clean and glowed in the soft light of the moon with the promise of imminent death just seconds away.

Wind rippled over the top of the ridge, sending leaves cascading over one another in the stillness. The owl started in again, hooting long and slow, as though he knew what was about to happen, and he was mourning the disturbance of his forest retreat. Reed checked the AR-10 and removed the lens caps off the scope before lifting the weapon. He slipped fifty yards down the ridge, ducking under limbs and between the dense shrubbery before stopping in a tiny clearing between two evergreens. He laid the rifle down between the trees, propped up on a stubby bipod, then checked his view of the cabin.

It was perfect. Oliver couldn't possibly escape without exposing himself to Reed's field of fire. The cabin was ideally defensible in that it was impossible to reach without being detected. But in that same way, it was impossible to escape without being cornered. Oliver must have known that. He must have bet on the secrecy of his forest home more than its impregnability.

That's a bet you'll regret for eternity, old man.

Reed left the rifle and retreated back to the mortar, then settled down behind it and lifted the first red shell. It would take a few seconds for the high-explosive round to arc through the air and make contact with the cabin's roof. Within that time, Reed could launch the second shell. The third and final shot would be in the air at the moment the second one detonated. After that, he'd have to run like hell. If Oliver had any unseen defenses in place outside his cabin, Reed's position would be exposed and wide open to them by the time the third round left the tube. His best and only bet would be to move like greased lightning.

Reed set the first shell in the top of the tube, holding it for a moment and feeling its weight and gravity under his fingers. Looking back at the cabin where it lay in silence and stillness, alone at the end of that ridge, it was so quiet and peaceful—a happy place under different circumstances—the kind of place you never wanted to leave.

But not tonight.

Go to hell, old man.

Reed released the shell at the same moment the phone buzzed in his pocket. He jerked his hand back from the tube and lifted the second shell. The first launched with a resounding *whoomp,* flashing through the darkness like a giant spit wad. The second shell launched as the first crashed through the trees and landed on top of the awning. It detonated with a blast so strong the trees over Reed's head swayed, sending dry leaves and dead pine needles showering over his back. The second shell detonated, again sending fire and fury ripping through the log walls as pieces of the pickup truck and shards of shingles rained into the ravine. Reed dropped the final shell into the tube, then dashed for the rifle.

Every part of his body pounded. Foliage exploded in a shower around him as he landed behind the rifle, lifting it and pressing his eye against the scope. The third and final shell landed outside the cabin in a blinding flash of white, sending burning phosphorous showering across the ridgetop and lighting up the area around the cabin as bright as day. The fire burned on, leaving Reed's field of view fully illuminated and at the mercy of his rifle.

The crosshairs of the optic swept over the cabin, first to the rear, then back to the front. The roof of the cabin was blown off, and one wall caved in, now ablaze as greedy flames licked up the dry timber. In moments, the cabin would flood with smoke, and anyone left inside would be forced to flee. The truck also burned, filling the sky with a column of dark black smoke that rose a hundred yards before it began to dissipate. Everything was chaos—the ruined wreckage of two high-explosive rounds and one illumination shell.

Reed flipped off the safety and rested his finger against the trigger while checking the surroundings for any sign of Oliver attempting to flee via a hidden tunnel or a rappelling rope down the cliff. There was nothing but the crackle of the flames and the whistle of the wind as the hideout of the old killer descended into flames. Once more, he swept the crosshairs over the burning wreckage, pausing over every shadow, every possible shelter. There was nothing.

Reed pivoted the scope over the forest, through the flames, and between the trees. Each inhale whistled between his teeth as fresh adrenaline pumped into his blood.

"You son of a bitch. Where are you?"

One more pass of the rifle. The scope was filled with the golden flames and the smog of smoke, reminding him of ancient Catholic paintings of Hell. Everywhere the chaos reigned, but there was no sight of humanity—nobody fleeing the smoke and running for their life into the trees.

The glint of steel caught his eye first: a white flash that reflected the moonlight and contrasted with the blazing orange all around it. He refocused the optic on the spot nestled a hundred feet from the cabin amid the trees. Bushes and shrubs clouded his view, obscuring everything but that hint of steely glow. And then there was a twitch of movement, barely noticeable, but enough to cast a shadow and reveal the full silhouette of the shape.

Oh, shit.

Fire blazed from the trees, filling the scope and blinding him a split second before a whining roar burst across the ravine. Bullets ripped through the trees all around him, shredding limbs and downing saplings in mere seconds. Dirt, rock, and forest debris exploded and rained down on all sides, fogging his vision as the minigun on the opposing ridge continued to rain fire and brimstone on his position.

Reed snatched up his rifle and broke into a run down the ridge, away from the mortar. He ripped his way through the trees and brush, clawing dirt and grime from his face. The ground quaked as small trees toppled down behind him and broken rocks rained down like hail. And still, the gun didn't stop. Hundreds of .30 caliber slugs tore into the ridgetop as the electric gun continued to thunder. Reed's mind began to tunnel on the path ahead, and each step further disoriented his focus.

One thought rang clearly through his panicked mind: *Run like hell.*

A bullet struck the ground inches from his foot, and another sent an explosion of pine bark shooting into his chest like the blast of a shotgun. A limb fell from overhead and struck him in the face. Reed stumbled and almost fell, then burst through a row of evergreens.

By the time he saw the drop-off, there was no prayer of stopping. His left foot gave way first, flying out from under him as he lost hold of the rifle and grabbed at the trees. Sticky green evergreen needles were stripped from the tree as Reed dangled in midair at the edge of the drop-off. Fresh gunfire shredded the evergreens in front of him, and then he fell over the edge and into the darkness below.

12

With perfect clarity, Reed remembered he hadn't purchased rental insurance on the pickup truck.

What a stupid decision.

Then he saw blackness again as he toppled over, free-falling into darkness. For a moment, he couldn't tell if he'd stepped off a cliff or simply overstepped onto a steep slope. The question was answered a second later as his ass collided with the muddy side of a hill. It was steep and wet, leaving nothing for him to grab onto as he rocketed downward. Rocks and sticks tore at his legs and back, and the shadowy silhouettes of trees flashed by on either side. He clawed at thin air, saw the moon, and then he felt the ground vanish beneath him as he left the end of the slope like the end of a water slide and shot into open air.

This time it *was* a cliff, with tall evergreens growing directly beneath him. Reed fell five feet before the first limb struck him in the middle of his lower back. Leaves and branches surrounded him as he crashed through the tops of trees, frantically attempting to grab anything to stop his fall. The blast of the minigun was distant now, drowned out by the pounding of blood in his head. Something tore through his jacket and scraped his ribcage, then a larger limb struck him right in the stomach. The air rushed from his lungs as he clawed at the branch, fighting to hold on. His legs fell, and the limb slipped out of his hands as he went crashing toward the ground until his back collided with the frozen earth.

The wind was ripped from his lungs again, and the sky spun. Reed was vaguely aware of something hot and sticky seeping from his torn jacket. The fear of moments before faded into a blur, along with the vague realization that this was his fault. He had walked straight into a trap.

The minigun stopped firing, and he thought he heard an engine roar to life—a truck, maybe, or an all-terrain vehicle. Tires spun far away, but the sound carried across the empty ravine as clear as though it were right next to his skull.

Reed moved his legs, twisting one at a time to check for functionality. Pain shot through his body, but his legs still worked. Nothing was busted. He grabbed a tree and fought to pull himself into a sitting position, clenching his teeth to fight back a scream. He could feel the tear in his side now, and when he placed his hand over it, fresh blood oozed between his fingers, sticking to his skin. Bits of dirt and sappy needles clung to his jacket and pants, and the dirt further blurred his disoriented vision.

I have to move. He saw me fall.

Reed's legs were stiff as he forced himself to a standing position. Nausea and dizziness racked his brain, but now that he could stand, he managed to focus on a tangible thought to clear his mind.

I'm alive. By some miracle, I'm alive.

He dug out a small LED flashlight from his pocket. It clicked on, but he didn't hear the sound through his ringing ears. One foot forward, then another. The dry leaves rattled against his boots and crunched against the earth. His head still pounded, but thoughts came more clearly now.

My rifle. I need my rifle.

Reed stumbled back toward the base of the cliff and swept the flashlight through the brush. Broken limbs and felled saplings lay everywhere, victims of both his fall and the raking fire of the minigun. He fought his way through the mess and kicked up showers of leaves, but he couldn't see the rifle anywhere. He redirected the light up the thirty-foot cliff to the steep slope above, all the way back up to the top of the ridge.

Damn.

From the moment he'd stepped into thin air Reed had descended almost two-hundred feet, most of it a reckless slide down the muddy slope. He could see his trail between the trees, only narrowly missing mortal collisions with trunks on several occasions.

If the slope had been a cliff, he would be dead now. Hell, if the evergreens at the end of this hellish mudslide hadn't been there and he had free-fallen the last thirty feet, he'd probably be dead. Or have a broken back.

Instead, he was bruised and battered with a few cuts, but nothing fatal.

That's more luck than I can count on.

A thud rang out from behind, jarring Reed from his wonderment. The sound was followed by the roar of an engine. Reed switched the light off and turned back toward the first ridge he had crossed. It was too dark to see, but in the distance, the roar of the motor grew louder, followed by the flash of headlights a hundred yards out, crashing across the forest floor like a tank. He couldn't tell if it was a Jeep or a semitruck, but either way, it was almost on top of him.

Reed broke into a run back through the trees, rushing amid the brush and limbs, away from the ridges, and into the open valley ahead. The river churned on his right, rippling over rocks and gurgling amid the roar of the engine. A gunshot rang out, and the bullet tore through the evergreens, sending yet another shower of sticky needles raining down. Reed dug under his jacket and pried the Glock free, then fired twice. He heard glass shatter, but the engine still roared, almost on his heels. Blood streamed down his side, soaking his jacket and seeping into his pants.

I've got to shake this prick.

Another ten yards of crashing through the brush and a row of giant fir trees loomed up ahead, five yards from the river's edge. Reed dove behind them, rolling to the ground and clawing his way beneath their thick foliage. For the first time, he turned back and peered through the brush at the oncoming vehicle. It was tall, with lights blazing, and big, meaty tires crushing everything in front of it. Definitely not Oliver. The old man had never been one to be this brash or loud. Oliver was more surgical, like Reed. Whoever the hell was driving this thing had no concern for subtlety or discretion. He was here to crush and nothing more.

The Jeep slid to a stop fifty yards away, the big motor rumbling as the dust began to settle around the tires. Reed couldn't see the man inside, but he could see the weapon mounted on the rear bumper of the vehicle. It was the minigun, still piping hot and smoking from the assault of ten minutes before.

He won't leave the Jeep. He can't. Somebody heard the mortars. Cops will be here in another half hour, and he can't afford to be found.

Reed slid the handgun out of his jacket and rested it against the forest floor. The night sights radiated neon green as he aligned the gun with the front tire of the Jeep. A vehicle this big and robust wouldn't be stopped by a single flat tire. It might still limp on, crashing after him, but with two tires down, the party stopped there.

The Glock popped, recoiling in his hand and spitting a 9mm slug fifty yards across the valley floor and directly into the heavy rubber of the tire. The second shot came a moment behind the first. Air hissed from both tires as the engine rumbled, and the driver turned toward the evergreens. Reed jumped up and dashed to the left moments before the front bumper of the vehicle, with two tires flopping against their wheels, hurtled through the fir trees.

By the time the driver realized his mistake, it was much too late to stop. The brakes screamed, but the Jeep hurtled onward, past the trees, across the bank, and nose-first into the river. Water splashed, drowning out the powerful headlights and sending a cascade down over the bank. Reed didn't wait to see what happened next. He turned back through the trees and broke into a run, shielding his face from the whipping branches as he melted into the darkness. In the distance, he heard what he thought sounded like police sirens, but his ears still rang from the explosions and machine-gun fire of the last half hour. Either way, he wasn't waiting to find out what it was.

His lungs and muscles burned, but the running felt good. With each powerful stride, fresh energy and renewed focus filled his mind. He could hear the sirens for sure now, coming from the south, rising and falling as the police drew closer. Another few minutes, and they would be at the cabin.

Reed stopped at the base of the cliff and peered upward, back to the place he had fallen from minutes before—a full hundred feet up a sheer wall of mud and rock. There was no way he could fight his way back to the top, and even if he somehow managed the impossible, the police would quickly blanket the woods before he could sneak the three miles back to the pickup.

He turned to the west and resumed jogging through the forest. His muscles ached and his right side burned like hell, but he blocked it all out, pounding onward. Miles passed under his boots before he broke out of the trees and onto a narrow gravel road that he remembered from studying maps of Oliver's cabin area. There was a hunting camp another few miles away, and with luck, there would be a vehicle he could hot-wire and use to get back on the road.

All of his gear was back in the truck. After the police cleared out, he would return to recover his weapons and work on a new plan. For now, he needed to get as far away from the mad killer as possible and figure out where the hell Oliver disappeared to.

13

Western North Carolina

Reed drove north out of Cherokee and into Graham County. The sun broke over the horizon, draping the rural mountain roads in a warm glow that reflected off the frosty tree limbs. In the tiny town of Robbinsville, the old truck squeaked like a rusty tractor as it rolled to a stop. It was a Ford, maybe a mid-seventies model, with rotten floorboards and a cracked windshield. A few years' worth of mud and grime clung to the body panels, covering the faded bumper stickers and empty soda bottles. The power steering was gone, and the alignment was way out, making it a constant battle to keep the battered vehicle on the road. But the truck ran, and at this point, that was all he could ask for.

Still better than walking.

At a gas station, the engine died as Reed pulled the ignition wires apart. His head ached. His body ached. The muscles in his toes ached. The injuries from the chaos in Atlanta were far from healed, and the bitter wind that swept through the open floorboard of the truck served to numb the skin and make every part of him stiffen. Add to that the injuries and battering of the night before, and he felt about as worn and creaky as his ride.

He dug through his pockets and found the bottle of heavy-duty pain killers that Kelly left him. The pills tasted bitter as they rolled over his tongue, and he swallowed them dry. He was reluctant to dull his mind with an opioid, but at this stage, the surging pain was a greater threat to his focus.

In a few moments, he took a mental inventory of what gear he had left on his person. It wasn't much—most of his essential equipment had been in the backpack, and everything else was in the truck. The only things he had on him were a knife, the Glock, a few magazines, a flashlight, a fake South Carolina driver's license, sixty bucks, a lighter, and half a dozen cigarettes—hardly the stuff of a war-ready killer. Not even any communication.

Wait.

Reed suddenly remembered his phone in the interior pocket of his jacket. The phone had vibrated right before he launched the first mortar, but at the time, he hadn't given it a second thought. Now the reality rang clear in his tired mind: His phone vibrated only for a few critical contacts.

When he unlocked it, the first notification he got was for a low battery. He dismissed the warning and navigated to the single text message. It was from Oliver.

Nice try Reed. Enjoy The Wolf.

Reed cursed and slammed his hand into the steering wheel. He started to reply to the message, but the phone's screen went black, and the *"charge battery"* symbol flashed.

Shit!

Reed had been a fool to assault the cabin so brashly. It was a rookie move—the kind that belonged in open warfare, not the art of assassination. He wasn't even sure whether Oliver was in the cabin at all, yet he had shelled that place and lit it up like a damn fireworks show.

I didn't care if he was there. I wanted to make a statement. I wanted to shit on his porch the way he shit on mine. Such a fool.

He drummed his finger on the wheel and stared out the window.

Who is The Wolf? The man in the Jeep?

Reed had never heard of a killer named *The Wolf*. All of Oliver's contractors had nicknames or call signs. Reed's was *Prosecutor,* and he knew every other killer by theirs. The Wolf wasn't on the list. It had to be somebody external to the company. Somebody willing to kill another contractor.

The next thought that rang through his tired mind was more chilling: *Oliver wouldn't hire somebody outside of his own company.* It was contrary to the old man's standards of operation. He didn't trust people he didn't control, and even though Oliver would be reluctant to set one of his own killers against a fellow contractor, it might be better than letting loose a rampaging madman with a minigun.

But Oliver *had* unleashed a madman with a minigun, which could only mean one of two things: Either Oliver had lost his mind, or he was no longer calling the shots. Reed remembered the contract for Mitchell Holiday, a state senator for Georgia he had been hired to kill right before Oliver turned on him. Who wanted Holiday dead? It was a question he had never been able to answer, and now it seemed more pivotal to this entire mess than ever. Somebody bigger than Oliver wanted Holiday dead, and now they wanted Reed dead.

Reed closed his eyes and thought back to his last encounter with Oliver—at Pratt Pullman Yard, in east Atlanta. It was there that Oliver admitted to his dastardly scheme to send Reed back to prison, there to be murdered in his sleep, removing him from Oliver's list of outstanding liabilities and loose ends. But Oliver wasn't the one who ordered the Holiday hit. No, Oliver had said the job was legitimate, ordered by the men Salvador worked for.

Salvador. The shady South American who had stood beside Oliver at Pratt Pullman. It was Salvador who hired the goons that Reed killed in Atlanta. Salvador who kidnapped Banks, and represented the interests of the people who wanted Holiday dead.

Salvador, not Oliver, was the link to these people—these people who would stop at nothing to destroy Holiday, and now Reed.

And I don't know who they are. That thought was the most terrifying of all. Reed could take on a battalion of Army Rangers if he had to, as long as he knew more about them than they knew about him. Information was his greatest asset, and right now, he had none.

Reed shook his head to clear it.

Time to get moving. This prick will be back.

He dug through the glove box, dumping the contents onto the passenger seat. There was a vehicle registration, a box of replacement fuses, and a folded map of the tristate area. Nothing else.

He pocketed the map, then slammed the box shut and stepped out of the truck, kicking the mud off his boots as he went. He glanced around the small service station and noticed a couple locals watching him from adjacent pumps. He wasn't sure if it was his angry body language or the rattletrap truck that was drawing more attention.

The clerk inside the store appeared much less inquisitive. He stared through the window with a dazed look, as though his mind were a thousand miles away in another universe. Reed picked up a bottle of water and walked to the counter, dropping a twenty-dollar bill onto it.

"Ten on three. And can I get some quarters?"

The attendant accepted the money and handed Reed his change. Reed cracked the water bottle open and took a swig as he walked back to the truck. He put ten dollars into the almost empty tank, then drove across the street to a Dollar General. A narrow metal roof sheltered a payphone next to the store. He dropped two quarters in, then dialed the phone.

"Lasquo Financial. How may I direct your call?"

Lasquo financial was the banking headquarters for the criminal underworld. Reed held most of his assets and loose cash with them and enjoyed the luxury of conducting business anywhere in the world with a quick phone call. After repeating his memorized series of coded phrases, he asked for Thomas Lancaster. The phone went silent for a moment, then the familiar New Orleans drawl of Reed's personal banker rang over the phone.

"Reed, good to hear from you. What can I do for you?"

"I need you to send me a couple grand by Western Union to the Dollar General in Robbinsville, North Carolina."

"Right away. Anything else?"

"No, that's everything. Thank you."

Reed hung up and dropped two more quarters into the phone. It rang twice.

"Winter."

If Lasquo was the criminal world's banking institution, Winter was its eye in the sky. A nameless, genderless, faceless entity on the other side of the phone who answered questions that needed to be answered, found people who needed to be found and dealt with information as a commodity. Reed had called Winter before when things went south in Atlanta, and Winter had been uncharacteristically unhelpful. This time, Reed wouldn't take silence for an answer.

"No bullshit, Winter. Where is Oliver?"

The phone was silent.

Reed wrapped his fingers around the metal roof over the phone. His knuckles turned white. "I know you know. You've been in on this shit from the start. Now you better start talking or—"

"You would be prudent not to threaten me, Reed." It was the first time Reed had ever heard emotion from the ghost on the other end of the line. "I'm not your ally. Don't make me your enemy."

Reed slammed his fist into the wall of the store but didn't snap back. "All right. Fine. So, I'm going to ask you some questions, and you're going to find the answers. That's what you do, right?"

"That depends on the question."

"How about this? Who ordered the hit on Mitch Holiday?"

The phone was silent. Reed gritted his teeth again and waited. Finally, Winter answered. The voice was soft, and Reed almost thought he heard fear in the tone.

"I don't know."

"*What?*"

"I launched an inquiry. My sources are . . . unhelpful."

"Okay, so where's Oliver?"

"I don't know."

Reed shook his head. "No, that's not how you work. You always know, remember? Now I just burned Oliver's cabin to the ground, and he's not there."

"Good for you." Winter sounded almost sarcastic. "I don't know where he is."

"Okay, then tell me something you *do know*."

"I know that if I were you, I'd stop asking questions and get lost while I still had the chance. I've been around for a long time, Reed. Long enough to know when something smells like death."

"That's not good enough!" Reed snapped. He waited, but the phone didn't cut off. Reed relaxed his clenched fist. "Just point me in the right direction. I've always taken care of you. You know I'm the real deal. Cut me some slack, and I'll cut you loose."

Winter's methodical breathing hissed over the phone, and Reed waited patiently against the phone booth.

"I know somebody is behind this," he said. "Somebody bigger than Oliver."

"Yes."

"They want me dead. They want Mitch Holiday dead."

"They do."

"So, who are they?"

Now Reed couldn't even hear Winter's breaths.

"Watch your back, Reed. Don't call me again." The line went dead.

Reed cursed and slammed the handset back onto the receiver. He spat on the sidewalk and walked inside the Dollar General, where the Western Union wire waited for him. Two grand, sent from a shell company out of Arkansas. Reed accepted the cash, then walked back to the truck and got in, rubbing the folded bills between his fingers as he watched the passing traffic.

There's a bounty on my head. This Wolf guy was hired especially for me.

Without knowing who was after him, there was little Reed could do besides run and be reactionary. He didn't know this man, and he didn't know his tactics, although it was obvious he had a flair for the dramatic. That was certainly outside the realm of Oliver's contractors, who would always prefer a knife to the throat over a minigun mounted on a Jeep. The Wolf was different. He was brash. Unpredictable.

Reed tapped his finger on his knee and looked up the highway. The temperature had dropped another few degrees. An occasional snowflake drifted past the cab, landing on the ground and fading into the concrete. Even though it was hardly midmorning, there was already a small crowd of bustling locals moving in and out of the gas station and the local diner. It was fifty miles back to Oliver's cabin—plenty of space to buy Reed a little time before he could expect The Wolf to come sniffing around.

He rubbed the exhaustion out of his eyes and started the truck. Half a mile down the road, he found a small grocery store with an empty lot behind it. He parked the truck next to a dumpster and double-checked to make sure the doors were locked, and then he lay across the bench seat. He would sleep for a couple hours, refresh his mind, and reset his battered body. Then he would regroup and resume his hunt for the kingpin killer.

Reed's eyes snapped open as though prompted by a gunshot. Even before he sat up, he knew he had slept much longer than he intended. A glance at his watch confirmed what he already feared: It was four p.m.

Shit.

It was the drugs. It had to be. He never slept that hard, especially under these circumstances. Sitting up, Reed blinked back the fog of sleep and scooped up the bottle from the convenience store.

The icy water cooled his dry throat, and he drained it before taking a quick glance around the pickup. From his position next to the dumpster, Reed could see half of the main intersection, along with a good portion of the grocery store's parking lot. A couple women walked next to each other toward the store, while a single man in a blue jacket hurried toward his car with a bag of groceries. The sky, once bright with sunlight, was now blanketed by dark grey clouds, and flecks of snow drifted through the air and landed on the hood of the truck. Reed couldn't tell for sure, but the wind that whispered through the cracks in the floorboard felt colder than before. The temperature was still dropping.

He reached for his phone then remembered that it was dead. That left him with nothing but a handful of quarters and a single payphone, but there wasn't really anyone to call. Without Winter, finding Oliver would be next to impossible. He hoped to get lucky back at the cabin, but that turned out to be a trap from the start. Oliver must have anticipated his arrival. He probably wasn't even in the country.

Reed's thoughts were broken off by the sight of a silver Mercedes with jet-black windows—definitely a coupe, but as big as a sedan, not more than a year old, with gleaming trim and wide black tires. It rolled gracefully down the street, well under the speed limit, sticking out like a sore thumb amid the battered SUVs and rusted pickups.

Nobody in a town like this drove a car like that. Reed sank back in the seat and laid his hand on the Glock. The pickup was fully exposed to the view of the Mercedes, and Reed felt suddenly vulnerable and wanted to jump out, but he sank deeper into the seat and waited.

The Mercedes rolled up to the intersection, thirty yards down the street. It stopped at the sign, its nose pointed directly at the side of the pickup. A cloud of grey vapor built behind the rear bumper, rising toward the sky as the car idled. Reed could see the man behind the wheel now. He was trim and fit, clean-shaven, with short black hair, sitting with one hand on the wheel at the twelve o'clock position, and the other out of sight beneath the dash. In the dying light, Reed could make out the veins in his neck, bulging and contracting with each breath. The quiet, collected calm of his features mixed with his narrow, darting eyes.

It was The Wolf. Reed knew it without ever having seen him before. The cold in his eyes, and hard lines of his face told the story better than Winter ever could.

The reality hit him just as the black eyes twitched to the right and locked with his. For a moment, the man in the Mercedes stared at him without blinking, and then a tight smirk spread across his lips.

Reed's hands darted to the ignition wires. The sharp copper dug into his fingers as he separated the red from the black, the blue from the yellow. The bite of wire in trembling skin hadn't changed over the past ten years since he hotwired his first car back in Orange County. He remembered the sweat that puddled in his palms as he fought with each wire, trying to ignore the frantic badgering of his stressed-out accomplice from Oakland. Even months later, after dozens of stolen cars, his fingers still shook. Over time, the tremors that ran down his arms felt less like fear and more like excitement.

But not now. Now those tremors felt like nerves that might well cost him his life.

Reed rubbed two exposed copper tips against each other, and a loud click rang out from beneath the floorboard, but the motor didn't turn. A fresh shiver racked his arms, and he fumbled to pick up a dropped wire, then pressed them together again—another click, and then silence.

Run.

The big motor of the Mercedes rumbled from the intersection. Reed kicked the door open and flung himself out, making a quick dash for the shelter of the alley behind the grocery store. He remembered the night before—the thunder of the minigun as brush and trees crashed to the earth—fire, hot lead, and total chaos. This man was insane, whoever he was. A complete maniac.

Allowing a repeat of that performance in the tight confines of this small town would result in a bloodbath of innocent civilians, and Reed couldn't live with that. He imagined the avalanche of bullets blasting holes through the Wendy's across the street or tearing through the Family Dollar straight ahead. He wouldn't allow The Wolf to go to war in this place. Reed would lose him first, then find his way outside of Robbinsville to a more isolated locale—someplace he could ambush and kill this rabid dog without needless death.

Reed jogged across the street, leaving the shelter of the alley and huddling close to the front wall of the Family Dollar. Locals bustled back and forth between SUVs and minivans, their shoes knocking against the frozen pavement. He felt the comforting hard plastic of the Glock beneath his jacket and tossed another glance around the parking lot for the Mercedes. It was nowhere in sight.

Come on, you bastard. Take it out of town.

Drops of sleet flashed past his face. Somebody honked, and a child cried. Reed ducked behind a pickup truck and turned away from the store. A mother herded her screaming toddler toward her Honda and shot Reed a suspicious glare as he stumbled past her, his gaze still sweeping the streets.

He started back toward the main road, and then he saw it. Black on silver, purring down the street only fifty yards away, with the giant Mercedes logo glowing in the middle of the front grill. A split-second passed, then the Mercedes coughed, and the back tires spun. Reed stepped away from the mother and child and wrapped his fingers around the pistol.

"Chris?"

14

The voice sent a shockwave ripping through Reed's body. He twisted on his heel, back toward the store. She stood outside the Family Dollar, bundled in a thick red jacket with a snow-white knit cap pulled down low over her golden hair. Her cheeks were rosy red in the bite of the wind, and her eyes, once as bright blue as the Gulf of Mexico, were now frozen sapphires, shining just as bright and beautiful.

Banks.

Reed's mind shut down, and the world around him ceased to exist as he stared at her. The curve of her body beneath the jacket. Her delicate fingers curled around a plastic shopping bag loaded with groceries. She was as perfect as the first moment he met her, and in a flash, his mind was ripped back to Atlanta. Back to the hospital hallway where he looked her in the eyes and said goodbye. The hardest thing he'd ever done. Walking away from a woman he cared for—cared for so deeply he didn't believe it could be real.

Her eyes broke right through his carefully orchestrated detachment and sank into his soul. In an instant, all the confused emotions of the past few days returned—the longing, self-doubt, obsessive affection. It took all the willpower he'd ever mustered to walk away from her three days before in that hospital. And here she was, in the middle of this isolated little town, with a killer just around the corner.

"Chris . . . what are you doing here?"

The words had barely left her lips before Reed heard the snarl of the Mercedes, now only yards away. The car was rocketing through the intersection and roaring toward them. There could be no mistake now. The driver was here for him.

"Get down!" Reed lunged forward and grabbed Banks, pulling her with him behind the nearest SUV. A second later, gunshots rang out across the parking lot. Reed recognized the chattering snarl immediately—rapid shots stacked on top of each other in a constant spray of lead. It was an Uzi—short-barreled, nine-millimeter. Not the glovebox gun of your average North Carolina redneck.

More gunfire roared from across the parking lot, and glass shattered from the rear of the SUV, pelting down over their heads in tiny black cubes. Reed pulled Banks lower and jerked the pistol from beneath his jacket. Twisting around the end of the SUV, he pointed it in the general direction of the Mercedes and fired twice. Another blast from the open window of the coupe sent a storm of bullets slamming into the rear hatch of the SUV and skipping against the ground.

Reed's infuriation grew with every twisting ache in his stomach. He grabbed Banks by the arm and jerked his head toward the far end of the parking lot. "Get up! Run!"

Banks's shoulders trembled, but she shook her head. "No! This way. I've got my car!"

Before Reed could stop her, Banks jumped to her feet and ran around the front of the SUV. He scrambled to follow her, weaving between the parked vehicles as the Mercedes roared again. Banks's bright yellow Super Beetle was hidden between two pickup trucks at the back of the lot, a dusting of snow building on its roof. Banks stood by the door, fumbling with her keys, when they slipped out of her hands and hit the concrete. She cursed and picked them up, dropping the groceries.

Reed snatched the keys from her hand and jerked the door open. "Climb in!"

"My snacks!" Banks objected.

"*Leave them*. Get in!"

He shoved Banks through the door and piled in after her, smacking his head against the low roofline of the car. He shoved the keys into the ignition and pressed the clutch against the floor, remembering the last time he and Banks had taken a drive in the vintage German car. The Beetle hadn't started; he prayed this time it would.

The motor turned over with a low whine, then coughed to life. Reed's knees were crowded against the dashboard, spread out on either side of the steering wheel, with barely an inch to spare. The Mercedes snarled from someplace behind, and he slammed the Beetle into first gear before planting his foot into the accelerator.

The rear tires of the little car squealed and spun on the frozen pavement. Reed swung the wheel to the right, and the Beetle shot forward, sliding between parked pickup trucks and into the parking lot. Another string of automatic gunfire ripped between the trucks, and bullets smacked the rear hatch of the Beetle, shattering the back glass.

Banks screamed, "Oscar!"

Reed jerked the wheel back to the left and turned the car toward the street. Lost behind them, the Mercedes was caught amid the tangle of bigger vehicles, and the mountain walls echoed with the clatter of the Uzi and the desperate whine of the undersized Volkswagen engine. Reed shifted into second gear and launched the Beetle onto the street. The front windshield was all but obscured by frost and fog, and Reed squinted through it, shifting into third gear as the speedometer passed forty miles per hour.

"Clear the windshield! I can't see!"

Banks leaned forward, jerking her hat off and pawing at the glass. Her hair exploded in a cloud of static, obscuring his vision as he fought to see through the fog. She sat back, leaving a cleaned section of windshield about the size of a dinner plate.

"Dog!" Banks shouted.

Reed jerked the wheel to the left just in time to miss a Labrador standing in the middle of his lane. Houses flashed past, and he swerved back to the right as a school bus blasted by them, blaring its horn. Small stores and restaurants rocketed by on both sides.

A street sign read State Hwy 129. Reed looked into the diminutive rearview mirror and caught sight of the Mercedes a couple hundred yards behind. Gears shrieked and groaned as Reed shifted into fourth and pressed the gas pedal to the floor. The motor strained, and the speedometer bounced at the sixty-five mark.

"Doesn't this thing go any faster?"

"He's old!" Banks shouted. "Don't yell at him!"

Reed swung the little car into a wide turn and downshifted. The tachometer rocketed up to the red line, and the motor whined like it was about to explode. Above it all, Reed heard the thunder of the big Mercedes, and the silver sedan closed the ground behind them in mere seconds. He could see the silhouette of the driver now: tall, lean, staring straight ahead with that same smirk plastered to his lips.

"Get down!"

Reed grabbed Banks by the neck and shoved her forward. He saw the muzzle of the Uzi pass through the open window of the Mercedes, and orange fire blazed through the twilight. Bullets zipped toward the Beetle and crashed through the thin metal. The windshield shattered as Reed jerked the car to the left into the oncoming lane. The Mercedes followed behind him, and Reed pulled back to the right. Once more, the big coupe swerved to follow. More gunshots rattled in his ear, and the rearview mirror affixed to the driver's door exploded and vanished as 9mm slugs tore into it. Reed slammed the Beetle back into fourth gear and jammed his leg so hard into the accelerator he thought he might punch straight through the floorboard. The car strained and gained a couple miles per hour, but it wasn't enough. He would never outrun a modern performance car. The killer behind him in the coupe would shoot him or run him off the road long before Reed could hope to lose him.

Banks spat hair out of her mouth and sat up, looking through the shattered rear glass. "Gun!" she shouted, and grabbed the wheel, jerking it to the left.

The Beetle swung back into the oncoming lane just as another burst of automatic gunfire shredded the air behind them. The driver of a pickup truck twenty yards ahead laid on its horn. Reed shoved Banks away from the wheel and pulled back to the right, swerving out of the way of the oncoming truck with milliseconds to spare.

"Chris!" Banks screamed. "What the *hell* is going on?"

Reed's mind raced, and he looked out the window to the right. A steep hill rose directly from the shoulder of the lane, with metal mesh staked into the frozen dirt to keep falling rocks off the road. To his left, the hillside dropped off into a short cliff, followed by another narrow ledge. Straight ahead, the highway continued, weaving its way into the mountains and toward Tennessee. A single sign protruded from the frozen earth:

DEALS GAP MOTORCYCLE RESORT — 1 MILE.

Reed had been there before. The previous summer, with his Camaro. He drove his car into these mountains as part of a charity cruise, just past the motorcycle resort, right on the state line.

"Buckle in!" he shouted, then swerved to the left as another string of gunfire roared from behind.

The Beetle topped a slight rise in the road, and Reed swerved into the left lane before stomping on the brakes. The little car's tires screamed on the pavement, and the Beetle slid twenty yards down the far side of the hill. The Mercedes flashed past on his right and continued down the hill before the driver could apply the brakes.

Reed planted his foot into the gas pedal again and continued down the hill a hundred yards before turning sharply to the left at an intersection. The new road was two lanes wide, with wide yellow stripes down the middle. Reed heard the Mercedes roaring back up the hill behind him as he worked his way through the gears. The Beetle groaned and squeaked at every bump, and what was left of the windshield was covered in frost, but Reed could now see through the shattered hole in the middle.

Banks clicked her seatbelt into place and watched through the rear glass, her eyes wide with fear. "He's coming, Chris. He's coming back."

Reed looked into the rearview mirror once, then ahead. The road curved to the right, then back to the left, and another intersection flashed by. The motorcycle resort sat between the trees where two roads intersected, and fifty yards past the resort, a yellow sign mounted on a metal pole stood beside the road.

WARNING: TAIL OF THE DRAGON PASS. 318 CURVES NEXT 11 MILES.

Memories from the previous summer came rushing back. Hairpin turns wrapping around empty drop-offs, often without so much as a guardrail for protection. Car clubs from all across America traveled annually to ride the famous Tail, testing their curving performance against one of the most challenging natural tracks on the East Coast. But that was during the summer—never during the winter. Never with ice on the road. The pile of scrapped cars was high enough when the pavement was hot and sticky—racing the Tail during the winter was a death wish.

Reed shifted into fourth and pressed the pedal to the floor. Just this once, daring the Tail in winter seemed the safer option.

Banks saw the sign and then shook her head as she reached for the steering wheel. "No, no, Chris! What are you doing?"

"I can't outrun him," Reed shouted over the roar of the wind. "I'm gonna have to out-drive him."

The first turn snapped back to the left out of nowhere, completing almost 180 degrees as the road dove downward. Reed relaxed on the gas and pulled the parking brake. The rear wheels locked and screamed, and the tail of the car pivoted outward as a rock wall passed directly in front of them. Banks screamed. The car rolled to the right. Reed slammed his shoulder into the door, shifting his weight back to the left as he released the brake and stomped on the gas again. The car swung out of the turn with another screech of tires, and Reed spun the wheel to the right just in time to slide into the next curve. In the rearview mirror, he caught sight of the Mercedes laying on its brakes. The bigger car slid and fishtailed as the driver struggled to reduce his speed without flying off the road. The distance between The Wolf and his prey was increasing as Reed powered into the next curve.

The Beetle was no drift car. It had barely enough power to break each slide, and the suspension was too loose and too high to control the body roll. With every turn, the car swung wildly to the outside of the curve, and he imagined the wheels lifting off the ground. The only saving grace were relatively new tires that gripped the pavement well enough to overcome some of the loose suspension.

"Grab the dash!" Reed shouted. "When I say, lean toward me."

He downshifted and dumped the clutch. The motor howled as though it were about to burst. Reed planted his foot against the brake and swung the wheel to the right as the next hairpin curve enveloped them.

"Now!"

Banks leaned against him, and Reed pressed his weight against the left window as the car slid around another curve. The rear bumper swung out, and this time Reed was certain the driver's side wheels left the ground. The car tipped and hopped, and Reed slung his weight into the door. The tires hit the ground again, and the stench of burnt rubber filled the cabin. A blast of bitter wind ripped through the shattered rear glass, and Reed couldn't help but feel a bolt of lightning streak through his veins.

This was it. Even here, in a race for his life, this was the thrill that kept him coming back for more. The addiction of too much speed and not enough safety. It was what made him love the

Camaro, love the chase, and love pushing himself to the limit. Because in this moment, The Wolf didn't matter. His confused feelings for Banks were less overwhelming. Only the thin line between himself and certain death held his attention as he danced down it, one hairpin curve after another.

In the rearview mirror, the Mercedes had fallen back a full hundred yards, struggling around a curve in the road. The big car struggled to make the tight turns, and the back tires were sliding off the road, slinging dirt and leaves in a cascade of brown.

Rejuvenated by his inevitable triumph, Reed smacked the steering wheel. "I've got you now, bitch."

"Congratulations!" Banks snapped. "Now, slow the hell down and get us out of here!"

Two more curves flashed past the car, and Reed alternated leaning into his door and leaning toward Banks, keeping the car planted on the pavement. White flecks of snow appeared on the frozen asphalt, sparse at first, but starting to thicken. The sky boiled with grey clouds, and the inside of the car felt like the interior of a deep freezer.

"Chris! Slow down. He's gone now."

Reed couldn't see the Mercedes, but he knew the driver wasn't far behind. He needed to put at least a mile of distance between them before the road ended. That would give him maybe ninety seconds to find a place to hide the Volkswagen and take cover.

Reed relaxed off the gas a little and screeched into another curve. The mountains rose on either side of the road in steep, tree-covered slopes, with the occasional ravine in between. He couldn't see more than fifty yards ahead through the curves. Large flakes glided off the hood of the car and gathered against the base of the windshield, perfectly white against the dirty yellow. The wind whistled and beat against the loose windows, making every part of the car rattle as they started down a hill.

"He won't be far behind," Reed muttered. "Once we get through the pass, we've got to ditch the car."

"Why is he shooting at you?" Banks still gripped the dash, her fingers the same color as her pale cheeks. In spite of the cold, beads of sweat gathered on her forehead, and her upper lip trembled.

Reed felt no fear. His hands were steady as he gripped the wheel with his left and rested his right against the gear shifter. Nothing about death scared him, but her eyes, so clear and enchanting—the fear and strain he saw was overwhelming; it pierced him to his core, making his stomach twist and his mind go blank. As the thrill of the run began to fade, the longing in his heart returned. All he wanted to do was hold her.

"Watch the road!"

A turn loomed ahead, veering sharply to the left as a steep hillside rose up directly beyond. Reed jerked the car out of gear and slammed his foot against the brake. Something snapped, as sharp and loud as a gunshot. The brake pedal went limp, and Reed's chest tightened. He snatched the emergency brake. The rear tires locked and screeched as the Beetle began to fishtail. Reed struggled to direct the car around the turn, but the back end swung out too far. Banks's mouth hung open, but no sound came out as her nails dug into his forearm.

Panic dulled his finer senses. The windows turned black in a storm of dirt as the air filled with Banks's screams. In what felt like slow motion, he reached out and grabbed her hand. The car lurched over an obstruction in the ditch and hurtled forward as their eyes met, building what might be the last memory he'd ever make.

I love her.

15

Tennessee/North Carolina State Line

The rear bumper of the Beetle dug into the hillside, and Reed's head slammed against the steering wheel as metal and glass crunched all around him. The engine hatch buckled in the rear of the car, sending a wave of heat flooding through the busted rear window. Reed coughed and clawed at his eyes as he spilled out of the VW and into the snow. The forest around him danced as though the ground were a magic carpet, rippling with every blast of the frozen wind.

Banks. Where's Banks?

He stumbled back to the car, still swaying on his feet, and reached through the mangled doorframe, fishing for her arm. Banks moved and coughed, and his fingers found her shoulder.

"Can you hear me? Are you okay?"

"You wrecked my car, you deadbeat!"

The muscles in his chest loosened at her emotional outburst. At least she was alive. Reed staggered into the ditch, the world around him wavering as he leaned against the smashed car. Tree limbs danced and swayed overhead, furthering his disorientation as he took stock of his surroundings.

The Beetle was done. One tire was blown, the back hatch had buckled as it collided with a boulder, and oil streamed over the clay. The frame must have twisted on impact—the entire car was warped, and both windows were shattered.

Reed stumbled around the front bumper and jerked on the passenger's door. It took him a moment to pry it open, but when he did, Banks fell out, coughing and rubbing her eyes. The cold sweat glistening on her face was already freezing under the sting of the wind.

Reed grabbed her by the hand and motioned at the hillside. "Come on! We've got to go."

They fought their way up the hill, using trees and fallen logs to help pull themselves up the slope. Banks coughed and fought her way up behind him, slipping on rock-hard clay. In the distance, a roar echoed through the mountains. He wasn't sure if it was the voice of the wind or the snarl of the Mercedes. Either way, they didn't have much time.

A fallen log lay halfway up the hill where the slope moderated and opened up onto a narrow plateau running along the side of the mountain. Farther on, the hillside became a rocky cliff face and shot skyward another forty yards, with trees growing out of the rock.

The spray of snow raining from the sky had become a shower, larger flakes falling closer together and obscuring his view. The leaves were speckled white now, with fading patches of brown. Reed stopped just past the log and panted, glancing back toward the Beetle. They had cleared a hundred yards up the hill, leaving the road a winding grey snake, rapidly turning white.

The Mercedes roared.

"Get down!"

Banks gasped as he grabbed her, and they crashed to the ground behind the log. New frustration clouded his mind as their situation unfolded. For the moment, they were hidden, but there was no egress off of this hill without exposing themselves.

He held her trembling fingers between his and nodded. "Stay quiet. It's going to be okay."

Moments slipped by. Reed heard the Mercedes rumble around the turns and then glide to a halt at the bottom of the hill. Propping himself up on his elbows, Reed crawled to the right as his heart thumped like a drum.

"What is it?" Banks whispered.

Reed held his finger to his lips and peered around the end of the log. The tinted windows of the Mercedes at the bottom of the hill were too dark to see through in the gathering darkness. Snow melted and streamed off the silver hood under the heat of the big motor, while exhaust billowed from the rear bumper. After almost a minute, the driver's door opened, and a slender white male stepped out. He was maybe five-ten, with skinny arms, holding what looked to be a glass Coke bottle in his right hand. He set the bottle on the roof of the car and stretched, rolling his neck to either side. The Wolf wore black slacks with shiny dress shoes. His torso was wrapped in a thick peacoat, but beneath the V of the collar, Reed could make out a suit jacket and a dark blue tie. The man's hair was close-cropped, almost shaved on the sides, and just long enough on top to comb over. He wore dark, aviator-style sunglasses, and black leather gloves.

Gloves. Who the hell wears gloves while driving?

Banks lay on the ground with her elbows dug into the leaves, biting her lower lip as she peered over the top of the log.

Reed shook his head and pulled on her sleeve. "*Get down.*"

Banks glared at him and swatted his hand away. Reed heard a crunching sound at the bottom of the hill and turned to see the man stepping gingerly through the snow toward the Beetle. He walked as if he were crossing a frozen lake—as if each step might break the ice—and he set each foot against the ground, feeling out the clay before placing his weight on it. He approached the Volkswagen from the rear and peered into the shattered glass, then walked back to the driver's side of the Mercedes, high-stepping the whole way.

Bent over, he gazed into the rearview mirror, brushing snow off his coat before adjusting his tie with a careful twist of both hands. He straightened, then adjusted his sunglasses as he walked to the rear of the car and swept his foot beneath the bumper. The lid of the trunk popped open automatically, and he dug inside for a moment.

Reed reached beneath his jacket and checked for his pistol. It was still there, only half-loaded now. He couldn't guarantee a lethal shot at a hundred yards. It was just too far. He might miss or hit an inessential body part, and then they'd be exposed and still short on firepower.

The Wolf emerged from the trunk with a long black case in his hands. He set it on the ground and snapped it open, then withdrew a black rifle-style weapon with a thick barrel and a wide drum mounted beneath the receiver. Reed squinted and tilted his head for a better view, watching as The Wolf pulled the charging handle on the side of the weapon.

"What the hell is that?" Banks hissed.

The Wolf lifted the Coke off the roof of the car, took a long swig, and then adjusted his sunglasses again. He set the bottle back down and raised the weapon into his shoulder, directing it into the trees.

Oh, shit.

A *shoonk* echoed from the roadway, followed by a brief pause, as something grey and golfball-sized arced through the air and thudded into the hillside to Reed's left. A deafening blast shook the mountainside, and snow and forest debris exploded over the hill amid a cloud of smoke.

Shoonk, shoonk, shoonk!

Banks jumped to her feet and dashed into the trees, shouting at Reed to follow. More explosions detonated against the hillside, throwing sticks and rocks around him as Reed fought to catch up with her. The grenade launcher continued to fire from the roadbed below, and each blast fell a little closer to home. Something sharp and hard tore through his pants and bit into his leg, and one more explosion blasted from above, sending a torrent of rocks crashing down over their heads.

"Banks! Get down!"

Reed slid to a stop behind a tree, Banks only feet away behind another trunk. He looked down the hillside and made eye contact with the black-clothed killer. That dancing smirk returned beneath flushed cheeks as The Wolf fed fresh grenades into the drum of the launcher.

Shoonk!

Another grenade exploded only a few yards away.

Banks shouted, then tumbled through the brush and crashed to the ground beside him. "Give me the gun! I'll cap that son of a bitch!" Her eyes were consumed by wildfire.

She's crazy.

Shoonk! Shoonk!

"Run!" Reed wrapped his fingers around hers, and they took off into the trees, running along the plateau. The slope beneath them was still gentle, but the frozen ground was slick, and they struggled to find footing as they crashed between the trees. The snowfall thickened as grenades detonated behind them, but the killer's aim was obstructed by the forest. Footsteps pounded behind them, and then they heard a fresh noise—the hissing, popping snarl of a suppressed assault weapon. Bullets ripped through the undergrowth around them.

"Who *is* this guy?" Banks screamed.

Reed ducked behind a tree as a string of bullets ripped over his shoulder. He pointed the Glock back toward the shooter and pulled the trigger. The gun clicked over a bad primer and didn't fire. Another roar of gunfire shredded branches and rained bark over their heads as Reed pulled back behind the tree.

"Here. Give it to me!" Banks jerked the gun out of his hand before he could stop her, and with a quick twist of her wrist, she ejected the bad cartridge and pumped a new one into the chamber.

She moved as though she were on skates and slid out from behind the tree, then raised the gun. The Glock barked, spitting hot lead through the trees, and a shout broke out from far behind them. The assault rifle fell silent.

Reed stared as Banks lowered the gun and turned back to him, her eyes blazing with vicious fire. "What?" She tossed him the gun. "Never seen a girl defend herself? I'm southern, bitch. On your feet!"

She offered her hand and jerked him up. He fumbled with the gun as the two of them crashed down the hill, deeper into the shadows. The sky grew darker by the moment as the snowfall increased from a steady shower into a howling swirl. Banks panted as she ran beside him, and they stumbled over fallen logs and small depressions in the ground.

Reed's stomach twisted in panic. He could make out the shadowy figure of the shooter behind them a hundred yards back. He saw the rising muzzle of a rifle and the tilt of the killer's head as he leaned into the stock of his weapon.

A fresh string of gunfire tore through the forest. The ground gave way, and Reed tumbled backward, free-falling down a new hillside, rolling head over heels as Banks tumbled down beside him, scraping past trees and sliding through valleys of leaves. Snow and mud clogged his vision as he tumbled down the hill, rocks and fallen logs slamming into his shoulders as he slid and rolled toward the valley floor.

The gunshots faded. He swung his arm to the left, and a rock tore at his hand as he tried to locate Banks, but she was gone. A splash and then a shriek from Banks came moments before the frigid water closed around his own shoulders—and then his face.

Kicking and fighting to the surface, the chill from the wind was a distant memory as the immediate, cutting cold of the water sank straight to his bones. Frigid air whistled between his teeth as his head broke the surface. He kicked out with both legs, treading water for a moment before his head descended beneath the surface again.

They had fallen into a creek. He couldn't tell how wide or how deep as he fought to keep himself above the surface, but the saturating cold told him all he needed to know about their situation. They had only minutes to live if they remained in the water.

No. I won't die here.

His head broke the surface again, and he struck out with both legs, kicking toward the bank. "Banks!" He pulled himself out of the water and back onto the mud, coughing up water and bits of ice.

It was almost dark now, and he couldn't see more than five feet ahead. The snow was a thick blanket, almost as impenetrable as fog. His whole torso was racked with violent shivers as his body fought back hypothermia. But there were no more gunshots.

"Banks! Where are you?"

Reed dug for the flashlight in his pocket. He knew the bright LED was little better than a flashing beacon, marking the killer's target stranded in the bottom of the creekbed, but he didn't care. He had to find Banks.

Charging through the creek, he swept the light along the far side of the bank. Trees and bushes, cloaked in snow next to the water, were now ghosts in the darkness. Amid chunks of ice, a limb drifted down the creek and over a short waterfall.

Then he saw her. Banks clung to a bush on the far side of the creek, not far from the waterfall. Gasping for air and kicking out with both feet, she fought the current as Reed launched himself through the water, fighting for footing as the powerful push of the water dragged him toward the drop-off.

"Hold on! I'm coming!" He clicked the light off and jumped for the creekside, ten yards upstream from Banks. Praying that the killer had lost them in the roar of the gathering blizzard, he grabbed a low-hanging tree limb and hauled himself out of the water. The snow that blasted Reed obscured his vision beyond more than a few feet. The killer couldn't hope to track them in this soup.

He clawed his way back onto solid ground, then ran toward Banks, who continued kicking against the water without screaming.

She was smarter than that, he realized. The sopping wet blonde focused all of her energy on survival instead of wasting precious breaths on expressing her fear. But he could tell she was only moments from giving out.

Reed scooped Banks into his arms and hauled her forward onto dry ground as she coughed. Particles of ice had formed on her nose and eyebrows, and patches of her face were flushed blue.

"Hold on, Banks. I've got you."

She staggered to her feet and spat creek water out between blue lips. "C-c-cold," she whispered.

Reed struggled with the zipper of her jacket, then ripped it with a powerful jerk. She fought him, huddling closer into the sopping garment.

"Take it off, Banks! Hypothermia will get you long before you freeze."

A fresh blast of wind tore straight through his body as he ripped off his own jacket. His torso felt frozen, and he pulled her close, rubbing her arms and back, and trying to keep the shirt from freezing to her skin. Nothing compared to the desperation he felt. Not the roar of gunfire snapping at his heels as he hurled himself off a cliff. Not the panic of the truck failing to start as The Wolf stared him down. Her life was here, in the balance.

Reed smacked her gently on the cheeks. "Banks! Stay with me. Focus!"

"I can't... breathe."

"Find a way, dammit. You wimpy Mississippi—"

Banks shoved him back, spraying creek water over the ground. The whites of her eyes were laced with red around pools of perfect blue. "When you almost drown, you can't breathe!" she snapped. "That's how that works!"

A hint of red returned to her cheeks—not enough to drive back encroaching hypothermia, but enough to bring hope into his desperate heart. Reed's mind raced, but he felt locked by indecision.

What now?

"What are you looking at?" Banks's words fell over one another as though she were drunk, but she gestured toward the forest. "Do something!"

Do something. Find shelter.

Reed wiped his face and peered down the creek into the whistle of wind and winter. Far ahead, nestled amongst the storm-torn brush, he caught sight of something mechanical.

"This way!" He took her arm and pulled her close, dragging her wet jacket along with him as they started through the trees. "Keep moving."

They crashed down the bank while Reed held the flashlight at eye level, spitting snow and feeling the tension grow in his body. He negotiated the side of the hill beside the waterfall. He had to find shelter immediately—a cave, or a recess between the hills—someplace he could build a fire and fight back against hypothermia. Banks wouldn't last much longer as the temperature dropped and the snow gathered around her ankles. Hell, *he* wouldn't last much longer. They needed shelter first, and then warmth. Without both, it would be less than half an hour before the forest swallowed them into the belly of the blizzard.

Reed's foot struck something hard, and it rang with a *thunk*. Momentary elation was drowned by disappointment as he shone the light down onto the object. It was an overturned canoe, left in the mud between the trees and bushes, and not wide enough to provide even a hint of shelter from the cold that sank into his bones and tore the life from his blood.

We're going to die. She's going to die, right here in my arms.

The cherry-red was gone from her face, leaving behind a blue that was rapidly turning to pure white.

No, dammit. Not here.

"Banks, run. You have to run now!"

Her eyes gleamed up at his. With a voice barely strong enough to carry over the wind, she said, "Where?"

Reed pulled her closer to his side and shined light through the trees. Each second that ticked by felt like a drip of life flowing from his bones. Only moments remained. He searched between the trees for any hint of a path.

Nobody leaves a canoe in the middle of nowhere.

There had to be some kind of camp or maybe a cabin nearby. As he peered into the snow, the outline of a narrow clearing between the trees appeared, leading away from the canoe and deeper into the storm.

"This way," he said.

16

The onslaught of the blizzard was overwhelming. Clouds of snow obscured the path, encircling them like the bodies of a million ghosts. Even with the bright LED, the path between the trees became harder to see with every step. Desperation overwhelmed Reed's mind as he pressed forward, kicking through the bushes and crashing over small depressions. For all he knew, they were running in circles. At any moment, they might collide with a tree or run off the edge of a cliff, but he couldn't stop moving. A moment lost in the single-digit temperatures could mean death for them both.

"Hold on, Banks. Stay with me."

Banks shivered like a puppy stepping out of a cold bath. Her hands were frozen in place around his arm, and her face was twisted into a pucker of pain and fear. "Hell of a third d-d-date."

Reed pulled her closer and turned a corner around a tree, tripping over something and feeling pain rip through his shin. He shined the light on his feet, where a chunk of wood lay on the ground. It wasn't a tree limb or a rotting log—it was a piece of firewood.

The glow of the flashlight illuminated the swirling snow as

Reed scanned the small clearing. He saw a splitting stump near the fallen firewood, and a little farther, a rusty steel barbecue grill like the ones in a state park, planted in the hard clay, leaning to one side. Across the far side of the clearing, nestled against the trees and almost obscured by the blizzard, a cabin squatted under the storm as though even it were freezing beneath the blast of the wind. Snow piled against its walls, and debris battered its single wooden door framed between boarded-up windows. It was built of pine logs with a cedar shingle roof—nothing as fancy as Oliver's A-frame, but to Reed it was the best-looking cabin he'd ever seen.

"Walk with me, Banks!"

His heart pounded, and Reed wondered if the cabin was locked. Was there somebody inside? Was the gunman still on their tail? None of that really mattered if he couldn't get them both out of the storm.

The latch was locked. Reed slammed against the pinewood door, framed by thick pine boards and hanging on heavy iron hinges, and was met by stiff resistance. He slammed his hand against the latch, but still, it didn't budge.

"Stand here, Banks." Reed placed her against the wall, then crashed into the door. Once. Twice. The blast of the wind tore so hard at his torso it almost pushed him off balance. Panic and sudden rage overtook his mind. It wasn't going to end this way. He'd rather fall on one of those damn grenades than watch Banks die.

Wood met flesh with a sickening thud as Reed slammed all two hundred thirty pounds of his body into the door. It crashed open with a splintering sound, and Reed fell inside onto the hardwood floor. His head smacked the planks, and the flashlight rolled out of his hand. He gasped for air, then rolled over and crawled back to his feet.

Banks huddled against the wall, but there was a smile dancing at the corners of her lips. "Not bad, Cowboy."

Reed hoisted her up and dragged her inside, then slammed the door shut. An entire chunk of it was missing around where the latch had been, and there was nothing to hold it closed. It blew open again, and Reed cursed. Why couldn't *anything* be easy?

He retrieved the flashlight and scanned the cabin's single room. Dust clung to the stained surface of each post on a worn, four-poster bed. Black ashes covered two rocking chairs next to a fireplace. The floor creaked under each footstep, and as he shined the flashlight toward the left half of the cabin, the pool of light illuminated a short counter and two cabinets with doors hanging on crooked hinges. The only other articles in the room were a table leaning on uneven legs and a large chest with drawers hanging half-open. Clothes spilled out, all dusty and old like nobody had entered this place for years.

Reed leaned against the dresser, sure it was loaded with bricks. He strained, and as it slid a couple inches, his back screamed in pain.

Banks stumbled beside him and placed her shaking hands against the chest. "On three," she whispered. "One Mississippi, two Miss—"

Reed broke into a soft laugh. "Just push, Banks!"

They slid the chest until it slammed into the broken door. The sound of the wind beating against the side of the cabin was muted now, even though the window panes still rattled in their frames. The cabin was dark except for the glow of the flashlight, and now that the door was finally sealed, it felt strangely still inside.

Reed panted and collapsed on top of the chest, his arms still trembling from the bitter cold. Banks slumped against the wall, and for a moment, they relished the peace. The relief from the wind was palpable. Reed said a silent prayer of thanks for the miracle of the cabin. He wasn't sure if anyone was listening way up there above the blizzard. He wasn't sure if he cared. He just wanted to breathe.

The stone fireplace held a rusting metal grate inside a hearth about a foot deep. Next to a large stack of firewood was a can labeled *"flammable."* He knelt on the hard floor and piled firewood onto the grate as a bug scuttled out of the stack. Reed tilted the can over the wood, and a clear liquid streamed out, splashing on the timbers and turning them a dark brown. From the first sniff, Reed recognized the acidic odor of kerosene.

Banks rubbed her hands together over the hearth, as though crimson flames were already bursting from the fireplace.

"Lean back," Reed warned as he peeled off a strip of bark and splashed kerosene over one end. He pried the lighter out of his pocket and flicked it with his stiff thumb, but the flint ground with a squishy sound. The lighter was still sopping wet from the creek.

Reed ground his thumb into the flint again. Once. Twice. Sparks flew from the wheel, then a flame burst from the mouth of the lighter. Reed waved it under the tip of the bark, gratified to see flames rising from the wood and sending a pale flash of heat over his face.

The bark found its home in the fireplace, and golden fire erupted from the grate, engulfing the logs and sending warmth rushing from the hearth. Banks and Reed huddled so close together that the flames almost licked their faces. Every tiny wave of heat was like heaven washing over their bodies and pouring life into their frozen veins. Banks's ice-encrusted hair dangled over the hearth.

"Damn that feels good." Banks rubbed her hands together in front of the flames. A hint of red returned to her cheeks, ushered on by a growing smile. That smile ignited a warmth someplace deep inside of him that was stronger than any fire ever could be. He didn't understand it. He had never felt it before. Even with Kelly and their whirlwind romance, it didn't feel this way—this felt stable and deep.

Reed watched as she combed the melting snow out of her hair. Each twist of her fingers around blonde waves produced new flakes raining down over the floorboards, there to melt under the rising temperature. She fought with a stick tangled in her bangs, and for a moment, the smile faded.

Reed touched her hand, and she froze as her bright eyes met

his. The flames in the hearth reflected in her crystal gaze, unbroken by the scourge of the blizzard.

"Let me," he whispered.

Her hands fell away from the knot of hair, and Reed twisted his fingers against the stick. It broke, then hit the floor as her liberated bangs fell over a damp forehead. He lowered his hand, still admiring her glistening face. She touched her fingers to his, and the lightning bolt that ripped through his body poured gasoline onto the warmth he already felt, turning a glowing ember into a raging fire. It numbed the pain and muted the wind, leaving only the beautiful woman kneeling on the floor beside him. It was a moment too perfect, too warm for any storm to break.

Whoever is up there . . . thank you.

17

Western North Carolina

The Glock hung faithfully at Reed's side, water dripping from the barrel. He unsnapped the retainer and dropped the magazine. Eight rounds left. The spare magazines were in the jacket pocket, somewhere outside, buried in the snow.

Shit.

Reed blew the water from the muzzle, then jammed the magazine back into the gun. There was no need to worry about the moisture—the durable weapon would dry quickly by the fire. Reed dropped the shoulder holster on the table, then pulled his T-shirt, dripping with creek water, up and over his head. Banks's mouth dropped open.

He coughed and looked away. "Sorry. It needs to dry."

"Oh my God." She hurried across the living room and placed her hand against his chest, tracing the dark bruises from around his side to the tear in his flesh. "Is this from the train?"

He'd mostly forgotten about the bruises. Some were from the train. Others were from the gunfight at the FBI field office the week prior. And, of course, the new ones were from the fall off the cliff the night before. They covered his torso like spots on a cow, both irregular and pervasive.

"Yeah. It's fine."

Reed pulled away but felt a sudden touch on his ribcage. Banks stepped closer. She laid eyes on him without reservation, but he could see questions, the sharp wit of a woman who wasn't fooled.

"You're not a venture capitalist, are you?"

Reed rubbed the back of his neck. "I invest in a lot of things."

"Things that get you shot up in a dollar store parking lot?"

Her stare exposed the simple soul deep within her. Not stupid. Not shallow. Just simple. The kind of simplicity that saw the world as it was and took life one day at a time—a happy, realistic simple. A simple he didn't understand.

"That was just a misunderstanding. That guy, um . . . he's grouchy."

She folded her arms. "Well, I hope he has insurance. Somebody owes me a Beetle."

"I'm sorry about that. I'll replace it."

"Are you sure you can afford it?" She ran her fingertips up his arm, stroking the outlines of a half-dozen scars. Her eyes danced with distant fire and not a hint of fear.

"I don't have the cash *on me*," he said.

"Is that right? Have to arrange a payment plan, won't you?"

"I guess . . ." Reed's words trailed off as he lost himself in her gaze. Wit and intelligence still shone in those bright eyes, but nothing else clouded her gaze. It was deep and honest and totally open. As though she wanted him to see her not just for what she was, but who she was. What she felt.

Banks ran her hand behind his neck and pressed her lips against his. Every bit as strong and overwhelming as he remembered, the kiss sent waves of thrill, fear, and elation rushing through his body like no drug ever could. She pulled his body into hers. Her hands were strong and soft and warm, running up his back and behind his neck.

He sank closer into her embrace as the moments stretched out, distorting his perception of passing time. Their clothes fell to the floor, and he slid his hands over each perfect curve of her naked body glowing in the firelight. Renewed passion surged into his mind, and the room around him faded from view as he pulled her closer, kissing her as long and slow as he had that first night in Atlanta. As she kissed him back, he heard the breath rush into her lungs and felt her body come alive. Her arm slid behind his back, and they tumbled to the floor next to the fireplace. He was vaguely aware of the dirt and grime that covered the floorboards, but he didn't care.

He lay on the hard floor as she moved on top of him with gentle twists of her curved form, cries of passion escaping her lips. Reed closed his eyes as her fingers slid between his. Every brush of her skin unleashed new levels of pleasure. The ache in his bones was driven back, overwhelmed by warmth and love. He slid his hand behind her neck and sat up, pulling her in for another kiss before rolling over on top of her. Banks closed her eyes and bit her lip. Firelight danced across the floorboards and sparkled against the melting snow on her cheeks. He lost himself in her face, memorizing every curve, every line and perfect detail. His mind faded back to the moment at the top of that parking garage in Atlanta, the moment when her beauty and grace enchanted him. Every deep longing that was awakened at that moment, then imprisoned as he walked away from the hospital, burst free from deep in his heart and overwhelmed his soul. He needed this woman. He adored this woman. She was the first thing in his entire life that felt completely safe. Completely home.

The rush of passion grew so strong his mind went numb, but beneath it all, he felt something else—something stronger and more stable. Something he hadn't felt in twenty years: belonging. It felt right in this moment—deep and real. Being with Banks, being close to her, sharing every intimacy, he was risking his entire shadowy persona to a person he really didn't even know, yet he felt like he'd known her his whole life. No matter the bloodshed or the money or the endless mountaintops of accomplishment he put beneath his feet, he couldn't outrun the reality that something was missing—something like Banks.

He kissed her neck and shoulders and pulled her body closer to his, drinking in each moment—the electric pleasure tearing through his body more powerful than a bullet.

He pressed his lips against her cheek and held her close. Held her like he'd never let go.

Banks rested her head on his bare chest. "Is your name really Chris?"

Reed lay back on the bed, enjoying the warmth and relaxation of the fire. Her voice, as soft and pure as her skin, sounded like music—like a waterfall trickling into a quiet valley.

"No." Why did he say that? He couldn't tell her his real name—it wasn't safe for either of them. But something in his soul wouldn't allow him to lie.

"I didn't think so." She stroked his stomach. "Are you going to tell me your name?"

This time he waited before answering, savoring the touch of her fingers on his skin. "I liked Cowboy. You could call me that."

She laughed. "I don't think I can call you *boy* after a performance like that."

He smiled but left his eyes closed, running his hand over her exposed back. She moved in closer, and for a moment, the only sounds that joined the crackling of the fire were their gentle breaths.

"Where are you from?" she asked.

"I was born in Birmingham."

"England?"

Reed snorted, and she giggled. "Alabama. But I grew up in Los Angeles. Moved there when I was ten."

"Your parents still live there?"

"My mother does. I haven't been back in a while."

"And your father?"

Once more, Reed hesitated, then relaxed. "He's elsewhere."

"I see." Maybe she knew when to stop pressing, or maybe she was saving it for later. "So, how did you wind up in Atlanta?"

"I was a Marine. Served overseas for a while. . . . Iraq, mostly."

"Is that where you got the scars?"

"Some of them."

He stroked her hair, pushing it behind her ears and over her shoulders. She lay perfectly still with her cheek on his chest. He couldn't see her face, but he imagined that her eyes were closed.

"After I left the military . . . well, lots of things happened. I went into business for myself, found my way to Atlanta, and . . . I guess it just seemed like a place to land. So here I am."

"Here you are . . . investing in billion-dollar firms in the middle of the Appalachian wilderness." She ran her finger down the center of his chest.

He could hear the sarcasm in her voice, but it wasn't cutting. It was honest, like everything else about her. She knew he was lying, and she wanted him to know she knew, but she wasn't going to press it. Not now. Reed was grateful for that. He didn't want to lie to her. Something about her open sincerity made him want to tell her everything, to spill his guts and shed every mask he'd ever worn.

But he couldn't. He never could. Not only would he lose her, he'd lose himself.

Reed shifted against the bed and cleared his throat. "Okay, your turn. What's your story?"

She sighed. "My story? I'm afraid it's pretty dull, honestly."

"I doubt it."

"Why do you say that?"

Reed shrugged. "I've met a lot of people in my line of work. None of them have dull stories."

She lay still, and her chest rose and fell in gentle waves. "I was born in Tupelo."

"Hence the sexy accent."

She laughed. "Yeah . . . hence a lot of things."

"So, who were your parents?"

"My parents were wealthy. My mother is heir to this big oil business out in Texas. Extended family are all multimillionaires, but I don't know much about them. I just know she always had a lot of money. She liked to spend it, too. We lived in this giant house on a small estate, and they called it a plantation, which is pretty standard in Mississippi, I guess, but it always bothered me. I always felt like a rich white girl living it up in the rural south, surrounded by some of the poorest people in the country. I mean, my first car was a Maserati. At fifteen."

"No shit?" Nothing about the woman lying in his arms impressed him as being a spoiled rich girl.

"Yeah, I never liked it. All my friends had pickup trucks and old beat-up Mustangs. We used to go down to the river and drink, skinny-dip under the moonlight, and smoke cigarettes. Mom would've killed me had she known. She wanted me to graduate and go to an Ivy League school and study law or something. Prep me to be the next heir to the family empire."

"I'm guessing you had other plans."

"No, I was going to do it. I had applications at half a dozen schools in the northeast. I was already looking for apartments."

"What happened?"

"My father . . ." Her voice broke. "My father died. He was on business in New Orleans and was hit by a drunk driver. They say he died instantly. . . . I hope it's true. He was such a good man—a kind, gentle soul. He spoiled me rotten, but not like my mother did with money and things. Daddy really spent time with me. We would sneak out and get ice cream and watch movies when I was a kid, and when I was in high school, he would take me to Memphis, and we'd slip into bars and drink. He was cool like that. He said I was his girl. That was all he ever called me, actually—'*my girl*.'"

Banks sucked in a deep breath, and her fingers tightened around his skin.

Reed spoke softly. "What did he do?"

"He was a doctor, but not like a physician. I mean, he had a medical degree, but it was mostly research. He was always driving up to Nashville and working at Vanderbilt. I like to think he did a lot of good in the world."

He squeezed her shoulder. "I know he did. What was his name?"

"Francis."

Reed's brow wrinkled. The name sounded vaguely familiar, as though he had heard it recently, but he couldn't place it.

"After he was buried, Mom became horrible, working all the time and always flying to Texas. She was really mean and intense about me going to school. I guess I just broke down. I ran out late one night and took a bus to Atlanta to see my godfather—Senator Holiday—the one you met in the hospital. He and Daddy were close friends. I stayed with him a while, and then I just knew I wanted to be on my own. I was sick of being the rich girl everybody takes care of. I wanted to take care of myself, chase my music, and just be alive for a while. And that's about it. That's my story, I guess. See? I told you it was boring." Her laugh was soft.

He nestled his head close to hers, then kissed her forehead. "Not for a moment."

18

Reed slipped out of bed, leaving Banks sleeping in a curled-up ball. His dry clothes smelled of river water and smoke, and they stuck to his skin as he pulled them on.

I wish I could stay in bed with her forever.

The fire had gone out in the night, and now the cabin lay in stillness as cold air seeped through the crack beneath the door. Reed peered out of the window. A field of white blanketed the woods around them, broken only by the tall grey trunks of the trees that shot toward the sky. Snow was built up at least a foot outside the cabin, laying in thick drifts where the wind had left it.

Reed's stomach growled, and the bed creaked behind him. Banks sat up, and her blonde hair fell in tangled waves. She smiled, and without a word began to dress in front of the vacant fireplace.

Reed rifled through the cabinets, searching for anything edible, though all he could find were a couple old cans of baked beans. He cut the lids open with the tip of his knife, then handed one can to Banks, who sat at the table and ate the beans without comment, scooping them out of the can with her fingers.

"No utensils?" she asked.

Reed sat down across from her and dug his fingers into the

sticky beans. "Just the one I used last night. I still have it on me if you're interested."

She rolled her eyes. "Too big for the can."

Reed grinned and shoveled more beans into his mouth. They were ancient but didn't taste half bad. Through a mouthful, he said, "You never told me why you're here."

Banks grunted. "My godfather has a cabin a few miles from where you found me. After that stuff in Atlanta, the FBI thought it would be a good idea for him to get out of town for a while, so I drove up for a visit."

Godfather. Holiday.

Reed wanted to kick himself. He remembered reading in Holiday's file that he owned a vacation cabin up here in the mountains, but even as Reed journeyed to hunt Oliver, he never considered the possibility that Holiday may have retreated to the cabin.

Not that it should have mattered either way, really. Not until Reed ran into Banks.

He finished the beans and set the can on the table. For a moment, he stared at the girl sitting cross-legged next to him, and his mind was lost in her simple beauty. But not just her beauty—her mental fortitude, also. He marveled that this woman, who had endured a brutal kidnapping only two weeks prior, and now was huddled inside a cabin in the middle of nowhere after running for her life from a maddened killer with a grenade launcher, could be so composed and calm. He wondered how that could be natural. Were he in her shoes, with no prior experience in warfare or bloodshed, he would be freaking out right now. Did she not grasp the reality of the terror that had befallen her, or was she simply that much stronger than he realized?

Banks looked up and lifted one eyebrow. "What?"

He shook his head and rubbed his fingers against the table, smearing the bean residue off his skin. He pushed away the confused thoughts about Banks and forced himself to refocus on the problem at hand. Or, rather, the *problems*. There were several of them.

After escaping The Wolf in the woods, his focus had been staying alive long enough to find Oliver. Now that goal seemed even further out of reach. If Mitch Holiday were in these mountains, it was only a matter of time before Oliver knew about it, and after that, the senator would be anything but safe. Whoever The Wolf worked for, he might be just as interested in killing Holiday as he was in burying Reed.

"I think you should leave me here." Banks leaned back in her chair, her arms folded as she stared out the window.

"What?"

"Whoever ran us off the road will be back. You should probably get back to town before he finds us. He won't hurt me."

The calm frankness of her words took him off guard, and he wondered for a minute if she was completely ignorant of the severity of their situation. But no, she wasn't dumb. She was just rational.

"I think we should get you back to your godfather, first."

Banks shrugged. "I can see to that. Where are we, anyway?"

Reed twisted his neck until it popped, then scooped up the cans and walked them to the empty trash bin in the corner. "I'm not sure. Either North Carolina or Tennessee. We were pretty close to the state line when we wrecked. Robbinsville is east of here."

"Are there any highways?"

"Highways? No. State roads, maybe. Places where we could pick up a ride."

"What about the Beetle?" she said.

Reed lifted Banks's bright red coat off the counter and dusted it off. It was mostly dry from the night before. "The Beetle is beyond the help of AAA, I'm afraid. We'll have to walk."

Banks slid the jacket on, then wrapped it around her slim body before standing on her tiptoes and kissing him on the lips.

"Well, all right, then. Let's roll, Cowboy."

The forest outside the cabin was a winter wonderland, a field of frozen trunks buried in drifts of perfect white. Reed had no clue where the nearest road lay or how to get back to a main highway. For all he knew, they would have to walk miles before encountering any life. He guessed that the cabin wouldn't be too far from civilization, so they started through the trees. Birds flitted, tweeting to one another as they swooped down between limbs and played in the snow. An occasional chipmunk bounded in the soft white snow, staring with beady eyes at the human invaders as they trudged onward. There was something perfectly serene about this place, now muted with snow and accented with icy diamonds.

Miles passed before the trees parted at a hilltop, and Reed caught sight of a two-lane roadbed a hundred yards below. It was covered in a thin sheet of snow, but tire marks ran back and forth in both lanes. There was traffic, at least, and maybe it wouldn't be long before the next vehicle happened along.

The exact position of the sun was difficult to determine through the mountaintops and trees, but hoping they were headed east, they faced the general direction of the light and marched on.

Banks looped her arm through his, her cheeks now flushed. "So. Coke or Pepsi?"

Reed laughed. "What?"

"It's a game I read about one time. Twenty questions to learn about a person—or, you know . . . a lover."

Reed shot her a sideways look. "Is that what I am now?"

"Well, you're definitely not a venture capitalist, so . . ."

He looked away. "Okay, fine. Coke."

"Ooh, nice."

"You?"

"Mountain Dew."

He poked her in the arm. "That wasn't an option."

She shrugged. "What can I say? I'm a rule breaker."

"Clearly. Ask me another."

She pursed her lips and looked up at the tree limbs hanging over the road. "Beach or mountains?"

"Beach. All day. You?"

"Same. Florida coast. Destin is my spot. Sports or movies?"

"Sports. Baseball and drag racing."

She giggled. "Yeah, don't quit your day job. You suck at racing."

"Well, if I had a decent car." He jabbed at her, but she moved to the side and danced backward, her hands in her pockets as she stared at him.

"Okay," she said. "Now for the tough ones. Don't think, just answer. Red or blue?"

"Red."

"Cold or hot?"

"Hot."

"Men or women?"

"Wait . . . what?" He wrinkled his brow, and she laughed, her eyes alight as she skipped backward, her feet moving over the road with deft accuracy. Her laugh was so light and gentle. Reed had never heard a sound so lovely. So much like home.

He broke into a run, pounding through the pavement as she slid to the side. His arms closed around her stomach, and he hoisted her off the ground, cradling her in his arms in the middle of the roadway. Bits of fresh snowfall stuck to her hair as she stared at him, her smile wide and bright. Reed kissed her, and she kissed back, wrapping her hand around his neck and pressing in close.

Tires ground on the pavement behind them. Reed flinched and jammed his hand beneath the jacket, wrapping his fingers around the grip of the Glock. His feet were rooted to the ground as the rumble of a big motor pounded closer. A lifted pickup truck hummed down the road behind them, its diesel engine rumbling over the asphalt. Reed relaxed his shoulders and held out his hand, thumb up. The truck bounced to a stop, and the passenger side window slid down. Even from his six-foot-four vantage point, Reed could barely see inside the cab.

"You folks lost?" The big man in the cab wore camouflage hunting clothes and a bright orange hat. His wide smile was missing teeth, but it was friendly.

"We broke down a few miles back, and we're trying to get back to town. Mind giving us a lift?"

"Which town?"

Reed shrugged and offered his most disarming smile. "Dunno. We're traveling through. Not exactly sure where we are."

Banks shoved Reed out of the way and hopped up onto the truck's running board before he could stop her. She shoved her head into the cab and offered her hand to the driver. "Hell of a rig you got here. You ever run biodiesel in this baby?"

The big man grinned. "What, you a motorhead? Climb in, darlin'. I'll get y'all back to the big city."

19

Lake Santeetlah, North Carolina

As it turned out, the "big city" was Fontana Dam, a tiny community nestled in northern Graham County, with a resident population of thirty people. George, their driver, was planning to do some shopping at the local general store. But by the time they rolled into the little community, Banks had him so warmed up talking about engines that he readily agreed to drive them another thirty minutes in the opposite direction, to Lake Santeetlah, a booming metropolis, population forty-three.

Reed rode in the back seat, jammed up next to a pile of smelly hunting clothes, while Banks took shotgun, carrying on a boisterous conversation with George about the understated performance power of diesels and their unappreciated racing capacity.

Banks's thorough understanding of engines was impressive. At the time, Reed assumed Banks's opening comment to George was designed simply to disarm him and secure their ride, but he quickly realized she had a genuine interest in the subject. Her technical knowledge of motors and performance, while a lot different than Reed's, was nonetheless enchanting.

How many times in a lifetime do you meet somebody like this? Somebody so sincere, and happy, and content with themselves?

As they piled out of the truck, George called after Banks, adding some last-minute wisdom about turbo-diesels. Banks waved, and George turned his toothy grin toward Reed, addressing him for the first time since picking them up.

"You take care of her. You hear me, boy? Got a good un, right there!"

The truck roared and bounced off. Standing at the edge of the small town, Reed shot Banks an inquisitive look.

She laughed and shrugged. "What? I told you I'm a southern girl."

The town of Lake Santeetlah sat right next to the water and consisted of a small gathering of homes and shops. Banks explained that Holiday's cabin sat fifty yards off the water, halfway back to Robbinsville.

Once again, the sky boiled with muddy grey clouds, sweeping in from the west over the mountains. Another snowfall was coming —maybe a bigger one. Reed didn't like the idea of staying with Banks while The Wolf was still on the prowl, but it was probably the best option if the weather took a turn for the worse. Because of the cold, there were no boats out on the lake, but Banks found a local with a pontoon boat down by the dock, and Reed paid him forty bucks to ferry them to Holiday's place.

As the water lapped and churned against the bottom of the boat, Reed stood at the bow with his arms crossed and tried to force his mind to relax. He didn't like crossing the open water, fully exposed this way, but he liked the idea of walking the narrow mountain roads even less. With luck, The Wolf was still snowed in ten miles to the west, and that would buy him enough time to get Banks to safety.

"Let her go, Reed . . . I saw the look in your eyes when you said her name. Take it from me . . . you break hearts a lot better than you break necks."

Kelly's warning echoed in his mind as he glanced back at Banks sitting next to the driver, chatting it up about fishing in the winter. The pilot was as engaged with her as George had been, laughing and motioning with his hands as he disclosed all of his secret fishing spots.

She's unlike anyone else on the planet—even Kelly.

Kelly. She was a lot of things—wild, ferocious, somewhat abrasive—but she had rarely been wrong in the two years he'd known her. Their love, for however long it lasted, felt real. Maybe it even felt like the kind of thing lifelong partnerships were made of, but looking back now, Reed could see the gaping cracks in their union. It was never meant to last, yet he put a lot of faith in Kelly's opinion. Her condemnation of his interest in Banks shook the foundation of the longing that boiled in his soul. Ever since David Montgomery was hauled off to prison and Tabitha dragged her son to the far side of the country, Reed never felt at home. But here, standing on this boat and watching Banks laugh . . . it felt more like home than anything he remembered.

Reed rested on the railing and watched the black water ripple and churn under the pontoons, vanishing from sight beneath the deck of the boat. Life was like that: It was here, so vibrant and active and beautiful, and then it was gone, swept away, and vanishing into the darkness of the world around it.

Banks can't be swept away like that.

He made the choice at the hospital to walk out and leave Banks standing in the hallway with tears streaming down her beautiful face. He remembered *why* he made that choice, and the reality of his situation hadn't changed.

I'll get her to Holiday. Make sure they're both safe again. Deal with The Wolf and deal with Oliver. And then I'll disappear. She deserves that.

The boat's motor whined down as the pilot allowed the pontoon to glide the last twenty yards until it ground against the muddy bank of the lake. Banks gave the driver a fist-bump, then walked through the front gate and jumped ashore. Reed waved at the pilot and followed, looking to the cabin that sat at the top of a hill.

It was nothing short of spectacular—obviously kit-built, but still refined. Giant red logs formed an A-frame sheathed in dark green sheet metal. Glass lined the front of the cabin, facing out toward the water and exposing a brightly lit interior on the other side. A tall man wearing a dark grey uniform and carrying an assault rifle stood by the door, monitoring the lake as though it were the most boring view in the universe.

Banks slid her fingers between his, and he looked down at her soft white hand.

God, this woman.

She pulled him up the hill, and Reed followed without protest, nodding at the guard once before Banks opened the door.

"Uncle! I'm back!"

A clattering sound rang from the other end of the cabin, and Mitch Holiday appeared at the door. He wore loose blue jeans and a turtleneck shirt, and his hair was perfectly combed back—the picture of political composure. But beneath that practiced pose of collection, the clear traces of Holiday's recent misfortunes were evident—bruises still clouded one cheek, and his right knee bulged beneath the blue jeans where a hefty brace encased it. Reed remembered what had happened to that knee—remembered the sickening crack of bone caving in as Holiday fell off the ladder outside the FBI field office.

It was a wonder Holiday could walk at all. The man must be tougher than he looked.

"Banks!" Holiday limped across the living room and wrapped her in a tight hug.

Reed scanned the small cabin, noting the pile of legal documents heaped on the coffee table next to an open laptop. A gas fire burned in the hearth, sending silent flames dancing amongst fireproof logs. His stomach growled, and he turned back to the senator.

Holiday still held Banks close to his chest, both arms wrapped around her shoulders. "My God, girl. I was so worried. Where the hell did you go?"

Banks turned to Reed. "Oscar broke down, but look who I found!"

Holiday looked up, his eyes settling on Reed for the first time. His gaze was clouded by uncertainty for a moment, quickly melting into a warm smile. "Chris!" He wrapped his long and powerful arms around Reed in a big bear hug.

Reed stood awkwardly while the senator finished the hug, then watched Holiday stumble back. He moved slowly, with pain flashing in his eyes. Thick bandages were visible, wadded up beneath the turtleneck and over the wounds he still didn't know Reed had inflicted.

"How are you, Senator?"

Holiday sighed. "I'm better, Chris. Got this shit patched up and getting back to work now. You can see they've got me bottled up here like a prisoner. But that's part of it, I suppose."

Banks gave Holiday's arm a squeeze, then hurried past him toward the open kitchen. "We haven't eaten. What's for lunch?"

Holiday waved her aside. "Get out of here. I'm fixing lunch. Chris! You like steak?"

"Sure." Reed sat down at the bar and bit back a grunt. Flashes of new pain pulsated through his torso, erupting from the bruises and cuts that crisscrossed his ribcage. Taking another one of Kelly's pills would only cause exhaustion, and he couldn't afford that. He needed to focus now.

Holiday limped about the kitchen, throwing pots on the stove and digging in the fridge. Banks sat beside Reed and put her head on his shoulder. Once again, he marveled at her composure and calmness. She had just been shot at, run through the woods, almost drowned, and starved to death. Yet here she was, relaxed and warm, acting as though nothing in the world could steal her peace.

This woman was bulletproof.

"Why did you lie?" Reed whispered beneath the clang of pots.

"About what?"

"What happened in the woods?"

Banks shrugged. "Because I still don't know the truth."

Fair answer.

Reed adjusted himself on the stool, then cleared his throat. "Could I borrow a phone, Senator? Mine is dead."

"Mitch. Call me Mitch. And sure, mine's on the table."

Reed smiled at Banks, then scooped up the phone and stepped back through the door. The guard cast him a casual, uninterested glance, then resumed his surveillance of the lake. Reed walked into the woods, putting enough distance between himself and the guard to prevent his voice from traveling, and then he dialed.

"Winter."

"Don't hang up."

The line went silent, then Winter snapped back with a hint of venom. "I told you not to call me again. I can't get involved in your little war."

"This isn't about that. I have another question. Legitimate business. Will you talk to me?"

Winter's silence was noncommittal, but Reed took it as acceptance.

"I need a personnel file. Just a basic sum-up."

"Name?" Winter spat the word.

"I don't have a name. But I think he's called *The Wolf*."

Dead silence returned to the line, then grinding teeth resounded through the phone. "I *told you*, I'm not getting involved in this war of yours."

"So you know him? Who is he?"

"Somebody you really don't want to cross. Is that enough information for you?"

"Who does he work for? Oliver?"

Winter's groan was full of derision and impatience. This was more emotion than Reed had ever heard from Winter.

"Oliver couldn't afford him. He's a free agent. A top-shelf killer. Much better than Oliver's crew."

Reed leaned against a pine tree. "I'm flattered."

"And why is that?"

"Because he's trying to kill me."

"In that case, nice knowing you. This is the end of your rope."

"I'm not that easy to kill, Winter. What else can you tell me?"

"Only what I've already told you. You're in way over your head. Remember when I said so before? This is what I was talking about. Never call me again."

The line clicked off, and Reed stared down at the blank phone screen.

If he's not working for Oliver, who the hell is he working for?

Reed swiped at the number on the outbound call list, but there wasn't an option to delete it from the history. He cursed, then turned and smashed the phone against the tree. On the third strike the screen shattered.

Walking back toward the cabin, he kicked at the dirt, trying to make sense of Winter's evolving behavior. Was the ghost afraid, or was Winter simply maintaining absolute neutrality?

"I dropped your phone, Mitch." Reed set the busted device on the counter. "I'm sorry. I'll get you a new one."

Holiday looked down at the phone, a brief frown crossing his face. He flicked his hand in the air. "No worries, Chris. Grab a chair. Lunch's almost ready."

20

Holiday never stopped talking. He sawed through his steak, rattling on about everything from Georgia politics to peach ice cream, filling the meal with a steady stream of pontifications and musings. Every time he asked Reed or Banks a question, he took so long to clarify what he was asking that the actual inquiry was lost in the weeds. Reed took a sip of expensive craft beer, watching Holiday guzzle hundred-dollar bourbon while he launched into a dissertation on coastal shipping outside of Savannah. With each key point, he tapped the tip of his steak knife on the wooden table.

He's scared shitless. But why?

"And that's why I support local tariffs, you see? Everybody has to get paid."

Reed finished the beer and set the bottle on the table. "Do you spend a lot of time in Brunswick, Mitch?"

Holiday shook his head, pushing the plate back and letting out a sigh. "Not as much as I'd like. Always in Atlanta these days."

"I thought the general assembly was almost finished for the year."

"Sure, we are. But then there's other work . . . Anyway, what do you do again?"

"I'm a day trader."

"I thought you said you invested in businesses?" Holiday's eyes were bloodshot, and his gaze seemed unfocused.

Reed shrugged. "Well, you know. . . . You don't put all your eggs in one basket, right?"

Holiday smacked the table. "Exactly! That's what I tell people all the time. You have to diversify. That's what I told them when . . ." He trailed off suddenly, then shook his head. "Wow, I think I've overindulged a little. My apologies, Chris. Would you like dessert? I was thinking maybe some peach—"

"Actually, Senator, I was hoping you had a cigar handy."

Holiday's eyes lit up like Christmas lights, and he broke into a grin. "A cigar man, eh? I knew I liked you. Let me fetch my humidor, and we'll step out on the porch."

Banks patted Reed on the hand. "I'm going to take a shower in something other than a creek. See you in a minute."

She kissed him on the cheek, her lips lingering a moment longer than was necessary. That warm rush flooded through his body again, and he closed his eyes. Then she squeezed his arm and walked toward the bathroom.

Holiday reappeared from his bedroom, holding a small wooden box and a Zippo. Reed returned his smile, then stepped out onto the front porch. The guard had moved farther down the lot toward the lake and joined an identically dressed man carrying a shotgun. It was barely one in the afternoon, but the boiling clouds blocked the sun, leaving the surface of the water a churning black beneath the wind.

Reed accepted a cigar and snipped the end off with his teeth, then dangled the tip over Holiday's outstretched lighter. The smoke tasted sweet and strong, definitely Cuban, and well-aged. Reed took a long puff and wished like hell it was a cigarette instead.

"So tell me, Mitch. How long do they expect you to be up here?"

Holiday rolled the cigar between his fingers, then took a slow puff. "Who knows, kid. Nobody talks to me."

"Do they have any leads, at least?"

"Yeah . . ." Holiday stared at the lake with empty eyes. "Got some guy on videotape. The guy who busted me out of the FBI office. Working on running him down now."

"Well, I hope they find him."

Holiday just stared at the water over the front rail of the deck, wearing only the turtleneck but not shivering in the cutting cold.

"Why do you think they want you dead? Some legislative business?"

"No, nothing like that." Holiday stuffed the cigar back between his teeth and puffed, long and slow. Reed decided to wait for him to speak, trusting the alcohol in Holiday's blood more than his own ability to worm out the truth.

Holiday spoke in a low monotone, still staring into space. "You ever do something you think is the right thing and it just kind of . . . becomes something else?"

Reed grunted. "Yeah. Several times. What did you do?"

Holiday shook his head and closed his eyes. "Protected a friend. Somebody I would've died for. And then . . ." The words blended into the whistle of the wind on the water. Holiday took another puff on the cigar, then tilted his head toward Reed. "You sure we haven't met before? I swear there's something familiar about you."

Reed forced a smile and looked away. "You probably saw me at a fundraiser. I have some business down in Savannah."

"No shit. Well, proud to represent you."

"No offense, Senator. I voted for the other guy. But I'd vote for you next time."

Holiday laughed and jammed the cigar between his back teeth. "There won't be a next time, kid. If I ever get out of this cabin, I think it's time I retired and found a quieter life."

Reed watched him out of the corner of his eye, studying Holiday's every movement. The twitch of his eyes, the way he rubbed the railing with his right thumb. He radiated stress like a nuclear reactor.

"Well, I need a beer," Holiday said. "Can I get you anything?"

Reed knocked the ashes off the end of the cigar, then extinguished it against the railing. "Actually, I wondered if I could borrow your vehicle. I need to run to town and get some fresh clothes."

Holiday raised an eyebrow. "It's not going to end up in a ditch like my phone, is it?"

Reed laughed. "No worries, Senator. I'm a careful driver. I'll grab you some beer while I'm out."

Holiday's eyes lit up at that, and he waved the cigar toward Reed with a drunken flip of his hand. "You've got my vote, Chris Thomas! Here"—he dropped his keys into Reed's hand—"get a case."

Reed dumped the cigar into the snow, then jumped off the deck and hurried around the cabin to a jet-black Land Rover, mud and snow clinging to the fenders. It beeped once when he hit the unlocks, then roared to life as he slammed the door. He slid it into gear, then turned back down the drive and toward the highway.

It was time to find some answers.

21

Cherokee, North Carolina

Forty-five miles east of Lake Santeetlah lay Cherokee, North Carolina. Predominantly a tourist town, it was the closest city of significance that could promise the refitting Reed required. It took him over an hour to negotiate the narrow, slick mountain roads, but once he reached the city limits, he replaced his clothes at a department store, then purchased new bandages, over-the-counter painkillers, and a toothbrush.

A quick trip to a convenience store bathroom allowed him to change clothes, wash the wound in his side, and wrap it in gauze.

At an Internet café, he sat down at a computer with a tall cup of coffee. In spite of the full night's rest, he could feel the wear and tear of the last few days dragging at the edges of his consciousness, threatening to pull him down. It was already growing dark outside as the building bank of clouds suffocated the sunlight. Within the hour, full darkness would fall, making it even harder to keep awake and alert.

Holiday made a comment on the porch that finally connected two dots Reed had struggled with all afternoon. When Banks mentioned her father, Francis Morccelli, the name rang a bell, but he couldn't place the memory. Holiday's brief mention of a friend he tried to protect brought to mind Reed's last intense conversation with the senator, back in the trailer outside of Atlanta. Reed had kidnapped Holiday and interrogated him in that trailer while wearing a mask, but during the process, Holiday asked a peculiar question of his own. He said, *"Did you kill Frank?"*

Frank must've been Banks's father and Holiday's frat brother. Reed remembered Winter mentioning it two weeks prior when Reed first began to dig into Banks's identity. Winter had said Frank and Holiday attended Vanderbilt University together, birthing a friendship that lasted into their professional lives. Banks believed her father died at the hands of a drunk driver. But Holiday's morbid question while lying on the floor and staring into the eyes of his potential killer indicated otherwise.

Why does Holiday think Frank was murdered?

Reed searched online for *"Dr. Francis Morccelli."* The resulting listings were overwhelming—much as he anticipated. He narrowed the search by adding *"New Orleans"* to the field and found a local news article detailing the accident, dated June of 2013.

> Dr. Francis D. Morccelli of Tupelo, MS, was tragically killed last night around 12:45 a.m. when an intoxicated driver lost control of his vehicle and hit Dr. Morccelli three blocks off of Bourbon Street. Dr. Morccelli is survived by his wife, Samantha, and his daughter, Banks.

Reed scanned the remainder of the article, but it recorded nothing helpful about the incident other than intended police investigations. He searched again for follow-up articles. *Why were you in New Orleans, Doctor?*

"He was always driving up to Nashville." Banks's words echoed in his mind, and he placed his fingers on the keys again. *"Dr. Morccelli, Vanderbilt, research, 2013."*

This time the results were much more specific. Research papers written by Frank were all available for public consumption on

Vanderbilt's website. Apparently, Frank often partnered with Vanderbilt on research projects but wasn't directly employed by the university or the hospital. He specialized in pharmaceutical research and had a great many radical theories about the possibilities of DNA-inspired synthetic drugs.

> ". . . the epicenter of my theory is this—a genetic disease is, by its nature, caused and extrapolated by the mutant, damaged, or underdeveloped genes of the host subject. These genes are the factory wherein diseases of all sorts are birthed and fostered. People with healthy genes don't struggle with these illnesses. Why? The secret is in their DNA. They are wired and written differently from unhealthy people. It follows, therefore, that if we can synthetically replicate DNA that is healthy, and form that into an active agent that will replicate those healthy cells, we can rewire unhealthy DNA and breathe fresh life into a broken species."

Reed took a deep sip of coffee and scanned the remainder of the article. It was a transcript from a talk Frank delivered to a research class in 2012.

Well, that doesn't sound at all like a mad scientist.

Another article was titled "Cancer: The Secret to Replicating Cells, by Dr. F. D. Morccelli."

So, Doc . . . you had a fascination with genetics. What did Mitch need to save you from?

The remaining articles were about various research projects. The most recent was dated twelve months before his death and detailed a special research grant from a medical company named Beaumont Pharmaceutical. For a research scientist, that seemed like another day at the office—certainly nothing that appeared murder-worthy.

If Frank was killed by the same people who were after Holiday, the link between them had to be the reason for their assassinations. But, assuming Morccelli's death six years before wasn't an accident, why wait this long to follow up with Holiday?

He was still in on it. Whatever's going on here, Holiday has been involved ever since. It's the only reason he would still be alive.

Reed sat back in his chair and rubbed his chin while staring at the screen. The reality of what he was looking at sank in slowly, then took hold of his mind. Oliver wasn't the villain here. Oliver was just another pawn. Somebody darker and bigger and lost in the shadows lay behind the curtain, calling the shots. They presumably killed Frank, and they now had reason to kill Holiday.

These people weren't killers, though. Criminals, for sure, but not hitmen. That's why they hired Oliver to get the job done, and Oliver passed the contract to Reed. When he realized that Reed had no intentions of continuing employment after his thirtieth kill, Oliver decided to set Reed up and have him thrown in prison for the Holiday murder.

There to die.

It hit Reed so hard he sat forward. Paul Choc, the Latino he killed in prison to secure his freedom. Was Choc another one of Oliver's henchmen who refused to continue employment? Somebody Oliver needed to be rid of?

This was a system. A machine for Oliver. Hire new people, run them until they quit, and then burn them. Only now, Oliver had lost control. He had failed to burn the Prosecutor, and whoever Oliver was hired by had turned elsewhere to finish the job. They had turned to The Wolf, this third-party assassin, and deployed him to destroy Reed by any means necessary.

Reed cleared the search history on the computer, then waved at a nearby barista and held up his phone. "Hey, do you have a charger for this?"

The kid pointed to a bank of wires along the far wall, then shuffled off without further comment. Reed jammed the charger into the phone, then leaned against the counter. If Holiday was in on it, he must have screwed up or outlived his usefulness. That would explain the sudden desire of the players behind the curtain to end his life. Either way, Reed was no longer comfortable leaving Banks with the drunken senator. He was probably harmless himself, but he was also a target, and not a very streetwise target at that. A cabin on the lake with an open wall full of windows was a dumb place to hide. A sniper of subpar skill could take out the senator from across the lake in broad daylight, and the FBI would have nothing to do about it. It was only a matter of time before Oliver, or whoever the hell was after Holiday, made another attempt. Banks needed to be gone before then. He would drive back to the lake and make arrangements to secure her somehow.

Reed closed the door of the coffee shop's restroom. It smelled like too much bleach sloshed at random over the tile floor. On his way to the urinal, he did a double-take of himself in the mirror. He looked like hell—messy hair and grime on his skin, and dark bags hanging under his bloodshot eyes.

This job is killing me, one way or the other.

"Welcome to Evan's." It was the sulky kid behind the counter.

"Thank you." The voice was clear and strong, late-twenties, brimming with confidence. "I'm Wolfgang."

Reed started, then zipped his pants as he stood in front of the urinal and waited.

Wolfgang. That's too much of a coincidence.

"I'm looking for my friend." Wolfgang spoke again, more casually this time.

Reed pictured the handsome man in the peacoat from the day before. Imagined him leaning against the counter, drumming his fingers on the tip jar, and shooting the cashier a wink.

"He's a big guy," Wolfgang said. "Brown hair. A real bad case of RBF."

Reed reached under his jacket and unholstered the pistol.

"He's in the restroom." The kid spoke without hesitation or interest.

Shit.

Reed press-checked his handgun and laid his finger on the trigger. Feet clicked on the hardwood floor, and somebody laughed.

"Great. Thanks, man."

"Hey, dude, what the—"

The kid's voice was broken off by the thunderous roar of a gun. The latch to the bathroom door exploded, sending shards of metal flying into the mirror as the door blew back on its hinges. Reed instinctively ducked as bullets tore through the wall just over his head, shaking the walls with each deafening clap.

With his hand cocked around the doorframe, Reed fired toward the attacker. The smaller-caliber handgun snapped like a popgun next to the bellow of whatever the hell was being fired at him.

Glass shattered, and the screams that ripped through the café were joined by the clatter of chairs colliding with tables. Reed pivoted around the door. Already swinging with his left fist, his knuckles connected with the metal slide of an enormous handgun just as The Wolf pulled the trigger again. The gunshot detonated, and the shock wave of the bullet passed by Reed's head as the muzzle flipped upward. Blood streamed from his ear, and every noise around him turned into ringing.

The man standing directly in front of him was of average height, just under six feet. His hair was close-cropped, and his eyes were crystal blue—deep and penetrating. He wore a black trench coat over a full suit—the same suit Reed had seen him in the day before outside the Mercedes. But the most striking thing about his appearance wasn't the suit, or the eyes, or even the oversized handgun he held. It was his smile. No, it wasn't a smile. It was a full-blown grin. And not the menacing, evil grin of a mob boss in a movie. This was more like the wild, unbridled grin of a kid with a new bike—pure, genuine joy.

Reed assimilated the entire scene in a millisecond and dismissed it all. He twisted his right hand and pressed the trigger of the Glock. It recoiled in his hand, and the bullet tore through the trench coat, just above the waistline, but he didn't hear the shot. The grin faded, and those crystal eyes flashed in pain. The man stumbled back, coughing and grabbing at his side as Reed followed the shot with a swift punch to the shoulder, knocking him farther back into the café. The gun clattered out of The Wolf's hand as he fell onto the floor, his face still awash with pain, but no blood seeped from the coat.

Body armor.

Reed kicked a chair out of the way and followed him, raising the Glock to align its sights with his forehead. He never got the chance to fire. The man on the floor twisted with blinding speed and swept his right leg against Reed's ankles. He stumbled to keep from falling, catching himself on the counter, but before he could adjust his aim, Wolfgang was already on his feet and spinning toward him. The grin was back, flashing at him a millisecond before a sweeping roundhouse kick knocked the Glock out of Reed's hand and sent his face crashing into the counter.

The room spun as Reed pushed himself up and snatched the Ka-Bar from underneath his shirt, then lunged toward The Wolf with an aggressive sweep of the blade. The man ducked and dodged the stroke with ease, then followed it with a rabbit punch to Reed's chest. The blow struck him with surprising force, knocking the wind out of his lungs and sending him stumbling backward.

"You don't disappoint, Montgomery. They told me you were good."

The Wolf reached into his pocket. A snapping sound rang out through the café, barely puncturing the ringing in Reed's ears. The bright outline of a switchblade knife glistened in The Wolf's right hand.

Reed steadied himself and adjusted his grip on the Ka-Bar, holding the weapon at shoulder height and keeping his eyes locked on his attacker. He spat blood. "I was a Marine."

"So I've heard."

"You know what the Marines say about knife fights?"

The Wolf grinned. "Let me guess . . . Don't get in one?"

"That's right. Because *everybody* gets hurt." Reed jumped a fallen chair and threw himself toward Wolfgang. He kicked up with his right foot, landing his boot into the man's knee as he swept the Ka-Bar toward his attacker's throat. The blade missed The Wolf's neck and tore into his jacket, shredding it and drawing blood from just above his body armor. The switchblade clattered to the floor a moment before they both followed, rolling onto the hardwood in a death lock. Reed fought to raise the knife still clutched in his right hand, but The Wolf's crushing grip closed around his wrist and kept tightening, squeezing the blood from his veins and paralyzing his fingers.

Reed rolled onto his back, and all he could see was The Wolf, leaning over him, his face still alive with that delighted grin. The knife's gleaming tip dangled inches from Reed's throat, and all at once, everything faded. He saw Banks's face again. The bright, honest smile. The way she touched his chest. Her gentle words and radiating warmth. It felt like home.

Home?

Wolfgang bore down on him, pushing, shoving, driving Reed's own knife closer to his jugular with every passing second.

I want to go home.

Wolfgang threw his shoulder into Reed's arm. The knife twitched, then fell half an inch closer.

22

Reed flailed out with his left arm, searching amid the table legs and spilled bagels. He backhanded a coffee mug and sent it spinning across the linoleum, then his fingers closed around something metallic—a spoon. He rammed the utensil into Wolfgang's temple, digging through the skin and sending a stream of blood spurting over the floor. The Wolf shouted and released the pressure on the knife, crashing to the floor beside Reed. The Ka-Bar clattered down behind him, and Reed jumped to his feet, though he could barely see through the blood and adrenaline. As he searched for either gun on the floor, he heard The Wolf struggling to his feet behind him.

Reed grabbed the nearest chair and swung in a wide, powerful arc. The metal chair slammed into Wolfgang's upper arm, knocking the switchblade from his hand again and sending him crashing backward. Reed dropped the chair and dashed for the door, scrambling for the Land Rover keys in his pocket as he rushed into the parking lot. The all-too-familiar sound of sirens rang in the distance as he jerked the driver's door open and jumped inside.

Wolfgang appeared in front of the SUV, the giant handgun clutched between his fingers. He raised it, the grin returning as he laid his finger on the trigger. Reed ducked and shoved the vehicle into gear, slamming on the gas as the handgun thundered again. The bullet busted through the windshield as the tires bounced over the curb and the bumper collided with Wolfgang. Reed kept his head beneath the dash as he shifted into reverse and planted his foot into the accelerator again.

The big British motor rumbled, and the tires spun before catching on the frozen pavement and launching him backward. Reed sat up and turned the wheel to the right before slamming on the brake. The SUV slid into the street, the nose swinging around until he faced the oncoming lane of traffic. The top-heavy vehicle swayed as he completed the turn, and for a moment, he thought it would roll.

Reed threw the shifter back into drive and shoved the pedal to the floor, lurching the SUV forward in a screaming chorus of tires and swerving onto the main avenue of the tiny community. One headlight was out, and there was a big dent in the hood, but the Land Rover drove with surprising force. In mere seconds, the speedometer crossed sixty miles an hour as Reed turned around a tight corner, narrowly missing an oncoming police car. Blue lights blinded him, illuminating the inside of the SUV as bright as day. He jerked the wheel back to the left, sliding around the rear bumper of the squad car and redirecting the Land Rover down a new street.

Reed sucked in a deep breath and leaned back in the seat. His left arm stung and was soaked in blood. The interior of the SUV faded to dark as the lights of the town vanished over a hill. Reed checked the rearview mirror. No sign of The Wolf.

The split-second survey was almost a second too long. The Mercedes coupe spun out of a side street and into his path, leaving him just enough time to jerk the Land Rover toward the ditch and avoid a collision. A rattle of gunshots pounded over the wind, and the back glass exploded.

"Damn Uzi!" Reed pulled the wheel back to the left as the Land Rover bounced through a shallow ditch. Every time he tried to get back on the road, the front tires lost traction, and the Land Rover slid deeper into the ditch.

His search for the four-wheel-drive selector switch inside the console was futile, but just above the shifter was a silver label: FULL-TIME 4WD.

Let's see what you got.

Reed twisted the wheel to the right and redirected the SUV farther into the ditch. The tires locked on the mud, and the four-wheel-drive kicked in as the Land Rover hurtled out of the far side of the ditch and onto a city playground. A wooden tower next to a swing set exploded over the front bumper. Reed shouted and swerved to the right, barely missing a merry-go-round. Sand mixed with the snow, blasting into the air around all four corners of the SUV as bushes, playground equipment, and park benches were blown out of the way by the rampaging vehicle.

Reed hit the windshield wipers, and they bounced over the cracked glass, clearing his view to the edge of the park. He swerved around a picnic table and between two oak trees, then slammed on the brakes. The SUV slid to a halt, rocking on its heavy-duty springs as the back end swung around.

Stillness descended over the park. The hum of the engine was disrupted now by the irregular clicking of the damaged radiator fan. The hood was bucked upward, and steam rose from the engine bay, but the motor still rumbled.

Reed looked around, searching the far side of the park for any sign of the Mercedes. The Wolf hadn't followed him into the park, but his tracks were clear, marked by a war zone of broken playground parts and rutted snow. He wiped the sweat from his face and placed his hand on the shifter.

The Mercedes appeared to his right just as the cops showed up on his left, both cresting the hill outside the playground and driving toward him at different angles. Reed deliberated only an instant before turning away from the flashing blue and red lights. He couldn't kill the cops, but he was damn sure going to kill this Wolf.

Shoving the shifter back into drive, he planted his foot into the accelerator and turned toward the Mercedes. The four-wheel-drive locked in again, and the SUV hurtled over the railroad tie retainer of the playground before bouncing back onto the road. Each landing sent jarring shocks ripping through his spine, igniting fresh pain in his pounding head. He turned the nose of the Land Rover directly toward the Mercedes and stomped on the gas again. All four tires spun, and then the SUV sprang forward as though it were launched out of a catapult, rocketing directly down the middle of the two-lane road.

"Come on, bitch! Come get some!"

The speedometer passed seventy miles an hour as the space between them faded like ice in a skillet. The gleaming Mercedes logo hovered directly over the double yellow lines as The Wolf piloted his car down the middle of the road, straight for the Land Rover.

Reed tightened his fingers around the wheel. *I'll crush you.*

He heard the chatter of the Uzi first. Bullets slammed into the windshield and tore through the SUV's roof as The Wolf swung to the right at the last minute. A snap rang through the cabin as the front corner of the SUV's bumper collided with the Mercedes's side-view mirror, ripping it off. The silver coupe flashed past Reed without an inch to spare, leaving a rush of cold air and gasoline fumes in its wake.

Reed punched the steering wheel. He heard the squeal of tires behind him, then the sound of the coupe sliding around to give chase. He whipped the SUV off the street and back onto the state highway toward Lake Santeetlah.

"Come on, Wolf. Let's see if you run like you howl."

The accelerator bottomed out against the floorboard, and the speedometer rose—one hundred, then one twenty—as the wide, straight highway stretched out in front of him. The needle kept rising as the motor roared louder under the rattling hood. Reed tightened his fingers around the wheel and pushed his foot to the floor.

One forty-five. The motor capped out as the SUV seemed to hover over the asphalt, rushing past the mountains in a blur. He had pushed the Camaro well into the triple digits many times before, but this was an entirely different experience. With no snow tires or racing suspension to press him into the pavement, he stood one breath of a crosswind from being hurtled off the road to his imminent death.

Torrents of nervous sweat ran down his chest as he searched for the Mercedes. Nothing but darkness filled his mirrors, and he relaxed just a little off the pedal, letting the engine wind down a few octaves. Blazing through the rear glass and illuminating the SUV, the unmistakable Mercedes rocketed toward him as though it was powered by jet engines.

Reed jammed his foot into the accelerator again, negotiating around a gentle curve on the highway. The SUV rocked as though it were about to fly free of the pavement.

I'd give anything for my Camaro right now. This jerk would be history.

Reflective mile markers flashed past like Christmas lights as the Mercedes closed in on the Land Rover. The road began to rise and fall more aggressively, forcing both vehicles to decrease their speed, but leaving the clear advantage to the sport coupe. What had once been two hundred yards of buffer quickly shrank to twenty as The Wolf powered closer to the SUV. Any moment now, the chattering roar of the Uzi would open up again, slinging pounds of deadly lead through the back of the Land Rover and toward Reed's head.

Another curve appeared in the road, followed by a hill. Reed topped it first, followed by The Wolf a second behind. A piece of loose bodywork broke free of the Land Rover and flew over the roof. Something metallic clacked inside the engine bay, and a red light flashed next to the speedometer. With the radiator drained of coolant, the engine was starting to overheat.

Reed pressed the gas, sliding around a tighter corner of the road with almost too much momentum. The Land Rover slipped dangerously close to the edge of the highway before the tires caught and pulled him back to safety. The active four-wheel-drive was his only saving grace.

Another straightaway opened up a full hundred yards of flat pavement. The Mercedes was too quick. It lurched forward, closing the gap between them in seconds. He saw the driver's window slide down, followed a moment later by a hand clutching the small black submachine gun. Reed ducked and gripped the steering wheel, waiting for the burst of gunfire to tear through the back of his head.

Moments passed, and Reed looked back to see the Mercedes slowing behind him. The gap between them grew wider as the German coupe rolled to a full stop, now fifty yards back. No cops or anything in the road before them warranted the sudden stop. Behind him now were the bright red taillights of the Mercedes.

What the hell?

The realization hit Reed like a fist in the face. There could be only one reason The Wolf would cut him loose so suddenly—only one reason he would break off the chase.

Banks. God, no.

The SUV creaked and groaned as it shot forward into the darkness. The blast of the wind burned his eyes and chapped his skin as it howled through the open windshield, but he couldn't stop. He had to get back to the cabin.

23

Lake Santeetlah, North Carolina

Smoke poured from the engine bay of the SUV as Reed rolled to a stop beside the cabin. Darkness hung over the A-frame like a blanket, thickened by a dense screen of fog that descended ahead of the coming storm. Reed slammed the door, circling the smashed front end of the Land Rover before pounding up the steps and into the cabin. The currents of tension that ruled his body made every motion feel overpowered and reckless, as though he were no longer controlling his own actions. The front door creaked on its hinges, and Reed searched the kitchen and dining room. Then he saw her.

"Chris!" Banks looked up from the couch, her eyes traveling over his disheveled clothes and bleeding arm. "My God! What happened?"

Reed motioned her toward the back of the cabin. "You have to get behind the wall. Where's Holiday?"

"He got drunk and went to bed. Chris, what's happening?"

"Come with me. Don't ask questions." They hurried into the

master suite, the only room not fully exposed to the bank of windows covering the A-frame.

Reed hit the light switch. "Senator! On your feet!"

Holiday sat up on the bed, covering his ears and groaning. His face was pale and wrinkled into a deep frown. "Chris, what the hell? Get out of here!"

"Get up, Senator." Reed slammed the door shut and flipped the thumb latch.

Banks hurried past him and sat beside Holiday, patting him on the back. "Wake up, Uncle." Her voice was calm, reflecting her continued mental fortitude in the face of yet another wave of chaos.

Reed peered through the four-pane window at the empty woods outside, then pulled the curtains closed. "Do you have any weapons? Firearms?"

Holiday ran his hand over his face. "What are you talking about?"

"Guns, Senator. I need a gun."

Holiday shook his head as though Reed were speaking a different language, but he motioned toward the closet.

Reed jerked the door open and rifled through the clothes, digging past jackets and three-piece suits until he found a hard case nestled in the rear of the closet. A sinking feeling washed over him as the contents were exposed: a single, break-action shotgun. It was an over-under model, with fancy scrollwork carved into the walnut stock, and a frame inlaid with gold etching, tracing patterns down the receiver and toward the barrel.

"Is this it? Do you have a rifle?" Reed lifted the shotgun from the case and opened the breach. It was empty.

"That's all I have." Holiday glared at him. "What the hell is going on?"

Reed returned to the closet and dug into the darkness again. His hand landed on a paper box of twelve-gauge shells. As he read the label, his heart sank again.

Birdshot.

Reed slipped two shells into the open double chambers of the weapon, then slammed the breach closed before dumping the remainder of the box into his pants pocket. "They're coming for you, Senator. Right now."

The color drained from Holiday's face. "Who's coming?" His words slurred, spilling over one another as he tried to stand up.

Banks forced him back onto the bed.

"That's a damn good question. One I'd very much like you to answer. Who tried to kill you in Atlanta?"

Banks frowned at her uncle.

Holiday buried his face in his hands. "No. They can't get to me here. I have guards. The police. They're outside right now!"

Reed returned to the window, peering through a slit in the curtain. "The police can't save you, Senator. Maybe I can, but you need to start talking. Who wants you dead?"

Holiday shook his head again, more adamantly this time. "No. I'm not talking to you about this. I don't know who the hell you think you are, but—"

"Don't test me, Senator!" Reed barked into Holiday's face, grabbing him by the shoulder and shaking him.

The senator's head rolled back, and his mouth fell open. His memory, once fogged with confusion and intoxication, suddenly cleared. "You.... It's *you*!"

Reed cursed under his breath and took a step back. He should have seen this coming. How many times had the tired Senator told Reed he looked familiar? The cat was out of the bag now.

"You kidnapped me! You beat me in that trailer! '*Don't test me.*' That's what you said to me then!"

Holiday dove toward him, and Reed turned with a quick twist of his hips, raising his fist and driving it straight into Holiday's temple with the full force of a left-cross. The senator's assault stopped mid-strike, his eyes rolled back in his head, and he crumbled to the ground without a sound.

Banks gasped and jumped from the bed. "Chris! What the hell! What are you doing?" Her voice cracked with emotion and panic.

A sudden thud resonated through the window, followed almost

immediately by a cry of pain, and then the unmistakable sound of metal slicing through flesh.

Reed shouldered the shotgun and hurried into the living room. "Stay here. Lock the door!"

The words had barely left his lips before a loud pop rang out through the cabin, and the power went out.

They're here.

Reed whispered this time. "Shut the door. Don't come out for anyone."

He heard Banks turn the lock behind him as he slipped across the living room. The front door swung open and the hinges groaned again. In the distance, the lake lapped against the shore, while trees creaked and rustled. Reed waited for a moment, listening for any sign of the guards pacing outside, waiting and hoping for a reassuring shout from someplace in the shadows. Nothing. With the shotgun lifted, he stepped out onto the porch, adjusting his vision to the inky darkness. Nervous tension commanded every inch of his body. He had no idea what he was walking into or how many men waited in the darkness. The Wolf could be one of them, or maybe an army of goons wielding submachine guns stood amongst the trees. There was no way to know—no way to prepare.

Where are you?

His boots sank in the loose snow as he moved away from the cabin. Each step was measured and slow, bouncing back and forth between the shadows like a lynx on the hunt.

The first guard lay face-up, his throat sliced ear-to-ear. Both his sidearm and rifle were gone, leaving nothing but a growing patch of scarlet snow and a corpse already stiffening in the sub-freezing temperature. Reed cursed and moved away from the body, sinking deeper into the shadows. A faint outline of footprints led away from the corpse, toward the lake, but they were rapidly filling as the snowfall returned, drifting down between the trees in a thickening cloud.

Dry chills ripped through his chest, and his fingers tingled around the stock of the shotgun, turning red as he tightened his grip. The trees around him were conspicuously silent of the forest sounds he had become accustomed to—the scampering of a squirrel, the hoot of an owl. Only the wind and the creek of the trees broke the stillness, each step bringing him closer to the lake and deeper into the shadows.

A scream ripped through the forest. Loud and long, then cut short. It was a man's scream—another one of the guards. Reed jerked the shotgun to his shoulder and spun around. The muzzle rose and fell with each breath, and once again the forest fell into deathly stillness.

Where are you?

Reed crept back toward the cabin. Slipping behind a tall red oak, he knelt in the dirt, watching the A-frame through narrowed eyes.

There.

It wasn't movement or even the sound of a twig breaking in the stillness. It was a shadow with a hard outline—too hard and defined to be natural—huddled behind a bush twenty yards away. Reed held the shotgun just below his eye line and faded between the trees like an apparition. Each footfall was slow and deliberate, minimizing the sound of collapsing snow. The wind picked up around him, howling through the trees, as he moved another ten feet around the back of the bush and toward the man on the other side.

He pivoted the muzzle of the shotgun around the bush, coming to rest on a body lying on the other side. The second guard lay on his back, his throat torn open, and his vacant eyes filled with death.

The realization hit Reed a moment too late. He turned and ducked, but couldn't avoid the blow to the back of his neck with the force of a baseball bat, knocking him to his knees and sending the shotgun tumbling from his fingers. Reed hit the ground and rolled to the left, twisting his body to avoid the next blow. Bone cracked as something hard and cold collided with his shin, and the pain that rippled through Reed's leg was almost as powerful as the fear that dominated his mind.

A mountain of a man leaned over him—a full seven feet tall, with gargantuan hands, gripping a four-foot metal pipe. The moment their eyes met Reed's heart skipped a beat. The big man grinned with gapped teeth. One eye stared at Reed while the other wandered at random, gazing into the forest.

The goon from prison. Did he work for Oliver all along?

His thick lips sneered down at Reed as he swung again, straight for Reed's chest. Reed rolled to the left, and the metal pole slammed into his hip with bone-crushing force, igniting pain that shot down his leg and flooded his brain.

The shotgun. Where's the shotgun?

Reed clawed at the dirt and swept his arm through the low piles of loose snow. He fought to pull himself backward, then felt the smooth metal of the double-barrel shotgun beneath his fingers. Before he could snatch it up, he saw the glint of the pole arcing through the air toward him. He rolled, and the weapon glanced off his shoulder.

No. I'm not dying this way!

Reed lifted the gun and swung the muzzle toward the giant's torso. The big man was already mid-swing when Reed pressed both triggers, dumping two twelve-gauge shells directly into his chest. The thunder of the shotgun shook the forest as the birdshot tore into the man and launched him backward.

Reed snapped the breach open and dug fresh shells out of his pocket, slammed them into the dual chambers, and flicked it shut again. The snowfall that swirled around him assumed the shape of a vortex, mixing with the wind and tearing at his hair. He spun back toward the forest and raised the shotgun. Twenty yards away, circling between the tree trunks, a shadow ran away from him, deeper into the woods.

The shotgun boomed like a cannon, and Reed dumped the empty shells and replaced them, breaking into a jog toward the elusive shadow. Blinding rage and the will to destroy overcame his awareness of the world around him, creating a tunnel that led to his next target.

The shadow faded into the forest. Reed swept the shotgun through the trees, searching for the outline of the running man. He was gone, swallowed by the storm.

Reed lowered the weapon and sucked in a breath. Only the whistle of the wind joined him in the forest now. Everything else was cold and empty. Why was life always a vapor between his fingers?

As he turned back toward the cabin, a dull orange lit the forest on the far side of the howling curtain of snow. A leaden weight descended into his stomach as he began to run again, crossing ditches and ducking under trees. As the yards passed under his feet, the orange glow clarified, joined by a trace of warmth.

The cabin was engulfed in flames.

24

Tall columns of smoke poured from the metal roof as fire consumed the log walls, filling the front porch. Glass shattered and a window frame collapsed. The Land Rover was also on fire, blazing beside the cabin with oily smoke clouding over the engine bay.

"Banks!" Reed dashed for the front door, but an overwhelming surge of heat stopped him in his tracks. He screamed into the fire. "*Banks!*"

"She's right here, Reed!" The voice carried over the wind behind him. Strong. Defiant. Just a hint of a British accent.

Reed spun and jerked the shotgun to his shoulder, aiming it at Oliver Enfield, his former employer, longtime mentor, and personal Judas. Banks was pinned under his left arm, standing on her toes as Oliver held a polished 1911 pistol to her temple. Just beside them, Holiday knelt on the ground with his hands in the snow and his head bowed as the giant pointed a massive revolver at the back of his skull. The big man's shirt was shredded from the shotgun blast, revealing the battered and torn surface of a Kevlar vest beneath it. His good eye glowed with devilish glee as actual drool dripped from his lip.

Reed slowly lowered the shotgun, keeping his fingers on the dual triggers of the weapon as he walked down the hillside, stopping twenty feet away.

Oliver grinned. His bald head shone in the dancing light of the flames, gleaming over a row of perfect white teeth. Tears streamed down Banks's face as she gasped for breath under the suffocating grip.

"Well, Reed, you found me. You here to pay for my cabin?"

Reed switched his gaze from the tall killer, to Banks, to Holiday kneeling in the snow. "Let her go."

Oliver laughed. "Who? This bitch? You know, I've hired a lot of military washouts, Reed, but I miscalculated with you. I thought somebody who gunned down half a dozen military contractors must be a coldhearted killer, but what I failed to appreciate was the *why* of it all. You're just a little superman, aren't you? Always looking out for the little guy."

Without blinking, and with a mind dulled beyond any perception of precise emotion, Reed stared at Oliver. He felt angry, yes, but more than that, he felt cold. For three years he surrendered his soul to this man, traveling around the world to gun down whoever he was told to kill. He never questioned. Never objected. He accepted the reality as his job, and he accepted Oliver as his boss—a man to obey, if not to trust. That had been the worst decision Reed ever made, not because it resulted in his ultimate betrayal, but because it ended here. In the snow. With Banks's life hanging in the balance.

Oliver jerked Banks's hair back, exposing her neck. "Tell me, girl. Who did he say he was? Let me guess . . . a *venture capitalist*."

Confusion and hurt poured into her soul as she looked at Reed and then squeezed her eyes shut. That pained look of desperation and fear tore Reed to his very core, shattering every confidence and justification he ever had, stripping him all the way to the foundation of who he really was: a heartless killer. A man who had sold his soul.

Oliver laughed. "Of course he did. That's what I trained him to say. I mean, he can't walk around bragging about being a cold-blooded murderer, can he?"

Holiday's eyes were still clouded with drunkenness, but there was a clarity that burned through the fog—a single point of focus strong enough to draw Reed's attention. "Did you kill him?" Holiday asked.

The years of pain and insecurity and whatever horrible secrets Holiday bore wore down his tired features, making him look years older than he was. The circles under his eyes were darker and heavier than before, and he sagged in total defeat. But Reed could still see him clinging to this one point of tension—the burden Holiday had carried ever since his best friend had been murdered in New Orleans. The guilt that Holiday himself was responsible.

"No." Reed met his tired gaze with all the honesty and integrity he had left in his blackened soul. Holiday nodded once, and Reed turned back to his old mentor. "*Paul Choc.*"

Oliver tilted his head, feigning confusion, then he laughed. "Oh, you mean Blazer. The man you killed."

"He was one of yours, wasn't he? A contractor you needed to burn."

"Killer in, killer out, Reed. It was his choice to walk away from me, just like it was yours. And he paid for it, just like you will."

Reed spat the remnants of blood from his mouth. "Okay. Well, I'm here. What do you want?"

Oliver grinned. "Thirty lives, Reed. I want you to finish your job."

Reed's fingers tightened around the grip of the gun, the barrel hovered at waist-height, pointing at the gut of the cross-eyed man. Through bared teeth, he hissed, "*Let her go.*"

Oliver's grin perished, and he jammed the gun deeper into her temple, pressing until Banks cried out in pain. Streams of tears ran down her face.

"Do it, Reed. Finish your job!"

The senator looked at Reed with steady, unblinking eyes, and slowly, Reed dropped the barrel of the shotgun over the groin of the giant, over Holiday's face, and then centered it on his chest.

"Don't.... Please don't do it." Banks sobbed, her neck twisted as Oliver drove her head into his shoulder with the pressure of the pistol.

"Pull the trigger, Reed, or I'll pull mine!" Oliver's expression reignited into a vicious smirk.

The desperate pleading in Banks's eyes tore straight through Reed's heart like a rifle bullet, making him go weak at the knees. The snowflakes that fell against her elegant features faded quickly to raindrops as thunder echoed overhead. She looked so perfect, even with the pain that dominated her face. She looked like everything he never knew he always wanted.

Oliver jerked upward, lifting Banks off her feet by her neck as she choked and scratched at his arm. "*Do it, Reed!*"

The senator still stared at Reed, but a calm settled over his tired eyes. He nodded once. "Save my goddaughter."

The giant cursed, his guttural voice booming over the wind. He jammed the barrel of the massive revolver into Holiday's back and pushed him forward onto his hands and knees, his head bowed directly beneath the twin muzzles of the shotgun.

Reed settled the butt of the weapon into his shoulder and stared down the barrel at Holiday's forehead. He placed his index finger over the front trigger and closed his left eye, then drew in a deep breath.

Banks fought against Oliver's grip and reached out for her godfather. "Please ... don't ..."

"It's okay, Banks." Holiday's voice was soft. "I love you."

Holiday's left hand twitched, and his palms settled into the slurry of snow and mud. His left index finger rose and tapped down. Once. Twice.

On the third tap, Reed spun to the left at the same moment Holiday launched himself to his feet. The revolver barked, and the shotgun spun upward, still swinging to the left as Reed depressed the trigger. The world around Reed descended into a chaos of slow motion. Blood exploded from Holiday's back, knocking him to his knees even as the senator fought to turn and assault the giant. The shotgun recoiled, spitting a deadly spray of lead birdshot over Oliver's right shoulder, inches from Banks's head. The edge of the shot pattern caught the right side of Oliver's face, shredding the skin and flesh from his cheek and neck. The kingpin killer screamed and fell back, dropping the handgun and releasing Banks. He clawed at his face, shrieking as though he were on fire.

Reed redirected the shotgun and depressed the second trigger. The back of the giant's head vanished into a blast of hair and brain matter as he crumbled to the ground. Reed snapped the breach open as he stepped over Holiday and toward Oliver, ejecting empty shells over his arm. He dug into his pocket for the next load, grabbed two shells, and lifted them toward the breach.

Oliver's face was a clouded, distorted mess of flesh and bone. His right eye was gone, and a bloody socket was left behind. He launched himself forward with unprecedented ferocity, grabbing the shotgun and jerking Reed off balance. They crashed to the ground as blows rained down on Reed's exposed face. The fresh shells slipped from his fingers and he released the shotgun as they tumbled through the snow.

Reed's fingers closed around Oliver's arms, and he dug in, channeling all of his strength and anger into this moment. This man had become the monster in his closet—a lying, thieving conniver who dangled freedom in front of his nose then snatched it away at the last moment. He would rip Oliver limb from limb before he walked away.

A knife flashed, clenched between Oliver's white fingers. It sliced through Reed's shirt, leaving a gushing red line behind it. Reed screamed, hurled Oliver off of him, and drove his left fist into Oliver's stomach. The slick mud gave way beneath him as he followed up the punch, and Reed fell forward over Oliver as both men rolled down the steep lake bank. Icy water closed over Reed's head as the knife flashed again and dug into his side. Oliver landed on his stomach, pressing him deeper into the water and pinning him against the mud.

Reed couldn't breathe. Darkness closed overhead. The knife dug into his shoulder and stuck there as Oliver's big hands closed around his throat and slammed the back of his head into the muddy lake bottom. Reed kicked and struggled, clawing for any leverage to shove his attacker off. His fingers dug through the mud for a rock or a stick, but nothing except the slimy lake bottom touched his fingers as life slipped from his lungs. Oliver bellowed, pushing Reed deeper into the mud. Each heartbeat that pounded through his skull came slower than the one before as death encroached on his consciousness.

The thunder of the shotgun rang out from the edge of Reed's reality, and a rippling shockwave shot through Reed's body as Oliver fell forward. The mutilated features of the killer crashed into the lake. The iron grip loosened around his throat, and Reed launched himself out of the water, gasping as he cleared the surface. Oliver flopped and screamed on top of him, but the power from his body was gone.

On the shore, Banks stood in the pouring rain with the shotgun in her trembling hands. Tears streamed down as she stared at Reed, full of so much pain and sadness. In an instant, that stare communicated all of the anger, hurt, and agony of the betrayal she felt. All of it directed at him.

Reed met her gaze and shoved Oliver back, then reached out for her. "Banks! Wait!"

She dropped the shotgun and shook her head once.

"Don't go!"

Water splashed around him as Reed fought to his knees.

"Banks!"

She ran up the hill, vanishing into the rain and darkness, and leaving him in the shallows. Reed screamed into the howling wind, feeling his throat choked by cold and emotion and so much pain.

His hands trembled and he started to slog out of the lake, but she was gone. In that split moment, the woman he loved slipped away like water between his fingers.

Reed's fingers closed around his limp mentor's arms and he hoisted him out of the water and hurled him onto the bank. The effort almost exhausted him as ripples of agony swept down his arms from his shoulder, mixing with blood and lake water. But he didn't stop.

The old killer landed on the bank with a grunt and looked up at him through a single bloodshot eye. His entire right cheek was gone, exposing missing teeth and a shredded ear. A tongue covered in blood lapped against the roof of his mouth as his torn lips lifted into a twisted grin. "Look at you . . . saved by a bitch."

Reed retrieved Oliver's fallen knife and slammed it into his stomach, digging in and twisting. Oliver's head lifted off the bank as a scream ripped free of his mutilated throat. He coughed up blood, spraying it over Reed's chest before his head slammed back into the bank again. Reed shoved the knife in deeper, pushing it until it slammed into Oliver's spine.

"Who are they, Oliver?" Reed screamed over the rain, bellowing right into Oliver's face.

Oliver spat, then gasped for air. The sound rasped and choked as blood puddled in his throat. "Don't you wish . . . you knew?"

Reed screamed again and drove his fist into what remained of the old killer's face. "Tell me, Oliver! Who are they? Who ordered the Holiday hit?"

Oliver rasped for air, his roving eye settling on Reed. Calm fell over the pain, and his torn lips twisted into a slight smile. "Maybe . . . you should ask . . . Kelly."

Without another breath, his head fell back against the mud, and the life vanished from his body.

Reed jerked the knife free and threw his head back, screaming into the rain. Rage and unbridled madness overtook him, and he jumped up and drove his foot into Oliver's ribcage, but the old man already lay still and lifeless—as dead as the hundreds of men and women who died under his command.

Reed turned away from the fallen killer and scanned the hillside, screaming again for Banks. Only the rain answered his cries, mixed with a cough and a soft voice from farther away from the water. Reed fought his way up the bank and followed the sound, running through the mud and staggering amongst the trees.

The voice came from the far side of the giant's body. Reed slid to his knees and lifted Holiday's head. The senator blinked once as he stared at Reed and then smiled softly. "Damn . . . venture capitalists . . ."

"Senator, you're dying. I need you to talk to me. Who wanted you dead?"

Holiday coughed up fresh pools of blood, and he shook with a violent tremor. Then he closed his eyes.

"Senator! Talk to me!"

Holiday's lips twitched, and Reed leaned down, pressing his ear close to the senator's mouth.

"From end . . . to end."

"From end to end? I don't know what that means!"

Holiday's neck went limp, and his head rolled back. Reed laid him down, then stood up slowly. He looked down at the dead senator, then back at the bloodied, crushed body of his mentor. Of all the gory scenes of carnage he had experienced in his life, this one gripped him more deeply. It sank into his heart and enflamed anger like he had never felt before.

Oliver's last words echoed in his tired mind. *"Maybe you should ask Kelly."*

Panic pushed back his anger as the reality sank in. Reed fell to his knees again and rolled the giant over. The big man's face was gone, and his jacket fell open. Reed searched the pockets, dumping out wads of gum wrappers and a pocketknife, and then his fingers hit something hard and heavy. As he pulled it out, the light from the distant cabin fire glinted off polished metal. It was an aluminum card about the size of a credit card, painted black with nothing but a single image etched on one side: a silver badger. Reed shoved it into his pocket, then resumed his search until he found a pair of car keys with a Cadillac logo emblazoned on them. He snatched up the massive revolver lying in the mud beside the body, and turning toward the hill, he broke into a run.

25

Reed found the Escalade parked a hundred yards behind the cabin on the side of the road. He slammed it into gear and shoved the accelerator to the floor, spinning the big SUV around and back onto the road. He swerved past oncoming police cars as he wound his way through the mountains, topping hills and crashing through canyons.

Blood streamed from his arm. He tore off a shred of his shirt and jammed it into the knife wound, maintaining pressure on the wad of dirty cloth as he crossed out of the lake town and blew through Robbinsville. Everything fogged around him, blurring almost out of view. It was all he could do to keep the SUV pointed straight down the road, but he didn't relax on the speed. Only one thought pounded through his skull: *Please let her be alive.*

The one hundred twenty miles back to northern Atlanta blazed by him in ninety minutes, swirling into a series of highways and small towns that were more like a memory than an experience. As he crashed into the outskirts of Canton, he could already see an orange light in the back of the neighborhood and the column of smoke that blackened the sky.

Reed screeched around a corner on the narrow residential

streets and slammed on the brakes. He left the revolver in the passenger seat and jumped out, still holding the shirt against his wound as he raced the last few yards down the street. Fire trucks lined the sidewalks, blocking his view as dirty, tired firemen walked back and forth between them. He pressed through the crowd, ignoring several shouts for him to stop as he slid around the last truck and faced the house at the end of the cul-de-sac.

Nothing remained of the home. Black ashes were soaked but still smoldering at the bottom of fallen brick walls and the remnants of a pine wood frame. Firemen lined the edge of the lot, showering the foundation with streams of pressurized water, but it wasn't necessary—the flames were gone, leaving only charred emptiness behind.

Three men in white plastic suits stood by two stretchers near a white van marked *"County Coroner."* Reed stumbled toward the stretchers, his hands hanging limp at his sides. The ache of irrefutable reality sank into his soul as he shoved the first man aside and stared down at the small, charred body on the first stretcher. He collapsed to his knees, tears gushing from his eyes as he fell forward. He couldn't feel the hands on his shoulders or the ground beneath his legs. Racking pain ripped through his body, starting at his throat and burning through his stomach.

"Sir . . . you need to stand up. Come with me." The cop's eyes were filled with compassion as his firm but gentle grip descended on Reed's arm. "Sir, stand up, please. We'll get you help."

Reed watched the stretchers as they vanished inside the van. The last glimpse of the bodies faded inside, and the doors crashed shut.

"Can you tell us who they were? We haven't identified the bodies."

Reed forced back the tears and ran his tongue over dry lips. He closed his eyes and bowed his head. When he spoke, he didn't recognize his own voice. The toneless words sounded as though they came from another world. Another man. "Her name is Kelly Armstrong."

"Thank you. I'm so sorry." The officer patted his arm. "Come with me. You need medical attention."

A soft whimpering rang from beyond the fire engines. Reed's eyes snapped open, and he looked back toward the burned-out house. He heard it again—barely audible but strong.

"Baxter?"

Reed pushed past the policeman, around the firefighters, and through the rubble of the house toward the burned-out backyard. He heard the whimper again—stronger this time. He grabbed a picnic table half-consumed by the scalding flames, and pain shot up his arms as the embers of the dying fire burned into his skin. With one powerful push, he threw it back and looked down.

Baxter's short brown hair was singed from the fire, and his big black eyes were bloodshot as he stared up at Reed. Swollen red burn marks crisscrossed his skin, and his breaths came in short, whistling bursts. He lay on the ground, barely moving, his paws and legs blackened by ashes and soot.

Reed scooped the big dog up, holding him close to his chest as tears streamed down his cheeks. "It's okay, boy. I'm here. I've got you."

The bulldog whimpered again and pressed his wrinkly face close to Reed's chest. He smelled of ashes and smoke, and his skin trembled when Reed touched the burn marks, but he didn't fight as he settled into Reed's arms.

Reed turned back to the street but stopped as he saw the officer step forward, his head tilted toward the radio clipped to his uniform. The cop nodded once, then reached for his gun. "Sir, stop where you are. Put down the dog."

Reed didn't wait for the gun to rise from the holster. He dashed back through the ashes of the home, slipping through the backyard as men shouted behind him. With Baxter clutched in his arms, he ran through the yards of half a dozen homes before dashing between two houses and reaching the Escalade.

Shouts and sirens rang out, but Reed ignored them as he swept the revolver aside and set Baxter into the passenger seat. The tires spun, and the SUV slid around again, back toward the open street. Sirens faded behind him, wisping away as quickly and elusively as the smoke into the black sky.

Reed didn't try to hold back the sobs that racked his body. His arms shook as the tears streamed down his face. He could still see her small, burned body lying on that stretcher. Faceless. Nameless. Her unborn baby inside of her. The reality that it was *his* fault was inescapable. He had brought Kelly into this and made her fiancé and her innocent baby victims of his own failures. And these people, these shadows behind the curtain, these demons who called the shots, held Oliver on a leash, and released murderers into the world—he didn't know what they were protecting or why, but it was obvious they would stop at nothing to get what they wanted.

Baxter sat up in the passenger seat, his beady eyes fixed on the bloody revolver lying on the floorboard. His lip curled up over his jutting teeth as his chest rumbled into a deep, menacing growl. Reed placed one hand on the big dog, sinking his fingers into the singed hair and soft skin.

There was nobody left—no allies, no friends. Banks was gone. Holiday was dead. Winter had cut Reed off. There was only one choice before him—only one road to travel. He blinked back the tears and clenched his fingers around the wheel.

"Don't worry, boy. We're going to kill them. We're going to kill them all."

TOTAL WAR

REED MONTGOMERY BOOK 3

For my parents, Tony and Karen,

who taught me the spirit of a pioneer.

1

Atlantic City,
New Jersey

"Are you here to check in?"

The woman behind the counter wore a red velvet vest, black satin pants, and shoes that gleamed under the casino lights. Her hair was knotted behind her head, exposing the tight skin of too many facelifts and not enough vitamin D. The smile she wore couldn't hide the exhaustion in her eyes or the disinterest in her tone.

Reed pushed his aviator sunglasses closer to his eyes. He laid the metal business card on the counter, and the casino lights glinted off its glossy black surface, shining on the emblem of a silver badger etched in the center of the card.

"I'm here to see Mr. Muri."

A shadow of emotion broke the exhaustion in her vacant gaze. Or maybe it was excitement. Trepidation?

They so often look the same. I wonder if she knows what kind of man she works for.

The woman smiled again, nodded once, and disappeared

through a doorway. Reed replaced the card into his pocket and leaned against the counter. The edge of the granite bit into the back of his sport coat, colliding with his bruised back. Through the dark lenses of his sunglasses, the flashing neon lights were only partially muted. The *shrink* of slot machine levers melded with the clinking ring of the dials as they spun like Ferris wheels on crack. A craps table on the far side of the room was crowded by a dozen men in collared shirts, half-drunk, leaning in and shouting as the dice bounced over the scarlet felt. The faint odor of flowers wafted from an air freshening device buried in the vents of the overhead AC unit, a clever design that subdued the chaos and tension of the room and further facilitated reckless spending.

What a masterpiece. And people wonder why the house always wins.

"Sir?" The woman returned to the counter.

Reed stood up with a soft grunt as his aching muscles objected to the movement. Her smile was gone now. Two large men with emotionless stares accompanied her, both dressed in dark grey suits that bulged around oversized arms and barrel chests.

Why do all mob goons look the same?

"These men will escort you to Mr. Muri."

Reed stepped around the counter. The first goon pushed the door open and led the way into a hall while the second fell in behind Reed. Flashes of orange and blue from the casino floor vanished into a sterile white of LED overheads glaring onto the floor and walls. The hall reminded Reed of a sick ward in a hospital—bare minimum in every way with plain metal doors and cheap linoleum flooring.

The house doesn't waste money, either. Another reason it always wins.

Except for today. Today, everyone would lose. It was why Reed left Georgia and drove twelve hours to be there. It was why he jacked himself up on caffeine pills before leaving the rental car in an alley and slipping up to the casino like another drunk tourist—casual, but fully alert and ready to kill.

Today the house will burn.

Twin silver doors blocked their path at the end of the hall. The lead goon punched a button on the wall, and the elevator opened immediately, revealing an interior decorated with mahogany panels and gold rails. Gentle elevator music drifted down from invisible speakers. Reed walked in and waited while the two men swiped ID cards. The doors glided shut, and they turned on him as the car began to descend.

"Arms up." The command was as blunt and bland as the man who grunted it. Reed lifted his arms while the men felt down his legs, around his waist, and over his ribcage. The big hand running up his side stopped at the suede holster with the oversized revolver tucked inside. The retainer strap clicked, and the weapon fell into the goon's fingers.

The men looked down at the massive handgun. Even with a short, four-inch barrel, the .500 magnum revolver dwarfed their large hands. As the first man lifted the gun and raised both eyebrows, the gaping, .50 caliber muzzle stared Reed in the face.

Reed shrugged. "Bear hunting."

They sneered at him, and the revolver disappeared beneath one man's sport coat as the elevator bell rang and the doors rolled open. Reed was shoved forward into a hallway that couldn't have been more different from the stark white of four floors above. More mahogany panels framed dark red carpet, gold trim, and brass light fixtures. Shadows clung to the corners, and the big feet of the two men behind him barely made a sound as they propelled him down the hallway toward the tall oak door at the end. Both men placed their thumbs against a black panel mounted next to the doorjamb, and the lock clicked.

This Muri guy really thinks he's something. All middlemen do.

The door swung open without a sound, and once more, the meaty hands pushed him forward. Reed stumbled across the carpet onto a thick rug, his vision temporarily blinded by the flash of lights overhead. Built into the walls of the large room were tall bookshelves, and a giant leather couch faced him next to a glass table stacked with liquor bottles. A quick survey of the occupants revealed a tall, thin man in a suit standing in one corner, a whiskey glass in one hand and his black hair plastered against his scalp. Only one other person occupied the parlor, and he faced Reed from the comfort of the oversized leather couch, one leg crossed over the other and round glasses mounted over a pointed nose. His face was worn and pale, with a network of scars tracing his left cheek and leading up to his ear.

Reed heard the door click behind him, and he tugged at the bottom of his jacket, brushing out the wrinkles left by the thick fingers of the two goons. One thug handed the revolver to the man on the couch, who surveyed the weapon, then motioned toward a chair sitting across from him. Reed adjusted his sunglasses again, then took a seat.

"Welcome." The man's voice was smooth, laden with a thick Swiss accent, but he spoke with the relaxed tone of a person comfortable with English. "Charles, won't you pour our guest a brandy?"

The tall man with the black hair lifted a bottle of brown liquor, then handed Reed a tumbler textured with diamond stipples. The first sip revealed the unmistakable smoky smoothness of a high-dollar brand—something old and rare.

"Thank you." Reed lifted the glass toward the man on the couch and was answered with a slight bow.

"Whom do I have the pleasure of hosting?" The voice was still calm, but an air of directness slipped into the tone.

Reed set the glass on the table and popped his knuckles. "Call me Chris. It's not overly important who I am."

The man shrugged—slight and disinterested. "Fine. What can I do for you, *Chris?*"

"I understand you're in the business of brokering contractors. Specifically, the criminal kind."

The room fell silent. Reed was vaguely aware of the two big men standing to his left, and Charles stepped behind a tall armchair, his hands falling out of sight.

Probably to a gun or a knife. As if either will save him.

The man on the couch smiled. "You're quite mistaken. I'm a simple businessman. A casino owner. Nothing more."

Reed leaned back in the chair and crossed his legs. He flipped the card from his pocket and onto the coffee table between them, then returned the smile. "No, you're not. You're Cedric Muri. The goon broker."

The smile on Cedric's face faded as he eyed the card with the glowing silver badger. He took a long sip of brandy, then returned his gaze to Reed. "Where did you get that?"

"From a dead man. Big fellow, cross-eyed. Carried a rather large Smith & Wesson revolver. The one you're holding, as it happens."

Cedric's gaze fell to the weapon, then returned to Reed. Fire blazed in his eyes, and he dropped the brandy onto the coffee table. He sat forward. "Why are you here?"

"We'll get to that in just a moment. First, I need some information. Besides the big guy I killed in North Carolina, you also hired out some East European thugs to a South American prick named Salvador. While I was busy carving them up in Atlanta, one of them mentioned your name. So, my question is, why are you supplying soldiers to the people who want to kill me?"

Cedric's lips lifted into a smile. "Reed Montgomery. The assassin."

Reed nodded. "That's me, although I'm trying my damnedest to retire. People like you are making it difficult."

"That's because people like me are threatened by rogue assassins like you."

"You wouldn't be if you had stayed out of it. Those two Europeans I mentioned kidnapped a young lady on behalf of Mr. Salvador. I happen to like her a lot. And then, of course, there are the men I gunned down at Pratt-Pullman Yard in Atlanta. None of these shitheads were proper soldiers. None of them were Oliver Enfield's men. So they must've been yours, and you're going to tell me who paid for them."

Cedric drummed the tips of his fingers against each other, producing the only noise in the still room. He lifted one finger and motioned toward Reed. "I think we're done here, Mr. Montgomery. I'm sure Mr. Salvador will pay handsomely for your head."

Reed lifted the brandy glass and drained the contents. "I was hoping you'd say that."

The floor creaked under the weight of one of the big men, whose reflection Reed saw flash in the gold railing behind Cedric. As he leaned forward to deliver a death blow, Reed sprang from the chair, and without turning around, grabbed him by the arm. With a quick heave, he bent forward and dragged him over his back. The goon sailed over the chair and crashed against the tabletop in an explosion of glass. A gunshot cracked from behind Reed, snapping against the wooden walls and reverberating in his ears. Cedric dove to the carpet as Reed followed him, and Charles vanished behind the minibar.

The revolver's grip filled Reed's hands as he jerked it off the floor and spun it toward the thug lying amid the shattered table. With a quick pull of the trigger, the room erupted into an explosion. The man on the floor convulsed as his head was blasted apart under the smashing impact of the 350-grain projectile. The shockwave that tore through Reed's arm sent him hurtling back against the floor as though a horse had kicked him. Glass tore through his jacket and into his shoulder, sinking into flesh so bruised he barely felt the cuts. Reed redirected the revolver and fired again, sending the second goon crashing to the floor.

Two more shots tore through the paneling that sheltered Charles, sending shards of wood spraying over the floor amid the broken liquor bottles. The gunshots ceased. Reed picked himself up, rubbing a sore shoulder. The handgun kicked like nothing he'd ever fired before. His hand ached, and his ears rang from the thunderous blast.

But it damn sure gets the job done.

The two fallen gunmen lay still and silent, with none of the twitches or residual fighting power he was used to men having after he shot them in the chest with his 9mm. The Smith & Wesson 500 was the cannon of the handgun world. The last word.

A gasping, rasping sound leaked from behind the couch. Reed rubbed his thumb against the Smith and shoved the couch out of the way, exposing the groveling figure of Cedric Muri on the floor behind it. Slobber and spilled brandy coated the hardwood floor beneath him, and he scrambled backward as Reed advanced.

"You should've worked with me, Cedric."

"Please . . ." Cedric held out his hand. "Let's discuss this!"

Reed squatted on the carpet and grabbed Cedric by the hair, pulling him forward and shoving the Smith's muzzle against his neck. Patience and self-restraint vanished from his body as renewed rage replaced them, quickening his heart rate and making his hand shake against the handle of the gun.

"Listen to me, you *shit*. Last week, a house burned down in Canton, Georgia. Two people died. Were your men involved?"

Cedric choked and struggled against the gun. "I don't know!"

Reed shoved the gun harder into his throat. "Like hell you don't know. *Tell me!*"

"I swear I never know what my men are hired to do! I'm just a business—"

Reed smashed the revolver against the side of Cedric's skull. "No more excuses! Do I look like I care?"

Once more, Cedric clawed at Reed's arm and tried to look away.

Reed slammed his head back against the couch and screamed into his face. "*Look at me like a man when I'm talking to you!*"

Cedric shuddered, then slowly turned his head toward Reed.

"Were your men responsible? Answer the question."

Reed had stared into a lot of eyes in the moments preceding a kill. Sometimes those eyes were a hundred yards away, viewed through a scope. Sometimes they were only photos—images of the people he was hunting. In none had he seen such total terror like the complete, consuming fear that filled Cedric's.

The shuddering fragment of a man on the floor nodded his confession.

Reed threw Cedric against the floorboards and stood up. "Do you know her name?"

Cedric just sobbed.

"I thought not. Her name was Kelly Armstrong, and she was a good woman. I don't suppose you know what that means, but it's an incredibly rare thing to find anyone good in this world. Kelly was the best of the best. Your men torched her house and burned her alive."

Reed lifted the revolver and opened the cylinder. He ejected the spent .50 caliber casings, then fed new cartridges into the weapon. Cedric gasped for air, his wide eyes fixed on the handgun.

"Do you know what they call me?" Reed snapped the cylinder shut and faced Cedric. "I know you've heard. What's my name?"

Cedric's voice warbled over the bile that boiled out of his throat. "They call you The Prosecutor."

"That's right. They call me the prosecutor—because I'm all about justice. I lay down the law, balance the scales. Or at least that's what I told myself, so I could sleep at night. But all that has changed. I'm over it, you know? I've moved on to bigger things. So you can rest assured I'm not a prosecutor, and I'm not here for justice."

Momentary hope flashed in Cedric's eyes as he peered up at Reed, his fingernails sinking into the hardwood. That hope vanished the instant Reed laid the muzzle against Cedric's forehead and cocked the hammer.

"I'm an executioner. And I'm here for revenge."

"No . . . please . . ." New sobs escaped Cedric's throat as he stared down the barrel and into Reed's cold eyes.

"Who hired you?" Reed spat out the question like a bad taste in his mouth. "Was it Enfield?"

Cedric shook his head.

"So, who was it? Give me a name, and I'll make your death quick."

"Please . . . don't kill me. I have a family."

"*So did she!*" Reed screamed and kicked Cedric in the stomach. The man fell forward, coughing and spluttering over the carpet.

"*Who are they?*"

"I don't know. I never had a name. I only dealt with Salvador."

Reed gripped the revolver, wondering if he could believe Cedric, then decided that it didn't matter. "I should kill you. You deserve to die. Do you know that?"

Cedric convulsed on the floor and didn't answer.

Reed grabbed him by the hair and screamed in his face. "I said, *do you know that?*"

Tears streamed down his face as Cedric nodded. "Yes . . . yes. I do. I deserve to die."

Reed released him and spat on the floor. "I'm glad we're on the same page. It just so happens I'm going to let you live, because you have a job to do. Do you understand me?"

Cedric nodded emphatically. "What do you want?"

"I want them to know who's coming for them. I want them to know they rattled the wrong cage. Go back to your bosses and tell them Reed Montgomery has declared total war. Do you understand me?"

Cedric nodded again, sweat dripping off his sharp cheekbones.

Reed lowered the weapon, relaxing his finger off the trigger. He stared at the man on the floor, then walked away. Cedric gasped for air behind him, and Reed heard his hands hit the floor. A soft, metallic click echoed through the room.

In one fluid motion, Reed spun around, and the gun bucked in his hand as he pulled the trigger. The bullet smashed into Cedric's chest and sent him crashing to the floor as the pistol fell from his hands.

Reed holstered the revolver beneath his shirt and leered into the security camera on the ceiling. He lifted one hand and pointed into the lens. "I'm coming."

2

University of Edinburgh
Edinburgh, Scotland, United Kingdom

"A tradition of excellence in both academic achievement and the pursuits of human development is the most sacred value of this institution and has been since our founding. When calling to mind some of the greatest examples of students who have embraced these values over the course of my forty-year career, the young man who will speak next will most certainly be among the first names I remember. He is a sterling example of work ethic, dedication, and a relentless desire to push the barrier of knowledge as we know it. For the graduating class of Edinburgh Medical School, please welcome for the first time . . . Dr. Wolfgang Pierce!"

The old hall erupted in cheers from the hundreds of guests and students. Many of the voices that called out in excitement reflected accents from all over the world—Australian, Spanish, Indian, Polish—but the slender white male who mounted the steps was unmistakably American. With high cheekbones and a bold brow, his body language was consumed by overtones of excitement as he smiled at the crowd and waved at his fellow students. The spring in his step spoke to his youth—not more than thirty-five—but the quiet confidence that followed him as he stepped behind the podium felt older and more collected.

Wolfgang rested his hands on the worn mahogany. As the cheering died out, the hall was again swallowed in stillness and genuine anticipation, as though the guests in this hallowed place actually cared about what Wolfgang would say next. His fellow students knew him not just as the academic king of the university but as a friend—a smiling face with kind words for every class.

"Thank you, Dean Rostier. And thank you, ladies and gentlemen, for your generous welcome. My name is Wolfgang, and I'm from New York."

Before he could continue, another eruption of applause broke from the student body. He smiled warmly and nodded at them, waiting for the disruption to die out before he cleared his throat.

"I came to the University of Edinburgh after completing my graduate studies at Cambridge. Over the past three years, I have experienced the most sincere and overwhelming joy being a part of the outstanding program this university administers in the interest of advancing medical science. I consider myself to be amongst the most fortunate people in the world to have learned here and contributed to ongoing medical research. Today, as we gather to celebrate our achievements and prepare to take the next steps in our careers, I want to tell you a personal story. Something very dear to me."

The silence in the hallway was so perfect, Wolfgang could hear the softest breath in the back of the room. Excitement and nervousness warred with the practiced calm in his mind, threatening to overwhelm him. He didn't like crowds or stages, and he enjoyed delivering a speech even less than listening to one. But today was important—too important to worry about himself.

"As many of you know, somebody very special to me suffers from a terrible disease. Her name is Collins, and she's my twenty-year-old sister. From the time she was born, Collins has been a victim of the genetic disorder cystic fibrosis. It's a chronic disease that hampers a person's ability to breathe. Normal daily functions become a chore—strenuous physical activity becomes impossible. Although Collins should be enjoying the excitement of her sophomore year at college, she spends most of her days inside, plagued by painful coughs and a weak body. Worse still, her life expectancy is half the average of the western world."

Wolfgang hesitated as nervousness and emotion built in his chest, but he forced it back and wrapped his fingers around the edge of the podium.

"The amazing thing about Collins is that even though this disease has robbed so much from her, it hasn't touched her personality. She is a beautiful soul, with the sweetest and most generous temperament of any human I've ever met. She's an angel. We say that often about people who are dear to us, but truly, Collins is born straight from Heaven."

Wolfgang accepted a cup of water from a nearby professor and took a slow sip.

"My fellow graduates, we're not here for ourselves. We don't study and research and fight for breakthroughs to build our own résumés or add awards to our office desks. We're here because we all play a critical role in protecting the most precious thing on Earth—life itself. We all have a battle to fight, a mountain to climb, and a cause to champion. The best doctors and the finest scientists dedicate their every day to conquering those challenges and lifting those who are too weak to lift themselves. For me, my fight is cystic fibrosis, and my cause is the seventy thousand human beings around the world who suffer from it."

Wolfgang clenched his fist and rested it against the stand. His voice rose in tone, booming through the hall as he continued.

"Some will say that some dragons cannot be slain. Some mountains cannot be climbed. Some causes are lost. To these people, I have only this to say: If you won't join us, then stand back and watch us. Because we are the generation that *will* slay the dragon. They said smallpox couldn't be killed. Polio couldn't be healed. Soldiers with missing limbs could never walk again. The generations who came before us climbed those mountains, lifted us onto their shoulders, and now say to us that it is *our turn*. My fellow classmates, your fight begins today!"

Applause thundered against the wooden walls as the crowd stood and cheered. Wolfgang stepped away from the podium and offered a brief bow before shaking the dean's hand and smiling at his classmates. They smiled back with rosy cheeks, alive with the thrill and glory of the moment. He knew they felt like conquerors already. Most of them probably had no concept of the gravity of his words, which was precisely why he kept his remarks so brief. They probably wouldn't be willing to do what it took to reach those mountain peaks—or even begin the climb. But he was willing and able.

As the volume of the crowd increased, Wolfgang slipped through a door in the back of the hall and peeled off his graduation cap. He left it with the gown on an end table and adjusted his tie before stepping out into the brisk chill of the impending Scottish winter. He wouldn't miss Edinburgh, although he had hardly set foot on the campus over the last two years, anyway. It was time to head back to the States.

Twenty yards away from the hall, Wolfgang stopped under the skeleton shade of an elm tree and pulled his phone from his pocket. There was a missed call from an unknown number, but no voicemail. He hit redial and waited while it rang twice. Across the street, freshmen students walked between the old university buildings, knotted close together with their heads held low under the biting wind. They smiled and laughed, and the boys smacked each other on the arms. Wolfgang wondered if any of them took their studies as seriously as he did, if they understood the gravity of their role in this brief life.

Likely not.

"Wolfgang, I called you twice. Where the hell are you?"

The snapping voice on the phone was taut with the bluster of a man who felt out of control and wasn't used to it. His South American accent was hampered by anger, causing his mispronunciations of English words to become almost unintelligible.

"Salvador, I told you before. I don't tolerate profanity. We can speak to each other professionally, or not at all."

Salvador spluttered and then moderated his breathing. He spoke again, slower this time. "Very well, *Mr. Pierce*. Where are you?"

"Europe."

"*Europe?*" Salvador's voice cracked. "What the fu—"

Wolfgang hung up the phone. He retrieved a stick of gum from his pocket and chomped it between his teeth, flooding his mouth with mint as he resumed his surveillance of the passing freshmen. The boys still laughed and showed off while girls giggled and pretended to ignore them.

It was okay that they didn't take much seriously right now. Life was serious enough, and their days would come, but for now, they enjoyed the simple pleasures that Collins never had—of being young and free. In a way, this very trivialness was what he fought for.

The phone rang.

Wolfgang cleared his throat and spoke before Salvador could. "Listen to me carefully. I am a contractor, not an employee. Furthermore, I am disinclined to tolerate your primitive form of communication and will terminate our arrangement if you curse again. Are we clear?"

The breath whistled between Salvador's teeth. "You're an arrogant little snot, aren't you?"

"Hardly. I'm simply a man of self-respect who values the power of words. Now then, with regard to my present location. As a contractor, I am under no obligation to report to you my whereabouts or activities, and you will not challenge me on this issue again."

"As a *contractor,* you have a *contract,*" Salvador snarled. "Are you *reneging* on that contract, Mr. Pierce?"

"Points for the correct application of an excellent verb. No, I am not reneging on anything. I will kill Reed Montgomery. I just haven't done it yet. I pulled back in North Carolina because you assured me that Oliver Enfield and his men had things under control. It appears you were mistaken."

"What happened in North Carolina has no bearing on our contract. I want him killed, and I want him killed *now*."

Wolfgang indulged in a tired sigh. "Very well. I'm headed back to the States. I'll start in Atlanta and keep you posted."

He ended the call before Salvador could add any last-minute outbursts. The students were gone now, and a taxi waited at the end of the street. Wolfgang slid into the back seat and smiled at the driver. "Edinburgh Airport, please."

3

Atlanta, Georgia

Reed handed the Uber driver a twenty before stepping out of the Prius and into the warm sun. In stark contrast to the whistling wind and damp air of New Jersey, late fall was kind to Georgia. Orange and brown leaves skipped over the pavement, complementing the Christmas decorations adorning homes and businesses. The scent of dying vegetation and a dropping temperature drifted between the buildings and breathed fresh energy into his lungs—a welcome relief after months of a thick, humid summer.

The auto shop at the corner of two residential streets consisted of a block building with hand-painted letters advertising the services its owner provided. Half a dozen beater cars were parked out front, and the pop and click of a welder rang from the garage in the back. It looked like the kind of brake-swapping, oil-changing place that had been servicing cars since the roads around it were paved in dirt, but Reed wasn't fooled. Hidden behind the dirty blocks and dusty yard was a precision racing shop that rivaled NASCAR's best pits—a true hidden gem amid the bustling city.

Reed shouldered his backpack and stepped around the open gate into the fenced yard. The clicking of the welder was louder now, joined by the whine of an air wrench. Everything smelled of oil and grease—a scent Reed would buy a candle in if he could. He indulged in a brief smile, then ducked into the shop.

Mike Wooster looked up from his workbench when Reed slipped in. The big man was covered in grease up to his elbows and had smudges on his face. He wiped his hands on a cloth and shot Reed a wide smile. "Welcome back. I was about to call you."

Reed accepted the crushing handshake and glanced around the shop. A Corvette Z06 hung six feet off the ground on a lift, while a mechanic worked beneath it with a welder. Sparks rained down beneath the bright yellow car. Farther down the bay, a Porsche 911 sat with its hood open, another mechanic buried in the engine bay.

"You're staying busy."

Mike shrugged. "There's a track rally in Charlotte next month. Last-minute mods. We swapped out the gears on that 'Vette. Adding long tube headers now."

For a moment, the two men surveyed the graceful curves of the sport coupe, admiring every detail and precise crease of the bodywork. It was more than a car to them; it was art itself.

"Is it ready?" Reed asked.

Mike motioned to the back of the shop, and Reed followed him into another section of the building. Bright lights glared over a spotless double-bay garage with blue concrete floors and paint equipment lining the far walls. In the middle of the garage, Reed's 2015 Camaro Z/28 sat alone, its black tires gleaming. Bumper to bumper, the car was a deep, seductive red, with the Z/28 badges removed from the fenders and nothing left to identify it as the jet-black vehicle that ripped through Downtown Atlanta three weeks prior.

Reed ran his hand over the hood of his car. Even though the metal was as smooth and glossy as a brand-new Ferrari, he knew it wasn't painted. The car was still black but now sheathed in a high-performance synthetic wrap that perfectly conformed to the vehicle's every contour—a masterpiece in every way.

"I installed the supercharger and cranked it up to twelve pounds of boost," Mike said. "It's putting about six hundred eight horsepower to the wheels at full throttle. I also swapped the driveshaft with a carbon fiber replacement to sustain the added torque and switched out your lower control arms to help with traction issues. Oh, and I put wider wheels on the back. With that much power, you're gonna need all the rubber you can get."

Reed stuck both hands into his pockets, still staring at the car. "It's perfect."

Mike shoved a wad of chewing tobacco into his cheek. "You sure you don't wanna add some better pipes? With all that power, it could sound incredible."

Reed shook his head. "I'm not trying to make noise. Just speed. What about the transmission?"

"Tranny should be fine. It's well made. Just watch out for the brakes. They're too small for this much power. You really need bigger discs, but I didn't have time to replace them. You're gonna need some room to stop."

Reed nodded and retrieved a thick roll of hundred-dollar bills. Mike accepted it without counting and passed Reed the keys.

"You know . . . rumor has it a black Camaro made quite a lot of noise downtown a few weeks ago." A playful light danced in Mike's eyes.

Reed opened the driver's door. "Wouldn't know about that, Mike. My car's red."

The metal door of the garage rattled as Mike rolled it up. Reed twisted the key, and the engine rumbled to life, flooding the small space with the voice of freedom ready to be unleashed. He tapped the gas and listened to the subtle whine of the supercharger kick in, forcing air into the motor and churning out new levels of power.

Reed shifted into first and waved at Mike before rumbling out through the yard and onto the street. Somewhere out there, north of the city and in the mountains, there was a man they called The

Wolf—a killer—an assassin's assassin. Two weeks prior, while Reed had been hunting Oliver Enfield amid those mountains, The Wolf had chased him twice in a silver Mercedes coupe with enough power to run down anything on the road.

Until now.

Reed scrolled through a short list of contacts on his phone. That list had grown shorter over the past few weeks as more and more of his former friends and colleagues faded into a grey area of untrustworthiness. Prior to Oliver Enfield's betrayal, Reed counted himself among an exclusive fraternity of elite killers, many of whom also worked for Enfield. Now, he couldn't be sure which of them might sell him out at the first opportunity. Reed was more limited than ever in who he could trust.

He hit the dial button and waited for the car's Bluetooth system to take over the call. The phone rang five times before a clattering sound rang over the speakers, then a nervous voice.

"Chris! Hey. Um, my phone was on the floor. Hold on a second."

More clattering. A dog barked in the background, and a child cried.

"Hey. Okay, I'm here now. Had to get my headphones."

"Is that a baby?" Reed snapped.

"What? Baby? Oh, no. That's the TV, man. Got my Netflix rolling in the background. You know what I'm saying?"

Reed rolled to a stop at a traffic light and ran his hand over his forehead. He tried not to sound as frustrated as he felt. "Dillan, I hired you to conduct research, not to watch Netflix."

"Oh, yeah, man. No worries. I work best with a little background noise."

"Okay . . . so do you have any results yet?"

"Results. Um, let's see here. . . ."

Each second that drained by grated on Reed's nerves as though it were a knife digging into his spine. "Dillan, have you found her or not?"

"Um, well, no. Not strictly speaking. But I'm pretty sure she's in the country!"

"What do you mean, you're *pretty sure?*"

"Oh, you're gonna like this. So you told me what bank she uses, right? I have this buddy who works there, and I got him to run a check on her account to see if there's any out-of-country spending. And there wasn't. Badass, right?"

Reed slammed his hand into the console of the car. "You involved a *third party*? Dillan, I told you this is highly confidential!"

"No worries, bro. My dude is totally discreet. He's also my weed dealer, so he knows how to keep things on the down-low."

"Did it ever occur to you that his computer use might be tracked? He might not be the only one who knows he checked into her accounts."

"He said it wasn't a problem. I'm not worried."

Of course you're not.

"Did you check to see where she *is* spending her money?"

"Yeah, well, I asked about that. Apparently, she took out a lot of cash in Atlanta, and nothing's happened since. But he's gonna check back in—"

"*No.* No, he's not. I don't want any more poking around at the bank. Banks are some of the most high-security, sensitive institutions in the world."

"Okay, how do you want me to find her, then?"

Reed spoke through gritted teeth. "*I don't know how.* That's why I hired a private investigator. Can you get it done or not?"

Dillan sighed. "Chill out, dude. I'll get it done. Just give me a few more days, okay? I'll holler at ya later."

The phone clicked off before Reed could add any further admonitions. He wrapped his fingers around the wheel and took a slow breath, forcing his tense muscles to calm. He didn't want to hire Dillan. It was anything but an ideal situation. In years past, he would've made a single phone call to the legendary sleuth of the criminal underworld known only as Winter, and within twenty-four hours, there would be an email in his inbox with his target's precise location. Winter was crazy good like that, but the genderless ghost wasn't accepting Reed's calls anymore and hadn't been since the events in North Carolina. That left Reed alone, blind, and without any hope of finding Banks Morccelli on his own.

He let his mind drift back to the last time he saw her, standing amid the trees next to the lake as rain washed over her pale face. Her eyes, so bright and beautiful, were strained with the pain and agony of betrayal as she stared down at the man she thought she loved. Reed stared back into the soul of the woman who held his heart in her hands, the only person he had left to hold. She didn't say a word as she turned into the trees, vanishing into the night and leaving him alone with the body of his former mentor lying at his feet.

In the two weeks since that night, Reed had searched all over Atlanta for Banks. It was only after days of fruitless searching that he hired Dillan, a local private investigator, to track her down. It was a desperate move, but he had to find her before anyone else did. The Wolf was still on the prowl, Oliver's shadowy employers were still at work in the dark, and Reed was likely the only person on Earth who could protect Banks from the war he had just started.

4

Lake Santeetlah, North Carolina

Special Agent Matthew Rollick of the FBI spent well over a decade as a homicide detective for the Los Angeles PD before making the career switch to federal investigation. During those long years, he'd seen everything from suicide by drowning to execution-style gang murder. Dozens of cases crossed his desk, and more than half of them were never solved. Blood, carnage, and the worst humanity had to offer were all par for the course during a normal day at the office.

But even after all of that, nothing could prepare him for the war zone beside the lake. By the time local law enforcement advised the FBI of a quintuple homicide outside of Lake Santeetlah, North Carolina, the bodies had long since been removed and the ashen remains of the cabin taped off, but the photographs were all there. Three males, all white, slaughtered by the river. The first was a bald man in his early sixties. A massive chunk of his lower back had been blown out by a shotgun, leaving dozens of tiny lead pellets embedded in his skin. His stomach, chest, and throat all sustained multiple knife wounds, and the left side of his face was missing, apparently also blown off by a shotgun.

Then there was the giant. A man of seven feet tall, no less than four hundred pounds, lay on the riverbank with the back of his head blown off by a shotgun. Two Georgia state policemen—state government guards, assigned to the cabin—lay farther up the bank, both with their throats cut.

And finally, stretched out in the mud, by himself, with a gunshot wound to his middle back, was Senator Mitchell Holiday. His face was the only one of the three still fully intact, leaving cold white skin and the lifeless eyes of a man who died in tremendous pain.

Agent Rollick stood next to the lake and closed his eyes, trying to visualize every angle of the crime scene as it must have looked when police first arrived. Shoe prints indicated four men, possibly five. A torrential downpour had begun close to the estimated time of death for all five victims, washing away most of the tracks and prints left in the mud, and leaving investigators to piece together the rest as best they could.

Four men. One of them with a shotgun.

Local police had indeed recovered a shotgun—an expensive twelve-gauge break-action weapon whose serial number was traced back to a purchase at a sporting goods retailer in North Georgia. A few hours of research produced a bill of sale from two years prior with Mitch Holiday's signature on it.

So the weapon belonged to Holiday, but it was difficult to believe that he used it. For one thing, there were at least two different sets of prints on the gun, and neither one of them matched the senator. And secondly, if he used the weapon, why was it found thirty feet away from his body?

Rollick walked back from the lake, gaining a vantage point over the crime scene where he could survey the whole area. It was a trick he learned back in LA—remove himself from the middle, gain a bird's eye view, and use his imagination to fill in the gaps.

Assuming there were four men in addition to the Georgia state policemen, that might explain why the shotgun was dumped thirty feet away from the bodies. It could also explain the multiple empty shotgun shells recovered farther up the hillside, near where the senator's two bodyguards were found dead. The fourth man was armed with a shotgun, directing gunshots toward everyone but the senator.

So was this guy protecting the senator? Holiday appeared to die from some manner of a large, heavy-caliber handgun or rifle fired close to his back. That explained the burned gunpowder residue that coated his shirt. Did the giant fire that weapon? If so, where was it?

"What do you think?" The voice came from behind, startling Rollick out of his muse. He turned to see Agent Liz Fido standing a few feet behind, a clipboard clamped between her petite hands. Fido had been his investigative partner for two weeks since his case involving Mitchell Holiday migrated from Atlanta and into the mountains of North Carolina, where Holiday was supposed to be under protective custody.

So much for that.

"I think we're screwed. Holiday was only weeks away from testifying. Now we'll never know what he had to say."

Fido twisted a toothpick between her lips. "You still think there was a fourth man?"

Rollick shrugged. "I don't see how there couldn't be. The fingerprints on the shotgun don't match any of the victims. I just don't get why all three men were so close to the lake while the cabin burned. Seems like they would've retreated to the parking lot."

"Holiday's Land Rover was pretty much totaled. Reports have it crashing through Cherokee County shortly before the estimated time of death. Maybe the fourth man used it, then returned, set fire to the cabin, and killed everybody down by the river."

"If that's the case, he must've been here before. The Land Rover was with Holiday when he arrived here. Unless this guy stole it, we can conclude this fourth man was a friend."

Fido plucked at her bottom lip with an index finger. "So then, maybe he didn't set fire to the cabin. Maybe it was already burning when he got back."

Rollick ran a hand over his face. His back ached, and he hadn't slept well in days—both compliments of the cheap hotel room the FBI rented him. "I don't know. We're working with too little information. The bottom line is we dragged our feet, and now our lead witness is dead."

Rollick started back toward the pile of ashes and charring timbers that remained of Holiday's lakeside cabin.

"What were you investigating him for anyway?"

Rollick kicked through the loose ashes of the burned-out home, toeing around for anything that survived the ravenous fire. "That's the weird thing. We got a tip about some smuggling operations down in Brunswick, and interviewed Holiday because we thought his logistics company might be inadvertently involved. He wasn't even a suspect at the time, but he flipped out. Got real jumpy, then eventually claimed he had proof of some kind of big conspiracy. But he wouldn't share anything without all these weird guarantees. I was stalling for time, hoping his nerves would get the better of him. He was clearly rattled."

Fido tossed the toothpick into the dirt. "Guess you stalled too long."

"I guess so. Look, we need to get the original DNA samples from local PD. I'm not satisfied with their analysis. I wanna run everything through DC."

"Have to get the new kid to do it. I'm being transferred to Charlotte."

"You're shitting me."

Fido shook her head. "Nope. New assignment of some kind. They're giving you a rookie fresh out of the Academy. Ex-Marine. I don't know much about him, but at least he's a blank slate. You can train him your way."

Rollick spat into the ashes and ground his heel over the mess. From day one, this entire investigation felt cursed. Bureaucracy, red tape, repeated partner changes, missing witnesses, and dead ends plagued his every move. Things looked up when Holiday was recovered from a trailer outside of Atlanta after his violent kidnapping from FBI custody, but everything fell apart when the senator still refused to testify. Everything about this case stank of organized crime—the kind of thing an FBI agent dreamed of investigating.

But no matter how hard he pushed, he hit nothing save block walls.

"Does this kid know *anything* about homicide investigation?" Rollick asked.

Fido shrugged. "Ask him yourself. That's him pulling up now."

Rollick peered through the trees as a Jeep Wrangler wound its way into the parking lot. The vehicle was old—at least twenty years—and red in color. Suspension groaned and exhaust gurgled as the Jeep rolled to a stop next to Rollick's agency-issued Impala, then the engine cut off.

"So long, Rollick. Good luck." Fido tossed him a two-finger salute, then walked toward her car.

Soft grey ashes spilled over Rollick's boots as he turned away from the parking lot and waded through the burned-out home. He knelt under what remained of the kitchen cabinets and sifted through the dirt and debris with his bare hands. A bent spoon, two glass beer bottles, and what appeared to be a double-A battery turned up, then Rollick's fingers collided with something hard and cold.

Boots crunched through the debris behind him. Rollick could feel the tense, all-business attitude of the rookie investigator spilling into the atmosphere. Damn, he hated ex-military agents. Sure, they were disciplined, hardworking, and universally respectful of the rules, but they lacked the outside-the-box imagination that, in his opinion, made for an ideal investigator.

"Agent Rollick?"

The man behind him spoke with a thick Southern accent. Rollick glanced over his shoulder, squinting through the sun at the broad-shouldered, thick-jawed man ten feet away. Yeah, he looked like a Marine.

"Get over here, kid. Help me with this." Rollick pried at the metal object, running his fingers around its smooth, round edge.

The big man knelt beside Rollick, and together they dug through fallen timbers, chunks of foundation, and sections of metal roofing. After a few minutes, the object became more visible amid the ashes. It was a large Dutch oven, turned upside down with the handles burned off. Rollick muttered a curse and kicked at it.

Another piece of shit.

The pot clicked against his foot, then rolled over, exposing a small rectangular object buried beneath. Kneeling back down, Rollick scooped it up and blew the ashes off.

Score.

It was a cell phone. The screen was busted, with chunks of glass missing and large cracks ripping through the remainder of the face. But the phone was still intact, and the best he could tell, untarnished by the flames.

Rollick handed the phone to his new partner. "Get this back to the lab. Have them run a full inventory of the memory. If they can recover the phone number, we'll subpoena the carrier to provide us a full list of the most recent calls and text messages."

The big man nodded. "I'm on it, sir."

Rollick turned toward his car. "I'm not your sir. I'm your partner. You can call me Rollick—or just Roll. If you want to thrive in the FBI, you work hard and keep your ear to the ground. Whatever you learned in the Marine Corps, you'll have to unlearn here. This isn't the military. This is an investigative agency. Our job is to find the bad guys, then supply enough evidence to the prosecutor to charge them. Then we're out. Understand?"

"Yeah. Got it."

Rollick stopped beside his car, dug out a stick of gum, then looked back. "You got a name?"

The big man offered his hand. "Rufus Turkman. Everybody calls me Turk."

Rollick grunted and accepted the handshake. "Welcome to the FBI, Turk."

5

The hotel room was small and dark, with peeling wallpaper and the kind of lumpy mattress that made you wonder what deformed dragon slept inside. That said nothing of the mold growing in the shower stall or the unidentifiable stains on the carpet. Baxter looked even less thrilled with the accommodations than Reed felt, but neither one of them commented as Reed closed the door and sat down on the bed.

"Baxter. Beer me."

The bulldog's wrinkled, scalded skin was a patchwork of singed hair and crimson. He peered up at Reed through beady black eyes and snorted, spraying snot and slobber over the floor.

Reed laughed and unzipped the suitcase. "I'm only kidding. Here. Time for your medicine."

Baxter dutifully climbed onto his dog bed, sitting silent and still as Reed massaged a medicated salve onto his wounds. When Reed's fingers traced the burn marks and swollen scars that crisscrossed his pet's back, Baxter cringed, but he didn't whine. He huddled against the bed until Reed was finished, then settled down.

"That's a good boy," Reed whispered. "You're getting better already."

The soft snores that rumbled from Baxter's open mouth weren't as smooth or peaceful as they used to be. There was pain in each labored breath, a hallmark of the trauma the dog had experienced two weeks before when he was caught in the midst of the house fire. Reed studied Baxter's slack lips, then scratched gently behind the bulldog's ears. In a lot of ways, Baxter was his only friend—his only companion during the long nights and bloody days that characterized his existence in Atlanta.

"We'll get them," Reed said. "We'll burn them the way they burned Kelly. I promise."

A thick binder at the bottom of the suitcase was bent and dirty, packed with folded papers, wrinkled photographs, and two or three pens. Reed spread the contents across the bed and sorted through each item until he located a small notebook. He pulled a pen cap off with his teeth and sat cross-legged on the bed with the notebook. A list of names lined the faded yellow paper, each scrawled in his own spidery handwriting. Oliver Enfield's name topped the list, with a thick red line scribed through it. The next name on the list was Cedric Muri. Reed scraped the pen across the name, obliterating it in an identical red line, then he tapped the third name. *Salvador*.

Reed didn't know his last name, but that didn't matter, because Salvador probably wasn't his real name anyway. A man in Salvador's line of work was certain to have multiple aliases. Whoever the unidentified South American truly was, he belonged on this list next to a kingpin killer and a mercenary broker. Salvador was the man most directly connected with the shadowy organization who wanted Mitchell Holiday murdered. He hired Cedric Muri to supply henchmen for Oliver's use in setting up Reed, and those same henchmen were responsible for kidnapping Banks and killing Kelly.

"Who are you, Salvador?"

Was he the head of the snake, or just another piece in a massive machine? Nothing about the events of the last month felt like the manipulations of a single man. If Reed knew anything about the criminal underworld, it was that nothing was ever as it seemed, and there was almost always another layer of puppet masters behind every fiendish action. Salvador was most likely just a boss, calling the shots on behalf of a bigger boss, and so on. The only way to know was to find him.

Reed stuck the list of names to the wall in front of the bed. One at a time, he taped each picture, note, and news article to the wall. Headlines documenting the events in Atlanta hung beside campaign photos of Mitch Holiday and charts outlining the structure of Oliver Enfield's criminal empire.

Reed stepped back and rubbed his chin, staring at the mess of data. He drew in a long sigh and turned to Baxter. "We're gonna be here a while, boy."

The dingy room was quiet, and though Baxter lay on the end of the bed with his eyes closed, Reed knew he wasn't sleeping. The old dog never slept without snoring, and now his breaths came in gentle wheezes between his teeth.

He's in so much pain.

Reed's eyes stung, and his head felt numb. He tipped the beer bottle and drained it, then tossed it on the floor next to half a dozen others. The carpet, a worn pattern of green with red flowers, blurred out of focus, and Reed didn't try to blink his way back into clarity. The flowers were dyed into the carpet's fibers, now flattened by years of dirty feet. He imagined he could see the bacteria and grime clinging to each twisted strand, crawling toward the beer bottles like an army of disease.

He embraced his headache and nausea. It was probably hunger, but he didn't have an appetite or any desire to leave the hotel room. A part of him wanted to stay there forever, lie back on the bed, let his mind drift into oblivion, and let them find him a week later.

Kelly. He saw her seductive smile as bright and dangerous as the first day he met her. He remembered that moment so clearly it almost felt real, as though it were happening all over again, here in his mind. Reed exhaled, savoring the memory. He could still feel the hot Mediterranean sun on his face, flushing his skin red as his heart pounded and sweat streamed from his face. The place was Monaco; the date was sometime in June of 2016. It was a memorable date because it was his first international contract. A casino drug lord crossed the wrong *hombre* back in Mexico City, and that *hombre* hired Oliver's company to settle his score. Oliver dispatched Reed. It was Reed's sixth hit, and in a lot of ways, it was the trickiest. Reed decided to conduct the kill by strangulation, inside the drug lord's penthouse, high atop a downtown tower.

Everything went perfectly, right up until nothing did. There was a prostitute in the penthouse, and even though she was high as a kite on some narcotic, Reed knew she would remember everything. He had hesitated over the bed, staring down at the slain mob boss, then turned toward the prostitute with the choke wire still dangling between his fingers.

That moment of hesitation almost killed him. His original egress plan had been to take the service elevator to the bottom floor, hijack a car, and make his way to the coastal town of Cannes. Oliver would extract him via a charter boat two miles off the coast—a difficult but manageable swim. In the years that passed since that pivotal moment, Reed often wondered what would have happened if he hadn't spent those crucial twenty seconds standing over the prostitute, struggling to decide whether he should kill her. Maybe he could have dodged the security officers who came barreling through the penthouse door with their guns drawn. Maybe he wouldn't have been shot in the arm or forced to take the stairway, falling down the last two flights and breaking a rib in the process.

He escaped the guards, thanks to his rapid descent, but every breath was agony and his arm still bled. He ran from the lobby to the parking garage, his vision bloodshot and his head swimming, still clinging to his initial plan of hijacking a car.

And that's when it happened. He slammed into Kelly at the

same moment she burst out of a service door and skidded toward a cherry-red Ferrari Spider 458. She wore a black sweatshirt with the hood pulled over her dark hair and a face mask covering her mouth and nose. When their eyes locked, a recognition of criminal kinship instantly registered in their eyes, and Kelly didn't hesitate.

After a quick manipulation of the ignition wires on the Ferrari, she jerked her head toward the passenger seat and slammed the car into gear. "Let's roll, kid. We're in this together now."

Reed piled into the car without question, ignoring the flashing red flags that erupted throughout his mind. Kelly stomped on the gas and piloted the vehicle out of the garage and onto the street. French police cars were already barreling toward them from all directions, but they didn't stand a chance. The shiny red supercar slid in and out of alleys, screeching around apartment buildings, and leaving the squad cars in a shower of golden Mediterranean sand.

Reed had never seen a woman drive like Kelly. With every twist of the wheel, her eyes shone as though she were a kid on a pony, working the paddle shifter with the grace and agility of a practiced master—a true racer.

Even now, Reed could still feel the wind whipping through the windows, tearing at their hair.

Ten minutes later he passed out from blood loss, remaining unconscious until he awoke in a hut buried deep within the French countryside. His wounds were stitched, his ribs braced, and Kelly sat beside him, watching the sunset over the gleaming outline of the supercar.

Her hood and mask were gone, exposing the sharp curves of defined features—a small mouth, a sharp nose, and high cheekbones. She wasn't beautiful in the traditional way, but at that moment, Reed had never seen a woman so gorgeous.

"That's not your car, is it?" he asked.

Kelly faced him with a broad, childish grin. "It is now."

Reed swallowed past a dry throat as the memory faded back into the foggy mist of the past. The months that followed with Kelly were a whirlwind of encounters around the world, carefully orchestrated to mesh with her car boosting and his assassination schedules. He never asked her about her curious career, and she never asked about his. From the start, they both knew it wasn't meant to last, but for an instant, he hoped it would.

He remembered Kelly's gentle words after the literal train wreck in Atlanta. *"I would have married you if you weren't such a walking disaster."*

She had left her successful career as a supercar thief after she found faith—some form of Christianity. He didn't understand it, and at the time, losing her to this strange, legal lifestyle ripped deeper than a simple breakup would have. Looking back now, he admired Kelly for making the jump that he only dreamed of—getting out, moving on, living a normal life.

And she almost made it.

Reed put his feet on the floor and fumbled with the phone. The tears that stung his eyes made it difficult to dial. He put the phone on speaker and cleared his throat.

"Lasquo Financial. How may I direct your call?" Lasquo Financial was a bank of sorts based out of New Orleans, specializing in managing the financial needs of the criminal underworld. As a contract killer, that included Reed. He read off his memorized series of coded passphrases, then requested to speak to Thomas Lancaster, his personal banker.

"One moment."

The hold music was gentle and soothing, but it couldn't fill the void that shredded through his soul. It only made it feel deeper and wider, every musical note echoing off the canyon walls in his heart and reminding him just how dark and empty he felt.

"Reed, my boy. Good to hear from you."

Reed cleared his throat. "Hey, Thomas. I wanted to check my investment balance."

"Let's see here . . ." Keyboard keys rattled. Thomas hummed a little. Reed ignored it all and thought about the French sunset falling behind the Ferrari.

"As of today you've got three-point-three million on investments. And change."

"That's perfect. Can you cash out a million for me?"

"Um, sure. May I ask why?"

"I lost somebody dear to me. I want to send some money to their parents."

"I'm so sorry to hear that, Reed. I can arrange it for you."

"Could you make it anonymous?"

The keyboard clicked again. "You know I can, Reed. What I usually recommend to my clients in this situation is to let me mail the money to the beneficiary as a life insurance check. I can set it all up through a shell company, and they'll be none the wiser."

"Perfect."

Thomas asked for names and addresses. Reed consulted his notebook and rattled them off, his mind still lost in a fog. Thomas read off a confirmation number but didn't hang up. Reed could hear the hesitation in his voice.

"Reed . . . there is another matter. Something happened a couple days ago."

"Yes?"

"A, um, gentleman came in inquiring about you. Small, South American fellow. Wanted to know about your recent spending, current location, etcetera."

The words rang in Reed's ears as facts with no emotional implication. What Thomas said should've concerned him, but he was too tired to be worried. "What did you tell him?"

Thomas snorted. "I told him what any self-respecting banker would tell a stranger inquiring about one of my clients. I invited him to have intercourse with himself."

Reed tried to smile. "Thanks, Thomas."

"I'm sorry I wasn't able to get his name."

"His name is Salvador, and I'm dealing with it. Thank you for letting me know."

Thomas coughed, his tone returning to its traditional, all-business formality. "Of course, Reed. Let us know if there's any way we can help."

Reed dropped the phone on the bed, then drew in a long, deep breath. He envisioned the flashing smile of the dark-skinned South American standing beside Oliver at Pratt-Pullman Yard, the first and last place Reed saw the man who called himself Salvador.

Regardless of whoever was behind this tangled mess of crime, deceit, and bloodshed, Salvador was to blame for what happened to Kelly. Her death, the death of her fiancé, and the death of her unborn baby were all on his hands. And Reed was going to roast him alive for it.

6

Baton Rouge, Louisiana
State Capitol Building

"Madam Governor! A moment of your time!"

"Madam Governor, can you comment on your administration's intentions concerning offshore drilling initiatives?"

"Madam Governor, has your cabinet reached any decisions with regard to a new attorney general?"

Maggie Trousdale stopped at the foot of the Capitol steps and turned to the crowd of reporters bustling in around her. The crush of bodies, the flash of cameras, and the clamor of voices overwhelmed her senses, igniting her trepidation about the office she had just been inaugurated into. When she first announced her candidacy for governor only fourteen months prior, she never imagined she would actually win. What business did a small-town girl from the Louisiana swamps have in running an entire state? She ran because she wanted to make a point—that corruption and bureaucracy had saturated her state for far too long, and that the new leader of Louisiana should be prepared to take on the challenges of Baton Rouge and the swamp of political mire it contained.

She had no idea how strongly that message would resonate with the people of Louisiana, or how ferociously the citizens of Louisiana's rural towns would rally around the prospect of electing one of their own.

But it did, and they had, and now here she stood—a thirty-four-year-old governor of one of the most culturally and legally unique places in the country—overwhelmed beyond her mind.

The state troopers who stood at her elbows closed in and held out their hands, barking at the reporters. "Stand back! Stand back now!"

Maggie's shoulders slumped in exhaustion. It wasn't yet noon, but she had already put in an eight-hour workday. She couldn't remember her last shower, or whether she had eaten breakfast, but she wasn't going to ignore the reporters. They were the mouthpieces of the people, and the people were the reason she took this damnable job in the first place.

"First of all"—Maggie raised her hand, quieting the crowd—"I want to restate my extreme sorrow and sincerest condolences to the family of Attorney General Matthews. He was a good man, a loyal servant of Louisiana, and an outstanding prosecutor. My cabinet is shocked by his sudden passing and will be providing the Louisiana Bureau of Investigations every available assistance as they pursue an inquiry into his death. We—"

A reporter shouted over his colleagues' heads. "Does that mean you believe he was murdered, Governor?"

"I didn't say that." Maggie faced him directly. "At this time, I have been advised by Lieutenant Colonel Jackson of the LBI that there are no indicators of—"

"Yes, you said that yesterday. Shouldn't we know more by now?"

"As I stated already, we are not—"

A new reporter broke in. "Who will be his replacement?"

Maggie felt her cheeks flush, and she bit back the urge to curse. Enduring the constant interruptions and disregard for anything she was saying was an element of political pandering she was neither accustomed to nor predisposed to tolerate.

Instead of objecting, she decided to answer the question with a challenge of her own. "Ms. Simmons, isn't it?"

The reporter nodded, tapping a pen on her lip.

"Ms. Simmons, are you at all familiar with the Louisiana Constitution?"

The crowd was quiet now, and several of the reporters shot Simmons crooked smirks. She didn't answer, and Maggie cleared her throat.

"I thought not. If you were, you wouldn't have asked that question. Per our constitution, anytime the attorney general's office is unexpectedly vacated, the assistant attorney general assumes the office *unless* the remainder of the attorney general's term exceeds one year, in which case the governor calls a special election. Since Attorney General Matthews's term extends another twenty-two months, I will be announcing the scheduling of a special election for a replacement within the week. You can direct all further inquiries as to the identity of the new attorney general to the people of Louisiana."

Another outburst of questions blasted from the crowd. Maggie waved her hand and offered a tense smile. "That's all for today, everyone. Thank you so much."

She mounted the steps, turning back toward the Capitol. At four hundred fifty feet tall, Louisiana's Capitol building was the tallest in the nation, rising above the streets of downtown Baton Rouge in polished white marble. In Maggie's early days as a pre-law student at Louisiana State University, she often sat in the sprawling thirty acres of state gardens that surrounded the building and studied under its magnificent shadow. At the time, the building inspired her. It felt majestic, powerful, and secure. Now it only stressed her out—a pit full of political vipers, half of whom wanted to take her out as violently as possible.

Her shoes echoed on the marble floor as she crossed the main atrium and approached the elevator. Maggie never wore heels—she hated them with a passion. Most days, she wore simple brown hiking boots, only donning flat dress shoes when tradition absolutely commanded it. It was an odd choice for somebody who also had to wear dress clothes every day, but her supporters loved it. They called her Muddy Maggie, The Swamp Girl. One of their own.

As soon as the door smacked shut on her executive office, the voices began. Daniel Sharp, her lieutenant governor, rambled on about press releases and issues with the media. Yolanda Flint, her chief of staff, waved a handful of papers and entered meltdown mode over logistical problems for her visit to New Orleans the next day. Half a dozen aides talked at once, crowding around the board table and freaking out over ten different subjects Maggie didn't care about.

"Everyone!" Maggie clapped her hands, and the room fell suddenly silent. She rubbed her temples and pushed out the mental clutter of the press conference. This wasn't the time to join the mayhem. "I think it's time you all had a break. Take a twenty and get some fresh air."

Everyone exchanged tense looks, hesitating where they stood.

Maggie snapped her fingers. "That wasn't a suggestion, people. Let's roll."

The aides began shuffling toward the door, and Maggie redirected her attention to Dan and Yolanda. "Not you two. We've got a call to make."

The doors clapped shut behind the crowd of aides, and Maggie sat down at the head of the board table, pouring herself a tall glass of water and sucking down half of it while Yolanda launched into her spiel about logistics.

"Yolanda." Maggie tried not to snap. "I really don't care. Just make it happen."

"But what are you going to wear? I need to coordinate your appearance given the current nature of—"

"Yolanda. Did my predecessor have to coordinate his appearance every time he set foot outside the Capitol?"

"Um . . ." Yolanda twitched and clicked a pen in her hand.

"No, he didn't. And don't tell me it's because he was a man.

We're not coordinating a dinner party, we're running a state. It doesn't matter what I wear. Now sit down, and chill out with the details."

Yolanda reluctantly settled into her seat, and Maggie finished the water. Dan sat next to her, interlacing his fingers and waiting for Maggie to speak. It was perhaps his most underrated talent—knowing when to shut the hell up.

Maggie punched the speaker button on the desk phone and waited for her secretary to pick up.

"Yes, ma'am?"

"Get me Lieutenant Colonel Jackson, please."

"One moment, ma'am."

Calm settled over the room, broken only by the occasional click of Yolanda's pen. The twitch grated on Maggie's nerves, but she chose not to comment. There were bigger fish to fry.

"Madam Governor." Jackson's booming voice carried all the command and directness of a life spent serving the military and then the law enforcement needs of Louisiana. After twenty-three years in the National Guard, Jackson switched to the LBI and quickly rose in the ranks as one of the chief investigators of the Bureau, and then as their executive director. Maggie didn't know much about him, but she liked him. He never had time for bullshit.

"Lieutenant Colonel, thank you for taking my call. I have Lieutenant Governor Sharp and Chief of Staff Flint in the office with me. I wanted to see if you had an update on the Matthews investigation."

Jackson cleared his throat. Maggie could already detect his hesitancy.

"At this time, Madam Governor, my office is unable to provide a confident determination as to—"

"Lieutenant Colonel, I'm so sorry to interrupt you, but I'm not a politician. I'm a swamp-raised gator hunter. I will never hold your instincts against you, and I don't expect you to be infallible. All I expect is for you to be direct and honest with me at all times. Tell me what you *know*, and then tell me what you *think*."

Dead silence hung in the air. Dan raised both eyebrows, and Maggie shrugged—she had to try.

"Yes, ma'am. At this time, we know that Matthews was found dead at his lake house yesterday around six forty-five a.m. Initial impressions are that he died of heart failure. There are no apparent wounds on his body, and no one was present at the time of his death."

"Did he have any known heart conditions?"

"We're securing his medical records and running a full toxicology panel on his body. A complete autopsy could take as long as forty-eight hours."

"What are the initial impressions of his manner of death?"

"Like I said, we believe congestive heart failure—"

"You know what I'm asking, Lieutenant Colonel."

Jackson sighed. "Murder is a distinct possibility, Madam Governor. We found a broken whiskey decanter on the floor beside him. The contents were mostly evaporated, leaving us to believe he died no later than around three a.m. We're running tests on the residue, but initial results indicate the presence of toxic substances. We'll know more soon."

Maggie leaned back in her chair. "Very good. I want you to move your investigation in the direction of a homicide, then. If there's any chance Matthews was murdered, I don't want a second to be lost. Whatever resources you require will be made immediately available."

"Thank you, Madam Governor. If that is all, I'll get back to work."

"That's all. Thank you so much."

Maggie ended the call and turned to Dan. He cocked his head and pursed his lips but didn't say anything.

In typical fashion, Yolanda spoke first. "Madam Governor, I think it's imperative that—"

Maggie held up an index finger. "Hold that thought, Yolanda. I want to hear what Dan thinks first."

Dan took a sip of water, then set it down. "Well, there are only two options. Either he was murdered, or he wasn't. Jackson will find out soon enough. My initial impressions are that we need to be careful throwing around the M-word. If it was a natural or accidental death, we don't need the press storm that will come with accusations of homicide."

"I agree," Yolanda burst in.

Maggie knew the demon of rationale had possessed her to hire Yolanda, and though Yolanda was the most annoying person in the state, she was also the most organized and the best at managing staff.

"Why would someone murder an attorney general?" Maggie drummed her fingers on the desk.

Dan grunted. "I mean, I guess there could be a lot of reasons. It might be personal. Might be random."

"Not if it's poison. A gunshot to the chest with a shattered window and a missing jewelry collection is random. A kitchen knife to the gut is personal. But poison . . . that's premeditated. That's assassination."

Maggie relaxed back into her chair and enjoyed the silence that followed her comments. Her head pounded, but headaches were such a common part of her daily regimen that she hardly noticed.

Dan's words were soft but strong. "I think we should be extremely cautious with that line of thinking . . ."

Maggie sat up. "I know. But I want you to consider this. There might be a lot of reasons to murder an attorney general, but there's only one reason why you would *assassinate* him: because he was in your way. That means somebody out there is up to something that Matthews wasn't having any part of, and I'm not having any part of it, either. I want to hold a special election for a replacement as soon as possible."

Yolanda sat forward. "Madam Governor, I want to advise *extreme* caution with that proposal. Rushing into a special election doesn't provide people enough time to grieve, and it could be interpreted as an extremely insensitive action on your part."

"Yolanda, I'm not here to manage public perception. I'm here to lead this state. Without an attorney general we are left wide open to all manner of corruption. I will not leave the state crippled. Dan, assemble a proposal regarding the earliest possible date we can hold a special election and have that on my desk tomorrow. Thank you."

Without another word, Maggie walked out of the office and into the Capitol hallways. She breathed in a deep lungful of musty air and smiled at a couple state representatives. Never had she been so surrounded by people and felt so alone.

7

Midtown, Atlanta

"Can I help you, sir?"

Reed laid the ID on the counter and spoke quickly, the way he imagined an impatient investigator spoke. "Chris Thomas, Georgia Bureau of Investigation. I'm here to have a look at Senator Holiday's residence."

The clerk behind the front desk gave the ID a glance, and then she shot Reed a wide smile. He was used to that smile. It was the one every nervous girl gave him when he played this impersonation game.

It's days like these I don't completely hate myself.

"Mr. Thomas, I'll just need to check with my manager."

"Agent." Reed forced himself to lean on the counter as he subtly replaced the fake state ID into his pocket and shot the clerk a wide grin. "It's Agent Thomas, actually."

The woman—she couldn't have been more than nineteen—blushed and nodded, then hurried off. Reed kept his head down and his fingers off the counter.

In the main lobby of the condominium tower were two security cameras in the back corners, and the best he could tell, as long as he kept his face down, they wouldn't record anything but the top of his head.

Seconds ticked into minutes, and Reed rubbed his fingers against his sleeve. He misread her, he thought. Maybe she wasn't as girlish and smitten as she at first seemed.

"Agent Thomas?"

Reed straightened and turned, still keeping his face ducked beneath the rim of the nondescript baseball hat he wore.

A chubby man with a goatee stood behind him, his chest puffed out and his shoulders thrown back with the air of somebody who wanted to look important and impressive but didn't feel that way. Reed had seen it many times before. You rarely had to convince somebody you were an agent, or an investigator, or somebody with governmental authority if you could *impress* them with the importance of your presence. Self-inflation took over at that point and drowned out the better judgment of your average American.

Reed shook the manager's hand and shot him a friendly but serious smile. At least he hoped that's what it looked like.

"Don Burk," the chubby guy said. "Assistant manager and activities director at this property. Elizabeth tells me you were inquiring about Senator Holiday's residence. May I see your ID?"

Reed passed him the card. "That's right, Director."

Don's cheeks flushed at the word *director*. He made a show of examining the card, but Reed could tell he had no actual idea what a GBI ID should look like.

"I'd love to help you," Don said. "It's always my pleasure to cooperate with law enforcement. Unfortunately, I cannot allow entrance into a resident's unit without a warrant. I'm sure you understand."

Reed nodded. "Of course. My office faxed you the warrant this morning."

Don frowned, then shot Elizabeth a semi-accusatory glare. She shook her head once, then turned to check the printer.

"I'm afraid we didn't receive that fax, Agent," Don said. "Are you sure they had the number right?"

Reed made a show of running his hand over his face and sighing. "I'm sorry. It's been a hell of a week. You'd think something as important as the *assassination* of one of our own senators would garner a little more support from downtown. Nothing but yahoos down there."

Don's shoulders slumped a little, and Reed patted him on the arm with an understanding smile. "Don't worry, Don. I know you'd help me if you had the power."

Reed turned away.

And three, two . . .

"Wait!" Don snapped his fingers, then motioned Reed toward the hallway. "Step this way, Agent."

Reed followed the chubby manager into the hallway.

Don spoke in a conspiratorial whisper, his cheeks jiggling with every step of his stubby feet. "Strictly speaking, this is against corporate policy. But as the manager on-site, of course I have the power to make emergency exceptions in the name of public security. Can that be our little secret?"

Reed winked and patted Don on the back. "You got it, Director. Can't say how much I appreciate this."

"No problem. Anything for the GBI. Just get me a copy of that warrant, ASAP."

Don led the way into the elevator and mashed the button for the fourteenth floor. Reed crossed his arms and waited as the elevator groaned and began to rise.

Don wiped the sweat from his forehead and adjusted his vest in the way only a self-conscious man would. "You know . . . I knew the senator. Used to say hello every time he came in."

"Is that right?"

"Oh yes. Senator Holiday and I were on a first-name basis. I was pretty messed up when he passed. Seemed like a good man."

"He was." As the words escaped his lips, Reed wondered if they were true. He thought back to the cabin and Holiday's words on the front porch while they shared cigars. How broken the senator sounded, speaking of his mistakes. Maybe Holiday wasn't a good man at all. Maybe he was conflicted and war-torn. Certainly, there were redeemable things about him. He treated Banks well, at least.

The elevator ground to a halt and the doors rolled back. The hallway that stretched out ahead of them was pretty much what Reed expected for a building of this class—smooth hardwood floors with clean walls painted in a soft cream. Gold knobs and locks adorned every door, with golden light fixtures mounted overhead. It smelled clean, too.

Reed followed Don down the hallway and around a corner to a doorway mounted in the far wall. The numbers "1409" hung on the door—also in gold. Don fished a key from his pocket and pressed it into the lock. The door opened without a sound, exposing a dark room on the other side.

"Here you are. Senator Holiday's residence."

Don made no move to leave, and Reed smiled at him. "Thank you so much. If I could have the room, please."

The chubby manager nodded and cleared his throat. "Of course. Let me know when you're finished."

He disappeared back toward the elevator, and Reed stepped inside the condominium. He pushed the door shut with the toe of his boot, then tugged a pair of surgical gloves from his pocket. They snapped around his wrists as he pulled them on, sucking tight against his big hands.

The metal switch on the wall snapped with surprising aggression as Reed flipped it on, flooding the kitchen with white light. A thin layer of dust already clung to the surface of the counters and appliances, but nothing was left out of place. The room was orderly, right down to the neat row of coffee mugs next to the sink.

Reed moved into the adjoining living room. Through the floor-to-ceiling windows, he looked out over the Millennium Gate Museum, the duck pond that sat beside it, and the park beyond that. In the far distance, over seven hundred yards away, the outline of Ikea sat amid the low hills and thick trees of North Atlanta. Reed remembered lying on top of that Ikea only a month prior, staring through the scope of a high-powered rifle as he aligned the crosshairs with this very living room. He remembered watching Holiday laugh and talk on his cell phone as he walked back and forth across the room, drinking wine. The senator looked relaxed as Banks walked through the door.

Banks.

Reed closed his eyes and again saw her walk into the kitchen through the magnification of his rifle scope. He saw her embrace her godfather and accept a glass of wine. That was the moment his whole universe turned upside down—the moment worlds collided, and he made the decision not to press the trigger.

I had no clue what I was stepping into.

No, he hadn't known. He had no way of knowing. But even now, in the middle of it all, the reality of his decision paradigm hadn't changed a bit.

I'd do it again.

Reed turned away from the window and stepped back into the kitchen. A quick search of the cabinets revealed nothing but a sparse collection of dishes and a few canned goods. Past the bare living room, a single door blocked off the bedroom. Reed tried the knob and found it locked.

Who locks their bedroom when they leave?

A quick manipulation of the keyhole with his lock pick produced a satisfying click, and the door opened. If the living room and kitchen were sparse and clean, the bedroom that opened beyond the door was anything but. Mounds of dirty laundry, books, newspapers, and every manner of trivial trash were heaped against every wall, barely leaving room for the twin-size bed in the middle. The reek of unwashed clothes, stale food, and God knew what else filled his nostrils.

Reed took a step back and held his hand over his nose. As his eyes adjusted to the dimmer light of the room, he surveyed the mountains of trash. In one corner, a stack of six file boxes leaned to one side with sheaves of paper falling out. Bold black letters were written on the boxes, labeling them as case files from Georgia's third state senate district. The piles of newspapers were wadded up beneath stacks of old, dusty books—everything from murder mystery novels to medical research textbooks. Reed retrieved his flashlight and clicked it on. The pale pool of light spilling over the room illuminated more dust and dirt. Reed sighed and began to sift through the books.

"What happened, Senator? Who broke you?"

He thought about the carefully manicured and poised individual he confronted at the cabin in North Carolina. Even the slobbering, terrified version of Mitch Holiday that he kidnapped in Atlanta was more collected and mentally refined than the bedroom indicated. Senator Holiday was a man of deep and dark secrets, and Reed wondered if his mental state was less stable than it appeared.

Also piled with books and case files was a nightstand next to the bed, from which a small brown notebook stuck out. Reed pried it free and sat down on the bed, flipping open the worn leather cover. Dust ballooned into the air as he flipped the crinkled, water-damaged pages. Most were empty, but as he thumbed toward the back of the book, a short scrawling of black ink in strained handwriting filled the pages.

September 3

Agents from the FBI have contacted me regarding the investigation. I'm working with a man named Matt Rollick. I don't know what he knows. I'm afraid to talk to him. I'm afraid of what will happen to Banks, or what they'll say about Frank. I didn't mean for any of this to happen—I just wanted to make things better. I won't talk to the FBI. I won't do a damn thing until they can promise Banks will be protected. I'll take my secrets to the grave if I have to. Oh, God . . . I'm so sorry. I'm so sorry. I'm so sorry.

Reed flipped the page, exposing a crude drawing of a farmhouse in the mountains, surrounded by apple trees. The next several pages were sketches of farms, empty roads, and valleys between the mountains. Reed flipped through the notebook, searching for more diary entries. He stopped over an entirely black page colored in with a pen. He froze over the drawing, maneuvering the flashlight until it illuminated the whole page. A black hole was surrounded by more darkness. In the middle of the hole, wreathed in shadows, was the face of a devil, with sharp, glaring eyes, horns, and vicious fangs. At the bottom of the page, written in shaky letters, were two words: *He knows.*

Reed's blood turned to ice as the demonic face watched him, judged him. He slapped the journal shut and dropped it clumsily on the nightstand, his hands suddenly sticky and numb. The notebook slipped off the table, and as it hit the floor, a dull *clunk* echoed from beneath the bed. Reed dropped to his knees and ran his hand beneath the bed skirt. His fingers collided with something hard and metallic, and he dragged it out, exposing a small black box with a key lock.

Dust hung in the air as Reed settled on the floor and pulled out his lock pick again. His chest was tight with tension, and sweat dripped off his nose. The lock stuck and resisted his attempts to defeat it. He continued twisting and manipulating the tool, working the tiny keyhole until he felt the latch click.

The lid fell to the floor in a poof of dust, exposing a single blank white envelope. Reed tore it open and shook it until a wallet-size photograph spilled out into his hands. It was printed in color but was worn and faded, as though it had spent the majority of its life in an actual wallet or on the dash of somebody's car.

There were only two people in the photo. Right away, he recognized the young man on the left by his thick hair and bold features. It was Holiday. A much younger, thinner Holiday, for sure, but definitely him. The second person in the photo was also young, but a little older than Holiday. He had sandy yellow hair and piercing blue eyes—eyes Reed would've recognized anywhere. They were the same as Banks's. This had to be Frank Morccelli, her father.

Both Holiday and Morccelli were dressed in black robes, and neither one of them smiled, with expressions bridging beyond serious to grim. The backdrop behind them was a black wall with the face of an owl etched in silver between their heads. Its eyes were painted red and glared out over their shoulders.

What the hell?

On the back of the photograph, written in Holiday's now-familiar scrawl, were two short lines: *Vanderbilt University, 1989. ΩAΩ.*

Reed leaned against the bed and tapped the photo against his knee. He wasn't surprised by the Vanderbilt note—Winter had told him Holiday attended Vanderbilt University, which was where he met and became close friends with Frank Morccelli during the late eighties. He also remembered Winter mentioning that Holiday shared a fraternity with Morccelli, which would explain the Greek letters. What letters were they, anyway?

Reed tried to recall any residual knowledge he had about the Greek alphabet, though there wasn't much—he knew there was an Alpha and a Beta. He had encountered the Greek alphabet a couple times in church. David and Tabitha Montgomery were big on church when Reed was a child, and once or twice the pastor taught on the Book of Revelation, discussing the end-times. There was something about the Greek alphabet buried amongst those confusing prophesies, wasn't there?

Yes. He remembered now. It was something God himself said: "*I am the Alpha and the Omega, the beginning and the end.*"

Reed sat up. He held the photo into the light that spilled through the blinds. The Greek letters on the back of the photograph were "*Alpha*" and "*Omega*," the first and last letters of the Greek alphabet. Only they weren't written in that order; they were written the other way: last, first, last.

Holiday's final words echoed in Reed's head. He remembered kneeling beside the lake with the dying senator in his arms. He remembered leaning in and making out Holiday's final, whispered words. *"From end to end."*

From Omega to Omega.

Reed kicked trash away from his feet and hurried toward the door, pocketing the photo. Whatever dark, terrible secret lay behind the tragic life of Mitchell Holiday, it began at Vanderbilt University in 1989. It began with Omega Alpha Omega.

8

Salvador knew what death smelled like. Not the actual decaying part, where the body rots and the flesh falls away from the bone, but what *impending* death smelled like—that distinct, burning odor of something about to go terribly wrong. The stench of the grim reaper's rotting cloak as he stepped toward his next victim. After years of work on the dark side of the law, Salvador could smell the grim reaper a mile away, and today, the guardian of the grave smelled a lot closer than that.

"Give me your weapons."

At the front door of the lonely brick home, standing by itself on the outskirts of the city, Salvador shuffled from one foot to the other. His body ached from the sleepless nights and constant strain of the previous few weeks. He was used to it. He didn't mind the sleeplessness or the pressure, but he only appreciated the smell of death when he was the one bringing it. Feeling detached and out of control was perhaps the most terrifying reality he could imagine.

The cold European blocking his way was neither tall nor broad but still carried the savage air of a man who could squeeze the life out of Salvador with one hand. There was nothing but cold death in his eyes—no love, no warmth, no joy. This man was a killer.

Salvador unholstered his Italian-made Beretta .40 caliber pistol and handed it to the guard. The steel gaze didn't break contact with his own, and Salvador reluctantly pried the knife out of his belt and handed it over, also. The guard grunted then stepped to one side. Salvador sucked in a deep breath, forced himself to relax, and pushed the door open.

It was still midday, but inside the mansion was as dark and empty as the grave itself. Thick curtains hung over the windows, blocking out all light, and none of the fixtures mounted into the walls and the ceiling were illuminated. The rooms were bare—no furniture, decorations, or artwork. The home felt abandoned, as though it were going under foreclosure.

Another guard appeared out of the shadows and motioned Salvador onward. Their footfalls echoed through the whole house as Salvador followed him down a hallway, through two more doors, and finally into a sunroom on the backside of the house—or at least it was *supposed* to be a sunroom. The windows were painted black, and every corner was buried in shadows.

Salvador stopped just inside the room and turned toward the guard. The man was gone as quickly and suddenly as he'd appeared, vanished back into the shadows, and leaving Salvador alone in the shaded confines of the sunroom. He turned back toward the wall of glass panels and took a step farther into the shadows.

"That's far enough." The voice came from the far end of the room.

Salvador stopped and leaned forward, squinting into the darkness. "I can't see you."

"You're not supposed to see me."

A chill ran down Salvador's spine, and his feet were rooted to the floor. He listened for the breathing of another human being or the creaking of the floor beneath a footfall, but there was nothing.

"Gambit?" Salvador asked, his voice tentative.

"It was a simple request, wasn't it?" The voice rustled like wind over dry leaves. Empty. Unfriendly. Salvador recognized that voice

—it was the voice of the man who hired him to assassinate Mitchell Holiday. The voice of the shadowy apparition known only as *Gambit*. But before, when Salvador accepted the job and was paid, Gambit's tone was warm and calm. Almost friendly. Now each word sounded as though it were being dragged over jagged ice.

"What request?" Salvador played for time.

"*Killing Mitchell Holiday.*"

The knot in Salvador's stomach twisted, sending panic through his mind. He sucked in a breath and shoved his hands into his pockets to keep them from shaking.

"Yeah, well, I took care of it. I hired the best."

"You hired *Oliver Enfield*, and he made the crucial error of putting his own interests ahead of ours. Apparently he was more interested in framing one of his own contractors than he was in completing the job."

Salvador nodded. "Yeah, that's how he operates. When one of his contractors becomes a problem, he sets them up. Lets them take the fall for the kill, so it's a clean slate."

"Did I *ask* for a clean slate?" Gambit's voice rose into a shout, and the windowpanes rattled in their frames.

Salvador swallowed hard. "You—"

"*I didn't.* I asked for a kill, plain and simple. You left me with a dumpster fire and a rampaging assassin!"

"You mean Montgomery? Look, I can take care of that. I've got another guy who supplies me the men I need—"

"*Cedric Muri?*"

Salvador hesitated.

"Muri's dead. Montgomery killed him two nights ago in his own casino. We have the whole thing on the security camera. You see, Salvador, when I hired you, I was under the impression that you were the man to get the job done. But it seems you're incapable of doing anything on your own. In fact, your entire methodology appears to be that of a cheap middleman—brokering out the dirty work to one subcontractor after another."

The panic rising in Salvador's chest began to take over. He took another step back and held up his hands. "Look, I operate with subcontractors for a reason. It gives you multiple layers of insulation from the kill. You know what I mean? I underestimated Montgomery, I admit it. But it's okay. I've still got assets in the field. Have you heard of The Wolf? He's not one of Enfield's men. He's an independent. A freelancer!"

"The same freelancer who let Montgomery off the hook in North Carolina?"

"Right, I know. That was my mistake. Oliver wanted to handle it himself, so I called The Wolf off. But Holiday bit the dirt, right? The job got done."

"After *two weeks*."

Salvador tried to step back again, but his foot hit the wall. "Listen. I screwed some stuff up, but I've got it. Give me a couple more days. The Wolf can get the job done—he just needs the right motivation. He's got this sister with cystic fibrosis in New York. It's leverage, right?"

Silence answered his sales pitch. The room around him was all at once darker and more closed in, as though even the walls bent their ill will upon him. He wanted to start again, renewing his arguments and mixing in additional excuses, but his better judgment finally took over. Any excuses now would be met with cynicism and perhaps vengeance.

"My boss is a patient man," Gambit said at last. "I'm not. You have three days."

A rustle of footsteps echoed from the far end of the room, and the speaker was gone—a shadow fading into deeper shadows.

Salvador sucked in a breath, then gritted his teeth. His patience with The Wolf's quirky behavior was about to cost him his life. It was time to take off the gloves.

9

"Chris! I found her." Dillan's words fell over one another in an excited stream. "She's in Nashville."

Reed held the phone away from his ear, wincing at the shrill noise. "I know."

He could almost hear the air whistling out of Dillan's deflating chest. "You . . . know? How? It took me two weeks!"

"Basic deduction. Don't worry about it. I'll send your payment."

"But—"

Reed hung up and downshifted the Camaro into third. The massive motor bellowed, and the supercharger screamed to life, blasting air into the engine block and pumping out additional horsepower. The back wheels of the car gripped the pavement and slung the Camaro forward. Vehicles flashed by on all sides as Reed navigated onto the freeway and swerved past a semitruck. Baxter lay in the passenger's seat, his tongue lolling out of the side of his mouth, dripping drool onto the floor mat. For the first time since the fire, his eyes weren't completely dominated by pain.

After returning from Holiday's condo, Reed stripped the hotel of any identifiable material and packed his gear into the trunk of the Camaro, then loaded Baxter into the passenger's seat. The smart thing would have been to leave him at a local animal boarder, but Reed didn't have the heart to abandon the dog again. For better or worse, Baxter would accompany him on the four-hour drive through North Georgia and into Tennessee.

The realization of where Banks fled to after the slaughter in North Carolina hit him only moments after uncovering the secret of Holiday's association with Banks's father, Frank Morccelli. Vanderbilt University was nestled in Midtown, Nashville. "Music City" had grown explosively over the past decade, expanding into a thriving tourist town packed with live-music bars and college kids. Reed recalled Banks's decision to leave Mississippi after her father died and take shelter with her godfather in Atlanta. Now that he too was gone, Banks would take refuge in the next most familiar place—Nashville, the town of her father's alma mater, and a place she frequently visited as a child. She wouldn't go home to face her vindictive mother, and she wouldn't disappear into a strange and lonely new place.

Reed was grateful that Banks was in Nashville because he didn't want to have to choose between pursuing his investigation and finding her. As soon as he reached the city, he would find a place to set up camp and give Baxter a bed, then look for Banks. There would be time to investigate Holiday's fraternity ties and make progress on finding Salvador afterward.

The sun began its western descent as the big car purred over the Georgia mountains and descended toward Chattanooga. The old town sat on the state line between Georgia and Tennessee, in the bottom of a valley and wrapped on three sides by the Tennessee River. Reed had driven through it many times before and always appreciated the charm of the dusty brick buildings and slow, methodical, Southern lifestyle. In a lot of ways, Chattanooga was stuck in another time—a calmer time.

As the exit signs flashed by on his right, Reed made the impulse decision to turn off the highway. Exhaustion burrowed deep in his bones, and his eyelids were already growing heavy. After two days of sleeplessness and who knew how much alcohol, it was past time to get some rest. He would stop here for the night, get dinner, then arrive in Nashville well before lunch the next day. It would be better not to confront Banks exhausted.

In typical fashion, as soon as Reed located a pet-friendly motel and reapplied Baxter's salve for the evening, his sleepiness vanished, and insomnia returned. He lay on the bed, staring at the ceiling for half an hour before he pulled his boots back on and stomped down to the front desk. A dirty desk clerk with a stained shirt and greasy hair watched him through smudged glasses, his gaze hazed over by some type of narcotic.

"What do you do for fun around here?" Reed asked. It was a poor choice of words.

"I dunno, man. Get high, I guess. You want some weed?"

"No, I mean I want to stretch my legs. Is there any place to . . . hike or something?"

"Oh, yeah, man. This is Tennessee. Lots of hiking, man."

Reed waited. The clerk stared at him with a blank expression, as though Reed weren't even there.

Reed rapped his knuckles on the counter. "So, where do I go?"

"Oh, yeah. Sure. Sunset Rock, man. It's really nice this time of the day. I go up there and get high all the time."

"Thanks."

Reed piloted out of the city, turning down one winding road after another as he followed his GPS into the mountains. Naked trees clung to the sides of rock cliffs, their ghostly limbs trailing over the pavement. With each switchback and curve, Reed drove farther above the valley floor. Many of the signs he passed advertised a place called Ruby Falls, while others mentioned Lookout Mountain. He was vaguely familiar with both locations, but he'd never been before.

After twenty minutes of weaving through small neighborhoods, the GPS led him to a tiny parking lot directly adjacent to the road. He squeezed the Camaro between two SUVs and climbed out, enjoying the blast of chilly mountain air. It was thinner and fresher than the smog-laden humidity of Atlanta, and after only a moment, it bit through his shirt and sent a shiver down his spine. Reed pulled a jacket out of the trunk and slid it on.

A trail led from the parking lot and into the trees, paved in thick slabs of rock that were half-path, half-steps, winding down the mountainside. Reed's muscles ached with every footfall, refreshing the agony of a dozen minor wounds that covered his body. Matched with bruises and stitches, his skin looked like the patchwork of Frankenstein's monster. The last month hadn't been kind to him, but even so, the exercise felt great. It revived his tired mind and brought clarity to his thoughts.

After less than a quarter mile, the trees parted all at once, exposing a wide rock ledge that jutted out from the cliff face and hung over the valley. Air rushed from Reed's lungs as he stepped off the trail and admired the rolling valleys of East Tennessee stretched out in front of him as far as he could see—miles of perfectly clear landscape cresting into mountain ranges on every side. The freeway wound through the valley floor a couple thousand yards away, each passing car and truck cruising across the valley floor at highway speeds, but at this distance, appearing to move at little more than a crawl. To his right, the western edge of Chattanooga was barely visible around the curvature of a mountain ridge, tall buildings reflecting the sunlight as the wide Tennessee River wound its way alongside the freeway. It was the most picturesque, gorgeous view Reed had ever scene—perfect and calm.

He took another step closer to the edge and felt his stomach churn. From this angle, he knew he was a few hundred feet high—enough to send his mind spinning and his every instinct commanding him to return to the car. But the view was too calming and beautiful. Reed forced himself forward another few yards, then sat down on a rock with his feet inches from the cliff's edge. He released a deep breath, liberating his tension and fear to the valley floor below and allowing a deep relaxation to settle in its place. The soothing touch of the sun on his face and the wind in his hair loosened his taut nerves, bringing gradual relaxation to his body.

Nearby, a young couple next to the cliff were wrapped in each other's arms. Farther on, a photographer with a camera and tripod attempted to replicate the stunning view. It wouldn't be easy. Something about the magnificent experience of sitting this close to the edge, saturated in the kiss of the sunset, was too raw and real to be appreciated by a photograph.

Reed closed his eyes and savored the bite of the wind. It was too cold to be comfortable, but the chill reminded him of the snow falling around his face as he and Banks crashed through the North Carolina mountains, desperately searching for a place to take shelter. At the time, all he felt was panic and a dreadful sensation of failure, but those feelings quickly melted into passion and warmth as he stood in front of a crackling fire and embraced Banks. He remembered the touch of her skin, the elegance of her kiss. It was the most perfect, beautiful feeling, too overwhelming and gripping to resist.

He opened his eyes and squinted into the sun. There was something about Banks—something profound that felt more solid than the mountaintop under his feet. It was something he never found in the Los Angeles gangs, the Marine Corps, or in Kelly's arms. All of those places offered him thrills and belonging and the promise of fame and fortune, but with Banks, it was deeper. It was a place to let his guard down and *be*, as though she had no expectations of who he was or what he could do for her—only what he could *be* for her.

The thought ripped through his heart like a bullet. Banks never cared about his real name, his occupation, his paycheck, or the chaos that accompanied their every encounter. She only cared about who he was and the way he made her feel. Maybe he made her feel safe, too. Maybe he felt like home to her in the way she felt like home to him. It was such a simple, beautiful thing, and he shattered it right in front of her face.

Reed retraced his memories back to that moment on the bank of the lake with Oliver Enfield dying at his feet. Mitchell Holiday, only a few yards away, was also gasping on his last breaths. The rain beat down from overhead as Banks stared at him, heartbroken, her tears mixing with rain as she dropped the shotgun and turned away.

I failed her. I crushed all the trust and faith she ever gave me.

Reed stood up, swallowing back the fear that overwhelmed his body, then took a step toward the edge, his hands held at his sides, fingers clenched.

She believed in me, and I proved her wrong. I've never been good. I've never been a home for anyone.

The valley floor opened up beneath him as his toes approached the edge. He could see hundreds of feet down the cliff face, into the belly of the gorge.

What am I fighting for? Oliver is dead. Who cares whether Salvador isn't? I don't deserve to be alive.

The wind beat at his shirt, plastering it back over his torn and marred chest. His feet were glued to the stone, as though he were no longer in control of his legs. He focused on each muscle group, commanding them one at a time. Lifting his toes, he inched his foot forward until it overhung the cliff. He stared down to the rocks below and imagined the next step: leaning forward, opening his hands, and letting go of his will to live.

So close.

He saw Kelly's sharp features and imagined her in the fire, slowly burning alive as her home caved in around her. He pictured her that first day in Monaco, her face obscured by the mask as she broke into the Ferrari. He heard her sassy, snapping voice again. *"Let's roll, kid. We're in this together now."*

"Hey, man. You okay?"

The voice ripped through his mind, shattering the memory. His eyes snapped open, and he turned to his left. The photographer stood a few feet away, his face twisted into a concerned frown. Farther down the cliff, the young couple, still in each other's arms, stared in semi-panic.

Reed stepped away from the ridge, shoved his hands into his pockets, and brushed past the photographer. "I'm fine."

The mountain steps strained his legs as he fought his way back up the trail to the parking lot. By the time he slid into the Camaro, his breath came in short gasps, and sweat dripped from his forehead. He wasn't out of shape, but he ached from the perpetual abuse of the past month.

He set his hands on the wheel and returned to that memory, there in the cottage in the middle of rural France. *"We're in this together."*

Kelly didn't abandon him when he stood in that French garage, dripping blood, and chased by an army of cops. She didn't abandon him beside the train tracks in Atlanta when he lay with an unconscious Banks in his arms, only moments from impending death. She didn't even leave him when he intruded on her perfect suburban life and asked her to watch Baxter—a favor that cost her life. She never let him down, never cut him loose, even when she should have. He wouldn't let her down now. He would wage war until her death was avenged and her enemies joined her in the ashes.

Then, and only then, he would die.

10

Reed had never been to Chattanooga's riverfront before, but there was something altogether familiar and calming about the gentle breeze that churned off the dark water and whistled over the dockside. The Tennessee river wound in graceful curves through the heart of the old city on its long journey south, leaving ample room for riverfront next to a downtown park. A large paddle cruiser rested at anchor with the name *Southern Belle* scrolled over the front in decorative letters. Just next to the boat, a metal, grated pier shot out over the river.

The sun had long ago set over the mountains, leaving Chattanooga dark and quiet as cars faded from the streets, and the business district fell asleep. After spending a few hours sitting in the hotel room staring at his feet, Reed decided to venture down to the water's edge before popping a sleeping pill. He resented the idea of taking any drug that would alter his state of mind, but it was now close to midnight, and he felt too exhausted and too frustrated with insomnia to argue. Maybe the fresh air would help.

The pier's metal grate squeaked beneath him. The river water lapped gently against the pilings, reminding him of the days when his father would load up the family in his old 1969 Camaro, and the three of them would drive five hours to the beach for the weekend. The waves lapped against the piers in Panama City much the same way, but the air didn't smell of fish and oil. It smelled of salt and sun and all things summer.

At the end of the pier, five flag poles stood bolted to the railing, with American flags snapping in the wind at the top of each. As Reed approached, he made out the shape of small, steel plaques fixed to the railings next to each pole, and recognized the familiar outline of the Marine Corps symbol engraved at the top of the nearest plaque.

He clicked on his flashlight. A simple memorandum was etched into the steel next to the Eagle, Globe, and Anchor:

LET US NEVER FORGET . . . THIS IS DEDICATED TO THE MEMORY OF LCPL WELLS, WHO PROUDLY SERVED, PROTECTED OUR COUNTRY, AND GAVE HIS LIFE TO OUR COMMUNITY ON JULY 16, 2015.

A weight descended over Reed's chest, and he stepped back from the plaque. He bowed his head, breathing in the musty air of the river.

I should've died. None of this would've ever happened if I had fallen, and Lance Corporal Wells had come home. He deserved to come home.

Reed swallowed back the guilt and straightened his back, then lifted his hand to his brow in a stiff salute toward the flags. The Stars and Stripes flipped in the wind, hanging as eternal guardians of the fallen. Somehow, he didn't feel worthy of saluting that flag. He didn't feel worthy of standing next to the plaques and remembering the fallen. Yet, at the same time, he couldn't walk away without the salute.

"Wow. You're still a patriot."

Reed recognized the sharp tone and inflection instantly, and even before he turned around, he was already reaching for the revolver strapped under his coat.

The man they called *The Wolf* stood only inches behind him, his lips lifted into a grin as his fingers twirled around a long, plastic-coated choke wire. Before Reed could wrap his hand around the grip of the weapon, The Wolf stepped forward and flicked the wire with an expert twitch of his fingers. It glided through the air and encircled Reed's head, cutting into the back of his neck and pulling him off-balance in an instant. He fell forward with a grunt and clattered onto the grating, struggling to roll over as The Wolf landed on his back. An iron kneecap crashed down between Reed's shoulder blades just as the wire slid beneath his chin and then tightened around his windpipe.

It all happened in mere seconds. Reed's world blurred as the grating cut into his chest. He choked and flailed with both arms, but the wire cut deeper into his neck, sealing off his throat.

"Seriously." The Wolf spoke without a hint of exertion in his tone. "If I'd been through half the crap you've endured, I'd hate this country."

Reed kicked out with both legs, twisting and wriggling from beneath the weight bearing down on his back, but he couldn't break free or reach his attacker. The deadlock was perfect—enough to keep him planted on his chest while his thundering heart consumed what precious oxygen remained in his lungs.

"All right, my dude. You have to die now. Don't be so dramatic about it."

The words sounded from the far edges of Reed's consciousness. He wrapped his fingers around the grate and desperately attempted a push-up to dislodge his attacker. It was beyond futile—the weight on his back and the wire around his neck immobilized his core reflexes.

No way am I dying on this pier.

Reed pushed his head down with all the strength he could muster, digging the wire farther into his neck, but forcing The Wolf to lean forward. Then he shot his head back as hard and fast as he could, momentarily dislodging the choke wire from his throat and allowing him a sip of air.

It was enough.

Reed shoved down with his right arm and wrenched his shoulders to the left. The knee slid from the middle of his spine, and The Wolf toppled to the left, colliding with the grate as Reed slipped out of the choke wire. Torrents of vertigo sent Reed rocking back on his heels as he clawed at his jacket, searching for the revolver. The Wolf was already on his feet, spinning the long choke wire at the end of his fingers as he grinned and stepped toward Reed.

"You're just too good at staying alive."

Reed grabbed the gun by the end of the handle and tried to jerk it free of the holster, but it caught on the retention strap and refused to budge. He ducked a sweeping kick from The Wolf and dove toward the flags. His attacker followed, spinning the wire around his head like a lasso. Reed saw the choke wire coming toward him only an instant before it arced toward his head, and he stuck his arm up to shield himself from the noose.

The wire closed around his wrist, biting into his skin as The Wolf jerked backward. Reed grabbed the flag pole and yanked back, pulling on the wire and digging his toes into the metal grating.

The Wolf stumbled forward, the grin fading from his lips as Reed twisted, grabbed him by the collar, and lifted him over the rail. With one massive heave, Reed propelled the flailing assassin past the flags and over the railing. Metal screeched against metal as The Wolf plummeted toward the water, still clutching his end of the choke wire.

Oh shit.

The wire snapped tightly around Reed's wrist, and before he could regain his hold of the flagpole or dig his toes into the grate, The Wolf's full weight descended on his shoulder and snatched him forward, over the rail, and into midair beyond.

Both men crashed into the icy water. The wire jerked against Reed's wrist, pulling him deeper into the murk as his unseen enemy thrashed in the darkness somewhere nearby. His lungs throbbed, still starved for air, and he impulsively gulped down river water. Everything was black and cold, saturating his jacket and sinking straight into his bones.

The surface of the river broke over his face just in time to keep his lungs from collapsing on themselves. Reed sucked in a massive gulp of air and choked on water. The wire felt limp on his wrist now, and as he surveyed the surface of the river, he couldn't see The Wolf. Everything was eerily still next to the panicked chaos in Reed's mind. Nobody stood on the pier overhead, and no shouts of shock or offered assistance came from the riverbank. Only the wind filled his ringing ears, further numbing his chalky skin.

Where is he?

Fear overtook Reed's desire for blood, and he began to kick toward the shore. Mud closed over his boots only moments later, and he hauled himself onto the bank. Dry grass crumbled under his face as he fell forward, still panting for air. The water lapped at his ankles, and the wire still hung in a tangle around his wrist.

Picking himself up, Reed unwound the wire from his arm and flung it to the ground, then clawed at his jacket as he turned back to the lake. The comforting rubber grip of the revolver filled his hand, and he pried it free of the holster. All four inches of the massive barrel swung out, and Reed directed the muzzle toward the river. The water remained calm, with small ripples dancing against the shore as the river flowed slowly past.

Did he drown? No way.

Reed lowered the revolver and caught sight of something glimmering in the water twenty yards away. He leaned forward and squinted in the darkness, trying to making out the shape as it drifted closer to the shore. Trash? A body?

It's a stick.

The thought cleared his tired mind at the same moment a kneecap collided with his lower back. The revolver flew from his hand as the choke wire flashed over his eyes and clipped his chin before closing around his throat. Reed fell forward onto the bank, his chest crashing into the dirt as the full weight of his assailant descended on his back, and then his face was forced into the shallow water. The noose closed off his windpipe, cinching down so hard this time he imagined it slicing into his skin. Everything turned dark, and his eyes filled with dirty river water as his arms flailed against the shore.

There was no moving this time—no dislodging the killer perched on his back, jerking away at the wire. In a flash Reed saw distorted memories of prison. He saw Blazer—his first assassination on behalf of Oliver Enfield—from the far side of the prison fence. He heard his own voice as he lured his prey close to the fence, and then encircled the wire around Blazer's throat. He heard his victim cry out and struggle even as Reed snatched the wire back and twisted, slicing into his throat.

And this is how it ends.

The wire bit deeper into Reed's throat, and his windpipe closed off completely. The water covered his face, choking him, and the last tinges of panic faded from his body as his life continued to flash before him: his father, his mother, Baxter, Kelly . . . and Banks. Her face gleamed in his mind before the shadows engulfed him. A fading beep echoed in the distance, matching his slowing heart rate and slipping away into the far reaches of his consciousness. Then his entire body went limp.

11

Reed's ears hovered only half an inch over the water, allowing him to hear the distant electronic chirp.

Beep. Beep. Beep.

The wire loosened around his throat, and the weight fell off his back. His windpipe opened, but he was too weak to lift his face from the water. Only the darkness and the outline of Banks's fading features filled his mind.

Fingers closed around the collar of his jacket, and with a massive jerk, he was pulled out of the water and hurled onto the bank. His shoulders collided with the hard-packed earth, and water shot out of his throat as he gasped for air. The sky swirled overhead, twisting stars into streaks of lights that unleashed unprecedented surges of vertigo and nausea through his body. Reed coughed and spluttered on more river water, then felt concentrated pressure on the middle of his chest. He couldn't see the source of the weight but felt his ribs constrict and expand as the pressure increased, then alleviated.

Reed choked up more water, then sucked in a full breath of air. It whistled through his ragged and bruised throat, and his vision began to clear.

He coughed and fell over on his side. Black boots thumped against the ground only a few feet away, and the electronic beeping was suddenly silenced. Reed clawed his way into a sitting position and searched for the revolver as he rolled away from the boots.

"It's right here, dude."

The Wolf's voice sounded strained and breathless, but there was a hint of amusement in his tone. Reed rolled toward him and clenched his fingers into a fist, already raising his arms to defend himself.

Ten feet away, his assailant dripped with water and stared down at Reed. The choke wire dangled from his left hand, and Reed's massive .500 Magnum revolver hung from his right, but neither weapon was raised.

The Wolf curled the wire around his fingers, then twisted his neck until it popped. "You're one tough cookie, I'll give you that. Let the record state that I would have killed you."

Reed blinked back the water in his eyes. His throat hurt like hell, bruised and crushed by the weight of the wire, but his mind cleared as vital oxygen surged back into his brain.

"Why didn't you?" It was a stupid, pointless question, really. And yet the most obvious.

The Wolf ran a hand through his short hair, forcing the water out. His bright eyes glinted in the moonlight, a hint of mischief shining behind them.

"It's midnight. Didn't you hear my watch? I don't kill after business hours."

Reed sank his fingers into the sod, still fighting off the last traces of vertigo as he tried to compute what he just heard. Nothing made sense, and he tried to stand up.

"Well, I don't have business hours, so hand me that damn—"

"Don't curse." The Wolf lifted the revolver and wagged the muzzle toward Reed. "Or I might be inclined to reconsider my rules. And no, you're not getting this back. Just because I'm off the clock doesn't mean I'm going to let you kill me."

Reed stumbled to his feet. "Who the hell—"

"Uh-uh."

The muzzle of the revolver twitched again. Reed stumbled, almost collapsing as the world tilted beneath him. He vomited into the grass, a mixture of beer and bile splashing over his boots. His throat stung like hell.

"I see you've been eating well." There was more than a little derision in The Wolf's voice. Almost condescension.

Reed spat vomit from his mouth and straightened. "You listen here, you cheap shi—"

The hammer of the revolver clicked back, and the gaping barrel leveled over Reed's chest. The Wolf raised both eyebrows, and Reed sucked in a lungful of air. Stillness filled the space between them, and for a moment, Reed thought he would press the trigger. He could envision the blast of fire as the weapon belched thunder and hurled a thumb-sized chunk of lead straight through his heart.

The Wolf tilted his head and smirked, then lowered the hammer and shoved the revolver into his coat pocket.

"Kicking butt really awakens the munchies," he said. "I'm famished. By the look of it, you could use some sustenance yourself."

Reed relaxed his clenched fists. The Wolf kicked mud off his shoes, and then started up the hillside toward the city, two hundred yards away.

"Come along! I've got this outstanding spot a mile down the street. The onion rings are, simply put, absolutely scrumptious. And don't get me started on the *duck pâté en croûte*."

Reed shot a glance around the riverside park. The commotion of two men thrashing around in the shallows, desperately trying to assassinate one another, hadn't garnered the attention of any locals. Only The Wolf stood on the bank, dripping water like a sopping dishrag as he started toward the city.

He's got my freaking gun.

The thought ignited strange, irrational anger inside of Reed. A basic instinct deep beneath the whistling breaths and aching chest told him he should be more concerned about his near-death experience, or perhaps it was the fact that the man who delivered that experience was himself still breathing. But somehow, the only thing that seemed pressingly important was the revolver jammed deep inside The Wolf's pocket. Reed felt like a kid whose favorite toy had been stolen on the playground. It was a deep, instinctive outrage.

Reed broke into a run up the hillside, wheezing and clutching his stomach the whole way. His head erupted with pain, making the shadows around him dance with every step, and his swollen throat throbbed as though a hot poker were being repeatedly rammed up and down it.

I'm going to rip his head off.

The Wolf walked in mechanical strides that kept him a dozen yards ahead. Reed followed him up the hill, where they walked past the anchored *Southern Belle* and then through the trees for a mile along the riverside. An occasional car drove by, headed toward downtown, but the streets were otherwise silent and shrouded in darkness.

"Now, understand." The Wolf spoke in a clear, chipper tone. "This place closes at midnight. I have an arrangement with the sous chef, a rather rotund fellow from the New England coast. Grills a cod on white rice like you wouldn't *believe*."

The Wolf tilted his head back and groaned at the sky, then wagged his finger toward Reed. "Anyway, my point is, be polite. Rumor has it you have quite the temper. Dust off your manners or you can hit up White Castle."

Reed stumbled to a stop. He tried to speak past what was left of his throat, but the sound came out as a gurgle.

The Wolf lifted an eyebrow. "This is what I'm talking about. That's brutish."

The riverside restaurant was a small building constructed of cedar shingle siding with a metal roof and gas lighting on the exterior walls. The parking lot lay vacant except for a handful of cars in the employee parking section. The Wolf approached without any sign of hesitation and rapped twice on the front door.

Reed leaned on the wall and gasped for breath, his heart still pounding from the strangulation twenty minutes before. He eyed the bulge of the revolver in The Wolf's pocket and calculated the prospect of retrieving the weapon before The Wolf put him on the ground. It was beyond question now that Reed's hand-to-hand combat skills were far inferior, and whatever bizarre set of rules had prevented The Wolf from killing him before, Reed didn't think they would save him a second time. He would have to wait for the right moment.

The lock clicked, and the door swung open. A short Asian man with tiny glasses peered out, squinting at The Wolf a moment before a wide smile spread across his face. "Ah, Mr. Pierce! Such a pleasure. Please, come in."

The Wolf bowed, returned the greeting, then motioned Reed ahead. "After you, Mr. Montgomery."

Reed reluctantly slipped through the door and into the dimly lit restaurant. It was decorative—far more so than the humble exterior would have indicated. Gold trim lined the bar, and glistening chandeliers hung over the main dining room, casting dull pools of yellow over tables covered in soft white cloths. Staff bustled about the room, vacuuming the floors, replacing the tablecloths, and dusting the wall decor, but the Asian man motioned past the main dining room and led them to an alcove at the back of the restaurant with massive windows that overlooked the river. He bowed and gestured to a two-person table with large, leather-cushioned chairs.

"Please, have a seat. I'll let Alphonse know you're here. Would either of you care for a towel?"

Reed glanced down at the muddy river water pooling around his boots, then grunted and plopped down at the table. The host sighed and disappeared into the kitchen as Reed shot The Wolf a glare. "So, you've chased me through the mountains, tried to obliterate me with a minigun, strangled me within seconds of my life, and now apparently we're on a date. I think it's way past time you introduced yourself."

The Wolf sat down across from Reed and picked up a folded

napkin from the table. He brushed the mud off his hands, then dabbed at his forehead before refolding it and replacing it on the table. "Fair enough. I'm Wolfgang Pierce, professionally known as *The Wolf*. I'm an assassin for hire."

Reed snorted. "Is that right? You know, I'm something of an assassin myself, only I actually kill people. I don't take them out for steak."

Wolfgang laughed. "Is that what you would've preferred? Because we can go back to the river, and I can drown you again."

Before Reed could answer, footsteps thumped against the carpet, and a short man with an immense potbelly appeared, dressed in a white apron with a floppy chef's hat perched atop his bald head. When the chef saw Wolfgang, his eyes lit up, and a smile spread across a mouth that contained less than half the usual ration of teeth.

"Mr. Pierce! What an unexpected delight. How go your studies?" Laden with a thick French accent, his babbled words almost blended together.

Wolfgang bowed and returned the smile. "Excellently, Alphonse. Thank you for asking. I actually graduated yesterday."

Alphonse snapped his fingers. "Ah, then it is *Doctor* Pierce!"

"Well, more or less. I still have a dissertation to write, but the diploma is secured, as it were. Alphonse, I'd like you to meet my colleague, Mr. Reed Montgomery, of Atlanta. He's joining me for dinner tonight."

Alphonse redirected his gaze at Reed, but instead of a bow and smile, his expression turned critical, and he folded his fingers over his gut.

Reed leaned back in his chair and scowled. "What the hell are you looking at?"

Wolfgang sighed. "Reed, if you curse again, I'll be forced to kill you."

Alphonse broke out into a raucous laugh and slapped himself on the leg. "That's funny," he said. "Because he actually kills people for a living!"

Wolfgang joined in on the merriment, smacking the table before wagging a finger at the chef. "Alphonse, you're *too much!* You'll have to forgive Reed. His manners are a great deal less refined than ours."

Reed switched his glare between Wolfgang and the chef. *What the hell is going on here?*

The Asian man appeared with a couple of rolled towels. Reed used one to wipe himself down as best he could, and Alphonse bowed again before bustling off to the kitchen. The Asian man introduced himself as David and offered to take their drink orders.

"I'll have black tea," Wolfgang said. "With a spoon of cream and a pinch of peppermint."

"Very good, sir. And you?"

"Whiskey," Reed said. "A lot of it."

David raised an eyebrow, but Wolfgang waved his hand dismissively, and the waiter retreated to the kitchen.

"I imagine you're thinking of a way to kill me," Wolfgang said, unfolding the cloth napkin and laying it over his lap.

"I just want my gun back."

"It's a little overkill, don't you think? .500 Magnum?"

"I could say the same about that Glock 10mm you tried to blow my brains out with back in North Carolina, you thug."

Wolfgang sighed. "Don't act so butthurt, Reed. It's only business. You should know that."

"You tried to run me over in a *Jeep,*" Reed snapped.

Wolfgang laughed and lifted his water glass. "I forgot about that. You run like a jackrabbit."

David returned to the table with a cup of tea on a saucer, and a small tumbler with two shots of whiskey on ice.

Reed drained the tumbler before it even hit the table and handed it back. "Bring the bottle."

Once again, David shot Wolfgang a sideways look, and Wolfgang nodded.

As soon as the waiter was out of earshot, Reed leaned across the table and glowered at Wolfgang. "All right, we're all impressed.

You're fancy, refined, and the chef loves you. I want to know who hired you to kill me."

Wolfgang sipped his tea, then tapped a finger against the side of the cup. "Don't you know?"

"Would I have asked if I did?"

The teacup clicked back against the saucer, and Wolfgang stirred the jet-back tea with a silver spoon. "Usually, people know who they've crossed."

"Dude, I've crossed so many people, I've lost count. Any one of them could want me dead."

"Occupational hazard," Wolfgang said. "You certainly dealt with Oliver."

"I did. Along with his henchmen and the person who sold him those henchmen."

"Cedric Muri."

"Yes. Do you work for him?"

"Who? Muri? Absolutely not. I don't work for anyone. I'm a free agent."

Reed sneered. "Nobody's a free agent in this business. Everybody has a boss."

Wolfgang shook his head. "That's not true. I work for myself, take the jobs I want, decline the jobs I don't. It leaves me plenty of free time to pursue my interests."

"Isn't that nice." Reed crossed his arms. "I'm sorry if I seem cold, but you *did* try to strangle me just a moment ago, and you also tried to kill somebody very important to me. I'm not in the mood for banter."

"If you're talking about Banks Morccelli, you should know that I would've never hurt her. The grenades were necessary to dislodge you off the cliff, but you were the one who put her in harm's way. I cannot be responsible for collateral damage when you use women as human shields."

Reed's blood boiled, and he slammed a closed fist against the table, sending silverware raining down over the floor. Wolfgang didn't react, but sat with the teacup in one hand and stared at Reed.

"Did you do it?" Reed hissed. "Did you burn Kelly?"

Wolfgang set the cup down, wiped his mouth, then shook his head. "No, I didn't. I would never kill somebody that way."

"But you'd blow them up with a minigun. You'd gun them down in a coffee shop."

Wolfgang stared off with vacant eyes, as though he had left the restaurant, and his mind was now far away. "Reed, I don't want to compare rap sheets. We've both done some unspeakable things, and we've both had our reasons. As an independent contractor, I operate under my own rules. One of those rules is that I don't kill people between midnight and six a.m. That's my choice. I would enjoy a civil dinner with you, one professional to another, but I'm not going to continue tolerating these outbursts."

Reed's breaths hissed through his swollen throat. He accepted a full glass of whiskey from David and drained it, deadening the ache of developing bruises on his body. The preposterousness of Wolfgang's erratic behavior didn't register with him. The Wolf was eclectic in the extreme, and perhaps he had reason to be. Or maybe he was simply weird. Either way, Reed couldn't kill him right now, and he wasn't going to wait around for Wolfgang to kill him.

Reed stood up, dropping the towel on the table. "Tell your boss, whoever the *hell* he is, that I'm coming for him. I'm coming for them all."

Wolfgang twisted the teacup in his hand. His fingers turned white against the porcelain, and for a moment, Reed almost thought he saw sympathy, but that light faded, replaced by iron and darkness.

"I'm sorry to hear that, Reed. I'm sorry we fell on opposite sides of the ditch. You're a good killer, and if you allowed yourself, you might even be a good man. But next time I see you, I'm going to kill you."

Their gazes locked, steel clashing against steel, and Reed walked out of the restaurant without another word.

12

Lake Maurepas, Louisiana

Maggie never liked the governor's mansion. Large, overdecorated, and inspired by all things plantation, the official residence of Louisiana's executive leader was downtown, only a couple miles from the Capitol. It wasn't that she didn't appreciate the grandeur and status of the luxury residence, and she certainly enjoyed the private chef and quiet study, but it just didn't feel like home. It was too fancy, filled with too many breakable things, and altogether too clean.

Most nights, Maggie was forced to sleep at the residence by virtue of its proximity to the Capitol. Late-night paperwork and administrative tasks kept her at her official office until midnight or later, and early-morning meetings began as soon as the sun crested over the mighty Mississippi. But some nights, when the workload bore too heavy on her tired shoulders, she slipped away from the crowds of aides and media reporters and took a long drive south of the city, into the swamplands of Louisiana.

The old family lake house sat on the shores of Lake Maurepas, a brackish catfish lake with an average depth of fewer than ten feet.

People from out of town found the lake to be both smelly and ugly, but Maggie loved the calm and simplicity of the swampy landscape. Frogs croaked in the darkness, the wind rustled through the grass, and the occasional alligator crawled past the back porch, migrating from one muddy inlet to the next. It was home, even if it felt less private with the burly state policeman standing guard outside.

As the sun melted into the pines, the moon took over, filling the night sky with a blue glow that reminded Maggie of late-night 'coon hunting with her father. When she closed her eyes, she could still hear the howl of the hounds and the crash of the brush as the two barged ahead, shotguns at the ready, alive in the hunt.

She missed everything about those simple days. When she went to law school and first considered running for political office, it was out of frustration more than passion. After years of watching corruption in Baton Rouge overrun the simple, low-income families of her community, she wanted to make a statement—defy the system.

Funny how such a small spark could ignite a wildfire. And it wasn't just the people around her who burst into flames—Maggie herself became consumed with the campaign. The more she learned about the status quo in Louisiana's capital, the more frustrated she became, and the harder she campaigned. Her only goal had been to pressure the older, more mature candidates into appreciating the needs of her neighbors.

By the time she won the nomination, it was too late to turn back. Even when she accepted the concession call from her opponent on election night, she still clung to the hope that after a single term, she could have accomplished enough to hand the reins over to someone else and open the small community law practice that she always dreamed of. She wanted to live a simple life—be the friend of the people.

Those fantasies were long dead now. Baton Rouge was a machine—a vortex that pulled you in and pulled you down, regardless of the odds. She still didn't want to be there, but she believed more than ever that it was her responsibility to serve the people, and that obligation chained her down.

Maggie sat on the edge of her bed, and through her narrow window, watched the moon glinting off the water. Every few minutes, her guard would pass by, a shotgun swinging from one hand. Fish splashed from the lake's surface, conducting elaborate flips before vanishing into the murky water again. Everything was so calm.

She sighed and closed her eyes. Her dreams were selfish. She knew that. Her old man would be ashamed of her if he knew how badly she wanted to throw in the towel after only five months of serving as governor. There was still work to be done—still justice to be served.

"A Trousdale never quits." Her father said it a thousand times. It was her mantra and what pushed her through college and brought her out of law school. Surrendering was never an option.

Maggie lay back on the bed, kicking off her flats and resting her head against a worn pillow. It was cheap, like everything in the cabin. This was the mansion of the minimum wage—the palace of a working-class family. Nothing was nice, but everything was wonderful.

A creaking sound erupted from down the hall. Maggie's eyes snapped open, and she held her breath, listening carefully. She recognized that distinct grunt. It was the sound the third floorboard in the hallway made when somebody stepped on it. She used to avoid that board when she was a teenager and snuck out at night to meet her boyfriend by the lake. It was a unique sound—one she shouldn't have heard in an empty house.

She turned and looked out the window, still holding her breath while she waited for her guard to walk by, but he didn't pass. Only the wind rustled through the grass.

Then she heard it again.

Maggie set her feet on the floor and opened the nightstand drawer. An old Colt .38 Special revolver lay in the bottom, a thin layer of dust clinging to the metal cylinder. She depressed the release switch and checked the five bullets housed within before snapping the cylinder shut and creeping toward the door. Her fingers trembled, and sweat pooled on her lip. She wasn't sure if it was her imagination, but she thought she heard heavy breaths on the other side of the door and a faint scuffling sound, like a boot scraping a baseboard.

Maggie ducked into the shadows behind the door and held the revolver next to her ear. A few seconds dripped by, and the guard still didn't pass outside. She heard the soft squeak of metal on metal, and the doorknob twisted.

Her heart flew into her mouth, and she inserted a shaking index finger through the trigger guard. The knob twisted again, and the latch clicked, then the door swung open on silent, greased hinges, and a single black boot landed on the floor without a sound.

Maggie's stomach twisted, and her head felt light. She recognized the dull grey color of the pants with soft gold trim. The boots were the standard issue of the Louisiana State Police. As the intruder took another step into the room, she recognized the broad shoulders and short blond hair.

It was Officer Maxwell. The lead guard of her nighttime detail.

Maggie lowered the revolver, her arms growing steady as she watched Maxwell walk away from her, toward the bed. An unholstered pistol hung from his right hand, reflecting moonlight from its polished black barrel. The bed was saturated in shadows, disguising the presence, or absence, of anyone sleeping within, and forcing Maxwell to take another step.

Maggie cocked the revolver. The splitting click of the weapon shattered the stillness like a thunderclap. Maxwell froze as Maggie took a step out of the darkness and leveled the weapon's barrel with the back of his head.

"Turn around."

Maxwell turned slowly, the gun shaking in his right hand. As he faced her, the clouds parted, spilling light over his face and exposing his features. Maggie gasped and lowered the weapon. Blood covered his cheeks and streamed from a deep cut in his chest. His face was washed white, and his eyes were as wide and dark as the lake outside.

He took half a step forward and dropped the gun, stumbling to his knees. "Madam Governor . . . we have to go." His words broke and hissed between his teeth. A trail of blood oozed from between his lips and dripped on the floor.

Maggie slid to her knees beside him and caught the big policeman as he toppled forward. His weight was almost overwhelming, but she managed to prop him up against the end of the bed. He gasped for air, his body still shaking as she held him.

"Maxwell, where's Green?"

Maggie saw worlds of pain and fear unleashed behind Maxwell's watering eyes.

"Madam Governor, I'm so sorry . . . I couldn't . . . stop him."

"It's okay." Maggie placed her hand over the wide gash in his chest and pressed down, wadding his torn shirt into the wound. She jerked the radio from his side and hit the call button.

"Is anyone there?"

There was no response, and Maggie cursed before depressing it again. "I said, is anyone listening?"

The radio crackled. "This is a secure government line. Identify yourself."

"This is Maggie Trousdale. I'm at my lake house. One of my guards is missing, and the other is bleeding. I need immediate medical assistance."

"Who now?"

"I'm the governor, you dumb shit! Get some help out here!"

A snapping sound rang from outside the house, and Maggie's back stiffened as she looked up toward the window. Clouds blew across the moon, drenching the house in shadow. Among the outlines of tree limbs and bushes, she saw something hard and straight—too mechanical to be natural.

Maxwell was unconscious now, his eyes rolled back in his head. She laid him down and scooped up the revolver before ducking through the doorway and hurrying down the hallway. Her bare feet smacked against the hardwood, and the third floorboard squeaked as she stepped out of the hallway and into the kitchen.

The front door hung half-open, and bloody handprints coated the doorjamb. As Maggie crept closer and pulled the door back, her heart jumped again. Green, her second LSP guard, lay dead on the front porch, his throat sliced open.

Just past the porch, Maggie saw a shadow out of the corner of her eyes. She spun the revolver toward it and pressed the trigger without aiming. The little .38 cracked and spat a bullet into the darkness. After a scream of pain, something clattered onto the pinewood boards of the porch. Maggie lunged out from the doorway and fired twice more. Sticks and rocks dug into her feet as she stumbled into the mud. Heavy breathing carried through the fog, somewhere amid the sound of rustling grass and crunching twigs. The thick stench of blood invaded her nostrils as warm mud squished between her toes. Ahead, she could see the silhouette of a man running through the trees, holding his side.

Maggie raised the gun. "Stop!"

The shadow kept running, diving for the cover of the pines. Maggie aligned the sights of the snub-nosed revolver, cocked the hammer, and squeezed the trigger. The bullet split the air and sent a shockwave of burned gunpowder blasting back over her hand, but the running man didn't stop. In an instant, the darkness consumed him, leaving her standing alone over the bloody ground.

As the gunshot faded, the whisper of the wind filled the stillness, rendering everything empty and dark. Maggie dug her fingernails into the grip of the gun and searched the forest. Only shadows filled the spaces between the trees, consuming her with the gripping reality that she was alone, and they would be back.

13

Nashville, Tennessee

"It's a lot smaller than home, isn't it, boy?"

Baxter's legs were splayed out over the passenger seat as he pressed his flat face close to the window and peered out at the city. Trucks and cars whizzed past the Camaro, cutting in and out from each other as they surged toward downtown.

Nashville looked nothing like Atlanta. The skyline was half as wide, with shorter buildings all made of glass and shiny metal. It was a new skyline—the kind a millennial designed. The bulk of downtown was dominated by the thick, impending mass of the AT&T Building, a circular tower that culminated in a narrow, flat top, and twin spires that reached for the sky like bat ears.

It was a nice skyline, but Reed thought it lacked the grandeur and majesty of Atlanta. It was too young—too polished.

And still too large a place to locate a single woman.

Reed followed the bypass around downtown, admiring the open hulk of Nissan Stadium before exiting the freeway onto 2nd Avenue. Reed knew very little about this city, other than that it had recently gained a reputation as a tourist destination for bars and live music. Nashville supposedly now boasted the title of "Number One Bachelorette Destination of the Nation."

And isn't that every city's dream?

Reed drove only two blocks into downtown before the first Pedal Tavern crossed the street ahead of him—a peculiar table-on-wheels contraption with riders on both sides working pedals that propelled the bar through the streets. The passengers were drunk, at barely noon. He didn't make it another two blocks before he passed a tractor towing a wagon full of drunk women in their twenties, a modified fire truck with an open top, filled with the same, and more than a dozen peculiar electric scooters laden with overweight tourists. Reed had never seen so much crap on the streets—golf carts, Pedal Taverns, modified pickup trucks with extended beds full of partiers, open-top school buses with disco lights. Even some type of modified RV with a hot tub in the back, filled with bachelorettes. The bizarre assortment of vehicles and drunk tourists bridged beyond unusual into the obscene.

What the hell is this place?

The Camaro barked and rumbled as he swerved around a pack of scooters and moved deeper into the city. People—old, young, of every race and origin—were everywhere, packed onto the sidewalks and jostling each other between the bars. Reed wondered if this was typical of a Friday, and what this place must look like after dark.

With any luck, I'll never find out.

Reed used to enjoy crowded places. He remembered car shows and trips to Disneyland as a kid. They took the old Camaro everywhere as a family, and he relished the excitement of people packed into one place. All that changed when he stopped seeing other people as fellow tourists and started suspecting them of being fellow killers. In a place like this, thick with every type of traveling amusement seeker, any number of foreign threats could slip right in, and nobody would be any the wiser.

But this is where she is. This is the first place Banks would go. Lots of people to lose herself in. Lots of music to block out the world.

He pulled the car into a parking lot and cut the engine, watching the tides of people washing back and forth across the sidewalks. Two blocks down, the bright neon signs of the bar district connected 2nd Avenue with Broadway. More people packed in next to a string of bars and restaurants, clamoring against each other to gain access. Even through the Camaro's thick windows, the roar of voices was overwhelming, melding with the pound of a few rock bands performing on the other side of open windows.

Baxter snorted as he peered through the windshield with stress-filled eyes.

"I know, boy. Crowds aren't for us, are they?"

Reed rubbed the key between his fingers and forced out the cloud of emotions that tugged at the edge of his thought process.

Should I be here? Would she be safer if I left her alone?

He thought again of the last time he saw her, soaking wet and crying on the lake bank. She didn't deserve what happened to her in those mountains, but if it weren't for him, she probably would've died there. Sure, it could be argued that he kicked things off when he accepted the Holiday contract in the first place, but it could also be argued that Holiday was going to die anyway. Somebody, somewhere, wanted the senator dead. Reed just gave them more trouble than most.

If I don't find her now, I'll never have a chance to make this right.

"Get in the back, boy. Don't want somebody thinking you're abandoned and busting out my windows."

Reed cracked both windows as Baxter grunted and climbed into the back seat. It was sixty degrees outside, and with the fresh air streaming through the windows, Baxter would be comfortable and safe until he returned.

The crowd melded around Reed as soon as he stepped onto the sidewalk, accepting him as one of their own and crushing in so close several of them bumped into his arms. Reed held his jacket close over the compact SIG Sauer P365 holstered in his belt. The little 9mm held only ten rounds—far too little firepower for his comfort. After losing most of his primary weaponry in North

Carolina, and then the revolver in Chattanooga, Reed was left with nothing but his backup weapon, and he felt altogether undergunned. After he left Nashville, he would need to refit—find a broker and secure new hardware.

His boots splashed through mud puddles as he worked his way toward Broadway. Every bar he passed stood with wide-open doors and a heavy bouncer checking IDs at the sidewalk. Half a dozen types of music drifted through the air—pop, rock, country, classics, and even a little blues. All of the bands were good, and what vocals joined the mix were considerably better than average.

They don't call it Music City for nothing, I guess.

Reed followed the crowd through the crosswalk and onto Broadway. On his right, the street dropped down toward the Cumberland River, lined by restaurants on both sides. What stretched out on his left really took his breath away. Three solid blocks of three-story bars packed door-to-door. Lights, signs, and decor clung to the exterior brick walls while hundreds of people surged up and down either side of the street. Taxis, Ubers, and police cars jockeyed for position along the four-lane road, with more Pedal Taverns sprinkled amongst them. A horn blared, and Reed looked to his right just in time to jump out of the way of a green tractor towing a hay wagon full of drunk women, all swaying and singing *"Oh Canada"* at the top of their lungs.

What the hell is this?

There were too many bars, dozens of them, all stacked and packed together, and that was only on this street. Each connecting road boasted more signs pointing to additional bars and restaurants that clustered outside of Broadway.

This could take days. She could be anywhere.

Reed pulled himself away from the crush of people and leaned against a brick wall, taking a moment to survey the city. It made sense for Banks to be in a place that celebrated music this much. He wondered how many of these bands were regular attractions, and how many rotated new acts.

She'll be somewhere that hires new talent, where she can sing for tips like she did in Atlanta.

"Excuse me." Reed stepped toward a cop who stood on the corner. "Do you live here?"

The officer shot Reed a sour look. "Unfortunately," he said. "What can I help you with?"

"I'm looking for a place to sing. Someplace that takes new talent."

The cop burst out laughing. He paused a moment to blow his whistle and shout at a speeding taxi, then turned back to Reed and laughed again. "You and forty thousand others. I'm not a record agent, bro."

"Let me clarify. A friend of mine is the new talent. She came up here to sing, and I forgot the name of the bar."

The officer blew his whistle again and waved his hand at a couple of kids zooming past on a pair of electric scooters. They ignored him, and he threw his hands into the air. "Damn kids!"

Reed cleared his throat. "So, about the bar . . ."

"Try Sweeney's. It's on Third Avenue past FGL."

Reed nodded his thanks and stepped off as the cop resumed the whistle blowing. One block down and two to the left, clinging to the side of a building, was a large black sign with white letters: FGL HOUSE.

Just beyond it, *"Sweeney's Saloon"* was painted in gold letters on red brick. It was a narrow bar with the sort of old swinging doors that you see in cowboy movies. The bouncer blocking the doorway was big, fat, and appeared totally stoned, but he demanded Reed's ID.

Reed displayed a fake South Carolina driver's license labeled *"Christopher Thomas,"* then ducked into the bar. It was smoky and dark inside, with tables crammed together along both walls. Servers jumped from one table to the next, handing out beers and glasses of liquor, while a scrawny kid with long, greasy hair groaned into the microphone at the stage in the back.

Reed helped himself to a chair in the corner, leaning against the wall and inhaling a deep lungful of second-hand smoke. It took the edge off his nerves but ignited an almost overwhelming urge to smoke. He hadn't enjoyed a cigarette in days.

Nobody paid the kid at the mic any attention. His style was weak, with words strung together and overwhelmed by moans that sounded more like the overtures of a masturbating teenager than a vocalist. Reed eyed him and thought how strange it was to be in a place where so many people were hungry for the limelight. He never understood that. Power made sense to him, and so did money. These were tangible, actionable resources. But fame? Who wanted to be famous? Reed had spent the better part of his life trying to keep most of the world from knowing anything about him. Clamoring for attention didn't make sense.

The kid at the mic finally finished and dismounted the stage to a few scattered claps.

A dusty bartender in torn-out jeans and a black T-shirt got up behind him and spoke into the mic. "Let's put it together for Rebel Joe!"

This time, the scattered claps were a little louder but no more enthusiastic.

"All right, you guys. I know you're ready to get your country on. We've got one more independent act—"

From the back of the room, somebody bellowed, "Put on some real music!"

The bartender pointed at him and smiled. "Take it easy, friend. We'll have somebody up in just a moment. Y'all go ahead and order another round!"

The radio clicked on overhead, pounding a popular country song through oversized speakers as a server slipped up beside Reed. "Can I get you something to drink, honey?"

Reed's eyes darted from one corner of the room to the next, searching for any unseen threats amongst the tourists. He replied without looking up. "Got any whiskey?"

She laughed. "Honey, this is Tennessee. We brush our teeth with whiskey."

"I'll take a Jack. Neat."

"Coming right up."

She disappeared into the crowd, and Reed folded his arms. The bustle and noise brought comfort to his ragged mind. It made him feel a little less conspicuous amid all these people. It made him feel like there was a chance he could shrink away and not be seen at all.

The server brought the whiskey, and Reed sipped on it, still watching the crowd. Wolfgang would be back. More than likely, the killer had already left Chattanooga and was headed his way, blazing down the road in his big Mercedes.

I've got to tie that one up. He's been on my heels far too long.

The whiskey tasted weak on his tongue, as though it were cut with water. Or maybe he was still drunk from the previous night. He tipped the glass up and drained it, then dusted off his pants. He couldn't afford to wait around for what probably wouldn't happen. There had to be a better way to find Banks.

"All right, ladies and gentlemen. I've got a special treat for you all the way from Atlanta, Georgia. Put your hands together for Miss Sirena Wilder!"

Reed's gaze flew to the stage. Ripples of polite applause rose from the audience as the radio faded, and the lights dimmed. His own eyes blurred, maybe from the saturation of alcohol in his blood, or the residual effects of insomnia, but he blinked the fog away and held his breath.

Please...

She stepped out of the darkness behind the stage, floating across the hardwood floor. A ghost of grace and beauty, her blonde waves were held back in a ponytail, and an acoustic guitar swung from a strap around her neck.

Her eyes, so deep and bright. But Reed could see the pain in them, carefully hidden, masked behind strength and willpower. Even her insatiable ability to manage stress and ignore trauma couldn't defeat the red streaks and black circles. Heavy makeup—dark eyeliner with bright red lipstick—coated her face, and she wore a loose T-shirt with sleeves that hung almost to her elbows.

Banks leaned close to the mic and smiled. Reed remembered the last time he saw her on a stage, leaning into a mic. She smiled then, too, but it wasn't like this smile. It was free and weightless—the smile that stole his heart in a millisecond.

"How's it going, Nashville?"

The room cheered. A couple tables away, Reed heard a drunk guy lean in and grunt to his friend, "Damn dawg. I'd hit that."

Banks strummed her fingers across the guitar strings, unleashing a gentle melody into the room. Reed recognized it immediately, and it flooded him with aching memories of that bar in Atlanta—the first place he heard those chords. As Banks leaned forward and pressed her lips next to the mic, a new wave of guilt and passion swept over him.

"He was a vagrant, and I a gypsy. I lost my way when he first kissed me."

Reed looked away from the stage. The wrenching agony that cascaded through his whole body felt more real and painful than any fistfight or bullet wound. It was total, complete heartache.

I did this to her.

The bar sat in transfixed silence as Banks sang. The boisterous drunks in the back watched with their glassy, intoxicated gazes fixed on the singer as she whispered each delicate lyric into the mic. Nobody moved. Nobody talked. Banks enraptured them as much as she had enraptured him only four weeks prior.

But this time, he could tell the difference. He detected the missing passion, the cavern behind the words. Banks was too much a performer to relax on her delivery, but she couldn't fake the emptiness in her voice.

"Can I get you another?" Reed was suddenly aware of the waitress at his side, leaning close. He blinked away the fog in his eyes and shook his head. She turned and wandered off through the crowd, leaving him alone as Banks broke into the bridge.

"I give, I gave, I'd have given him everything. I just wanted to believe some things would last forever."

Each word shredded what remained of his stamina, emotionally bringing him to his knees. He didn't recall her singing this bridge in Atlanta, though perhaps it was a lapse in memory or the alcohol fogging his brain. Or maybe he had crushed her even deeper than he had crushed himself.

Banks's soft voice drifted away, and for a moment, Reed forgot about all the people pressed in around him. Then a wave of roaring applause filled the room, shaking the walls and pounding in his ears. Banks smiled, her bright lips lifting into what *looked* like true happiness, but he could see past the mask, through the charade of a performer. Her real smile could light up a tomb, and this wasn't it.

She played three more songs, all covers of popular country tracks, then she waved and bowed without a word and moved toward the back of the building. Reed dropped a twenty on the table, then pushed his way through the crowd and out the swinging doors. The chaos of the city streets crushed in around him as he forced his way along the sidewalk, fighting around the building to the nearest alley. Piles of pallets and empty alcohol boxes lined the walls as he pushed through them, splashing across mud puddles and around dumpsters to the back of the three-story bar and the connecting alley.

As he rounded the corner, he saw her. Banks sat on the back step next to a closed door, her guitar leaned up against the brick wall and her head in her hands as her shoulders rose and fell in gentle sobs. His world stood still, locked in a purgatory of her tears. Every protective and loving instinct within him ignited, thundering to life and commanding him to rush forward, take her in his arms, and sweep her off her feet.

But he couldn't move. His feet were frozen to the ground, locked down by guilt and uncertainty. He swallowed back the dryness in his throat and whispered, "Banks..."

Her blue eyes flashed as they met his. The cloud of confusion and hurt that filled her gaze clamped down on him, unleashing new levels of pain. She stood up and stepped back. Her hair, now a tangled mess hanging over her ears and eyes, was stuck to her forehead by a layer of sweat.

It's sixty degrees outside. Why is she sweating?

Reed took a step forward. "I need to talk to you."

She licked her lips, her face flushing a sudden crimson, and she shook her head once, then took another step back.

"Please." Reed waited, still holding out his hand.

She hesitated, and her lips parted. For a moment, he thought she was about to speak, but then he noticed her chest heaving in short puffs. Her flushed face faded to a pale white, and without a sound, she collapsed in the alley.

14

Salvador hated America with every part of his soul. Deep within him, in his very bones, this place felt hostile and cold. Maybe it was because of his line of work, or because he was hostile and cold himself. Maybe it was because America made him into a person he never wanted to be.

    The darkness of the small hotel room hung around him like a cloak, and the lights from his laptop danced in front of his eyes. The video feed was weak and broken, shifting and freezing from time to time, but the audio was clear. The familiar voices of his family, four thousand miles away in the midst of war-torn Venezuela, carried over the fickle internet connection, bringing the first warmth to his soul that he had felt in weeks. A smile spread across his tired face as the voice of his grandmother babbled on in hurried Spanish, discussing the local politics that ravaged his homeland. He listened to the words, but the only thing he heard was the voice. His sisters, two nephews, and his mother also appeared on the screen in turns, excitedly greeting him with smiles and blown kisses. Salvador waved back and asked them about school, work, and what books his mother was reading. Salvador sent books home every week for her, along with his weekly wire transfers. He could see the warmth in their cheeks and a little fat beneath their olive skin for the first time in months. Food was hard to come by in Venezuela, as inflation and political turmoil shattered the weak economy. The money Salvador sent home was the only thing keeping his large family alive. It was why he left South America in the first place—to find a lifeline that would keep his hungry siblings in school and his parents and grandparents out of the grave.

"How are things at the plant, Salvador?" His mother put down the book she had been reading to him and smiled with the sort of warmth and love that only a mother could express.

Salvador hesitated. "The plant . . . yes. Things are well. We're building parts for Nissan."

"Are you still enjoying the work? Are they treating you well?"

Salvador smiled. "Of course, Mamá. Things are different in America. The factories are safe."

"They pay you so much. It's hard to understand."

He shrugged. "I work hard for them. They give me extra hours."

The smile faded from her wrinkled lips, and worry crowded into her eyes. "Salvador, you don't have to. You should be pursuing your own life. Finding a nice girl. All this work is going to kill you."

Salvador shrugged. "I enjoy the work, Mamá. You know that. Is Papá home?"

The worry in her eyes faded to sadness, but she nodded. The laptop twisted, and the screen froze, then it was filled with the familiar features of his tired father—worn and serious. Salvador had never seen his father smile—not once in thirty-two years. He was more than a serious man; he was a severe one. But he loved his family, and he would do anything to protect them.

"Papá, how are you?"

The old man grunted. "I'm fine, Salvador. How are things at the '*plant*'?" Salvador's father never spoke of the plant without suspicion in his tone. Every time he asked about the work in America, his eyebrows furrowed, and he stared at Salvador with the intensity of a man who didn't believe anything he was being told. Maybe he saw through Salvador's farce, or maybe it was simply sixty years of programed distrust for America talking. Venezuela was, after all, a communist-leaning nation and a loose ally with the Soviet Union during the Cold War.

Salvador shifted but smiled. "Well, Papá, I'm getting promoted soon. I'll be able to send more home to the family."

His father grunted. "We don't need the money, Salvador. I can provide for the family on my own."

"The children need schoolbooks, and Mamá needs medicine for her back. I'm happy to help."

The suspicion in the old man's eyes remained, but he shrugged. The video feed faded and froze again, but the distorted audio continued to carry through the tiny laptop speakers.

"Salvador, there's something I want you to know."

The audio cut and warbled with electronic distortion. Salvador leaned closer to the computer, holding his ear next to the speaker. He still couldn't hear anything.

"Papá? Are you there?"

"... I know ... I should have ..."

The screen went black, and then a window popped up: VIDEO CALL FAILED.

Salvador closed the laptop. He ran his hands through his dark hair as exhaustion tore at his mind. It wasn't the kind that comes from the physical exertion he claimed to expend at the plant. This was the exhaustion of mental torment, months of self-doubt, and guilt. So much damn guilt.

He didn't want to become a killer. He didn't leave Venezuela to administer violence elsewhere. He came here to find better work and to find a way to feed his starving family. But the immigration system rejected him. He was deported twice, returning to Venezuela without visiting his parents or letting them know of his failures. Embarrassment and self-hatred wouldn't allow him to fail, and it soon became clear that if he wanted to get ahead in the world —if he wanted to win—he had to fight dirty.

The criminal underworld was a cold and ruthless place, but

working for men who lived in the shadows paid a great deal better than any Nissan plant ever would. Salvador was good at making things happen. He was good at being the hand of men who couldn't afford to leave fingerprints. Being the fingerprint himself, and risking his own demise, promised the payout his family depended on.

Salvador twisted until his back crackled. He picked up a photograph from the desk and walked through the connecting door to the adjoining suite. Six men stood around a table loaded with MP5 submachine guns and H&K pistols. Dressed in black combat gear, they were pale-skinned, broad-shouldered, Swedish by birth, and a solid eight inches taller than him: trained killers, all of them. The six men were members of the East European mercenary group, Legion X. After Cedric Muri was gunned down in Atlantic City, Salvador knew he might need backup, so he hired Legion X out of his own pocket, flew them into Atlanta, and now held them in reserve.

A seventh man lounged in a chair in the corner of the room. Unlike the others, he wore street clothes and tennis shoes, and his blonde hair stuck out from under an Atlanta Braves hat.

Salvador raised an eyebrow. "Well?"

The man in the corner nodded. He spoke in a heavy Swedish accent with weak English, but Salvador could make out the gist of what he was saying. "It is as you said. He did not kill Montgomery. They fought near the river, then The Wolf just . . . quit. I do not know why."

Salvador nodded. "We have work to do. Two of you are flying to New York immediately. There's a young woman at a special needs facility outside of Buffalo. Pick her up and take her to Detroit. Don't harm her, and wait for further instructions."

Salvador dropped the photograph on the table. It was of a young woman with dark hair. Her eyes were bright, but her cheeks pale. Her body thin. A lifetime spent fighting a chronic illness had taken its toll.

One of the men in black picked up the photo and regarded it through narrowed eyes. "Who is this woman?"

Salvador walked to the window and crossed his arms, staring out at the city. His stomach knotted, but he swallowed back the taste of bile in his mouth. "Her name is Collins. She's The Wolf's sister. If we cannot pay the man to do his job, we'll force him."

15

Nashville, Tennessee

Reed sat next to the narrow bed and stroked Banks's forehead with a damp washcloth. Her face had faded from white to red, and now back to white. Her skin was warm to the touch, and her palms were clammy. When he held his ear against her chest, he heard her heart thump at an accelerated pace. Banks inhaled in short gusts and breathed out just as fast.

He dipped the washcloth back into the bowl and wrung it out before touching it to her forehead again. Her nose twitched, and her head turned a little, but she didn't open her eyes.

Baxter lay on the floor next to him, drool pooling on the carpet beside his slack jaw. The bulldog's legs were splayed out behind him, but his eyes peered up at Reed with concern rippling through their inky depths.

Reed wiped the cloth across his own forehead. He wasn't sure why he confronted Banks in the alley behind the bar. He had to find her—that thought rang clearly through his head from the moment he accepted Kelly's death and drove away from the scene of the fire. For two weeks he searched diligently to locate Banks, hiring Dillan and implementing every Google search known to man. It was a fruitless, desperate search—something that consumed his every thought outside of destroying the people who murdered Kelly.

Now that he found her, he wasn't entirely sure why he started looking in the first place. Deep within his soul, he felt things for this woman that he had never felt for anyone. He cared for her in an instinctive, meaningful way that regulated his actions and filtered his intentions right to their core. But none of those feelings answered the dominating question of why he felt he had the authority to track her down. Did she deserve her privacy? Should he have let her go?

Baxter grunted, almost as though he understood Reed's internal conflict better than Reed understood it himself.

I can't let her go. I have to make this right.

Banks stirred, and Reed sat up. She had lain passed out on the bed for four hours now, with occasional twitches. But this time, her eyes fluttered, and her tongue touched her dry lips.

"Here, drink this." He held out a bottle of water with a straw.

Her eyes were still clouded with confusion as she accepted the straw and sucked down two greedy gulps of water, then fell back against the pillow. She blinked and turned her head toward him. "Chris."

Reed looked away, fiddling with the rag in the bowl.

She lay still, but he heard her breathing regulate as her full consciousness returned. Her voice turned cold as she spoke again. "No. Not Chris. *Reed*."

Reed folded the towel around his fingers, refusing to face her. Banks pushed her hands beneath her and began to sit up.

"You should lay down," Reed said. "You need to rest."

"I know what I need," she snapped. She leaned against the wall and grabbed the water bottle. Reed thought she might have intended to snatch it from him, but she was too weak to give it more than a tug. He released it, and she gulped down two more swallows.

"I'm home."

"Yes." Reed cast a glance around the tiny apartment. It was a studio with dingy yellow walls and carpet that somehow rivaled that of the hotel in Chattanooga.

"How did you find my place?"

Reed gestured to her phone. "Significant location on your maps app."

"My phone was locked." There was no grace in her voice. No feeling.

Reed shrugged. "Thumbprint."

"Nice. Glad to see you're still busy intruding."

Reed forced himself to face her, then rested his palms against his kneecaps and cleared his throat. "Are you . . . okay?"

Banks pushed sweaty hair out of her eyes and tilted her head. "Well, let me see. The man I thought loved me turned out to be a liar, a psychopath, a professional killer, and the kidnapper of my godfather—who, by the way, was brutally gunned down right in front of me. I have no family left, no friends, I'm living in this shithole trying to be left alone, and now *you're* here. How do you *think* I'm doing?"

Reed rubbed his fingers against his worn jeans, then took a slow breath. "I meant . . . physically. You seem sick."

Banks blew a fallen strand of hair out of her eyes. "Wow, you're a regular Sherlock Holmes, aren't you?"

"I know you have Lyme disease."

"Oh, do you now? Well, that shouldn't surprise me. You are, after all, a black-hearted criminal. Bet you know all kinds of things."

Reed looked away. Her every word bit like a knife, tearing into him. Igniting more pain than any of his dozens of injuries over the last two weeks. He wanted to spill his guts. Tell her everything about Iraq and prison and the bad choices he made that led him down this long, bloody path. Explain himself.

But no. She wouldn't buy any of it. The proof was in the pudding, after all, and the only pudding she had ever seen was the blood and carnage he'd left behind.

"I can't apologize for what I've done," he said. "I don't think there's anything I can say that will make it better. I'm willing to tell you anything you want to know. I'm asking you to believe me when I say I never meant for you to get hurt. I did everything in my power to protect you."

Banks snorted. "Well, aren't I a lucky girl?"

Reed looked up again. "You don't even know what happened . . . why your godfather was killed."

"Does it matter? He's dead. And as far as I can tell, it's your fault."

"It might matter, Banks. I want to explain. I want to make this all right, but I didn't come here to win you back. I—"

"That's good to know, because I'm done with you, Chris. Or Reed. Or whoever the hell you are. You're just like every other deadbeat on the planet. Happy to get into my pants on a dark stormy night, and just as happy to leave me high and dry when shit hits the fan. Only you're worse because you're actually a horrible person."

As she spoke, her words faded from angry outbursts to weaker and weaker sobs. She finally broke off and slumped against the wall, her face turning red as sweat dripped down her cheeks.

"What's happening?" Reed asked. "Are you sick?"

"Of course I'm sick. Don't you know everything?"

"Okay, well, where are your meds? What do you need?"

Banks closed her eyes and breathed heavily. Her fingers trembled, and she continued sweating, even though the A/C was set on full blast.

"I ran out. This happens sometimes. It's a flare-up."

"What do you need? I'll get it."

She glowered. "You got a bottle of fever-crushing antibiotics in your back pocket?"

Reed unzipped his backpack, digging through it before tossing three different medicine bottles onto the damp blankets. "Take your pick."

Banks picked up the first bottle and read the label, then snorted. "My God. You really are a killer."

"I prefer to think of myself as an adult Boy Scout. Always prepared."

Banks shoved two pills into her mouth and washed them down with another gulp of water before slouching back on her pillow. Her skin, a constant alternation of flaming red and snow white, now faded into an irregular blotchy pattern of both.

Reed took the bottle back. "What does it do? The disease, I mean."

"It's an infection that comes from ticks. It can lay dormant for years, then ignite out of nowhere. Fevers, nausea, insomnia, aches, muscle spasms."

"Fainting?"

She licked her lips. "Sometimes."

"I'm sorry."

She glowered toward him. "*Never* say that to me again. I'm nobody's victim."

Reed nodded slowly.

The glare faded, and Banks turned her bloodshot eyes toward the ceiling. "You're not leaving, are you?"

Reed shook his head.

"Then what are you doing here?"

Reed folded his arms. The silence that hung between them felt heavier than a loaded Marine rucksack on an uphill run. His mouth went dry, and he clawed at the edges of his mind, searching for an answer.

Why am I here? Did I honestly expect her to run into my arms?

"I'm here to protect you. You're not safe. And I'm here to find the truth."

Once again, her eyes closed, and her breaths came in ragged bursts. He thought she had faded away, sinking into a labored sleep, or fainting again. But then her lips parted, and she spoke in a calm whisper. "The truth about *what*?"

Reed stared at his worn and battered hands, crisscrossed with dirt, scars, and healing wounds. He didn't feel any pain, only numbness, and he was at a loss for answers. Should he tell her? Could he tell her?

"You told me your father died in a car wreck."

She gritted her teeth. "What does that have to do with anything?"

"You said it was an accident."

Banks didn't answer.

"Your godfather.... I spoke to him about your father. In detail."

Banks's eyes opened, and a tear slipped out. She faced him, the rage melting away into unsheltered heartache. "Let me guess. He told you it wasn't an accident. He told you Daddy was killed."

Reed tilted his head. "You know?"

"Of course I know. He told everyone that story. He spent months investigating it, badgering the cops, then one day, six months after Daddy died, he just quit. Went quiet. The police finally convinced him, I guess. Daddy died from a drunk driver. I guess Uncle Mitch wanted deeper justice."

Reed touched the bed next to Banks. She made no move to take his hand but turned her gaze to the ceiling. Reed withdrew his hand and clenched it into a fist over his knee. Every part of him ached inside, commanding him to hold her, to comfort her. To somehow take away the hurricane in her heart that ripped her apart from the inside. But he couldn't. Not now. The only thing he could do was what he should've done from day one—tell her the truth.

"It's true, Banks."

She faced him. "What's true?"

"Everything. My name is Reed Montgomery, and I'm a professional assassin. I was hired to kill your godfather by an underground organization that I believe he was associated with. I kidnapped him in Atlanta because keeping him alive was my best bet of saving you. While I held him captive, Mitch demanded to know if I had killed your father. The last thing he told me before he died was about the fraternity where he met Frank."

"What are you saying?" she whispered.

"I'm saying your father was murdered by the same people who murdered Mitch. They also kidnapped you, sent the assassin after us in North Carolina, and murdered a very dear friend of mine. I'm here because I'm going to find them, whoever they are. I'm going to make them confess what they've done, and then I'm going to destroy them."

16

Baton Rouge, Louisiana

"I'm sorry, Madam Governor. We did everything we could."

Maggie nodded once. The doctor's footsteps faded, and for a brief moment, the clatter and chaos of the emergency room faded with them.

Dan touched her arm. "Maggie, I'm sorry. We have to address the media."

Ah, yes. The media, already clustered around the sliding doors at the entrance of the ER, ready to descend upon their governor with all the wrath and ferocity of a herd of vultures. It wasn't that she hated the media or was unappreciative of their role in society; she simply resented their callousness. No matter the tragedy, the loss, or the heartache of the situation, the only thing a reporter cared about was the headline. That sort of detached mission-focus was the heart of Louisiana's problems. People forgot about people.

"Fine," she said. "Assemble them outside. I'll freshen up."

The bathroom at the end of the hall featured a small, dirty mirror and a counter that Maggie was afraid to touch. She brushed her hair back behind her ears and held it in place with a hairband, then refreshed her makeup and lipstick. A brief survey in the mirror left her satisfied she'd avoid any media gaffs about her appearance, and she turned to the door.

A crowd of TV and newspaper reporters was already knotted around the door, jostling each other for position as Dan called for them to calm down and wait for Maggie. He was good at that, Maggie thought. Dan was never designed to be an executive, but he absolutely thrived as a lieutenant governor. He understood people, understood how to get the sludge moving, and most importantly, he could tell the difference between overstepping his own authority and bothering Maggie with things he could manage on his own.

Maggie straightened the collar of her blouse and checked her reflection one more time in the sliding glass door, then straightened her back and stepped out in front of the flashing lights.

The questions started immediately, but before Maggie could speak, Dan stepped forward and barked into the microphone. "Let me be perfectly clear. The next time we hold a press conference and questions are asked before the governor has an opportunity to make a statement, there will be *no* questions answered for that conference. Are we understood? Thank you."

Maggie nodded her thanks at Dan, then approached the middle of the crowd. Several microphones were held out toward her, and she offered a polite smile. "Thank you all for coming out on such short notice. It is with tremendous sadness that I announce that Officers Green and Maxwell, two lead members of my personal detail, passed away early this morning of wounds sustained while protecting me against an attempted assassination."

A low gasp rang out through the crowd. One or two reporters leaned forward, indicating an impending question, but Dan snapped his fingers, and the reporter fell back. Maggie accepted a bottle of water from Yolanda, took a long sip, and blinked away her exhaustion. It still hadn't registered that two of her own men were killed. It still didn't make sense that somebody had tried to take her life. It all felt detached, as though it were happening to somebody else.

"Officers Green and Maxwell were more than servants of the state. They were my friends. I knew the names of their kids, and they knew how I liked my coffee. They were good men—the finest the state of Louisiana has to offer, and their sacrifice is a debt we can never repay. Having said that, I have already outlined an initiative with the LSP to ensure that both officers' families are financially sustained for life out of honor for their sacrifice. Investigations as to the identity of the assassin are underway, and we have very limited information at this time. I will now take a few questions."

One hand shot up before she finished speaking, and Maggie resisted a sigh. "Yes, Ms. Simmons?"

"Can you comment on the policy in place within the LSP for death pensions of this type? I wasn't aware that the executive branch had the authority to grant cash disbursements on command."

The muscles in her back tensed, and Maggie consciously relaxed to avoid appearing combative. "Existing LSP compensation programs will be leveraged to ensure the financial security of the Green and Maxwell families. Any further compensation will be arranged as required because that's the right thing to do. Any other questions?"

"Madam Governor, can you comment as to why this attempted assassination took place so far from the Capitol, in an unsecured rural area near Lake Maurepas?"

Maggie shot Dan a sideways look. He shook his head, and she turned back to the crowd.

"Details of the circumstance surrounding the attempted assassination will not be disclosed at this time to protect the integrity of the investigation."

"Madam Governor, don't you think the people will find it strange that our female governor was inexplicably absent from the Capitol, attended only by her two male guards?"

Blood and a growing rage surged into Maggie's skull. Before answering, she waited five seconds, staring directly into the reporter's eyes. "The Executive Office is under no obligation to report on the travel agenda or accommodations of the governor, and the people of Louisiana will have to content themselves with the public results of the investigation as soon as they are available. Thank you, everyone. That will be all."

Maggie turned away from the mics as questions continued to rise from the small crowd of reporters. Dan stepped in behind her and made a brief statement regarding the governor's gratitude to the press, then followed her across the parking lot to a jet-black Tahoe waiting for them. Maggie piled inside and slammed the door, resting her head in her hands. The exhaustion of the last twenty-four hours descended on her full force, making it difficult to think clearly.

"How did they know?" she demanded.

Dan buckled his seatbelt and leaned back, taking a deep breath before answering. "I don't know, Maggie. Somebody must have leaked it."

Maggie dug her fingers into the leather seat as the big engine rumbled and the Tahoe turned toward the Capitol.

"Dan, you *know* why I was at the lake house. It's disgusting that they would insinuate anything scandalous when two of my men are *dead*!" The end of her sentence cracked, and she leaned forward into her hands again, rubbing both temples.

"I agree with you, Maggie, but your parting shots only added fuel to that fire. They're journalists. This is what they do."

"That was *not* journalism," Maggie snapped. "That was fishing for tabloid gossip."

Dan handed her a bottle of water and waited for her to take a sip before replying. "Again, I agree. But you have to be very careful not to come across too aggressively. It will hurt you more than it helps. They're only looking for drama, and the way you manage that is by feeding them the drama *you* want to be proliferated. Do you understand? You have to play this smart."

Maggie stared out the window, watching the city streets and stoplights flash by. The exhaustion she felt in her soul was deeper than just a lack of sleep. It was true, total frustration with every aspect of her life.

"This is exactly why I hate politics," she muttered.

Dan grunted. "Yep. And it's exactly why the state needs you now more than ever. You're here to bring Baton Rouge back from the depths. But these things take time, and you have to work with what you have. That includes the media."

Maggie stared through the glass. Dan's ability to view things objectively was the counterbalance of her fire-and-brimstone approach to destroying corruption, and she knew she needed that. She knew she needed to listen.

But dammit, she was still pissed.

"Have you heard back from Jackson?"

Dan sighed. "Yes, I got an email an hour ago."

"And?"

"They confirmed the presence of poison. It'll take a day or two for the autopsy to confirm the exact type and amount, but we can now safely assume Attorney General Matthews died of unnatural means."

"So, he *was* assassinated."

"It looks that way. Again, we'll need more time to formulate an official report."

"That's fine. Where are you with the special election?"

"We can announce dates next week. My recommendation is to hold the general election no sooner than eight months from now, to give time for the primaries. I know you want to rush it, but—"

"No, I agree. Eight months is fine. What about an intermediary?"

Dan lifted his briefcase off the floor and clicked it open. "You'll need to appoint an acting attorney general—somebody to hold office until after the special election. I've already assembled a list of suggestions that—"

"Robert Coulier."

The SUV fell deathly quiet as Maggie rubbed her bottom lip.

Dan shut the briefcase. "Is that a *joke*?"

"Do I sound like I'm joking?"

"Maggie, he's been *disbarred*. He doesn't even live here!"

"He's been disbarred in Texas. His law license is still active in Louisiana. He maintains an address in Shreveport and has for more than five years. That makes him a resident, and qualifies him for the office."

"Maggie, look at me, please."

She took another sip of water and faced Dan. The fear in his eyes was that of a person who's been pushed too far out of his comfort zone. She had seen that look several times before. Dan never liked to play the wild cards.

Then again, Dan wasn't the governor.

"You can't put a man like that in office."

"Actually, I can. I'm governor. You said so yourself."

Dan laid both hands over his knees and wrapped his fingers into his cotton slacks. "What I mean is, if you do this, the media will have a feeding frenzy. It'll be open season on your every move. The critics will go wild. You could easily lose the faith of the public—"

"The public elected me less than a year ago. They elected me to do a job—to lead this state and destroy corruption. That's what I'm going to do. The worst that could happen is they don't reelect me. In the meantime, I need somebody in the AG's office with teeth. I have no guarantee who will be elected to fill that spot, or how spineless they may be. That means I have eight months to get as much done as possible, and I need a pit bull to make it happen. Coulier is a pit bull if ever I met one."

"You're right, and that's why he was disbarred. He pushes too hard. Gets too aggressive. You put a man like that in the Capitol, and you'll have every corrupt politician, aid, lobbyist, and pundit turned against you overnight. They'll panic. They'll band together."

A faint smile played at the corners of Maggie's mouth. "That's exactly what we want. Set up a meeting with Coulier."

17

Nashville, Tennessee

"I should gut you."

Reed sat with his hands in his lap, watching as Banks slurped down mouthfuls of chicken noodle soup. "That's a fair sentiment."

Banks scooped up another puny chunk of chicken and gulped it down, then leaned back and surveyed him through tired eyes. "What the hell happened to your throat?"

Reed touched his neck. He hadn't taken a look in the mirror since the incident in Chattanooga, but he imagined the skin to be purple by now. Every breath and swallow hurt like hell, only mildly subdued by the Tylenol pills he took earlier that day. "That guy from the mountains. Bumped into him again."

Banks grunted. "Pity he didn't finish the job."

The words stung, leaving Reed wondering if she felt any of the confused, twisted emotions that he had battled since they first met. Did she ache, longing for the way things had felt before? Or did she simply hate him beyond words?

"I'm sure he'll be back. Maybe you'll get your wish."

"Maybe I'll help him." Her tone was cold.

"Don't you want to know?" Reed asked. "Don't you want the truth about what happened to your father?"

Banks lingered over her bowl, staring into the yellow depths of the broth and poking at the noodles with her spoon. "What if I do?"

"That's something I can help with."

She glared at him.

"Banks, I'm not trying to win you back. I know I'm a horrible person. But there are people out there who are worse than me. They killed Mitch, and I believe they killed your father. I want revenge . . . for your people and mine."

"What was her name?" Banks spat the question.

"I'm sorry?"

"Your friend. It was a *she*, right? Another woman?"

"It wasn't like that."

"Don't bullshit me, dammit. What was her name?"

Reed averted his eyes. "Kelly."

Banks tipped the bowl up and sucked down the broth, then wiped her mouth with the back of her hand. "Did you love her?"

Reed thought back to the last time he saw Kelly standing by her kitchen counter, just the hint of a baby belly building beneath her shirt. She looked different than she had in Monaco—less fit, a lot less wild. She wasn't the girl who rescued him from the French police, but she resembled her.

"Yes," he said. "I loved her. A long time ago."

"Isn't that nice? Guess that didn't work out for her, either."

Reed gritted his teeth and stood up. "I'm sorry, Banks. I lied to you, I hurt you, and I hurt those closest to you. I'm a despicable, deplorable human being. There's nothing more I can say. I came here because I felt like you deserved the truth and an apology. I'll go now. Good luck with everything."

Reed started for the door, his own words echoing in his ears, ripping deeper than hers had.

"If what you say is true, those people are still alive. The people who killed my father."

Reed stopped and put his hands in his pockets. "Yes."

Banks stood up, and he turned to see her bright blue eyes blazing fire toward him.

"Then you're not going anywhere until you bring me justice. Am I clear?"

Reed nodded slowly. "Okay."

"Great. I'm going to change. I hope you know where to start."

He didn't hesitate. "Vanderbilt University. We're starting at the beginning."

"What the hell is this thing?"

Banks stood back from the Camaro, her arms crossed as she glared down at the car. She wore a loose Guns N' Roses T-shirt that fell over one shoulder, with torn-out jeans and tennis shoes. The color had balanced in her face, but he could still detect the effort it took for her to make every step.

"Camaro Z/28. Slightly modified."

"You drive it like you drove my Beetle?"

"It's a little faster than your Beetle."

"A little less destroyed, too."

Reed chose to ignore the comment and unlocked the driver's door. He leaned the seat forward and whistled softly. "Come out, boy."

Baxter lumbered out of the back seat. With each step, he grunted as his scalded skin rippled over his body.

"Oh my God," Banks cried. She rushed around the car and knelt in front of the bulldog. "You poor baby. What happened to you?"

Baxter tilted his head back, peering at Banks. She touched his head, stroking behind his ears as she examined the burn marks and singed skin.

"He's a rescue," Reed said. "He was in a house fire."

"You poor thing." Banks ran gentle fingers over his back and kissed his head. Baxter shot Reed a sideways look, his eyes laden with smug satisfaction.

"Oh, shut up," Reed snorted.

"I'm taking him inside. He can't ride around in that thing anymore." Banks tugged on Baxter's collar, speaking gently to the old dog as she led him up the sidewalk toward her apartment door. Baxter complied without complaint, his stubby tail twitching as Banks continued to stroke and console him with gentle words.

Reed slid into the driver seat and slammed the door. The motor coughed twice before its comforting purr filled the cabin.

Banks returned ten minutes later and plopped down in the passenger seat, shooting Reed another glare. "That puppy needs medicine, a decent diet, and a lot of rest. I don't know what you think you're doing, dragging him around in the back seat of a car."

Reed blinked. "Um . . . he's my dog . . ."

"We'll see about that, shithead. Now start driving. We've got work to do."

Reed slid the car out of the parking lot and back onto the street. To the southeast, the Nashville skyline rose above condominiums and shiny business centers. The Camaro roared through a small residential district before turning south toward Midtown.

West of downtown, Vanderbilt University, a booming medical and legal college, lay nestled amongst a crowd of restaurants, housing, and small businesses. Reed had encountered several graduates during his tenure as a professional killer, but he'd never laid foot on the university grounds.

"What's your plan, exactly?" Banks demanded. She looked out the window, watching passing buildings with her arms crossed.

Reed rolled to a stop at a light and fought to clear his tired mind. What *was* his plan? For some time now, his only objective had been to find Banks, then find the people who killed Kelly. After gunning down Cedric Muri, he wasn't entirely sure where to look next.

"Your godfather attended Vanderbilt the same time as your dad.

They were both members of a fraternity, and Mitch indicated that things began—"

"What precisely did Uncle Mitch say about the fraternity?"

"Well . . ." Reed searched his memory, trying to recall every moment with Holiday as the senator lay dying on the lakeshore. "His exact words were, '*From end to end.*'"

"'From end to end?' What the hell does that have to do with a frat?"

"I found a picture of him standing beside your father at a ceremony. The name of the fraternity was written on the back. *Omega, Alpha, Omega*—the last, first, and last letter of the Greek alphabet. From end to end."

"Seriously?" Banks rolled her eyes. "*That's* what led you to Vanderbilt? That could mean anything, shithead."

"You know, I liked *cowboy* a lot better than *shithead*."

"Well, I liked Chris a lot better than Reed. Shame we can't have what we like."

Reed dug his fingers into the Alcantara covering of the steering wheel, biting back the urge to retaliate, and refocusing on the task at hand. "We're going to find the frat house for Omega Alpha Omega and check the membership records. Find any photographs or meeting minutes we can. There had to be other members besides Mitch and Frank who can give us a clue where to look next."

Banks said nothing.

She's devastated. She's either aching inside or she hates me, but it's no more than I deserve.

Reed navigated the car off of West End Avenue and through the main entrance of the university. Large metal signs advertised Vanderbilt's founding in 1873. Trees, barren of leaves, overhung the parking lot, sheltering a string of fancy foreign cars sitting in front of "reserved for faculty" signs.

Reed parked at the back of the lot under a magnolia tree, then turned to Banks. "I get it. You hate me, and I can deal with that. But if we want to find what we're looking for, you have to work with me. Feuding like this isn't going to get us anywhere."

Banks rolled her eyes again. "Get your head out of your ass, shithead. I'll let you live a while longer."

She piled out of the car and slammed the door. Reed watched her go, then ran an exhausted hand over his face.

Here goes nothing.

18

State Capitol Building
Baton Rouge, Louisiana

The man that sat across the desk from Maggie was neither handsome nor homely. He wore a brown suit—yes, the man actually wore a brown suit—and a soft yellow shirt, unbuttoned halfway down with no tie. Bald, with a dusting of hair just above his ears, and a wiry goatee that matched his shirt. In spite of his frumpy appearance, his teeth were impeccably straight and white, his eyes sharp and bright, and his posture stiff. He had the look of a man who knew his worth and didn't give a crap if anyone else did or not.

Maggie leaned back in her chair and tried to appear casual. In spite of her title, she felt a shadow of intimidation sitting across from Robert Coulier. The man had a reputation in the greater Texarkana area—a ruthless, brutal, cold-blooded lawyer with absolutely no interest in cutting deals or taking prisoners. Disbarred in Texas for repeated witness intimidation, Coulier now practiced international law for Chinese businesses out of his Shreveport office, but he was never there. Known simply as "The

Dog," he was feared by defense counsel and hated by legal academia as a brutish example of what law could become. Vile, profane, grizzly.

In spite of all this, Maggie had always respected Coulier. It wasn't because he always won, although that certainly didn't hurt. It was because he was true to himself. He knew what he wanted, he knew how to get it, and he didn't compromise.

The only wild card? Sometimes what he wanted conflicted with standard ethics. The Dog would need a leash.

"Mr. Coulier, I can't thank you enough for flying out on such short notice. I know you have a busy schedule."

Coulier nodded once but didn't reply. He folded his hands in his lap and stared Maggie down, unblinking.

Maggie gestured to the decanter sitting on the end table nearby. "Can I get you a beverage?"

Coulier smiled. "I don't drink, Madam Governor. It disrupts my sleep patterns."

"Of course." Maggie offered a warm smile. "I hear you keep long hours. They say you barely sleep at all."

"I sleep for three hours every ten. This enables me to be the most productive."

"That's something we have in common. I usually sleep only a few hours a night, although I'm afraid it's not as regular as I'd like. The burden of the office, I guess. Do you use sleep aids?"

Coulier's smile remained plastered to his face, neither friendly nor cold. All business.

"Madam Governor, I appreciate your eloquence, but neither one of us have the time. Why am I here?"

Maggie placed her hands on the table, palms down. Her body language advisor told her this gesture displayed confidence and authority. It felt awkward.

"Right. Of course. Well, as I'm sure you know, we've recently lost out attorney general. The official statement is that the investigation is ongoing, but confidentially I can tell you his death was not an accident. We're pursuing a homicide investigation now."

Coulier didn't comment. Maggie shifted her hands on the desktop, then cleared her throat.

"As governor, it's my responsibility to appoint an interim AG until a special election can be held. I'm currently reviewing candidates, and—"

"I'll do it." Coulier's tone remained calm but confident. Maggie raised her eyebrows.

"I didn't offer you the job."

"You flew me from Beijing on taxpayer dollars, and we both know you don't have any other candidates. The only reason I came is because I want the job."

Maggie sat back in her chair and folded her arms. She wasn't entirely sure how to respond. On the one hand, his confidence and directness were exactly the reasons she wanted him in the first place. On the other, she wanted to ask him herself. She needed him to obey and respect her authority. This wasn't a great start.

"Why do you want the job?"

Coulier relaxed his shoulders and crossed his legs. "Why does anyone want to be the lead legal officer of a state? Power. Prestige. Influence. Access."

Maggie smirked. "I appreciate your eloquence, but neither of us has the time. Why do you really want it?"

This time Coulier's smile was genuine. He tilted his head and stared at her for a full minute, as though he were evaluating an expensive piece of art he was contemplating purchasing. She didn't blink and stared right back, arms still crossed.

"I'm sure you're aware that I'm not an altogether popular attorney," he said.

"I am."

"I'm sure you know why."

"I do."

"Only one thing makes me tick, Madam Governor. *Winning*. I live for the win. I breathe for it. Winning is in my blood. I don't care about money, fame, or renown. I just want to conquer. Five years ago, I was engaged in litigation against a large oil firm that operates off the Louisiana coast. The case started as a single-plaintiff lawsuit about unsafe work environments on their oil platforms. One of their welders lost his leg to a falling piece of steel, and he wanted compensation. Seemed like a home run case to me, so I took it. But as soon as I began litigation, everything spilled over. I found thousands of cases of muted OSHA filings, wrongfully denied workman's comp claims, workers who were fired for reporting unsafe working conditions, bribes paid to regulators, and every other type of corporate corruption. So, I advised my client to allow me to pursue a class-action lawsuit and involve other plaintiffs. I didn't see how I could lose."

"But you did."

Coulier's smile faded. "You're very astute. I was sabotaged. The defense delayed and dragged their feet every possible way they could. They insisted on a trial, and stacked the jury, all while launching a slander campaign against me for my difficulties in Texas. I fought to the end, but I lost. Not a single dollar was paid out to my clients, and no regulatory measures were improved. Ryman Offshore Partners continues unmitigated operations to this day."

Maggie lifted a glass of water from the executive desk and took a sip. Coulier waited, his expression impassive and unreadable.

"So," she said. "Now you want revenge."

"No, Madam Governor. Like I told you before, there is only one thing I want. I want to win. In this case, winning means destroying Ryman. And when I'm finished with them, I will win with the state judge who presided over the case, who refused the admission of key evidence and sheltered the jury. Then I will win over the defense counsel."

"Double jeopardy law prevents you from trying them for any of the regulatory infractions they've already been acquitted of," Maggie said.

"I won't need to. Dirty hands are seldom soiled with a single variety of mud. Trust me when I tell you, Governor, I've been collecting ammunition against my enemies from the day the ruling was issued. All guilty parties will be charged within two days of my inauguration."

Maggie laid her hands on the desk again and stared Coulier down. She tried to imagine what was happening behind that impassive stare and blunt honesty. She didn't think he was lying or would have a reason to lie, and she appreciated his absolute candor. This was exactly the sort of agenda-driven bloodthirst Coulier was known for, and she could only imagine the meltdown Dan would descend into if he were sitting in the room with them. Obviously, that was why Dan wasn't invited to attend the interview. She anticipated Coulier would have some type of personal agenda from the moment he readily accepted her invitation to the Capitol. Granted, this was a bit more extreme than she had hoped for. Somehow, it still didn't alarm her.

"Well, I appreciate your bluntness," she said. "Do you know what *I* want?"

The smile returned to Coulier's thin lips. "You want to fulfill your campaign promises. You want to destroy political and corporate corruption."

Maggie returned the smile. "Yes, sir. I very much do, and I need a pit bull to make that happen. They tell me you're a dog. Can you be a dog who hunts more than one raccoon?"

The smile spread into an unabashed grin, fully exposing the flawless white teeth. "Governor, I was born to hunt."

Maggie stood up and offered her hand. "Welcome to Baton Rouge, Mr. Attorney General."

19

**Vanderbilt University
Nashville, Tennessee**

Reed didn't have a great deal of experience with college campuses, but he guessed that most of them weren't as pretty as Vanderbilt—a fusion of old trees and older brick buildings, with sidewalks that wound between them like hidden paths in a magic forest. Students bustled back and forth across the streets, burdened down with backpacks and laptop cases. Some were teenagers, but many were much older.

They found their way to the student information hall, and Banks stopped Reed at the foot of the steps. "You're gonna need to look less like a killer, or the police will be here in no time."

"What do you mean? I look fine."

Banks rolled her eyes and ran her hand through his hair, ruffling it up before she yanked at his shirt, untucking it. "I'm not going down for your sins, you fool."

Fool is better than shithead.

She turned and started up the steps. "All right, shithead. Be cool."

Annnnnnnd we're back.

The big brick building at the top of the steps featured dual glass doors guarded by a concrete arch. Inside, small clusters of students gathered around desks with old, tired counselors seated behind. Must hung in the air, as though many of the books were far older than the librarians who kept them and would likely sit on these shelves long after their guardians had passed on.

Reed slouched his shoulders and leaned forward, trying to imagine what a college student looked like. The young males around him were as diverse as a promotional billboard. Some wore ties and button-down shirts, with slicked-back hair and rimless glasses. Others appeared more relaxed—sports T-shirts and tennis shoes.

"Can I help you?" The overweight woman behind the counter sounded as though she were interested in doing anything but. Even so, she offered them a polite smile as they approached.

"My brother is looking for information on fraternities." Banks smiled so sweetly, Reed felt his heart skip. He looked away and feigned interest over a poster on the wall.

The old woman grumbled. "Rush week is over. I can give you a list of on-campus organizations, though." She rustled through her drawer and produced a glossy brochure with a group of smiling kids wearing backpacks. She passed it across the counter, and Reed scooped it up. A quick scan of the names and addresses listed under the "*fraternities*" tab came up emptyhanded.

"What about Omega Alpha Omega?" he asked.

"I'm sorry?"

"I don't see them on the list."

She shook her head. "I've never heard of Omega Alpha Omega. Every Vanderbilt fraternity is on that list. You must have the name wrong."

Reed scanned the list again. Many names he recognized from years of reading assassination profiles, as some of his more professional targets were frat members. But Omega Alpha Omega wasn't on the list.

"Is there something else I can help with?" The impatience in her tone was evident. Reed shook his head and turned toward the door, leaving Banks to offer a quick thank-you before scuttling after him. The cold air outside the building flooded his lungs, bringing welcome relief from the stuffiness of the student hall. Once more, he scanned the brochure, but it was pointless. Holiday's old fraternity wasn't there.

"What now?" Banks snapped. "Did you get the name wrong?"

"No, I definitely had it right. The letters were very clear."

"Where's the picture?"

Reed tapped the edge of the brochure against his lip and pretended not to have heard her.

Banks pinched his arm. "Don't fool around with me. Where's the picture?"

He sighed and dug out his wallet, producing the faded photograph of Mitch Holiday and Frank Morccelli in fraternity robes. Banks snatched it away and fixated on the image. Her eyes turned red before she flipped it over and read the back.

"See? Omega Alpha Omega," Reed said. "I had the name right. And that *does say* Vanderbilt University."

Banks tapped the photo against her fingers. Confused emotions clouded her face, and Reed guessed it had little to do with the location of the mystery fraternity.

"Let's head over to the row and take a look around," she said.

"The *row?*"

Banks rolled her eyes. "Wow, you really are a moron. The row—where all the frat and sorority houses are. Every campus has one. Look at the addresses."

Reed scanned the brochure again, and sure enough, several of the headquarters' addresses were on the same street. The pamphlet's map guided them through a series of tree-sheltered sidewalks deeper inside the campus.

In spite of the bustle of students, everything was calm. Reed wondered what it must feel like to be one of them—jogging to their next class, the most stressful thing in the world their latest grade or midterm. In times past, he hated people like them. As a gangbanger in Los Angeles, he viewed all college kids as rich, spoiled brats who wasted their lives away with their noses crammed into books.

Now, things weren't so black and white. Jealousy tugged within him, and he wondered what his life could have been like if he'd never joined the gangs, never ran into the recruiter, and never became a Marine. Would he have gone to college? Probably not a school like Vanderbilt—who was he kidding?—but maybe a state school. He could've studied something like business or marketing, worked in a tall, glassy tower like the ones in downtown Nashville, dated a nice girl, and had a couple kids.

"What's wrong with you?" Banks's snapping voice jarred him out of the daydream. He realized he had stopped on the sidewalk, his gaze transfixed by the crowds of students bustling by. Everything about his picture of another life, for another Reed, felt surreal and frail, built on a foundation of false realities that could never have come to pass.

I wasn't born to be like them. I was born for something different. Something hard.

"Let's move, dumbass."

"Look." Reed withdrew his hands from his pockets and folded his arms. "If you want to know the truth about what happened to your father, I'm the best way. I'm not asking you to like me, but I'm not your enemy."

"Not my enemy?" Banks wheeled on him and stepped so close he could smell her breath laden with tequila, even though he hadn't seen her take a drink since he found her at the bar. She jabbed a finger into his chest. "You *lied* to me—about everything. You kidnapped my uncle, brutalized him, and swept me up in this entire mess. I almost died *twice* because of you. If you're not my enemy, I don't know who is."

The fire that blazed in her eyes was every bit as bright and fierce as it had been the first night he met her, but these flames didn't speak of joy and ambition and a passionate hunger for life. This time, the dark embers smoldered with resentment.

"I understand that. Believe me. I hate myself more than you hate me. And when this is over, if you want to push me off a cliff, that's fine. But right now, we have a chance to discover the truth, and I have a chance to punish the people responsible. *They* are the enemy. If you want to do it on your own, be my guest, but if you can find it in your heart to suspend your hatred for just a few days, I can help you. I want to help you."

She stared him down, her finger still pressed into his chest. He thought she might slap him, but she turned away. "Fine. Help me. But this doesn't mean I've forgiven or forgotten."

They started down the sidewalk again, watching trees fade into small parks and brick buildings into old homes. Flags hung from the columns of front porches, displaying the proud symbols of a half dozen sororities and fraternities. A few homes featured Greek letters over the front doors, while a handful of kids shuffled in and out, backpacks over their shoulders, evidence of hangovers in their sloppy steps.

None of the signs or flags matched Omega Alpha Omega. Reed and Banks walked down the street, then turned back on the other side, stopping from time to time to ask passing students if they had heard of the fraternity. Blank stares and shrugs were the most expressive responses they received, except for one shirtless frat boy, still drunk, who grinned and invited them inside.

Banks leaned against a tree and pushed her hands into her jean pockets. Her face was flushed red again, and in spite of the breeze, sweat trickled down her neck.

Reed moved toward her. "Are you okay?"

She jutted her chin toward the street. "It's not here. This frat of yours doesn't exist."

"You saw the letters," Reed said. "It exists. Or at least it did at some point. Maybe they didn't have a frat house, and they met in the library or off campus."

"So how do we find them? It's a big city."

Reed looked back down the narrow street, his eyes coming to rest on a house three doors down that featured a blue flag with gold letters. The two-story house was white with strips of peeling paint hanging from the siding. Big windows framed the second floor, and a small skylight overhung what must have been the attic. Dead grass around the home was sheltered by untrimmed evergreen bushes, and compared to the surrounding rows of manicured homes with clean yards, the house stood out like a sore thumb. A small crowd of college kids were busy unloading a van, carting food and cases of beer into the house.

"What do you suppose they're doing?" Reed asked.

Banks shrugged. "What all frat boys do. Partying, or getting ready for a party."

"Yeah, I know, but look at the house. It's a shamble."

"So they don't take care of it. What's your point?"

Reed started down the street, walking along the curb as he surveyed the home. The paint clinging to the walls had peeled and dropped into the grass in sheets—everywhere except the fascia over the front porch. A towering oak tree sheltered the home, where the frat's three-letter name was mounted in gold letters. Each letter was clean, with fresh paint and not a speck of dirt—a sharp contrast to the wall they were mounted against.

The letters are new.

Banks stumbled to a stop beside him, peered at the house, then shook her head. "I don't get it."

Reed held up his finger as the clouds began to part. A sunray cut through the oak tree's ragged limbs and spilled over the fascia. The bright light exposed the shadowy outline of a sign: Omega, Alpha, Omega. It was hung long before on that same facade, protecting the paint beneath it from the scar of the sun, and leaving its outline, even after it was torn down.

Reed turned to Banks, and a slow smile spread across her face, spilling into her eyes for the first time since she took the stage at the bar earlier that day.

"They're taking over the house," she said. "It's been abandoned."

"Yes. For God knows how long. Those letters were probably

pirated for use on another house years ago, which explains why nobody knew it was the old Omega Alpha Omega headquarters."

"We've got to get inside. There could be old records. Logbooks. Information on who else was in the fraternity that might still be alive."

Reed started across the street, slumping his shoulders and trying to appear as casual as possible as he approached the kids unloading the van. "'Sup, guys? Need a hand?"

An underage redheaded teen took a sip of beer and poked his head around the back door of the van. He surveyed Reed with squinted eyes, then his gaze traveled to Banks. His demeanor shifted. "You guys students?"

Banks nodded and offered her hand. "Yeah, I'm Sirena. We're from Iowa."

"No shit!" He grinned and shook her hand. "So am I! What city?"

She had to pick Iowa.

"Iowa City. Born and raised. You guys prepping for a party?"

His grin widened, and Reed checked his first assumption when he noticed the black-and-yellow Hawkeyes baseball hat hanging on the van's rearview mirror.

She's a manipulative genius.

The frat boy ran his hand through his short red hair. "You bet. Gonna throw a little celebration party tonight. We just got a lease on this place. Dope, right?"

Banks pretended to be impressed with the shabby building, leaning back and tilting her head up.

"Looks great, man! Sounds like fun."

He nodded, still staring at her curvy body, then blinked as though his mind had come awake. "Hey, you guys should come! It's gonna be rad. Got a DJ and everything."

Banks shot Reed a smug smirk, then directed a grin back at the kid. "What time?"

"We're kicking off at eight. Bring booze!"

Banks gave him a fist bump. As they walked back onto the

street, Reed caught sight of a new wave of sweat dripping down her face, now faded from red to white.

She's barely standing.

"We should go back to your place. You need to rest. Then we can hit them up tonight."

"Oh, what a master plan. Come up with that all on your own, did you?"

Reed wanted to cringe but rolled his eyes. "Fine. *Thank you, you manipulative genius.* Your skills of sexual mind control are unmatched."

Banks turned off the street, back toward the Camaro. "You haven't seen anything yet."

20

Baton Rouge, Louisiana

The restaurant was quaint, dressed in white trim, and built inside an antebellum home with a wraparound porch now converted into an outdoor dining space. Maggie might have been impressed under different circumstances. Even excited. Instead, she surveyed the crowd of people sitting under whining ceiling fans on the porch and wondered if they were witnesses or potential victims.

On one side of her Tahoe, two men stood stiff-backed, surveying the downtown streets of Baton Rouge. She turned to a black-suited state policeman standing at attention next to her vehicle. "What's your name?" she asked.

"Officer O'Dell, Madam Governor." He spoke with a Cajun accent so thick and oppressive it was difficult even for her to discern the exact words.

She rested one hand on her hip. "Is that what your parents call you?"

Confusion flashed behind his eyes, and he shook his head. "No, ma'am. My first name is James."

"That's a great name, James. My first name is Maggie. We'll be spending a lot of time together from now on, so let's drop the formalities. Is that okay?"

Discomfort radiated from O'Dell's stiff shoulders and rigid arms like heat waves of a Louisiana bayou, but he nodded. "Yes, ma'am. If you prefer so, ma'am."

"I do. Now, James, I'm going to get a bite to eat. I want you to stay with the Tahoe. I'll be back shortly."

"Madam Governor, I'm afraid I can't allow that. I have to accompany you at all times."

Maggie raised an eyebrow. "Did your commanding officer tell you that?"

"Yes, ma'am."

"And who do you think he reports to? Don't worry, James. I can look after myself. Keep the motor running. I won't be long." Maggie stepped away from the vehicle and walked up the short row of white concrete steps.

A hostess greeted her at the front door, taking a small bow and motioning her toward the door. "Just one tonight, ma'am?"

"No, I'm meeting somebody. A gentleman."

"Yes, of course, ma'am. He mentioned you would be coming. Right this way."

The hostess led Maggie through a maze of chairs and tables, toward a small alcove in the rear. Full-length windows filled the whole wall, looking out over downtown Baton Rouge from the gentle hill the restaurant sat on.

A tall man in a grey suit sipped tea from a white cup as Maggie approached. He set the cup down at his table and offered his hand without standing. "Madam Governor, thank you so much for accepting my invitation."

Maggie ignored the hand and pulled back her chair, sitting without a word.

He tilted his head and smirked at her, then retracted his arm and lifted the cup again. "Would you care for something to drink? Dinner's on me."

"No, thank you. I won't be staying for dinner. I'm here because two of my men are dead, and you reached out to my office anonymously almost immediately after. Kind of strange, don't you think?"

The smirk remained plastered on his face. He stirred his tea with a silver spoon as the waitress approached.

"Ma'am, can I take your drink order?"

"Water," Maggie said. "Thank you."

The waitress retreated, and the man in the grey suit leaned forward, his lips turning down into a soft frown. "May I express my deepest condolences about your men. I read about the incident in the news this morning. What a tragic accident."

"Accident? Is that what they're calling it? News to me. You see, I was there. I saw the intruder. Shot him, as a matter of fact. Regrettably, he survived."

The smirk returned, and the man adjusted the teacup on its saucer.

"Maggie—may I call you Maggie?"

"You may not. I'm the governor."

"Yes, of course. Forgive me. Madam Governor, my name is Gambit. Well, that's not my actual name, but since you prefer titles, I suppose you can use mine."

"Gambit, I'm on a tight schedule. I've got a shitload of corruption to burn out of this state. I suggest you find your point."

"You're even saucier in person than you are on TV, Madam Governor. It's a true wonder anyone ever voted for you."

"Oh, plenty of people voted for me. Over six hundred thousand. It just so happens none of them were scumbags."

Gambit sat back. "Well, then, if you're going to be so curt, I may as well cut to the chase."

"You really should."

He sipped his tea, then cleared his throat. "I represent a *significant* organization of tremendous influence that would very much appreciate your partnership."

Maggie folded her hands. "So, you're a criminal, and you're here to enlist me in your elicit enterprises."

Gambit chuckled. "No, ma'am. As you said yourself, you're the governor of Louisiana. I wouldn't dream of involving you in anything less than legal. What my company proposes is more *mutually advantageous*. We simply want to count you as an ally. On occasion, we may ask you to redirect an investigation or help us with the approval of a permit. Perhaps offer us regulatory assistance. In exchange, we will ensure that whatever political initiatives you may have are completely successful—schools, roads, state parks . . . whatever you care about. We have the power to ensure you never lose an election. You can be governor for two terms, and then we might find you a home in the Senate. Who knows?" He took another sip of tea.

Maggie placed both hands on the table. "Well, Gambit, I believe this meeting is concluded. I'm afraid you have drastically miscalculated what type of person I am. I ran for the governorship to make a statement. I didn't even plan on winning. But I did win—and the reason I won is because scum like you have no place in this state, and the people of Louisiana want me to run you out. If you think for a moment that I'm going to have any part in whatever sordid activities you represent, you've got another thought coming. My *political initiatives* are to destroy people like you."

She stood up, and Gambit's smile faded. He stirred the tea again, then shook his head. "That's tragically unfortunate, Governor Trousdale. I always prefer honey, but I'm no stranger to vinegar. I understand you have a family who lives in the swamps outside New Orleans. I'm sure they're very important to you."

Maggie tilted her head and stared Gambit down. "My father can barely read, but he can hit a running rabbit at two hundred yards with a fifty-dollar rifle. My brother never finished high school, but he hunts gators for a living. My sister is a three-time national champion mixed martial artist. And my mom? The house was broken into last year, and she beat the burglar with a rolling pin. To my knowledge, he's still in a coma. If you'd like to threaten my family, Gambit . . . well, *good luck*."

Maggie walked past the oncoming waitress and back through the front door. O'Dell stood next to the Tahoe, his hand held close to the Glock .40 caliber mounted to his hip. He opened the door for Maggie, and she climbed in without comment. As the Tahoe pulled away, Gambit stood in the window, smiling at her. It was the smile of a man who enjoyed the hunt as much as he enjoyed the kill.

"James, I want protective details assigned to my family immediately. If the LSP gives you any flack about the cost, inform them that they can detract from my personal detail if necessary."

O'Dell nodded. "Yes, ma'am. Right away."

She folded her hands. "You know how to shoot that thing, or is it just a belt ornament?"

A smirk played at the corners of O'Dell's mouth, exposing the glint of a gold tooth in place of his lateral incisor. Their eyes met in the rearview mirror.

"Don't worry, ma'am. I know how to use it."

"Excellent." She closed her eyes and leaned back in her seat. "You just might have to."

21

Nashville, Tennessee

Reed whistled as Banks slid into the Camaro wearing skintight jeans and a crop top. Her hair, heavily fragranced with perfume, hung over bare shoulders. Red lipstick coated her mouth, and dark eyeliner complemented heavy mascara.

Banks glared at him. "Keep it in your pants. This isn't for you."

He shifted into gear, and the Camaro rumbled away from Banks's apartment, back toward Vanderbilt. The city lay in darkness now, but it was far from asleep. Cars, Ubers, taxis, and every manner of modified-party contraption rolled down the streets, honking and shouting at every intersection. Reed felt his blood pressure rise as he fought his way through the mess, giving lower Broadway a wide berth before he turned west toward the campus.

Even before they could see the frat house, the thump of rap music filled their ears. Dull lights flashed into the sky in half a dozen neon colors, and students gathered around the front porch. Reed parked the Camaro fifty yards down the street and watched the house. In a crowd this dense, it would be next to impossible to conduct a thorough search of the old home.

"We need a plan," he said.

Banks sighed and opened her door. "How about this? I flash the frat kids, you find what we need."

Well, that seems workable.

Reed checked the SIG handgun tucked into his belt before joining Banks on the sidewalk. He could tell by her soft, labored breaths that she still felt terrible, but it didn't hold her back for a moment. Her hips swung gracefully as she trotted in heels toward the house. He couldn't help but admire her gentle strut, confident and calm, completely masking the clutch of illness on her body. His mind faded back to the two of them standing on the parking deck outside Atlanta, gazing at the skyline, while Banks strummed her ukulele. She was happier then, but no less a rock.

I want her back. God help me, I do.

A tall frat boy with broad shoulders and a drunken glare stumbled at the bottom of the steps. "Hey, this is a pwivate pawty."

Banks shot him a seductive smile and tilted her head, but it wasn't necessary. The redhead reappeared from the front door and waved his hand. "Don't worry, Max. I invited them. Wassup, baby?"

He winked at Banks, and she batted her eyelashes.

My God. How does somebody this idiotic get accepted at Vanderbilt?

Reed followed Banks up the steps and into the house. The beat of the music pounded inside his head, jarring his shoulders and flooding his mind with new aches. He eagerly sucked down the cup of cheap beer that was pressed into his hand.

"Welcome, brother! How's it going?"

Reed smiled and gave the kid a thumbs-up. Banks was already lost on the dance floor, swaying under the neon lights with the redhead grinding against her side. Reed felt his muscles tense, and he reached for the gun before his mind regained control of his reflexes.

She's doing her job. Do yours.

He glanced around the living room, now so packed with kids he could barely distinguish the walls. The Greek letters of the new frat hung over the kitchen doorway, and pinned to the living room wall was a fraternity constitution. Reed pushed his way into the kitchen, where two guys smoked joints, and a third leaned against the wall, making out with a brunette. Much like the living room, the walls were bare, and nothing but alcohol covered the counters.

Reed pushed past the cloud of marijuana smoke and into the next room. It was the dining room, empty except for more cases of beer and a few cartons of fried chicken. He grabbed a drumstick and tore into it as he stepped into the hallway. His stomach grumbled from neglect, and the cold, greasy food relaxed his nerves. A frat boy—clearly a freshman—leaned over the toilet in the hallway bathroom and puked into the bowl. Reed couldn't resist a small smile.

Gonna be a long four years for you, my friend.

Inside a hallway closet built beneath the stairwell were a couple coats on hooks. A thorough investigation of their pockets produced nothing but cigarettes and weed. Reed mounted the steps and ascended to the second floor, softening each footfall as he drew closer. The music still pounded below, masking his footsteps as he passed the first bedroom. Empty. Light spilled out from beneath the next door. He placed his hand on the knob and started to twist, then heard soft moans and cries of ecstasy from the other side. He sighed and released the knob.

There has to be something more. They couldn't have cleared the whole house.

A window at the end of the hallway opened out over the backyard, where tall weeds were trampled under the feet of a few dozen more college kids, all sipping beer and swaying to the beat of hip-hop music. As Reed watched them, he marveled at how happy they looked—so loose and carefree.

Why does this piss me off? Am I seriously jealous of frat kids?

Reed started back toward the stairwell, then stopped. He remembered standing outside the house and staring up at the windows. There were skylights in the roof.

The attic.

A few paces down the hallway, Reed caught sight of the attic door. It was more of a hatch, really, about the size of a large pizza box, framed in the ceiling just above the window but obscured by shadows and cobwebs.

Reed stuck the light between his teeth and stepped up onto the windowsill. He pressed up with one hand on the tile, and it lifted free from the remainder of the ceiling with a shower of drywall particles. Reed shoved it aside and forced his head through the hole. Pine rafters and dust filled the space beyond, illuminated by the moonlight spilling through the skylights. He stuck both arms through the hole, then hauled himself above the ceiling. Flooring covered the upper side of the ceiling, providing a firm landing place as he rolled away from the hole.

Reed pulled himself to his feet and leaned against a rafter as his eyes scanned the plywood floor scattered with splotches of dark red. The residue was unmistakable. It was blood. Next to the blotches, systematic rows of dents in the wood lay in long, evenly spaced impressions. Chair legs?

Reed scanned the light around the room, hoping for an abandoned piece of paraphernalia from the vanishing fraternity, but found only dirt, dried blood, and shadows.

What the hell is this place?

Reed took another tentative step toward the end of the room. A board creaked under his foot, and he squinted at the far wall. It was different than the sloped roof that hugged his shoulders on either side. It was darker and softer looking, as if it wasn't built of wood at all.

Reed touched the black surface of the wall, covered floor to ceiling in dark cloth, confirming his suspicions. He wrapped his fingers into the fabric and jerked down. The breath rushed from his lips as the sheet fell, exposing the complete wall behind. Inches away, a large dark face stared directly into his. Reed leaped back and jerked the pistol from his hip, even as his mind recognized painted features on the wall.

It was the silver owl—the same one he had seen in the picture of Mitch Holiday and Frank Morccelli. Its blood-red eyes glared at

Reed with all the malice and rage a painting could express. Reed slowly lowered the gun, then shuffled forward and reached out his hand, tracing the painted outlines whittled into the blackened plywood. The eyes weren't actually painted. They were glass, flat-backed, and glued to the wall. Reed traced the owl with the flashlight beam, moving all the way to the floor where the LED light exposed a wide pool of dried blood.

This was no fraternity.

Reed traced the edges of the wall, searching for any hidden passage or retractable piece of plywood, but the entire wall was fit perfectly against the sloping roof, screwed into place at every edge. He returned to the owl and examined the wood beneath his feet more closely. Small indentions in the plywood, clearly engraved but unmarked by any contrasting paint, lined the wood beneath the owl's talons. As Reed leaned in closer, he recognized the familiar outlines of Greek letters, but these weren't the letters of a fraternity name—they formed a full sentence, written in ancient Greek.

Reed searched the internet on his phone for an ancient Greek translator, and it didn't take long to find a website that claimed to translate text instantly. Reed painstakingly matched each letter to the Greek alphabet. Beneath his feet, the music continued to pound while college kids laughed and shouted at one another.

He was ten letters in, with another ten to go, when he heard the first scream, shrill and panicked, coming from the front of the house. Reed's back went rigid as the first shout was joined by a second, then a third. Gunshots—fast and chattering—blazed into the house. Heavy thuds sounded beneath him, followed by doors slamming, more screams, and more gunshots.

Banks.

Reed started toward the hole in the ceiling, then stopped, knowing this might be his last chance to get into the attic. Whatever secrets were formed in this dark, strange place led to the deaths of Mitch Holiday and Frank Morccelli. The men behind this blood-eyed owl burned Kelly alive, and he had to know who they were.

Back at the wall, Reed frantically tapped each letter into the phone. Sweat pooled on the LED screen, making his thumbs slip. More gunshots ripped through the house, and two stray bullets blasted through the plywood a few feet to his right.

The last letters clicked into the translator, and Reed tapped the blue button. Seconds dragged by, scraping against his nerves and feeling like hours. The translation loaded, and Reed squinted at the words, whispering the convoluted stream of text back to himself. *"Our mother wisdom war conquest guard secrets beneath mighty feet."*

Reed stepped back and shone the light upward. The owl glared at him, bending invisible menace against his every move. The hellfire that burned in those red eyes spoke of outrage at the broken peace of this strange place. It was a dark soul eager to protect the secrets that Reed so desperately needed to uncover.

Reed eyed the owl. "Who's the mother?" he demanded. The painted bird didn't respond, but Reed imagined he could see renewed wrath in its scowl.

Reed snapped and slammed his hand against the wall. "Who *is* she?" His forehead collided with the wood, and he pressed his fingers against the carvings, retracing them.

The owl. The mother. Wisdom. War. Conquest.

Reed lifted his head and placed his hand on the face of the bird. The realization sank in, tearing through his mind like a thunderclap.

Owl. Mother. The goddess, Athena.

22

Reed's boots hit the floor of the second-level hallway at the same moment his pistol cleared the holster. At the top of the stairs stood a man dressed in black, wielding an MP5 submachine gun. A black ski mask covered his face, but blue eyes glinted behind it. Reed raised his SIG and fired twice, driving two 9mm slugs right between his eyes. The gunman dropped, but gunshots and screams from the first floor continued. Reed dashed toward the stairs, shoving the handgun in his pocket before snatching up the larger MP5.

At the bottom of the stairs, bullet holes decorated the walls and banister, and outside, the screams of fleeing college kids filled the air. Music continued to pound from the living room, now joined by the flash of disco lights.

Banks screamed again, and this time, Reed could make out her location. He crashed around the end of the banister and charged into the kitchen.

A man pressed Banks against the wall with a handgun jammed into her temple. He screamed at her, "Where's The Prosecutor?"

Banks kicked out with both legs, then spat in his face.

"Hey, you!" Reed screamed. "I'm right here."

The man released Banks and spun toward Reed, the gaping mouth of his weapon following. Reed pressed the trigger of the MP5. The gun fired twice, sending slugs whizzing past the man's arm before it clicked back over an empty magazine. Reed rolled to the floor as a heavy bullet whistled over his head. The MP5 clattered against the hardwood, and he fought for the handgun stuck in his pocket.

The mouth of the gun swung toward Reed. He kicked out with both legs, slamming his boots into the unprotected shins of the gunman. The handgun barked, and hardwood exploded into splinters next to Reed's head. The SIG still lay buried in Reed's pocket, but he managed to force his hand around the grip and reach the trigger. Without aiming, he pushed the muzzle away from his thigh and fired. A bullet rocketed out of his pants and struck the staggering gunman in the ankle. Another scream filled the kitchen, and Reed's attacker stumbled back. Before the masked man could regain his balance, Banks appeared from the back of the kitchen, a can of soup clenched between her fingers. She drove the makeshift weapon full force into the face of the gunman, and he crumpled to the ground as blood gushed from his mask.

Reed pulled himself to his feet as Banks delivered another blow to the top of her attacker's head, but it wasn't necessary. He was out cold already.

"There's more of them outside," Banks said. Fear plagued her eyes, but her voice remained calm.

"Through the front!" Reed shouted.

They crashed over piles of shattered bottles and abandoned cups, sliding through the door as fresh gunfire erupted from the front yard. The windows that framed either side of the door exploded and Reed grabbed Banks, crashing onto the front porch. She slipped and hit the planks with a muted cry. Reed slid to his knees beside her, raising the SIG and opening fire on the gunman. Three pops of the pistol silenced the MP5, and Reed pulled Banks upright.

"Quick, the car!"

They jumped down the porch steps and around the van. The screams continued from the shadows, and fresh gunfire erupted from behind them, back toward the house. Reed emptied the SIG into the home, sending bullets flying at random. The submachine gunfire ceased, and Reed grabbed Banks by the hand.

"Let's go! He's not dead."

Banks gasped for breath and slouched against his arm as they ran. He could feel the exhaustion and the weight of her disease sucking the life out of her and weakening her every step. She pressed on, one foot dragging over the street as they approached the Camaro. Reed slung the passenger door open and pushed her inside. As he jumped into the driver's seat he saw shadows moving inside the frat house, and somebody shouted in a harsh, east European language.

Panic and confusion clouded his mind. *Where the hell did these guys come from?*

The big engine roared to life, and Reed slammed the shifter into first. "Hold on to something!" he shouted, then dumped the clutch. The thunder of the motor was joined by the whine of the supercharger, and the back wheels lost traction. Tire smoke filled the air as the back end of the car fishtailed to the left, and then the tires caught, slinging them into the seats and causing Reed's skull to smack against the headrest. By the time the man in black stepped into the street, it was much too late for him to move. The Camaro launched forward like a rocket, hurtling down the road with the front end lifted an inch off the ground. Banks screamed a split second before the bumper collided with the gunman, sending him tumbling over the hood and back into the street. The front tires slammed against the pavement as Reed jerked the wheel to the right and pulled the emergency brake. The car spun a full one-hundred-eighty degrees, facing the way it had come. Police cars filled the street two hundred yards away, their blue lights ablaze as sirens screamed, and the supercharger whined again.

"Reed, don't do it!"

"Buckle up!"

The police cars swerved to either side as the Camaro screamed down the street like a cannonball. By the time the first car flashed past Reed's window, the heads-up display in the windshield read 63 miles per hour. Nothing he had ever driven compared to the raw power of the supercharged LS motor. Every imperfection in the road sent shudders through the car's tight suspension, though muted by the growl of the motor. A stop sign flashed on the right, and a horn blared. Twenty yards ahead, Reed cut the wheel to the left and redirected toward West End Avenue.

"I found it!" he shouted.

Banks clung to the armrest with wide, panicked eyes, sucking in air between blue lips and screaming as Reed swerved around a taxi.

"It wasn't a fraternity," Reed said. "It was some secret cult. They worshipped the Greek goddess Athena. I saw it all."

He relaxed off the accelerator as the Camaro merged into traffic, and the rearview mirror displayed nothing but an empty avenue behind him. The car shook as the tachometer dropped, but the exhaust still voiced the suspended power ready to be unleashed. Reed wiped the sweat from his forehead and turned abruptly off the road into a large park on the far side of West End. Tall trees overhung a curving road that wound past war memorials and small ponds.

Banks clutched the door handle and peered into the rearview mirror. "We have to go, Reed. They'll find us here. We're not far enough away!"

Reed shook his head. "No, we have to get the book. They hid it in the temple."

"What the hell are you talking about? What book? *What temple?*"

The car squeaked to a stop, the engine still rumbling. Reed nodded toward a wide field. Thin fog clung to the grass, shrouding the park in a cemetery-like mood, enveloping the single structure that dominated the middle of the park. *"That* temple."

Fifty yards away sat the towering bulk of the Parthenon. Constructed of sandy-brown concrete and illuminated by soft-yellow lights, the impending mass of the life-sized replica filled the windshield, commanding reverence. Columns lined every side of the temple, supporting a pitched roof rimmed with spikes. It was breathtaking. Monumental. Haunted.

The moment Reed connected the dots between the owl and the mother, everything fell into place. The owl was a Greek symbol—a sacred token of wisdom and conquest, dedicated to the goddess of the ancient Athenians. This goddess—their holy mother—was also the goddess of war, conquest, science, and mathematics. Athena was a virgin, the offspring of the mythological deity Zeus, and her home was the Parthenon—the temple built for her in the ancient city of Athens.

The concrete building that filled the windshield of the Camaro was a full-scale replica originally designed and constructed in 1897, and had sat in the Centennial Park of Nashville ever since.

Reed knew what was inside. He remembered it all from an eighth-grade field trip when Mountain Brook High School bussed his entire history class to Nashville to tour the Greek monument and learn about Athenian mythology. The featured experience of the trip had been the dominating forty-two-foot-tall statue of Athena herself. It was nothing short of glorious. And it was exactly the place where a cult obsessed with the mother of warfare and wisdom would hide their secret records.

"What is that?" Banks asked. "Is that a government building?"

"You could say that. For a government that died two thousand years ago. We have to get inside."

Banks shook her head. "No, we have to leave. *Now*. They're coming!"

Reed put his foot on the brake. "Banks, this is our best chance of finding them. Those men are just hired guns. Do you want to keep fighting the minions, or do you want to cut the head off the snake?"

Banks looked over her shoulder, back toward Vanderbilt. She licked sweat off her lip, then nodded once. "Okay. Let's hurry."

Reed released the clutch and put his hand on the shifter. He piloted the car around another curve in the asphalt path, weaving toward the parking lot at the main entrance. The closer they drew, the grander the temple appeared. It blocked out the moon, casting a shadow over them as deep and dark as the emptiness Reed felt. He stopped and craned his neck back. Above the tops of the columns, a row of masterfully carved figurines clung to the wall. Gods and goddesses, riding chariots and horses, jutted toward the sky. Their faces were vacant, again speaking to the deadly mystery that led Reed to this strange place.

They were here—Mitch and Frank. Whatever terrible secret cost them their lives, this place was a part of it. This place birthed the monster that killed Kelly.

Reed looked away from the carvings and down the stairs leading beneath the parking lot to the museum's entrance. "We'll only have a few minutes. I won't have time to disarm the alarm systems, so we have to assume that the police will dispatch immediately. Hopefully, the shooting will distract them."

Banks nodded, and sweat dripped from her nose.

He attempted to hold her hand, but she recoiled and shot him an icy glare.

"You ready?" he asked.

She wiped the sweat from her face and slung the door open. "Might as well be. Let's move, shithead."

23

The granite steps that led toward twin glass doors were slick beneath his shoes. Banks limped along on bare feet, her heels abandoned in the car. Her skin rippled with goosebumps, but she didn't complain. Reed felt the irresistible urge to wrap her in a hug, warm her body, and soothe her tired mind. But Banks didn't want comfort. She wanted justice, and it was time to find it.

Reed pushed the mental tumult away and stopped at the doors. A quick press against the handle confirmed they were locked. He pressed his face to the glass and noted an open lobby with restrooms on the left, a gift shop on the right, and beyond that, stairs leading toward the museum.

"Once we breach the doors, we have to move directly to the statue," he said.

"What statue?"

"There's a statue of Athena in the main temple room. When we were in that house, I found a script etched into the attic wall beneath a carving of an owl. The owl is one of Athena's symbols, and the script said secrets were housed beneath her feet—beneath the statue."

Banks shot him a glare. "Are you serious? We're breaking into a museum based on an owl and something whittled into a wall?"

Reed started to object, then stopped. "Yes," he said. "That's pretty much what's happening."

Banks looked back toward the university, then waved at the door. "Well, hurry!"

Reed pulled the SIG from his belt and checked the magazine. Four weeks ago, he possessed a collection of small arms sufficient to knock down a National Guard post. Now, only the backup handgun and the three bullets it contained stood between him and the army of gunmen on his tail.

Life's a bitch.

He pointed the little gun at the glass and pulled the trigger. Glass exploded, and only milliseconds later, the shrill ring of an alarm ripped through the air. Reed drove his boot through what remained of the door, sending a cascade of glass clattering against the granite. He jammed his hand through the hole and flipped the latch, then pushed the door open.

Banks jumped onto his back, wrapping her arms around his neck as her bare feet swung over the shards of razor-sharp glass. Reed rushed past the gift shop and pounded up the steps. The pressure of her arms against his bruised and cut neck blinded his mind with pain and restricted his airflow. He leaned against the wall, and Banks slid off, her feet smacking the smooth tile floor.

Dim light illuminated glass display boxes full of Greek artifacts and replicas. As they circled the tight halls and topped another set of steps, the blare of the alarm grew louder, bouncing against the walls and shrieking in their ears. Two more flights of stairs through more display cases and art galleries, and they burst through a door, skidding to a halt at the entrance of the main temple.

Even though he'd seen it before, the mass of the statue sent a shiver down his spine. It was all at once majestic and terrifying. On a raised platform in the middle of the giant hall, with columns on all sides, Athena wore a golden robe hanging from her white marble shoulders and draping down over her feet. A golden war helmet rested over her head, gleaming above piercing blue eyes.

She held the statue of an angel in her outstretched right hand, and a massive shield adorned with Greek art leaned against her left thigh. Between her left knee and the shield, a serpent reared its golden head, glaring out at them as they stood twenty feet away, staring back at the horrifying and magnificent recreation of Greek worship.

"My God..." Banks whispered.

Reed was jarred out of his stupor by the continued blare of the alarm. He shook his head to clear it, then pushed Banks toward the steps that led down to the main floor. "We have to hurry."

The statue was encircled by red velvet rope, and Reed clicked his flashlight on and scanned the pedestal beneath Athena's massive feet, where golden, mid-relief sculptures projected from the base. They were Greek characters—peasants, gods, warriors, all crafted in painstaking detail.

"What are we looking for?" Banks asked.

"I don't know. Something hidden. The script said the secrets were housed beneath her feet. That could mean directly under her shoes or anywhere in the platform."

Banks slid on her knees along the far side of the dais as Reed worked between the golden figurines of warriors, poets, and rulers standing in a tight row, wielding spears and riding horses. He moved his fingers against their feet and between their bodies, searching for any crack or hidden script—anything that might house the secret of a thirty-year-old cult.

"Reed! Come here!"

Banks shouted from the rear of the platform, and Reed hurried around the back corner. Over the alarm that shrieked overhead, he thought he could hear distant police sirens growing gradually closer, but there was no way to tell if they were headed for the Parthenon or the shooting scene on campus.

Banks knelt in the middle of the platform, where she pressed her fingers against a small symbol hidden between the legs of a horse. Reed saw the light of discovery in her eyes.

"It's an owl," she said.

Reed knelt beside her, shining the light on the dime-size spot nestled so far toward the horse's protruding chest that the only way to see it was to kneel. Etched in red ink, the clear outline of an owl's face, painted in reflective paint, glowed under his flashlight. Reed ran his finger over the carving, making out its rough texture. He pushed in, but the owl didn't move.

"What is it?" she whispered. "Can you feel anything?"

He shook his head and felt around the hooves and neck of the horse, searching for a crack or crevice—anything that moved or shifted.

"Wait," Banks said. "Didn't you say she was the goddess of wisdom?"

"Yeah. Why?"

"The scribe." Banks motioned to the figurine of a Greek man dressed in soft robes. He didn't wear armor, and unlike the others, he didn't carry a weapon. Held between his hands was a thick, gold scroll—the symbol of knowledge and understanding.

Reed wrapped his fingers around the scroll, pulling out, but feeling nothing. He twisted, and a dull click resounded from behind the stone. As he continued pulling on the scroll, the scribe shuddered, and dust fell from around the figurine's head and shoulders. It slid outward, grinding against the stone, then fell away from the platform, displaying a guide rod sticking out of his back that corresponded with a hole in the stone. Set in a cavity just beneath the hole was a small leather notebook with a red-eyed silver owl printed on the cover.

"That's it!" Reed hissed. He jerked the book out and ran his hands over the leather. Banks shoved the scribe back in place and twisted his scroll into the locked position while Reed pried dry rubber bands off the notebook.

"What is it? What does it say?" Banks hissed.

Reed shook his head and turned to the first page. It was covered in Greek symbols, filling every open space right up to the edges. He flipped a few more, exposing black-and-white pictures, all taken inside the attic of the frat house. He recognized the owl with the red eyes, and even though all the figures in each image wore black robes and full masks, he thought he recognized Mitch Holiday by his broad shoulders and thick neck—the frame of a running back.

Each photo depicted a ceremony. A table, covered in blood, was set up beneath the talons of the owl, and parts of various animals—rabbits, cats, a few birds—lay on the floor, all dismembered with their intestines strewn about amid the feet of the robed worshipers.

"What the hell?" Banks whispered. "Is that Greek worship?"

Reed shook his head. "Not like any I've ever read about. This is something else entirely."

He flipped two more pages, then stopped at an entry written in red ink. Unlike previous entries, these letters formed English words he could clearly read.

> Under the sacred eye of our mother, we pledge ourselves to her worship. We, the holy members of this sect, protectors of wisdom, embracers of conquest, warriors of the world, commit our lives to her service, and our bodies to this brotherhood. From end to end.

Reed glided his finger down the page, tracing a short list of biographies. Banks leaned in closer, her breath warm against his neck. His finger stopped at Mitchell Holiday, followed almost immediately by Frances Morccelli—names he expected to see. Reed pushed on down the page, skipping over anecdotes about Frank and Mitch's involvement, searching for the list of remaining members. He flipped the page and felt his heart stop. His vision blurred around the next name and he blinked himself back into focus. His fingers went numb, and the notebook slipped from his hand, clattering to the floor amid a confused gasp from Banks. She snatched the book up and flicked her way back to the page, holding it under the light. After a moment, she shut the book and turned toward Reed, her lips pressed into a demanding frown.

Reed looked away, trying to shut out the flood of questions pouring into his tired mind. There was no denying the clean handwriting on that page and no refuting the name written there. It was a name he knew all too well, and one he hadn't heard in years, but it was a name he would never forget.

David Montgomery.

24

"It's your father, isn't it? David Montgomery?"

Reed nodded but avoided her gaze. "Yes."

She grabbed him by the chin, wrenching his face toward her, and her voice snapped. "Did you know? Is this why we met? Why you kidnapped my godfather?"

"I had no idea!" He jerked away. "I barely knew my father. I haven't seen him in two decades. I don't—"

Gunshots cracked from outside. Men screamed, and a shotgun boomed.

Reed snatched the book back and crammed it into his cargo pocket, then hoisted Banks to her feet. "Let's go!"

He cast one more glance at the back of the statue, watching the dust drift through the air around the war helmet.

My father stood here. My father was a part of this.

They ran back up the steps, through the art gallery and the back of the museum. The gift shop flashed past on their right as they pounded through the lobby and toward the door. Banks swung from his shoulders again as he crunched over the glass, and blue police lights flashed through the shattered front door. Gunshots still popped from the park, and as they climbed the steps back to ground level, Reed's foot collided with a body. A METRO cop lay on the concrete, bleeding out as his hands twitched at his sides.

Reed dropped Banks and slid to his knees beside the officer, feeling for a pulse against the man's neck. "Can you hear me?"

The cop's gaze drifted toward him, but he didn't respond. Reed searched beneath the blue shirt until his fingers touched the wound. The bullet had passed just below the ribcage.

Two gunshots ripped through the air, and the edge of the sidewalk exploded into a cloud of concrete dust only inches from Reed's knee. He snatched up the cop's service pistol and directed it toward the trees, unleashing a string of shots at random.

"Banks! Get him down the steps. He can't be hit again!"

Banks grabbed the officer by his ankles and dragged him out of the line of fire as Reed turned toward the smoking hulk of a squad car twenty feet away. Bullet holes riddled the rear fender, and the back glass was blown out. Another cop, holding his side, lay against the sheltered side of the car, a bloody shotgun on the ground next to him.

Reed lifted the cop's sagging head. Faint breaths were warm against his hand, but the tension in the policeman's body was obvious.

"Stay with me, officer."

"I was going to get married," he whispered.

Reed ripped his shirt off and tore it into strips, searching the officer's body for the source of the blood. He found two gunshot wounds, both in the gut. Under the glint of the moon, he made out the officer's nameplate—B. Friz. That was a good name, he thought. The kind of name that didn't take itself too seriously.

"Listen here, Officer Friz. You're gonna marry that girl. You hear me? We're gonna get you home."

Reed wrapped the strips around Friz's middle, but even as he pressed against the wound, he could feel the life slipping away. Friz's arms fell against the concrete, and Reed withdrew from the body, searching for a pulse around his wrist, then his neck.

"No . . . Friz. Stay with me, dammit!"

Banks stumbled up beside him, blood coating her hands and smeared across her face. "Reed . . . the other cop. He's gone. I didn't know what to do."

The ache that descended over Reed felt more like a fog than any conscious pain. A distant agony of a traumatic injury muted by morphine, but still there, ripping through his heart. He slammed his hand into the side of the car and screamed.

Gunshots rang again, and Banks grabbed his shoulder. "Reed, we have to do something!"

Sirens screamed in the distance. It was the voice of more officers rushing into the jaws of death to protect people they might not even know.

Their blood is on my hands.

The thunder of a shotgun jarred Reed from his daze.

Banks leaned over the hood of the car, directing Friz's gun toward the trees. She pumped another shell into the chamber and fired again, felling limbs and spraying dead leaves across the grounds.

We have to run. We can't win if we stay here.

Shadows flitted through the darkness. Muzzle flash illuminated the space between the trees, and a shower of small-arms fire skipped over the pavement and slammed into the squad car. Banks covered her head and curled into a fetal position.

Reed grabbed Banks by the arm, pulling her behind the shelter of the patrol car just as more bullets tore over the hood. "We've got to get to the car! Come on, Banks. You've got to run now."

A brief pause in the gunfire brought welcome relief to the chaos, but the police car's siren and the alarms from the Parthenon still blared. Reed lifted Banks off the ground. She felt limp in his arms, and her skin was clammy, a now-familiar sign of her disease taking over.

She's almost done.

He hoisted her over his shoulder and sprinted toward the Camaro fifty yards away. Gunfire resumed behind him, bullets skipping against the pavement around his feet. One of them tore the toe of his boot, missing his toes by millimeters. Reed ducked and wove, jerking erratically back and forth as the gunfire intensified. His saving grace was the inherent inaccuracy of a pistol-caliber submachine gun fired in full auto mode. At a hundred yards, his chances of evading the scathing fire were about as good as being cut down by it.

His lungs were ready to collapse as he ground to a halt next to the Camaro. Banks hung limp in his arms, her strength fading. He opened the passenger's door and set her inside, locking the seat belt in place before he slid across the front hood of the car.

A blast of gunfire chattered against a Confederate memorial statue sheltering the Camaro. Reed cursed and dug the SIG from his pocket, unleashing his final two rounds. The puny pop of the handgun was insufficient to defy the fully automatic bursts, inaccurate though they were.

The shadows of two men began their approach. Reed slung open the driver's door and piled inside. Banks clutched the handle and groaned, and her head twitched.

"Hang on, Banks. We're getting out of here."

Reed shifted into first and stomped on the gas. An unearthly bellow burst from the engine, the familiar thunder of the big V-8 mixed with the whine of the supercharger. Both rear tires squealed, and the car launched out of the parking lot. Reed swung the wheel to the left, and the back end of the vehicle pivoted outward, sending clouds of tire smoke and bits of asphalt shooting into the air.

The two gunmen in the shadows—masked, tall, and wielding submachine guns—were now joined by a third. The Camaro hurtled straight toward them, leaping a speed bump and slicing through the parking lot with no sign of stopping. A panicked shout rose from the lead gunman, and he dove out of the way just in time to miss the car. Reed jerked back to the right and slid toward West End, slapping the shifter into second. Headlights flashed behind him, and a black pickup truck with fog lights mounted over the roof barreled out of the trees. Its motor howled, and he recognized the whine of a supercharger.

Shit.

Sweat coated the steering wheel, and his hands trembled as he worked the shifter and dumped the clutch, swerving around a garbage truck and whistling through a red light. Businesses, restaurants, and parked cars blurred around him as the Camaro kept climbing past eighty miles an hour. The truck was only a quarter mile behind and barreling toward him.

A green sign ahead displayed an arrow pointing to the right: 440 WEST.

They won't keep up on the highway.

Banks groaned, and her head rolled toward him. He placed one hand on her neck, bracing her as he swerved in front of a sedan and turned toward the on-ramp. Darkness clung around the road, shrouding his view. Yards away from the ramp, a stopped car in the middle of the road came into view. It blocked his path onto the highway as its flashers blinked a steady rhythm of yellow. Reed shouted and jerked the Camaro back to the left, hopping over a bump in the road and sliding back onto West End Avenue, still hurtling like a rocket.

He could hear the bellow of his pursuer, even over the howl of the Camaro. There could be no mistake—this guy was going to run him to ground.

"All right, bitch," Reed hissed. "You asked for it."

He downshifted into third and pushed the pedal to the floor. The front end of the car lifted away from the pavement, and every part of the car shuddered, sending shivers through Reed's body. A red light flashed from the dash, alerting him that the car had reached redline. He power-shifted into fourth and clung to the wheel, watching the speedometer pass 110.

"It's not just a car, Reed." Dave Montgomery's distant voice echoed in his mind, a memory from ages gone by. For a moment, the plastic dash and Alcantara trim of the fifth-gen Camaro was replaced by the hard metal and vinyl of Dave Montgomery's 1969

Z/28, and Reed was transported back to his first drag race—the way the car lifted free of the ground as Dave Montgomery slammed his foot into the gas while his eight-year-old son sat in the passenger seat, screaming with joy. *"It's art, son. It's you, the motor, and the open road."*

The blur of Midtown Nashville returned, and Reed clung to the wheel. He ignored the speedometer. Nothing mattered but the open road—this moment between himself, the car . . . and Dave Montgomery.

By the time he saw the bus, it was too late. The intersection loomed directly ahead, a sign reading White Bridge Pike. Small brick buildings clustered together on either side of the street. In the distance, a hospital towered in the sky. Reed saw it all in the same millisecond the long city bus pulled into the intersection, only yards ahead, loaded with a smattering of people sitting behind dirty windows. In the split second it took his mind to register the blocked pathway ahead, his foot was already slipping off the accelerator, colliding with the brake, and pressing toward the floor. The front tires of the Camaro screamed, and the car fishtailed as Reed jammed harder against the brakes, but the vehicle barely slowed. Smoke poured from both front wheels as the brake pads ground and slipped against the rotors.

"Watch out for the brakes. They're too small for this much power." The mechanic's warning about the Camaro's undersized brakes echoed in his mind a moment too late.

The bus flashed closer, and the world slowed around him as he made eye contact with a passenger in the rear of the bus, her grey hair pulled back in a ponytail, eyes filled with terror as she saw the car rocketing toward her like a cannonball. Reed snatched the emergency brake and jerked the wheel, sending the car spinning toward a wall of buildings.

25

The moment before the Camaro made contact was one Reed would never forget. Even though he wasn't looking at Banks, he saw her face as clearly as the first night they met. Her shining eyes, the bright smile, every gorgeous thing he loved so much about her, right beside him.

The Camaro collided with a tree first. The rear bumper of the car crashed against the towering oak, and a shower of metal ripped across the pavement as the car skidded across the sidewalk. A fire hydrant exploded, and glass rained down around them. The air was alive with the odor of burnt rubber and oil, and the seatbelt cinched down around Reed's neck. He reached out for Banks as the Camaro continued spinning, bouncing off a retaining wall, and hurtling toward another tree.

The hood of the car popped upward, and both airbags blasted into the interior of the car. Everything descended into a daze of crunched metal and smoke as the car finally screeched to a stop, and Reed pried his hands free of the steering wheel. His ears rang. Everything around him danced in a confused blur, and through the haze he heard his own voice calling for Banks. But he couldn't see her.

Fire erupted from the engine bay, and the reek of burning carpet filled his nostrils. He clawed at the seatbelt, clicking it free of the latch, and slammed his shoulder into the bent door of the car—once, twice. On the third strike, the door swung open, and Reed spilled out onto the concrete, gasping for air.

Where's Banks?

Panic overtook his mind, and he was vaguely aware of streetlights glimmering around him as people shouted. But none of that mattered. He stumbled back toward the car as flames continued building in the engine compartment, licking their way toward the gas tank at the rear of the car.

My God, no. Don't take her.

He slid around the rear of the car and reached the passenger's door, crunched together and impossibly distorted. He slammed his unprotected fist into what remained of the window, clearing out the shards of glass. Banks lay inside, slumped forward with a trail of blood dripping from her forehead. Reed leaned through the window and fumbled with the seatbelt, clicking it free as black smoke clouded his eyes. He could hear the roar of the pickup truck now, hurtling down the avenue half a mile away.

"Banks, come on. You've got to help me!"

Her head twitched, and she turned toward him. Her face was covered in soot, and her body so weak she could barely hold her head up, but she wriggled toward the window. Reed leaned back and pulled, clearing her shoulders of the window frame, then her stomach. The car shuddered against his efforts as flames filled the cabin. A cry of pain erupted from her swollen lips, and they crashed to the pavement. Heat flooded his face, singeing his hair as smoke clogged his throat. Banks lay on top of him, limp and unconscious, but breathing.

"Don't let go," he whispered. "I need you. God help me, I need you."

The truck behind him screamed to a halt, and three men dressed in black, wearing ski masks and wielding submachine guns, piled out. They stomped toward him in slow motion, the smoke of the car fire drifting around their tall frames and making them appear ghostly, like the villains of a slasher movie.

Reed choked for air and rolled over, stumbling to his feet and clawing for the SIG. He knew the gun was empty, but somehow pointing it at the oncoming killers still felt better than giving up. Snot drained from his nose as his lungs continued to flood with acidic smoke. The three men drew closer, closing the gap between the truck and the burning car. The lead man was shorter than the rest, and under the ski mask, Reed made out the dark tinge of olive skin. He wrapped his finger around the trigger of his gun, raised the weapon, and trained it on Reed.

Reed released the SIG, abandoning it in his pocket, then took a step forward, placing himself between the gunman and Banks. Everything slowed around him. Smoke drifted from his lips as he breathed out, exhaling the smog from the car fire. He stared into those dark eyes, and for a moment, the world grew still.

This is it. This is how it ends.

The glare of lights and the roar of a motor burst through the stillness. A split second of confusion flashed across the dark gaze of the gunman, and he turned toward the sound as a Mercedes coupe rushed toward them. The bumper of the big car rammed through the two rear gunmen, shattering their bodies in an instant and sending their guns flying.

Even before the car stopped, the driver's side door flung open. Wolfgang appeared in all black, his giant Glock 10mm pistol swinging from one hand. But he didn't turn toward Reed. He turned toward the short, olive-skinned man.

The gunman raised his weapon and clawed at the trigger, spraying shots around the scene of carnage. Wolfgang's giant handgun thundered, spitting a bullet through the smoke, and the slug crashed through the gunman's shoulder. The weapon fell from the man's fingers as he screamed and crashed to the pavement. Wolfgang followed him, shoving right past Reed and snatching his victim off the pavement with one powerful arm. Reed watched as The Wolf pivoted on his heel and slammed the gunman against the side of the Mercedes. With a quick flip of his fingers, the ski mask was ripped away, exposing the brown features and terrified eyes of the face beneath.

It was Salvador. Reed would have recognized that panicked face anywhere. The face of the man who kidnapped Banks, threatened Reed over the phone, and was the author of the fallout in Atlanta. Salvador, the only definite link between Reed and the shadowy men who wanted Mitchell Holiday assassinated.

Wolfgang shoved the mass of the Glock into Salvador's throat and snarled in his face.

"No!" Reed shouted. "I need him!"

Reed jumped over the bodies and rushed toward the truck, his mind pounding in a confusing swirl of desperation. Every step was agony, as though he were dragging himself through quicksand. Wolfgang's words warbled and echoed, distorted by Reed's frayed consciousness and pounding head.

"*Where is she?*"

Salvador shook, and Wolfgang backhanded him, shattering his nose and sending blood streaming over his lip. "Where is my sister?"

Salvador's eyes were bloodshot and draining tears, his face reddened under another brutal blow from The Wolf, but he didn't speak. The muzzle of the gun was jammed harder into his throat, closing off his windpipe.

"*Collins!*" Wolfgang roared. "Where is she?"

Reed slid to a stop and clawed at the gun in his pocket. It finally tore free of his pants, and he raised it, directing the muzzle toward The Wolf. "Wolfgang!" he gasped. "Don't do it. I need him to talk!"

Wolfgang glanced at Reed. Their eyes met, and fire clashed against fire. For a moment, Reed thought he might redirect the Glock away from Salvador and toward him—The Wolf's original target. Instead, he ignored Reed and turned back to the South American.

"Kill The Prosecutor," Salvador hissed. "And I'll tell you."

Wolfgang sneered and wrapped his finger around the trigger of the pistol. "If you wanted him dead, you should have never touched my sister."

The Glock swung downward, then thundered. Blood exploded from Salvador's thigh, and Reed started forward.

"Don't kill him. I need to know who he's working for!"

"*Stay back, Montgomery!*" Wolfgang swept the gun toward Reed, stopping him in his tracks. Salvador writhed in pain, trying to collapse against the concrete, but Wolfgang held him suspended against the car.

"I can do this all night." Wolfgang breathed malice over Salvador, placing the gun back against his stomach. "Where's my sister?"

Salvador coughed, spitting up saliva. "She's in an apartment . . . Detroit . . . Oak Ridge Place . . . unit B7. She's safe, I swear."

Wolfgang dropped Salvador and raised the barrel of the oversized handgun.

Reed rushed forward. "Don't!"

The pistol thundered, and Salvador's face exploded in a spray of blood. Reed stood over the dead South American, his hand trembling as he lowered the empty SIG. He stared down at the crumpled body and felt desperation take over. It blocked out his fear and panic, and nothing but defeat filled his mind.

Wolfgang stood next to him, staring down at the body, then spat onto the corpse. He turned toward Reed, and for a moment, neither one spoke. The soft breeze that swept over the crime scene carried the stench of blood and sweat and burning rubber. The Camaro burst into a total blaze as gasoline ignited, boiling the air around them.

"I'm sorry, Montgomery," Wolfgang said. "We all have rules. He broke mine."

"I needed him *alive!*" Reed snapped. "Who hired you to kill me?"

Wolfgang looked back down at the body and motioned with the gun. "He did."

Once again, the silence descended around them, broken only

by the crackle of the flames. Reed raised his gun, pointing it toward The Wolf. "You said you were going to kill me next time we met. I can't let you do that."

Wolfgang stared down the barrel of the gun to the blackened face of The Prosecutor. His finger relaxed around the trigger of his own gun, then he holstered it.

"It's after midnight," he muttered. "Good luck, Montgomery."

Without another word, Wolfgang turned back toward his car. The big German motor roared to life, tires howled against the pavement, and the coupe rocketed away into the darkness.

Reed slumped to the ground and rested his face in his hands. His body racked with dry sobs as the gun toppled to the ground beside him. The stench of blood that filled his nostrils was so familiar now, he didn't even notice it. He didn't recognize the carnage, or the chaos, or the death that hung around him like a cloak. The wreckage of war. And yet, at this moment, the weight of it all crashed down on him like a load of bricks.

Footsteps tapped on the pavement, soft and slow. Banks staggered toward him, clutching herself and pinning the burned and tattered clothes to her body as she surveyed the carnage with a blank face. She stopped a few feet away, then picked up his fallen gun.

The ache returned to Reed's chest, piling on to the defeat he already felt. "Are you going to kill me now?"

Banks looked down at the gun, then frowned. Her voice was weak and cracked. "What are you talking about? We've still got work to do."

Reed motioned toward Salvador's body. "He's dead, Banks. He's gone. Whoever he worked for . . . they're lost now. Another shadow."

She gazed at the mutilated corpse for a moment, then turned back to Reed. "And what about David Montgomery?"

A knot tightened in Reed's stomach. The name ripped through his heart and shattered every reality he had carefully constructed over the last nineteen years, every lie he ever crafted to forget the man who was his father.

"He's alive," he whispered.

"And you know where he is?"

Reed closed his eyes, then nodded slowly. "I do."

"On your feet, then. This isn't over yet."

The gun clicked, and Reed opened his eyes to see Banks's outstretched hand. Her face was still damp, and her fingers trembled, but there was steel in her eyes. Relentless resolve.

"I'll let you know when you can quit, Reed Montgomery."

Reed felt the blood return to his head. He pulled himself to his feet and caught her just in time to keep Banks from collapsing. She huddled close to his chest as he cradled her in his arms and stumbled toward the pickup truck. In the distance, the ever-present howl of sirens roared toward them. He cast a look around the blood and bodies piled near the truck. There was no way to hide the massacre, so there was only one option left. Keep running.

He laid Banks into the passenger seat of the truck, then hauled himself in behind the wheel. In the distance, locals gathered around the stopped bus, watching with gaping mouths. They would need therapy. After tonight, a lot of people would need therapy—one of the many costs of the bloodshed. But that didn't change the inevitability of it all. There was no other choice, no other way out of the twisted hell he found himself in. Salvador might be dead, but it was now clear how trivial a tool Salvador really was—a minion of a much larger villain still hidden in the shadows. The secrets he unearthed in the Parthenon would cost a great deal more blood before this was over.

More than that, it was personal now—more personal than Banks or Oliver could have ever made it. It wasn't about avenging the woman he used to love, or protecting the woman he would always love—now it was about him.

David Montgomery was there when this evil was born, and Reed Montgomery would be there when it died.

26

Bank of America Plaza
Atlanta, Georgia

Gambit could feel the twist of tension in his stomach and the dampness on his palms. His feet dragged over the carpet in spite of his efforts to walk normally. With each step toward the elevator, the weight on his shoulders grew heavier.

He mashed the button for the fiftieth floor and adjusted his tie. There was no one else in the elevator. In fact, at three in the morning, there were very few people inside the skyscraper at all. Other than cleaning crews and security guards, the hallways lay empty, lending a haunted aura to the giant building.

As each floor ticked by, Gambit fingered the sleeve of his custom-tailored suit and reviewed what he planned to say. Would it be best to lead with the Montgomery situation or discuss Governor Trousdale? He wanted to remain in control of the conversation—provide solutions, not problems. In his line of work, he found that people who provided problems found themselves out of a job, if they were lucky. The unlucky ones wound up six feet under.

The bell dinged, and the gold doors of the elevator rolled open.

Gambit straightened his back. He screwed up, and he wasn't going to deny that. Now he had to fix it.

Scarlet carpet lined the hallway. Gambit had traveled this path a thousand times, so much so that it felt more like home than his own penthouse. And yet, the grandeur of the fiftieth-floor suite still made him question his belonging. It was imposter syndrome at its worst. Gambit placed his hand on the gold handle, cleared his throat, and pushed inside.

The suite, complete with the scent of lavender and vanilla, was expansive, filling half of the fiftieth floor. Massive windows looked southward toward the heart of downtown. A minibar sat on one side of the room, and a massive executive desk on the other. Filling the space in between were lounge chairs and a chess table with ivory pieces standing five inches tall. Otherwise the room was bare, and sterile, reflecting the economic tastes of the man facing the skyline with his back toward Gambit. The door slid shut automatically, leaving Gambit standing in the relaxing darkness of the room.

"It's bad, isn't it?" The man standing in front of the glass didn't turn around. Hands folded behind his back, he spoke with perfect calm. His voice carried no edge, no tone, but Gambit knew the power hidden beneath the practiced posture. The venom.

"It's not good," Gambit said. "Things went sideways in Nashville."

"Why the hell was *anything* happening in Nashville?"

Gambit spoke with confidence. "It was Salvador, the man I hired to take care of Mitch Holiday. He made a mess."

"Sounds like it. I've read the news."

Gambit refused to hesitate or display any signs of the anxiety that plagued him. "I'm still collecting intel, but it appears there was a confrontation."

"A confrontation? Is that what you call this slaughter? They killed at least two cops. Montgomery got away. And then there's this Wolf. Somebody Salvador hired, I take it?"

"Salvador got sloppy. I take full responsibility and will ensure that he is removed from the equation."

The man at the window turned around, his hands still folded behind him. He was tall and slim, and with the moon at his back, his appearance was altogether impending. Greying black hair was swept behind large ears, with deep, penetrating eyes the hallmark of his face. He settled down behind the desk before motioning to the minibar. "Whiskey . . . on ice. Fix yourself something."

Gambit hurried to prepare the drink, splashing three fingers of bourbon into a glass for himself. He handed his employer a glass of expensive Irish whiskey, then took a seat.

His boss took a long sip of the drink. "Salvador is already out of the equation."

Gambit frowned. "How do you know?"

"Because Montgomery escaped. He wouldn't have left Salvador alive—not after all the chaos that fool caused. Our priority now is damage control. We're making entirely too much noise. There's already an FBI agent sniffing around—the guy who was hounding Holiday. Now we've got a rogue killer on our hands. Montgomery needs to be on ice, immediately, along with anyone working with him."

"I'll take care of it . . . personally."

"I know you will." The man took a sip of whiskey and met Gambit's gaze. There was ice in his stare—a chill that turned Gambit's stomach.

Gambit coughed and took a swallow of bourbon. "There's another issue. Governor Trousdale. She's going to be a problem."

"I thought you spoke with her."

Gambit nodded. "I did. I leaned on her pretty hard, but she's not budging. She's got this crusade against corruption. It's her whole campaign promise. I think she actually believes in it."

"You know how this game is played. Doesn't she have a family?"

"I tried." Gambit set the glass on the table. "I really think the harder we lean on her, the more she's going to fight back. She needs to be taken out, promptly, before she causes any more noise."

"You want to assassinate the governor of Louisiana?"

"We already sent a gunman after her."

"Only to scare her her into cooperation."

"I know. That backfired, though. She's a fighter, tooth and nail, and I don't think we can break her."

The silver-haired man stared at Gambit a moment, then stood up and gestured toward the chess table. Gambit followed him, feeling the knots in his stomach constrict. He stopped a couple feet away and watched as his boss lifted the white queen and traced the delicate outlines of each carving.

"Stephen, why do I call you Gambit?"

Gambit shifted, then cleared his throat. "Because that's my job. To take risks, implement deceit, and make things happen."

"That's right. And for almost a decade, you've been my most indispensable piece. Honestly, Stephen, this company would not be what it is today without your brilliance, dedication, and ferocity. Your hard work is appreciated more than you'll ever know."

Gambit glanced at the floor. "Thank you. That means a lot."

For a moment, the silence hung in the air, while the man gently stroked the queen, scraping his thumbnail over the polished ivory. "The funny thing is, Stephen, that a career full of highlights and trophies can be undone in a matter of seconds. Just a few critical mistakes. This company is a tower built on a delicate foundation— a foundation that depends on *every* piece."

Gambit felt claws of ice dig into his soul. He remained frozen, rooted to the floor, staring at the chessboard. Waiting for the next words.

The silver-haired man cleared his throat and set the queen down abruptly. It clicked against the marble chessboard.

"I don't want you wasting time lamenting the things you can't change. I want you to do what you do best—make problems go away. If you tell me Governor Trousdale is an irreparable liability, then I trust your judgment. Erase the liability."

"Yes, sir. I'll just need to find a way to keep it out of the headlines."

"She's the governor of Louisiana, Stephen. It's *going* to make headlines. May I make a suggestion?"

Gambit nodded hastily. "Of course."

His boss crossed his arms. "Montgomery is a wanted man suspected of killing a state senator. One could presume that he has a penchant for killing politicians. Perhaps that is because of his bad experiences in the Iraq war. Who knows? Why not use one liability against the other, and kill two birds with one stone?"

Gambit frowned. "You want me to pin the murder of Governor Trousdale on Montgomery?"

"No, I want you to have Montgomery kill her himself, and then make sure the FBI finds out about it."

Gambit tried not to grimace. "He's impossible to manage, sir. Salvador attempted to manipulate him by kidnapping Holiday's goddaughter, and it all blew up. I don't think we can force him to kill anyone."

Gambit's boss lifted the black king off the chessboard and set it in the middle. Slowly, he began to rearrange the white pieces, aligning them around the black king. "Stephen, I shouldn't have to tell you this. Everything is a matter of positioning. You place your subject alone"—he adjusted the black king in the center of the board, then placed a white rook within striking distance and a knight blocking the retreat—"then you surround him. Give him no other way out. Salvador screwed up because Salvador grabbed a tiger by the tail. You're never going to get that close. Drive Montgomery into a corner, and then open up a single route of escape— over Governor Trousdale's dead body. Don't tell him what to do. Just leave him no other option."

Gambit's eyes gleamed with excitement. "Do I use the girl?"

"No. You'll need more than that. Something that reaches deeper into his psyche, all the way back to his earliest memories."

Gambit tilted his head, and slowly, a smile spread across his face.

The silver-haired man thumped the black king, knocking it over. "Stephen, it's time we reconnect with an old friend. It's time we brought David Montgomery out of retirement."

THE STORY CONTINUES WITH…

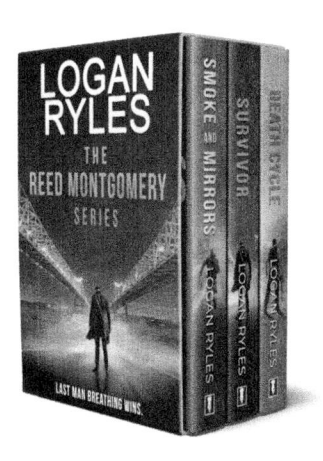

Turn the page to read the first chapter.

SMOKE AND MIRRORS
REED MONTGOMERY BOOK 4

Riga, Latvia
Eastern Europe

Even as the dying glow of the sun washed Juris's face with a kiss of warmth, the autumn wind blowing off the Baltic and across the weathered Latvian coast sank through his jacket and saturated his body. Every scar and fractured bone ached and burned in the cold —constant reminders of the bloodshed over the past decade. Juris couldn't remember the first time he fell off a building and listened to his leg shatter. He couldn't recall the first bullet that ripped through his flesh or the knife that shredded his pale, European skin. Now, the scars had lost their stories and become the faceless memorabilia of every *oh-shit* moment of his life.

He stared out at the Baltic bay and watched the fishing boats churn in and out of the marinas. Unlike the scars, the boats held memories. Each battered vessel reminded him of his father's boat, not unlike these, albeit older and filthier. Juris spent the greater part of his childhood on that boat, cursing its every smelly hold and tangled fishnet. He could still hear his father shouting from the pilothouse as waves battered the creaking fiberglass hull and the wind snapped against the boom. At the time, he couldn't imagine a more disgusting and unfriendly place to spend a childhood. Now, he would give anything to go back. Anything to stop himself from boarding the nameless freighter to Albania, and the doom of a loveless, violent life that it promised him—a life where everything was counted in bodies and American dollars.

Juris stared down at the cell phone in his hand, and once again, he refreshed the email inbox, but there were still no new messages. Cedric Muri's last email came five days prior, directing him to return home to Latvia and lay low after the chaos that erupted in Atlanta. Juris was more than happy to comply. He was beyond sick of the violence he triggered every time he visited the States. In fact, he was beyond sick of everything about his sordid, criminal lifestyle. At seventeen, running from the economic wasteland of a former Soviet nation-state and falling in with a group of organized international criminals promised excitement, fortune, and a chance to make a better life for himself than what his father, grandfather, or great-grandfather had ever dreamed of.

Funny how time morphed reality, stealing away what felt most important and replacing it with the things he could never have again—things like his father, that old fishing boat, and the quiet life he led on the Baltic coast.

Once again, Juris refreshed the screen, then cursed. The downside about making a lot of money, he found, was that you never had any. For years he drowned the nagging feeling of guilt that tugged at the back of his mind with every shiny thing his blood money could buy: fancy cars, copious amounts of alcohol, loose women. Even an endangered species of cobra that he kept in his basement and fed kittens to. It all failed to wash away the emptiness his lonely life drowned him in, and in spite of a multi-six-figure income, he lived paycheck to paycheck.

But not anymore. After nearly twenty years, Juris had finally had enough. As soon as Cedric wired him his payout from the last job, he would withdraw the cash and disappear. At least for a while. Maybe he'd go to Africa and find cobras in the wild, or to Australia and watch kangaroos. The money wouldn't last forever, but it would buy him time to catch his breath and search for new ideas about how to fill the void in his soul.

Juris turned away from the balcony and walked back inside the dilapidated apartment. He crashed down on the couch, then refreshed the email browser again. Still no word from Cedric. That was unusual. Sometimes Cedric would go dark for a few days, but never this long. The Swiss broker was always good about paying his contractors on time, especially on a job as big as Atlanta.

Juris ran his hand up his arm, tracing a couple of scars that were fresher and more tender than the rest. Burn marks ran down his arm—fallout from his partner's sloppy application of gasoline to the corner of the house. The images of the dancing flames flashed through his mind, and Juris recalled the screams from inside—a woman's scream, followed by a man's. Juris stood outside and shouted for his partner, but the blond-haired Ukrainian never appeared. The flames grew hotter, singeing his face, and that was when a renegade spark ignited the traces of gasoline on his left arm. His voice joined the screams as he stumbled into a park behind the home, beating out the fire with one hand.

And still, he could hear the screams.

Juris snatched up the phone and typed a quick message to Cedric.

WHERE'S MY MONEY?

He tossed the device onto the coffee table and ran his hands over his shiny, bald head. The wind rattled against the broken screen door, filling the apartment with a clamor. Juris cursed and stomped across the room, slamming the door shut. As he did, he felt the cold edge of a knife against the back of his neck, biting straight through his collared shirt and sinking into his skin with a sting. Juris froze, his hands erupting in a new series of shudders. His gaze wandered across the room to the handgun lying on a shelf, but it was too far out of reach. He would never make it in time.

"Turn around," a voice hissed. It was raspy and broken, but he could still make out an American accent.

Juris turned slowly on his heel, sucking in another breath as the blade traced his skin and nicked his windpipe.

He could tell it was a woman by the shape of her hips and shoulders, even though she was shrouded in a thick black burka. Only her eyes—dark, brown, and full of fire—were visible through the face mask. In her right hand she clenched a long hunting knife, its razor edge glimmering in the last light of the setting sun. She flicked her wrist, and the blade cut deep into his neck, sending a surge of blood shooting out over his shoulder and onto the wall. Juris shouted, and his hands flew to the injury, desperately attempting to restrain the bleeding as the tip of the knife hovered over his face.

"*Sit!*" The word snapped with lethality, and she motioned with her free hand toward a wooden chair. Juris tried to step back, but his shoulders collided with the balcony door. The woman flicked the tip of the knife across his nose. "I said, *sit!*"

Juris stumbled backward and sat down.

The woman followed, producing a pair of handcuffs and a roll of tape from inside the folds of her burka. Her hands shook as she tossed him the handcuffs and motioned with the knife toward the back of the chair. "Cuff yourself. Behind your back."

Before Juris could object, the knife flicked toward his eye, and he jerked his head back just in time to avoid being blinded by the weapon. He closed one cuff around his left wrist before pressing both hands behind his back and fighting with the second cuff. The woman stepped behind him, and he felt the metal click into place around his right wrist. The sharp *shrick* of the tape tore through the small apartment, and Juris shuddered as he felt his hands secured to the chair, followed by his ankles. Then two thick layers closed around his mouth, muting his pleas for mercy.

The woman appeared in front of him, the tip of the knife jumping as her hand trembled. Blood dripped from its gleaming edge, staining the dirty floor beneath her feet. She reached up and pulled at the burka from behind her neck. With a quick twist of her hand, the entire garment fell from her shoulders, leaving her naked in front of him.

Juris gasped for air, his stomach convulsing at the horrific figure exposed before him. She looked like the product of a horror movie, with massive red welts covering her entire body, from her ankles to her neck. The right side of her face was a swollen mass, twisting her lips into a hideous sneer that left three of her teeth permanently exposed. Dark, dirty hair fell down over her ears, with random chunks missing from her scalp, leaving behind red, scalded flesh. Scars and burn marks spider-webbed across her chest and legs, culminating over her swollen stomach. It was as though she were a couple months pregnant, with black bruises and brutal welts massed over her navel like cancer.

Vomit rose to his mouth, but he forced it back down to keep from choking. He turned his face away, but the woman grabbed him by the chin and swiveled his head toward her. Her hands still trembled, but there was no fear or trepidation in her eyes.

"Do you speak English?" she hissed.

Tears dripped down his face as he nodded.

Her breath was hot against his cheeks. So close it stung his eyes. "Three weeks ago, you were in Atlanta. With your friend."

It didn't sound like a question, but when the blade slid into his exposed arm, he nodded admission.

"You went to a house—*my house*—and set it on fire."

Juris tried to look away. The knife sank into his arm, and he thrashed, trying to break free. The woman's viselike grip on his jaw held his head in place. He couldn't budge.

A tear slipped down her distorted cheek as she continued, but her tone remained stone cold. "You burned my fiancé alive. Destroyed my home. *You took my baby.*" She grabbed him by the left ear and jerked his face down until he was forced to stare at the mutilated mass of her stomach.

She held him, pinning him down like a bug beneath a shoe. "I killed your friend and left him in the house to burn. When the police came, they thought it was me. Guess the body was pretty much ashes by then. But I knew he wasn't alone. I heard you screaming outside. I found your footprints in the park, and then I traced you all the way back here, to this hole you call home."

Juris sobbed. His lungs heaved as he struggled to breathe through his nose, but he didn't care. He couldn't feel anything except the crushing reality of the man he had become. The knife slipped down his arm, around his ribs, and to his stomach.

"You took *everything* from me. The only happiness I've ever known." Tears rushed down her cheeks in a waterfall now, and the blade began digging into his gut. "You took my future husband. You took my future child. People you didn't know and didn't love the way I loved!"

The knife twitched and lunged into his stomach. Juris screamed, but the sound was muted by the tape.

The woman twisted the blade and dragged it across his stomach, across his belly button, ripping the entire way. She grabbed him by the throat with her free hand, pushing his head backward and growling directly into his face. "Tell the devil to keep the door open. I won't be far behind."

READY FOR MORE?

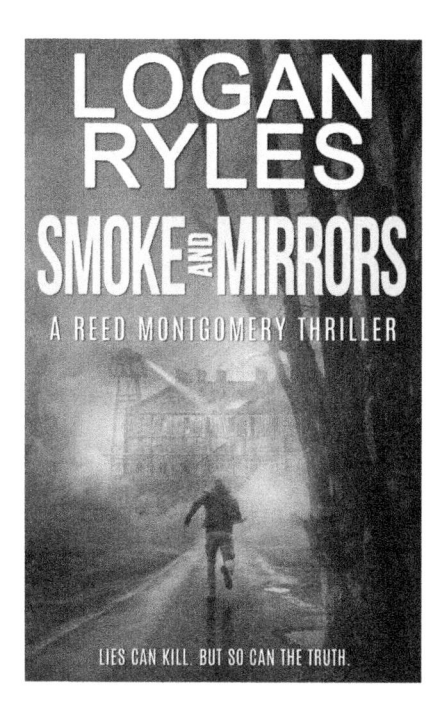

Visit LoganRyles.com for details.

ABOUT THE AUTHOR

Logan Ryles was born in small town USA and knew from an early age he wanted to be a writer. After working as a pizza delivery driver, sawmill operator, and banker, he finally embraced the dream and has been writing ever since. With a passion for action-packed and mystery-laced stories, Logan's work has ranged from global-scale political thrillers to small town vigilante hero fiction.

Beyond writing, Logan enjoys saltwater fishing, road trips, sports, and fast cars. He lives with his wife and three fun-loving dogs in Alabama.

Visit his website at www.LoganRyles.com

ALSO BY LOGAN RYLES

The Reed Montgomery Series

Prequel: *Sandbox*, a short story (read for free at LoganRyles.com)

Book 1: *Overwatch*

Book 2: *Hunt to Kill*

Book 3: *Total War*

Book 4: *Smoke and Mirrors*

Book 5: *Survivor*

Book 6: *Death Cycle*

Book 7: *Sundown*

The Prosecution Force Series

Book 1: *Brink of War*

Book 2: *First Strike*

Book 3: *Election Day*

The Wolfgang Pierce Series

Prequel: *That Time in Appalachia* (read for free at LoganRyles.com)

Book 1: *That Time in Paris*

Book 2: *That Time in Cairo*

Book 3: *That Time in Moscow*

Book 4: *That Time in Rio*

Book 5: *That Time in Tokyo*

Book 6: *That Time in Sydney*

LOGAN RYLES

LoganRyles.com

Printed in Great Britain
by Amazon